Kingston Raine
and the
Arena of Chaos

Jackson Lear

AKA

OISÍN RAYMOND

ISBN 978-0-9924320-4-1

By Jackson Lear

Kingston Raine and the Grim Reaper
Kingston Raine and the Bank of Limbo
Kingston Raine and the Arena of Chaos
Kingston Raine and the Starlight Muse

I

Just beyond the outer edge of reality lay the pit stop to the afterlife: Limbo. Every day a quarter of a million recently departed souls were shuffled through the system, processed by an army of office workers who used to be alive themselves, and then escorted to one of two destinations. The realm of Limbo was designed to reinforce the notion that once someone had arrived it meant there was no going back to Life. Despite the moving statues, wisps of smoke carrying messages through the air, the many grim reapers moving around and the occasional dragon standing guard, most of the recently departed were still under the delusion that they could talk their way out of being dead and return to Life by simply asking one of the thousands of sorters to bend the rules just this once. It never worked.

In another part of the realm, far from the headaches and miseries of reminding the dead that they were, in fact, dead, was a small office on the corner of Anubis and Niamh, where one slightly inebriated client was trying to get one particular bounty hunter to bend the rules to work in his favour.

"Please," slurred Montgomery Stup. "You used to work for the bank. It's only a hundred gold pieces."

Kingston Raine leaned back in his chair and raised his hands to form a steeple, and he rested them just in front of his chin. He was taller than average with his hair swept back in an executive wave, and he tried his best to ignore the rum coming off his client's breath. "I'm not about to rob someone's vault just because they owe you money, Montgomery."

"But please! We need to find Rufus. He can't have just dropped off the face of the realm. He can't have! If you met him you wouldn't like him either, you'd want to go into his vault and get the blueprints that he promised were mine. He's a liar and a thief."

"He's an apothecary," said Kingston.

"And an enchanter! You would hate him."

Kingston considered his words carefully before responding to Montgomery. "That's just the thing, I'm afraid. No one likes to be made a fool of, do they?"

"See! You get me," said Montgomery, beaming with a faux smile. It seemed to fit his faux suit as well, which was a sad and faded grey jacket with frayed cuffs and a tie that had never held a decent knot. Montgomery was now building up quite the sweat on the top of his balding head.

"And you're not the only one who's out there looking for him," said Kingston.

Montgomery stiffened and Kingston saw his breathing slow down. "What do you mean?" asked Montgomery.

Kingston rolled his eyes. "I mean you and several others are all looking for the same person. No doubt he owes everyone money and he has decided to run off because you lot keep threatening him."

"I won't tell any of them if you find him," spluttered Montgomery.

"Uh huh. The last time we met you gave me this to give to him." Kingston opened his desk drawer and removed a black leather wallet.

Montgomery glanced at the wallet and blinked back towards Kingston. "Yes. That's his wallet."

"Yeeeaaaah. No one exchanges a hundred gold pieces and offers their wallet as collateral. It just doesn't happen."

Montgomery blinked several times as his nerves got the better of him. "He dropped it."

"Oh, it's certainly his, no doubt about it," said Kingston. "He would be a remarkably clumsy thief if he took a hundred gold pieces and then dropped his wallet, and quite a fortunate one if he hadn't yet put the money into the wallet that he was about to drop."

Montgomery shook his head. "He had the money in his purse. That's just for his ID and cards and ... well, you've probably looked inside. I was hoping it would inspire an act of kindness on his part, that he would be so grateful that he would pay me back in a hurry."

"Uh huh." Kingston sniffed the wallet and handed it over to

Montgomery. "Notice anything about how it smells?"

Montgomery took a whiff. "Smells like leather."

Kingston drummed his fingers against the chair's arm rest. "It smells a lot like ostrich powder, which can be used as a tracking and listening agent. You thought you could get this to Rufus and then follow the scent, or simply eavesdrop on what he was up to. It's not very clever."

Montgomery stammered and looked over the wallet again. "Uh, my brother ... he's a lawyer."

"My condolences," said Kingston. "No, really. I am so sorry."

"He thought it was a good idea."

Kingston covered his face with one hand and shook his head. "Montgomery, your brother is a moron."

"He's quite gifted."

"You asked me to find Rufus."

"That's right."

"And Rufus used to run his own apothecary."

"... Yes."

"And so your brother bought this powder from the same apothecary that Rufus used to run, not thinking that it would be the first place I would go to find out if they knew the whereabouts of the former owner."

Montgomery blinked again. "... Yes."

"And at some point I'm bound to ask, 'Has anyone been in here lately asking about Rufus' current location?'"

Montgomery dropped his head. "Oh."

"Exactly. Madam Muira was quick to identify the ostrich powder. She also told me a little more about why you're looking for Rufus."

Montgomery spluttered and threw his hands out in defence. "I told you everything I know!"

Kingston nodded and felt a smile try to break through. "Yes, I do believe the sum of your knowledge could be passed on to me in a ten minute meeting, so let me ask you about your gambling debts."

With that, Montgomery froze. "I, uh, don't have any."

"You came in here last week with a black eye, Montgomery."

"I bumped into a statue."

"And clearly you lost," said Kingston. "I used to work for the Bank of Limbo, as you know. I still have some access there and

3

some old friends. You and your brother owe a lot of money."

Montgomery sunk lower into his chair, then he finally shook his head in defeat. "Rufus owes us money. He's quite a genius."

"Yes, borrowing money and dropping off the face of reality is the surest sign of intelligence. You wanted to find him, no problem. Perhaps you wanted him to honour your agreement, again I see no problem. You even lied to me and my business partner. I, personally, don't take much offence if someone lies to me. I'm quite used to it. My business partner, though, is a little sensitive on the matter. You hurt his feelings."

Montgomery cocked his head to one side and could barely look Kingston in the eye. "I'm ... sorry?"

"I also found out that you are not the only one who has loaned money to Rufus."

"He can pay me back, I know he can."

"He's utterly flat broke," said Kingston.

"But the bank keeps records. He told me. I'm serious! He's a master builder, you see. He can engineer any kind of mechanical device and enchant it to work against the laws of reality. All of his time in the apothecary paid off. He can enchant a mechanical clock with a cuckoo that does more than just chirp on the hour, he can make the cuckoo fly around as though it were alive. His attention to detail is remarkable, a true genius. But he couldn't have kept everything in his head. He had to write something down. All of his documents, plans, blueprints, notes, and theories are locked away in a vault. And not just his! Just about anyone who has ever come through Limbo has something locked away in the bank and that kind of information is valuable. I don't need Rufus to pay me back in gold. I mean, I'd like it, but this was his collateral. He promised that he could get me all sorts of plans and notes and that I could sell them to the highest bidder." Montgomery beamed with a desperate smile. "So you see, I just need to find him so we can go to the bank and get to his vault."

Kingston shook his head. "Bad news on that front. He doesn't actually own that paperwork. The bank does. Intellectually the information is his, of course, and the bank can't do anything with it, but the physical paper and ink that's stored in those vaults belong to the bank. Rufus doesn't have access to any of that. He never has, he never will. He offered you that collateral when he knew it didn't belong to him."

Montgomery wiped the sweat from his brow. "He ... knew?"

"Oh, he knew all right. You didn't know, and that's the important thing."

Montgomery's eyes darted from left to right as he tried to process a mixed bag of emotions and fears all at the same time. His jacket now looked far too big on him, as though he was an eleven year old wearing his father's hand-me-down. "Okay ... does he have copies of these plans?"

"He burned them."

"*What!* Why?"

"To stop people from stealing them. Tell me, are you now more interested in getting your money back from Rufus, or getting these plans for his cuckoo clock?"

"The plans! But not of the clock, of everything he ever built!"

Kingston sighed and leaned back in his chair. "So I feared. I'm afraid our business together has come to an end."

"But ... what? All I did was ask you to find Rufus. I can handle the rest."

"Should you require these sort of services again I'll let you know that your troubles no longer entertain me. Should you require future assistance in such matters, perhaps you could try one of the other bounty hunters."

Montgomery breathed in quickly, gritted his teeth and, like a nervous Pekingese, barked at Kingston. "You are contractually obligated to finish what I paid you to do."

"We didn't sign a contract," said Kingston.

"It was verbal."

"And you haven't paid me at all. You promised to do so when I located Rufus for you."

"Then you should deliver!" shouted Montgomery. He looked around the office frantically and his attention fell upon a curious painting hanging in the corner. It appeared to be an abstract watercolour of a zebra-striped dragon flying through the air. Montgomery shivered and looked away. "Hideous," he mumbled.

Kingston looked over to the door marked 'private'. "You have the five gold pieces on you? That was the figure we agreed upon."

"I can write a cheque when you find him," grumbled Montgomery.

"Fine. I don't know why you're so miffed all of a sudden. I located Rufus. He's in that room, listening to everything we said through your enchanted wallet there. You really should take note of your temper, it can be rather off putting."

Montgomery glanced at the wallet sitting right in front of him. "You indicated that you couldn't find him."

Kingston shook his head. "I said no such thing."

"You never said that you found him."

"I've never said many things. It would be quite difficult to keep track of everything I haven't yet said, wouldn't you agree?"

"You told me our business was done!"

"And that's true, because I have wrapped up our business successfully. Is this really how you deal with people?"

"How did you find him?"

Kingston was sure his answer was not going to make the slightest amount of sense to his somewhat challenged client. "I dropped a nearly invisible gold coin on the ground and sat in a café until someone tried to pick it up."

Montgomery shook his head a few times and leaned in across the table. "What? You ... what?"

"So that will be five gold pieces, if you will," said Kingston.

Montgomery scowled. "I demand proof that you caught him."

"You never asked me to catch him, just to find him."

Montgomery glanced towards the private door. "You said he was in there."

"I did. And he is. But you need to be careful with your choice of words. You never said anything about catching him. You said, exactly, *'I want you to find Rufus.'* And so I did."

Montgomery stood, went to the door marked private, glared at Kingston one more time, and he pushed on the door handle as hard as he could. "It's locked."

"Well, of course it's locked, you moron. It says 'private.'"

The door handle turned and Montgomery released his grip in surprise. The door swung open, revealing a mighty goliath of a man. He stood seven feet tall with broad shoulders and a thundering chest. He looked like he could bear hug an oak tree into oblivion. This man was Little John.

Montgomery wheezed again and stepped back to stop his head from craning up to the ceiling.

"John, you remember Montgomery?"

"I do," said John, glaring at the tiny man.

"Now behave yourself. I know he hurt your feelings and all ..."

"He did more than just hurt my feelings," said John, refusing to take his stare away from Montgomery. "And it sounded like he doesn't want to pay us."

Montgomery spluttered and backed away. "A bu ... bu ... no, no, that's not it at all."

"Then here's our bill," said Kingston, holding up the invoice. "Forty five days to pay, if you could."

"Of course," murmured Montgomery. He took the invoice and was relieved to have an excuse to move farther away from the hulking giant in the room. "But uh, on the matter of actually locating Rufus ..."

Kingston called out to the other room. "Rufus?"

A feeble voice echoed back. "Yes?"

"You told Montgomery that he could have access to your plans that are housed in the bank if you couldn't pay him back, right?"

"... Yes."

"You weren't entirely truthful, were you?"

"Not ... entirely."

Kingston smiled back to Montgomery. "Thank you. We hope you have a pleasant day."

"You owe me money!" Montgomery shouted into the private room. He then glared back at Kingston. "You. I will hire you to get him to pay me back the money he owes me."

"One hundred gold pieces?" Kingston asked.

"Plus the interest."

"Of five gold?"

"Yes."

Kingston laughed and shook his head. "He doesn't have that money. And no, I won't take you up on that."

"I'll get my money!" shouted Montgomery. He glared at Kingston, looked away from John, and backed himself towards the exit. "I can report you to the bounty hunter's guild."

"You could," said Kingston. "But it won't do much good. Forty five days. Don't forget."

Montgomery clenched the invoice tightly in his grip and pulled the front door open. He didn't bother to close it as he left and allowed Kingston and John to hear his tiny footsteps disappear down the corridor.

Kingston stood, fixed his pin striped jacket, and closed the door after his client. He could still smell the streak of rum on the man's breath and he was a little disappointed to see him leave in such a hurry; Kingston had a few more insults prepared that would now go to waste. He shrugged and went into the private room, which was the tea room in the back of Kingston's office. It was thin and cramped, with one sofa pushed against the wall, facing the kitchen counter and small fridge. It was so narrow that no one could pass if the door to the fridge was open.

At the far end of the sofa was Rufus, a thin man of average height with a trimmed white beard hiding his gaunt face. His glasses shimmered and Kingston knew it was because they had been enchanted to see the unseen, or at least the easily unnoticed, which was how he came across the nearly invisible gold coin that Kingston had laid out for him. Rufus cursed himself for falling for such an easy trap, but the surprise of finding something on the street while surrounded by hundreds of people had caught him off guard. His only moment of gratitude was that Kingston and John had not beaten him to a pulp when they finally caught him.

"He's going to tell everyone he knows I'm here," said Rufus.

"I know. And he's probably going to trash my office when he gets a chance," said Kingston. He looked over the enchanted leather wallet and held it out for Rufus. "Did you want this?"

"He's probably copied all of my details." He looked over Kingston and John carefully, weighing up the success of what he planned to say. "I need someone to hide me."

"You did a reasonable job of that yourself," said Kingston.

"I stayed out of sight for two months and got caught looking at the pavement. But I've heard about you. You can hide me where no one will ever find me. You two are really ... you know, fictional?"

Kingston and John nodded in unison. A cosmic accident happened not too long ago that sent Kingston Raine, the master of industrial espionage, from the pages of his own series of books into the real world of Limbo. When he was able to return to his own universe and rescue his girlfriend, Joanna York, he had managed to trample through several classics and picked up a couple of friends; Little John from *Robin Hood* and Catalina from *Don Quixote*. Limbo had become their new home since it was neutral territory. Death tolerated their existence, even if it did break some fundamental rules of the realm, being that only formerly living people could live in Limbo, but Death had to accept that he himself had never actually been alive, so he was a violation of his own rules.

Kingston was quite aware of what Rufus wanted help with. Kingston had some access in returning to the fictional universe and it was entirely possible to bring someone with him. "What you're asking could have serious consequences. Trust me, I've screwed up enough lives by being in the wrong place."

"I'd be safer there than here," said Rufus.

Kingston snorted. "Hardly. Macbeth nearly decapitated me."

"Well then, don't send me to Macbeth," said Rufus. "How about somewhere tropical?"

"And the bounty hunters will be after you to bring you back to reality," said John.

"They won't find me if you hide me really, really well."

"Or, you know, you could just stop picking up pennies from the ground," said John.

Kingston smiled at John and gave him a nod of respect.

Rufus fell quiet and shook his head. "I can't pay anyone back, you know that?"

"Oh, I know," said Kingston. "You've racked up quite the fortune in debt. But, sadly, I'm not here to protect you. You're free to go."

"What? But ... you guys help people."

Kingston looked over to John, a little surprised by the news. "Is that our reputation?"

"You guys thwarted a coup!" cried Rufus.

"By accident," said Kingston.

"And you toppled a secret organisation operating within of the Bank of Limbo!"

"That doesn't really mean we help people hide from debt collectors," said Kingston.

"Please? I mean, I can pay ... wait, no, I can't pay you. But I'm sure I have something to barter with. I mean, the Games are coming up soon. I can provide information. I know who the good competitors are. I know the betting system."

"What Games?" John asked.

"They haven't been announced yet," said Rufus. "But they come every ten years and this year is Games year. I could help you win a lot of money with some well placed advice. You can always tell a winner from a distance, and you can always tell who's going to take a fall to try and better their chances in the next round. Well, usually. Sometimes the odds are sixty to one!"

John glanced over to Kingston. "Is that good?"

"If they win, yeah, but has anyone with sixty to one ever won?" Kingston asked.

"Not as such, but they wouldn't have odds if it wasn't a possibility. Please? You can just hide me and I won't cause any trouble."

John looked back to Rufus. "What are the odds for the expected winner?"

"Even money, I suppose. But that's still a win, isn't it? The best was three to one. No one saw that one coming."

Kingston waved his hand in the air. "No longer interested."

"You will be as soon as you know the combatants," said Rufus.

John arched an eyebrow. "Combatants? Like ... wrestling?"

Rufus shrugged. "I guess, but there is fighting involved, so wrestling could happen."

"I'm in," said John, now beaming with a smile. "Put three to one on me and no one will see me coming. Three to one is good, right?"

"Yeah, that's pretty good," said Kingston.

"But not as good as sixty to one?"

"You're more likely to win at three to one."

"What if I'm three to one and fighting twenty guys at once? Would that put me up to sixty to one?"

"It might be a straight twenty to one. Or, more likely, eighteen or nineteen to one, giving the house a chance to take their cut."

"Ah. Gotcha." There was a slight pause, broken by John asking, "The house?"

"Please just hide me," said Rufus. "I've got skills. I have something to barter with, I know it. Anything you want!" He did his best impersonation of a broken man begging for mercy, but his eyes kept darting towards the door and Kingston knew that look. Rufus was ready to run at a moment's notice and he would cause undue trouble the moment someone's back was turned.

"Maybe we could use him, not just hide him," said John. "He's good at the apotha ... please don't make me say that word."

"Apothecary," said Kingston.

"And he knows all of that. Maybe we could use some concoction or whatever. Spells and stuff. Enchantments."

Rufus shrunk back into the sofa. "Oooo, that's ... no, I left all of that behind. I even sold my shop."

"But you remember how to do it," said John.

"I'm not very good at that, actually. A bit of a train wreck."

John snapped his fingers as though he had a brilliant idea. "We could use his glasses to see things. He can teach us that ostrich powder trick."

Kingston bobbed his head and knew a good idea when he heard one. He turned to Rufus and smiled, turning from a troubled rogue to a beaming employer in interview mode. "Well? We've found something worth bartering for, and considering how many people are after you it might be a good idea for you to agree."

"You want to learn to be an apothecary?" Rufus asked.

"Ha! No. You'll do all of that. We hide you and you help us out from time to time."

"Enchantments are really difficult and expensive. I don't have any of the materials. And if I'm honest, I drove my business into the ground. How does this not concern you?"

Kingston shrugged. "I'm sure we could set you loose, but we know how to find you. We know the people you trust and maybe they don't trust you quite as much as you'd like. So we could pop by whenever we wanted. I mean, when Montgomery tells everyone that we found you we're going to be quite rich in the finding Rufus business. We can keep dragging you back here and let you sweat it out while the guy who hired us demands that we hand you over to him. Eventually one of them will make us a reasonable offer."

"But I thought you lot helped people!" cried Rufus.

"I help John," said Kingston.

"I help Kingston," said John.

"Ugh." Rufus slapped his hands over his face and pulled them down over his cheeks, stretching his features wider. "If I agree, where would you hide me?"

"In Limbo, where we can find you and you'll know how to get your chemicals and powders and the like."

"Okay. Well, actually, I can go unseen in most places so I don't need much hiding. I was thinking more of a good book, like *Twenty Thousand Leagues Under the Sea*, something like that."

"I was thinking the basement of the bank," said John.

"Me too," said Kingston.

Rufus reeled back. "You're going to hide me in the bank?" Then something dawned on him and he warmed up to the idea.

"Actually, that might be a good idea."

"If you mess around in there they'll do a lot worse than Montgomery and his lawyer brother."

"If the bankers catch me, yes," said Rufus. His eyes narrowed. Kingston and John had the distinct impression he was plotting something sinister.

John's eyebrows and nostrils flared and he stepped forward, crossing the entire room in one stride. He sucked in a mountain of air and bellowed at Rufus. *"We are saving your life and you will not dick around with our gratitude!"* John raised one of his mammoth sized palms to the side. "Do you see this hand?"

"Yes," said Rufus, shrinking back into the sofa.

"Do you see how close it is to your face?"

"Yes!"

Like a dragon breathing steam out through its nose, John exhaled and the room settled into a controlled calm. "Good." He turned to Kingston and dropped the act completely. "I think he understands now. No dicking around."

John stuffed Rufus into a sack, told him to keep still, and carried him to the bank, where John still enjoyed some privileges as a former janitor, even if he no longer actually worked there. The senior janitor, Simon, had worked in the lower recesses of the bank for so long it had done a number on his memory, so it would take him years to realise that John hadn't been around for a while. Nevertheless, John fitted Rufus with a janitor's uniform, introduced him to Simon and Snowflake the cat, and he knew the two guys would avoid each other as much as possible.

Meanwhile, Kingston turned the idea of Rufus being an asset to his business over in his mind. He leaned back in his chair, tapping his two index fingers together against his lips, and worked through everything he had learned from Montgomery's blunders. He also needed to research something that both Montgomery and Rufus had mentioned. Kingston grabbed a pen and sheet of paper and scribbled a note to Joanna York, his girlfriend and partner in crime.

J, Rufus is now our ally, for the time being. There's a large gambling ring in Limbo. Are you able to track that down and see how Rufus and Montgomery fit into it? There are 'games' coming up, they happen every ten years. Dinner tonight? K.

Kingston sealed the note, wrote Joanna's name clearly on the front, and dropped it into the air. In a flash of light the note disappeared and would reappear instantly at Joanna's feet elsewhere in the realm. Kingston reached for another sheet of paper and scribbled a note to Catalina, John's girlfriend and occasional partner in crime.

C, John did very well today. Can you pick up a copy of any newspaper printed in Limbo from the last twenty five years? I'd like to go over the news a bit. Thanks a million. K.

Like with the previous letter, Kingston sealed it up and dropped it into the air. It disappeared in a flash, leaving Kingston to consider the details of Rufus' knowledge that was locked away in the bank. His thoughts were interrupted when he heard a gentle tap at his office door. It was not the secret tap that either John, Joanna, or Catalina used. Kingston rose out of his chair, quickly put the trip wire in place and closed all necessary drawers to his desk, then he stepped silently towards the corridor.

"To whom am I speaking?" Kingston asked.

"It's Michelle. May I come in?"

Kingston dropped his erudite dominance in an instant. He knew he was going to be delighted with Michelle's arrival and he was equally sure that she was going to bring on a whirlwind of problems. Kingston opened the door and beamed with a smile. "Michelle my dear, how are you?"

"I'm doing okay," she said. She was Death's personal secretary and was often credited for actually running the realm, though she always denied it. Despite being in Limbo for eight hundred years Michelle had the features of a young woman in her prime. Her brown hair was pulled back into a ponytail and she wore a dark grey business suit with a waist coat. Kingston was also sure she had a crush on him. "How are you?"

"Couldn't be better," said Kingston. "Please, come in."

"Is it safe?"

"Ah, let me just unbooby trap the place." Kingston quickly disarmed everything he could use in a surprise ambush. He showed Michelle inside and closed the door behind themselves. "Coffee?"

"Sure," said Michelle. While Kingston headed into the small tea room, Michelle glanced over his dinky office and wondered how a man like Kingston, with all of his considerable charm and ability to lie through his teeth, had settled for one of the smallest offices in the entire realm. It didn't seem to fit with his ego, but she reminded herself that he had only just started the business on his own and, despite receiving an allowance from Limbo, money might be tight.

Kingston returned with an espresso for Michelle and a cappuccino for himself. "Here you go."

"Thank you."

"So how's work?"

"Busy as usual," said Michelle. "And yours?"

Kingston shrugged. "A little slow but I'm sure it'll pick up."

"And Joanna and Catalina are well?"

"Very well," said Kingston. "I mean, there hasn't been much for them to do lately, so they're usually out making contacts, trying to rustle up our next client." Kingston gave Michelle a weak smile, and it was something Michelle read into.

"Are you and Joanna having some problems?"

"Not at all," Kingston said, upping the value to a million dollar smile. "We're actually being honest for once. But she did like being able to jet across Europe, and hide out in Morocco for a few days, then to slip over to the Andes without a care. Limbo has none of those things. It has a few restaurants, and a theatre of sorts, but ..."

Michelle gave Kingston a sympathetic smile. "She's bored?"

"She might be afraid that the best of her years are behind her."

Then came the secret knock and John walked inside. "Sorted," he said, and he glanced at their guest. "Ah! Michelle. Long time."

"John! How are you?"

"I'm the envy of men everywhere, so I'm doing quite well."

"And Catalina?"

"Enjoying herself immensely. She's picked up a few Latin dance moves and I've never seen a woman shake it like that. Neither has any other man in the realm, hence the admiration I receive."

"Lucky you." She turned back to Kingston. "I've come to liven things up."

"I thought you would," said Kingston, and he gave Michelle a cheeky grin.

"I don't always come with an assignment, you know."

"Not always, no. But when you do they are big and expensive."

Michelle dug into her bag and pulled out a freshly printed booklet. It was titled *The Guide* and featured a stylised drawing, circa 1930, of two robots in a gladiatorial battle. "Fresh off the presses. The Games will be announced tomorrow and here is most of the history you'll need as a casual observer."

"The Games, huh?" Kingston said. John picked up the booklet and started flipping through the pages, trying to understand what he was looking at.

"Death knows that the people here can get bored, so not long ago he set up a suggestion box on how to entertain the masses. We sorted through the ideas and put it to a vote among the population. The Games ended up winning. I take it from your stoic look that you are not entirely familiar with what I'm talking about."

"I'm about five percent aware of what the Games are, and I'm trying to figure out how I'm supposed to fit into all of this."

"Well, this is not entirely a social visit," said Michelle. She saw Kingston and John lean in with intrigue. "The people here are quite starved for entertainment, so when something does come along everyone gets involved and things get a little crazy. Everything gets blown out of proportion. You guys are getting a heads up because you are pretty good at thieving and espionage, and these Games require an enormous amount of both. If you get caught or pick the wrong team to root for, people are going to come after you with pitchforks. Or, more likely, bills and insurance claims."

Kingston leaned forward as he was now very interested in all of this potential thievery. "These Games require espionage?"

Michelle smirked. "You're giving me that look where you've already agreed to do anything to enter this tournament."

Kingston feigned a bout of innocence. "I haven't agreed to anything."

"And if I say the team with the best skills at espionage and stealing usually wins?"

"Damn it, Michelle! How am I going to say no to that?"

"Then hear me out. Since the industrial revolution there has been a fight to the death involving machines and, to some degree, magic. Mostly machines, though. No actual people. The to-the-death thing is a figure of speech. It's just machines pummelling each other into dust, although sometimes people do get hurt. The Games happen every ten years. It began as a purely Limbo thing where groups of mechanics and engineers built robots that would beat up other robots. A hundred years ago Hell was granted access to join in. There are several components to this battle with a lot of spectacle. There are battle royales and different weight divisions, power divisions ... it's your regular spectator sporting event, really, but mix in festivals, parties, egos, cheating, secrecy, false information, and you have utter mayhem. Enchanted robots slug it out against other robots until there is a final winner."

John bobbed his head, fascinated by what Michelle was saying, and finally he had to lean in towards Kingston. "Robot?"

Kingston nodded. "Think of a suit of armour that could walk and fight all by itself without anyone inside it."

"Ah, a golem," said John, and he beamed with a smile. "Gotcha. And there are kings involved?"

"A battle royale would be several of these things in the arena at the same time, all fighting each other."

John's eyes lit up. "Oooo! A free for all? I'm in."

"It's not for humans," said Michelle. "Though, humans still take a few beatings. They have a habit of picking a team and being a little too enthusiastic when their team wins, and the losing teams generally knock them senseless."

"Definitely in," said John.

"And this has what to do with us?" Kingston asked.

"You're celebrities and celebrity endorsements can be useful. But mostly you're thieves. If you're working for Team A then it would be good to steal the blueprints from Team B while keeping your blueprints a secret. That way you can prepare Team A's robot to fight effectively against Team B's. Usually there are dummy blueprints with false abilities or surprise tricks, so it's amusing to see when someone falls for believing a dummy blueprint or if they actually managed to get the real thing. Spare parts are also an issue. Teams raid everything they can, even their own offices and rip furniture to pieces just to get some oddly shaped hunk of metal, or they'll try to melt down a door hinge and use it to build their machine."

She caught John looking over the office for anything to steal, and she did her best not to smile. "The enchanting also requires lots of rare items, lots of exotic powders and mystical elements. Without those, your team doesn't stand a chance. But these things are ridiculously expensive and most of them come from Life. So, grim reapers are bribed and some of them get caught, because it's all cheating and all illegal to steal from Life for personal reasons and especially for profit, but Death tolerates it to some degree because it's better to have a disruption like this every ten years and get it over and done with than to have a constant annoyance every single day where people rip apart their offices for no other reason than because they're bored. But the thieves are probably the most important part of a team. Everyone thinks the builder is the number one person, but even the best builder doesn't stand a chance without all the parts they need, and to get all the parts you need a brilliant thief."

"Finally – a noble cause I can get behind," said Kingston. "I suppose there's a lot of gambling involved as well?"

"A ridiculous amount of gambling," said Michelle. "You can bet on anything. Who wins each fight, who's going to lose, who's going to win the first round but lose thereafter, who's going to be the first team disqualified for cheating, which team will be the first to be beaten up, which team is going to be arrested, and which team has no chance whatsoever. The list goes on but there's an official betting sheet that goes with the Games. Well, I say official … it's completely illegal, but since Hell got involved there's no way to stop it. Even if Limbo made gambling illegal, people would just find someone from Hell to bet against. So it's tolerated. But the gambling sheet is as thick as a book. I assure you, someone will be betting on you, even if you don't endorse a team."

Kingston arched an eyebrow. "On me? How?"

"Which team you'll support, which team will you come out the hardest against, which team will try to hire you, all of that."

"What about me?" John asked.

"You as well. Which team will you punch out?"

"Oooo, I like that. Can I bet on myself?"

"Of course, but I'd be careful about it. The odds can change and sometimes teams will bluff their way into the gambling association to turn things in their favour. If they're afraid that you're going to punch them out, they'll make it seem as though it's inevitable and your odds will be terrible. Say you bet a gold piece on yourself that you will beat up Team B, and they go to the commission and turn the odds so that if you do win, you'll get your gold piece back and an extra silver for the actual odd. That way it won't be worth fighting them in the first place."

Kinston glanced over the booklet and saw a familiar face on one of the pages. "Rufus?"

"Yeah, Rufus," said Michelle, with a sympathetic smile. "Oh

boy, is he terrible. He's a builder. Really he's an enchanter. He used to run the apothecary on Uka Pacha Way and I guess the fumes got to him. He's able to bring some of these machines to life. Not actual life, I should say. And not anything remotely life-like either. It's just an expression. But he can build a power source and make it work when, really, it shouldn't."

"Good for him," said Kingston, and he gave Rufus a nod of admiration.

"It's a remarkable talent," said Michelle. "But these builders always get in over their heads and competing is ridiculously expensive. So expensive that you need to take out a loan from the bank and the only way you can pay it back is if you rank in the top three at the end of the tournament. You can collect some of the prize money and any winnings from the bets you placed, and even then you have to sell your robot or break it down into spare parts. That's for third place. Second place, you will earn enough to either keep the money and sell your robot, or repay the loan and keep the robot. You'll end up with a neutral bank balance, give or take."

"I take it if the bank is after Rufus then he didn't break even?" Kingston asked.

Michelle nearly laughed, and shook her head. "Not even close. He's entered himself into every tournament. He's never won. I can't begin to imagine what kind of debt that would put him in, so I can't blame him for hiding at this time. If I were him I would be staying as far away from trouble as possible."

Kingston glanced back at the booklet and felt a rising possibility in his chest. "I suppose the odds of him winning will be terrible."

"Very," said Michelle, and she gave Kingston a knowing look.

"But you also said that the team with the best spy and thief has the greatest chance of winning."

"Yes, I did say that," said Michelle, and then she settled into something that looked a lot like defeat. "But there's no way he's going to compete. He swore off it after the last tournament. He owes too much money to risk it again."

Kingston kept his expression as neutral as possible. "I see. How many teams usually compete?"

"Around thirty. It's a roughly even split between Limbo and Hell. The Games are announced tomorrow, the teams will figure out if they can compete or not, and in a month they'll have their official entries. In three months the chaos begins. I suppose most of the teams started figuring it out the day after the last Games ended so they've had ten years to gather their materials and keep everything hidden away. The gambling, though, starts tomorrow. They'll bet on who's going to compete and who won't. The betting sheet will be updated constantly and you can get a short list that appeals to your interests, or the full thing which weighs the same as a brick."

"Interesting," said Kingston, his eyes glazing over as he imagined the possible glory.

"I thought it would be up your alley," said Michelle. She reached into her bag and pulled out a mass of paperwork, bound and held together with official tape. "Here's everything you'll need. You have a breakdown on Rufus' strengths and weaknesses, previous designs, details on previous competitors and winners, typical enchantments they use, and, most importantly, you're going to need to remember to cheat as much as you can." Michelle locked eyes onto Kingston. "You're going to ensure Team Rufus wins."

"Team Rufus for the win," repeated Kingston, with a nod.

"Good. I've been saving up for the last two years and this time I'm actually going to make some money out of this tournament. And by the time you reach the next set of Games you'll understand how bored everyone in Limbo can be. Just remember to be sneakier than any of the other teams." Michelle leaned back and the seriousness in her demeanour drifted away. "It was nice catching up. Say hi to Joanna and Catalina for me. I must be off." Michelle gave a quick and innocent smile to Kingston and John, and she slipped away.

"I guess the cheating has already begun," said John.

"So it would appear."

II

Kingston had more research to do on Rufus' gaming troubles before he got stuck into Michelle's mass of paperwork. He took John over to Muira's Apothecary, formerly belonging to Rufus, and saw her suspicions the moment he returned.

"Mr Kingston," she said in a raspy and scattered accent.

"Mr Raine, actually. Kingston is my first name."

"You've brought some muscle," Muira said, looking over the giant Little John. "I'll have you know I can knock you both out in an instant without resorting to fists or threats."

"We're not here for trouble," said Kingston, holding out his hands to try and calm the little woman. He handed over *The Guide* booklet and saw Muira's eyes narrow with interest. She was a slender woman with silver streaks in her long red hair, which was tied into a braid that stopped near her knees. She had a slight hunch to her shoulders and wore several necklaces of poor quality, though no doubt of sentimental value, and they matched the many rings on each finger. Kingston noticed that her nails were of differing length and he presumed she had little need to even them out. Muira took the booklet and headed down to the far end of the shop.

It was John's first time in the apothecary and he found it rather unsettling. It was a stupidly long and thin room, just six metres wide and sixty metres long. There were five long wooden shelves with barely any room to move, giving John the feeling that he was a little too robust to fit inside the shop. The shelves were stuffed with small vials and bottles, boxes and containers, bags and purses, each a different size, made from a different material, and in no order whatsoever. Nothing was labelled, either. There wasn't even a counter for Muira to stand behind, it was all shelving. John heard the sound of a gentle stream and wondered if it was one of those weird spinning wheels running against a tap, but he couldn't locate any such item. He opted to stay in the doorway in the hope of looking as inconspicuous as possible.

"You're still looking for him, I gather?" Muira asked.

"No, we found him," said Kingston. "He came to no harm and the matter has been resolved. I was wondering what you could tell me about the Games."

"Because you're new here," Muira mumbled.

"Exactly."

"Everything you need to know is in this booklet."

"Yes, I read through it a few times, but it's more of a publicity shot than actual information. I didn't know that Rufus was a competitor, or that he's competed in every single tournament."

Muira snorted, then she glanced around her shop. "The last time you were here, you bought an enchanted coin."

Kingston did his best not to sigh and knew there was very little in the afterlife that came for free. "What's on offer?"

"How about a necklace for your girlfriend?" Muira moved to the back end of the shop, hunted around for a moment, and return with a plain silver link necklace. "What do you think?"

I think it looks expensive, Kingston thought. "What does it do?"

"It makes people look at her neck and chest," said Muira.

Kingston smirked. "It's not enchanted?"

"I have a feeling if I offered you an enchanted necklace you would ask for something cheaper. This is one gold three silver."

Kingston looked it over and knew that Muira would have more inside knowledge on Rufus' gaming history than anyone else he could find on such short notice, and the sooner he could get to that the sooner he could turn a profit. "Knock it down to one gold, one silver, and you have a deal."

Muira peered at Kingston and was about to refuse, until Kingston pulled out his wallet and counted off the coins. "Very well."

They headed to the front of the shop and Muira found a small woven pouch for the necklace.

"So what can you tell me about Rufus and the Games?" Kingston asked.

"He was crushed in the last tournament and refused to compete again. People kept hassling him to continue, and to pay his debts, and he said as long as he owned this place he would keep on participating, but everything caught up to him in a hurry. At least, that's what he said. He sold it to me last year, and yet everyone seems to think this place still belongs to him and everyone keeps trying to track him down, starting here. I only bought it because it was cheap."

"Do you think he's planning a return to the tournament despite having sold his shop?"

"Everyone knows he'll return," said Muira.

"Even if he refuses?"

"He threatens to quit every time, but someone always finds a way to convince him. It might be with a lady admirer, even a gentlemanly admirer, but he spends the next ten years complaining about how he was duped again and how he will never fall for it again. It's really quite irritating listening to the same story over and over again."

"And he's never won?" Kingston asked.

"Never even came close," said Muira, shaking her head.

"Who usually wins?"

"The gamblers, mostly. No team has ever won twice. Last time one of Hell's builders, Kwon, won. Some compete again, but it's very expensive. I think only one team has ever turned a profit and it took them five tournaments to win just one."

Kingston cocked his head to one side and tried to figure out how that was even possible. "And all of their money comes from the prize at the end?"

Muira shrugged. "Unless they take a bribe. It's often the only way a team can make some money out of it. If someone pays the team a hundred gold pieces to fail it can be tempting." She looked Kingston up and down and narrowed her eyes. "You were wearing that suit the other day."

Kingston looked himself up and down. "Possibly."

"The tie as well."

"It's a good combination," said Kingston.

"Hmm. You came in here and you noticed my outfit and my nails. You always notice my nails. I notice your suit. You think my nails must serve some purpose or else I would cut them. I think you believe you are more successful in that suit and you may find it lucky. Does that sum it up?"

Kingston smirked at Muira. "Well played. I want to convince Rufus to compete this year."

Muira shrugged. "It's not out of the question, but he's more determined to lay low this time than any other. Maybe he wants to stick to gambling. It's hard to do both very well."

"Perhaps he could compete and I could bet on him."

"You're not the first to think he was a winning ticket, Mr Kingston."

"Raine."

"Why don't you bet on someone who wants to win?"

"I have a habit of fighting for the underdog," said Kingston.

"There'll be one favourite and thirty underdogs. Take your pick."

"I already have."

Muira studied Kingston carefully and hummed to herself.

"So what of the gamblers? Who's the most successful one here?" Kingston asked.

"No idea, they don't like to broadcast that information," said Muira. "You would be stupid to gamble alone, though. Us apothecaries usually stick together, pool our money and keep tabs on everything. The same with the reapers. Any trade, really. You'll be a fool to go alone."

"What if I only competed?" Kingston asked.

Muira sighed and shook her head. "You wouldn't last one minute in the arena."

"You never know."

Muira smirked. "I've watched every tournament closely since they started. I know."

"I could buy a team."

"Ha! What an imagination you have."

"Is that illegal?"

"Eh ..." Muira looked to the side, searching through the vast web of random knowledge. "Not illegal, no, but you would be sinking your money into a pit. You're better off taking that money and throwing it at the bookies, at least then you might make something in return."

"I could do both," said Kingston.

"Buy a team and bet yourself to victory? Preposterous. It's not just blind luck that ensures a successful bet, it takes years to perfect a system and to cover all of your bases, and even then your return is pathetic. Trust me. I never gamble more than one gold piece for the whole tournament. You should do the same."

"I do have a trick up my sleeve," said Kingston. "I could find the most successful gambler, or team of gamblers, and simply do that they do. They've done the research, I'll just bet the same."

"Good luck finding them," said Muira. "Anyway, I'm very busy and it looks like you're not buying anything."

"I might buy something. If I do finance a team how would you go about supplying me with some useful items?"

"I don't have enough to supply a whole team. No apothecary has everything. And you shouldn't irritate us either or else we might not deal with you. Then, if you try to use your own independent supplier they're just going to rip you off. I had one guy in here last week who tried to enchant a door knob with radish of skunk, and his dealer came from Hell. But he was supplied with male skunk instead of female and now he can't open his front door anymore. We've cut him off until the end of the year, so don't irritate us or we'll do the same to you. I also wouldn't limit yourself to just one business, you'll need to charm them all and pay in advance. No IOUs."

"Of course," said Kingston, and every secret play from Las Vegas and the sporting world from Life came rushing in all at once. "So what if I were to invite you to an exclusive builder's party? You could get some insight into the team, place your bets accordingly, and gain access to whatever happened behind the scenes?"

Muira peered at Kingston, furrowing her brow, and considered the Englishman carefully. "You're not clever enough to pull that off, Mr Kingston. Good day."

Kingston nodded politely and went to leave, then he found John holding his breath while rubbing his hands furiously against the door frame. "What happened to you?" Kingston asked.

"I held onto the door handle too long and it stung me."

"Ah. Well, I found out something useful."

"Good. Can we go?"

Kingston nodded and they headed outside. "It seems as though the trick is to set a trap for the gamblers. Invite all the interested parties over, schmooze them a little, and see how they gamble. I think with a few cocktails in them we could find ourselves the best people to follow. We just need to convince Rufus to build another robot."

"What if he likes being a janitor?"

"I bet you three silver that he hasn't even picked up a mop yet."

Even though the official announcement to the Games wasn't until the following day, the whole realm was spreading the news like their lives depended on it. Even Joanna could feel it in the restaurant Kingston had picked out for them. All the tables were excitedly hushed, repeating, "You remember the last time ..." and "... should do better this time." Kingston had never seen such excitement on their faces. Even more curious was knowing that the Games didn't actually start for another three months.

"Would you care for some more wine?" the waiter asked, holding a bottle of shiraz in front of Kingston and Joanna.

"Yes please," said Kingston. He looked over the various tables and leaned in closer to the waiter. "So who's your pick for the winner?"

The waiter smiled and leaned forward. "Whoever blows up in the first round is usually crowned the winner, so I'm waiting until then."

"Huh?" said Joanna. "They blow up and can still win?"

"Oh, yes," said the waiter. "In the future rounds all the teams are too afraid of engaging with them in case they blow up again. You take a hit on the first round and sacrifice your machine to scare off the competition until the last round. Your meal will be out shortly." He smiled and headed back to the kitchen.

Joanna shook her head. "I know they have a chance to repair and do some rebuilding, but to completely blow up ... surely that's against the rules."

"From what I read it's not the machine that wins, it's the team. As long as they have something that can compete, even if it's stolen or bought from another team, the team is still in the competition."

"That's hardly fair," said Joanna.

Kingston shrugged. "It will be interesting to see."

"That's certainly one word to describe it," said Joanna. She gently touched the silver necklace Kingston had bought her to remind herself it was still there. From under lowered eyes she peered at Kingston carefully. "You have that look again."

"I know," smirked Kingston.

"You spent the whole day researching this thing, didn't you?"

"Pretty much," said Kingston.

Joanna sighed with a smile and shook her head. "My dear, sweet, sometimes stupid Kingston. Whatever happened to the quiet life?"

"It doesn't pay very well," said Kingston. He leaned over the table and grinned at his girlfriend. "What did you find out about the gambling ring?"

Joanna shrugged and took a sip of wine. "They keep themselves quiet during the off season and are usually honest. Montgomery has a lot of debts with them, as does Rufus. You can still bet on anything around here. Aside from the Games the gambling in Limbo is pretty big, and they usually bet on people in Life living or dying. Montgomery has a thing for musicians. I'm sure he thinks he has a system, but he spends a lot of time at the bar whimpering to himself."

"That's too bad," said Kingston.

"Which is why the Games must be a big deal for him. Thousands of different bets, very good odds, and he might be able to influence a team or two."

"He seemed desperate to get to Rufus," Kingston said.

"I can't help you with that one, other than Rufus does owe him some money."

"And Rufus is a builder. He would have some insight into who would be a contender or not, might even help Montgomery place a few bets. Rufus is a long shot at winning, but a sure thing that he'll compete. The odds on him not competing would be tempting."

Joanna dug into the last of her garlic bread and ran through what Kingston had just said to her. "So Rufus could bet on himself to do nothing?"

"I suppose," said Kingston. "But that doesn't quite make sense."

"No, it doesn't."

Kingston stared into his glass of wine and an intriguing idea occurred to him. "They really bet on everything?"

"I was able to get a copy of the previous betting guide. It's huge, with lots of notes and scribbles. It's the kind of thing you're going to fall in love with. I had a flip through it and one of the craziest bets you could place was which team would accept the blame for something they didn't do, and it had various side bets like beating up another team or stealing another team's design, followed by a bet on which team paid them off to accept that kind of blame."

"So if I bet on Rufus losing everything, failing everything, being robbed, and I ensured that happened, we could make money?"

Joanna shrugged. "Maybe not a lot, but you would certainly make a little."

"And if I bet on him actually winning?"

Joanna rolled her eyes. "Honey, you might want to read up on everything you can before gambling away your life savings on a man who has never even competed in the last round. It's the most corrupt tournament I've ever heard of and ..." She saw Kingston beaming at her with a smile she had seen many times before. She shook her head. "Don't try to convince me."

Kingston winked at her. "Joanna, my love?"

"Don't."

"The light of my life?"

"Oh, come on."

"You and I are gifted with many remarkable skills. We can investigate, we can steal, we can charm people into giving us money. We're also a lot younger than most of the people around us."

Joanna's eyes grew wide with surprise. "How does that help?"

"Most of these people weren't around when sporting events sold out to sponsorship deals and endorsements. These days you don't need a team that can actually win, you just need a team that can sell tickets, sell your brand and be interesting enough for people to pay good money to collect t-shirts, or go to conventions or Meet 'n Greets. You and I know how far reality is willing to take it. We know about sponsorships and endorsements. Very few teams would be able to capitalise on that because they're a hundred years old."

"They will if we start them off," said Joanna.

Kingston grinned. "Then let's start them off. If we hold a fundraiser for a team, sell memorabilia and toys and do all the flashy gimmicks, we can make money on a losing team."

Joanna sighed. "Rufus' team?"

Kingston flared his eyes with delight. "*Our* team. Everyone loves an underdog. Everyone wants the underdog to win. No one likes the favourite because the favourite is boring."

Joanna groaned, finished her glass of wine, and set it back on the table. "Do we know anyone else who is competing?"

"I've heard Carmen Lucha is in the running."

"Ooo, she's in my yoga class."

"Great. Spy on her. More names will come soon but I do know Carmen has taken out a loan from the bank to pay for her machine. The Games start in three months and in that time we could distract everyone out there with our flashy spectacle. And ... and this is the important part ... you and I are famous."

"And fame attracts sponsors?"

"Oh, yes."

"And you think whoring ourselves out like this will be fun?"

Kingston smirked. "I think the level of insanity that happens during these Games will make the whole event a story worth telling. You *know* this is something we're good at. Plus ..." Kingston glanced over his shoulder to make sure no one was listening in. "We have inside help."

Joanna arched her head to one side. "Who?"

"Michelle."

Joanna raised her eyes in surprise, thought it over, and then shook her head. "Has she ever competed?"

"I don't think so."

"Then she's not inside help."

"But she has prime access to a lot of information," said Kingston. "We should sponsor a team."

"We don't have that kind of money," said Joanna.

"I still have some access to the bank."

"Please don't rob the only bank in town. They'll know it was you before you can even start to launder the money."

"I mean I can get a loan. A very good one. And the point isn't to win the prize money at the end."

"It isn't?"

"No, and it's not even to win at gambling."

"It's not?"

"No. It's not about winning the tournament, it's about making money out of it, through sponsorship deals, endorsements, advertising, and by cheating our asses off."

Joanna shook her head. "Just to ball park this idea, how much do you think you could make when this is all over, compared to how many people you will have pissed off to earn your fortune?"

"We will give the people the ride of their lives and it'll be worth them spending money to join in. As far as profit, I haven't run the numbers."

"What kind of price range would make you happy?"

"Ten thousand gold pieces?" Kingston asked.

Joanna raised her eyebrows in surprise. "Ten thousand? *Ten?* When we're currently earning one and a half gold pieces a day?"

"It will set us up for the next ten years," said Kingston.

Joanna raised her eyes in disbelief. "And this is divided between you, John, Catalina, and myself?"

"If we all work as a team, yes. Minimum." Kingston stretched his hand out and placed it on top of Joanna's. "Honey, we've created public relations nightmares for businesses and corporations throughout our entire lives. We've seen them in full damage control. We know the ins and outs of being sneaky and making millions of dollars, pounds, and euros without having a single asset to show for it. And we are popular. Every time we go to a restaurant, or to that sorry excuse of a theatre, people talk and they want to see the mythical Kingston and Joanna. We could run the sorriest excuse of a team into incredible popularity by not trying to win. We'll put on such a spectacle that when the next Games come along people will be begging us for help. They'll pay us to do what we did last time. We'll have a chance to go out there, meet people, interact with this new reality, and have a good time."

Joanna rolled her hand over and stroked Kingston's palm. "It's going to be more work than you realise."

Kingston fired back a grin and knew Joanna was warming up to the idea. "I look forward to it."

"It's not going to turn out the way you want it to."

"I like to be surprised."

"Other people are just as sneaky as you are."

"But they won't have you, and I do. You can handle anything I throw at you."

Joanna smiled. "Aww. Cheesy, but aww."

"And here's the number one reason why you're going to say 'yes'. It's intricate, very difficult, slim chance of success, but it's going to be a lot of fun pulling this off."

"You think I'm swayed by boredom?" Joanna asked.

"I think you're swayed by a challenge."

Joanna sighed and glanced down at the table. "Damn it, I should stop telling you things."

"It's a challenge that only the smartest and most studious of people can pull off," said Kingston. "It's the type of thing that has almost nothing to do with luck, but everything to do with strategy."

Joanna felt a groan coming along. "And you really hope to win ten thousand gold pieces?"

"Oh, yes. With eight hundred thousand residents in Limbo and just thirty teams, ten thousand is achievable. Either way we have a month to come up with a plan before we register. If something is impossible then we simply bow out and give it some more thought over the next decade."

Joanna hesitated.

"Come on. We're going to buy a losing team and ensure it loses so we can make money. We'll be the only team using that strategy."

"Didn't Michelle ask you to ensure that Rufus' team wins?"

"Yeah, and maybe we'll accidentally win."

"Will we lose money if we win?"

"No, we actually win fifteen thousand gold pieces."

Joanna arched an eyebrow at her boyfriend. "Just how bored are you to consider doing something this reckless?"

"Somewhere between 'very' and 'completely'. But here's the best part." Kingston reached into his jacket pocket and pulled out several pages of paper with scribbles and plans scrawled throughout. "I looked at every sporting event from Life."

Joanna held back a snort. "Every?"

"Well … I glanced … at a list. The Library of Limbo has every book ever written, and not only has secured every autobiography by a sportsman or team boss, but I've found every report, fine, and sanction on cheating from the last twenty years. *And* I've found manuals on every sporting fundraiser and sneaky tactic they used to earn a fortune."

"Have you read any of them yet?" Joanna asked.

"No, but give me a month and I'll have everything covered. It's not fool proof but it will be a work of genius by the time we're done with this!"

"So we can't lose?"

Kingston hesitated. "I wouldn't go that far, but if we're trying to lose on purpose then how could we possibly win?"

Joanna thought it over, but the look of determination in Kingston's eyes sold it. "We really need to find something more productive to do with our time."

Kingston beamed with a smile. "Is that a yes?"

"It's a cautious yes, but at any time over the next month we can cut our losses and go back to a normal life, right?"

"By all means."

"Then we might as well look into this thing and see if we're any good at it."

III

Kingston and Joanna headed back to their apartment on Cerberus Avenue, which felt like the size of a shoebox, since it was stuffed with an excess of clothes, maps, and guides to every union in the realm. Two floors below them lived John and Catalina, who had managed to acquire even more clutter than Kingston and Joanna. John had taken up painting with watercolour. Catalina had enrolled in a couple of introductory courses at university and had textbooks piled on top of their dining table.

John and Catalina were pacing back and forth in the corridor by Kingston and Joanna's front door waiting for the intrepid duo to return from dinner.

"It's about time!" cried John.

Kingston removed his keys and took one look at his friend's expression. "I take it our office was trashed?"

"Beyond trashed! I swear, when I find Montgomery I'm going to wring his little neck until his head pops off and explodes against the ceiling like a piñata."

Catalina looked at Kingston with the deepest sympathy. "I tried to calm him down before you got back. We only just arrived."

Kingston unlocked their door and led everyone inside.

"Is everyone okay?" asked Joanna, as she dropped her purse onto the sofa.

"We're fine," said Catalina. "Just a little agitated."

"Ah well, there wasn't much to trash anyway," said Kingston.

"That's not the point!" said John. "It's the principle! You don't just walk into a man's office and rip it apart like that!"

"John? You've done the same."

John paused and stared back at Kingston. "I had a very good

reason for doing whatever it is you remember."

"I know, we all have good reasons. But Montgomery actually did us a favour by trashing our place."

John pulled a face and, for a moment, looked as though he was stuck trying to swallow a lemon. "He ... did? How?"

Joanna nodded and slipped off her shoes. "Kingston has this thing about his offices being trashed. He likes to figure out how dumb the trasher is by what they touch and what they miss."

"They didn't miss much," said John.

"I bet they left the ashtray," said Kingston.

"Yeah, I saw it on the ground."

Joanna rolled her eyes. "I keep telling him that only a moron would take it."

"And I keep telling her that only a moron would leave it behind."

John shook his head and stared at his two friends. "You'll have to explain that one to me."

"It's Limbo!" said Kingston. "No one smokes here. You can't even get cigarettes. So why would I have an ashtray? Because there's something significant about it, maybe there's a clue hidden away and this provides the key. You can't leave something that sneaky behind, you just can't."

"Meanwhile I tell him it's an obvious trap," said Joanna.

"But to be fair, most of our clients are already morons," said Kingston.

"Maybe he just wanted to trash the office and not rob you?" asked Catalina.

"Montgomery wants to know about Rufus' involvement in the Games. Thankfully there was nothing left behind for him to take and Rufus is now in hiding. Speaking of which ..." Kingston pointed to a thick bundle of pages lying on the dining table. "Michelle has given us a hell of a lot of background information that we need to get up to speed on before we talk to Rufus tomorrow."

"Is anyone else concerned that my darling boyfriend decides things for the group without consulting us?" Joanna asked.

"Sometimes," said Catalina, with a sharp nod.

"Fine," said Kingston. "I would like to sponsor Rufus in this year's tournament, bet almost everything I have by following the lead of experts, and I'd like you three to help make us all a lot of money by being a little more creative than the other teams."

"I'm in," said John.

"Yeah, me too," said Joanna, with some degree of resignation in her voice.

"John promised there'll be parties," said Catalina.

John quickly nodded to Kingston, begging with him to agree.

"There will be lots of parties," said Kingston.

"I'm in," said Catalina. "I've been cooped up at home for so long that I'm starting to crash against the walls."

"Excellent," said Kingston. "I just need to find a way of convincing Rufus to join our team."

Catalina sighed and shook her head. "I can help."

Kingston ran through a list of all the possible things Catalina was supposed to say instead, and came up blank. "You can? How?"

Catalina pointed to her chest. She noticed that Joanna glared at her for a moment. "He's a little old man, right?"

"Uh, yeah," said Kingston.

"I had hundreds of little old men in my town. They thought I couldn't hear them describing me, but I could. They'd come to the bar and try to talk to me. After a few drinks they became a lot more juvenile, and I would slap them."

Kingston hesitated in trying to find the most diplomatic way to say this and knew there were two women in the room who would be pissed off with him if he ballsed up his handling of the situation. "I think it's a fantastic idea. What is your best outfit for negotiations?"

John snorted and quickly looked away. "Sorry."

Catalina glared at him. "I know what you're thinking."

"Still sorry," mumbled John.

Kingston was sure that John was imagining Catalina wearing nothing and trying to hold Rufus' attention to her eyes while she death-stared him during a negotiation. Kingston also felt Joanna glaring at him, now burning his soul as she figured out what Kingston was picturing.

Kingston quickly jumped back into reality. "I'll go talk to Rufus. If it doesn't go well I have no problem pulling out all of the stops and trying again later."

"I might have a problem with some of the stops," said Joanna.

"We'll cross that bridge when we come to it," said Kingston.

"Oh, we will, will we?"

"Yes. As a team," said Kingston, giving her a quick nod.

"Are you -"

"Sure? Absolutely."

Joanna sighed. "Fine. Go talk to our master builder."

Kingston smirked at his girlfriend. "I could bring back some gelato."

Joanna looked away sheepishly.

"Mango and lemon flavoured."

Joanna still looked away.

"With crushed chocolate and coconut."

Joanna gave Kingston a diplomatic nod. "That will do nicely."

Rufus stood in his janitor overalls and looked very uncomfortable hiding in the basement of the Bank of Limbo. He shook his head and turned away. "Not interested."

"I have a lot of resources at my disposal," said Kingston, wearing his best suit with his power red tie. "You do know that I used to work for the Bank of Limbo, right?"

Rufus shuddered and shuffled away. "Still not interested."

"What if I can offer you a deal?" asked Kingston.

"I've had too many deals in my day. They don't work out."

"As long as you're competing you'll have amnesty against any debts you owe," said Kingston.

"Ha! You think I haven't heard that one before? How else would you explain the last three tournaments I entered? Up to my earlobes in debt and still people tell me that this year will be better, this year will be worth it." Rufus shook his head and looked away.

"I'll sponsor you," said Kingston.

Rufus paused, then looked back to Kingston. "You what?"

Kingston smiled, and knew he was reeling Rufus in. "Teams can get sponsored, right? I read through the rules."

Rufus spied Kingston with considerable suspicion. "You didn't read all the rules, did you?"

"I did," said Kingston.

"Then clearly you don't understand them," said Rufus.

"How about I convince you to let me sponsor your entry into the tournament?"

Rufus squinted at Kingston and jutted his jaw out as he thought it over. "Go on."

"I will buy your entry into this year's tournament. I can rustle up some sponsorship deals and events and try some unique strategies. We can make money even before we enter the competition, all we need to do is promise that we actually enter."

Rufus cocked his head to one side. "How does that work?"

"I'm a local celebrity. As soon as we have a team the press will write about me, people will talk about us, we'll build up some public perception of what we're up to, and then there will be luncheons and parties. We'll gather donations, sign a few autographs, display your machine, and convince them it's a winner. You have the experience, I have the fame and know-how."

Rufus thought it over carefully and waited to see if Kingston was going to elaborate any further. "You'll cover all of our expenses for this tournament?"

"Of course," smirked Kingston.

"But I'm terrible at winning," mumbled Rufus.

"We're not here to win, we're here to make money."

"But people only make money when they win."

"We're going to be different."

Rufus shook his head in bewilderment. "What the hell does that mean? And what about my previous losses?"

"I'll handle the loans. The interest you would pay is ridiculously high. But because this will be my first loan my interest will be low."

"Until they find out you're sponsoring me, then it'll be high," said Rufus.

"Either way, it's doable. Before every new bash-'em and thrash-'em we'll hold a press release, a party, a donation for a good cause, and we'll recoup our money."

"And what happens if we place in the top three? You'll take every copper, I suppose."

"We'll split any profits evenly," said Kingston.

"Profits, eh? You'll cook the books just enough so that if we place first there won't be any profits for us to share?"

"I'm not like that," said Kingston. "I'll keep you up to date on just how much we're spending."

"I see you have really not thought this through."

Kingston dropped his shoulders. "Then what am I missing?"

"Last time there were thirty three teams competing. Fourteen were from Limbo. Do you know who the real winner was? The bank. There ended up being forty nine loans to the Limbo teams.

I'm not the only one who is flat broke and utterly in debt, you know. I'm just the one who's more utterly in debt than the others."

"I know, I did my research," said Kingston. "It's going to cost ten thousand gold to make it through to the end of the tournament in one piece, providing we get lucky. Whoever wins first place takes home fifteen thousand gold."

Rufus shook his head. "All it takes is one malfunction during a match and our cost to rebuild will cancel out any winnings we could hope to earn. And you have no idea how heart breaking that is working for months, even years, to build the best machine, and then rebuilding it over and over again, hoping to see the odds work so well in your favour that you can bet everything you have. And you know what? Other teams still win. I've competed eighteen times and have taken out fifty three loans at increasingly higher interest rates. I had to sell my apothecary and I still owe close to a quarter of a million gold to the bank because of these stupid tournaments. Do you know how long that would take to pay off? At best, that's three hundred and fifty years' worth of salary. So no. I'm out. I can't possibly afford to compete."

Kingston nodded and knew he had a final card up his sleeve. "I will cover all expenses for this year."

Rufus paused, working it through his mind, and he slowly turned back to Kingston. "All of them?"

"Within reason," said Kingston.

"No team ever makes money out of this."

"Just because they haven't, doesn't mean they can't. There's merchandise, fancy parties, gambling, insurance pay outs, product placement, endorsement deals, raffles, you name it." Kingston beamed at Rufus and, at the same time, felt his pulse drive a rampage of panic through his chest. The only saving grace was knowing that Michelle had given him a tonne of inside information already.

"And all I have to do is build a machine and you'll pay for it?" asked Rufus.

"Ideally a machine that could win if it ended up in the finale, and no, there will be other obligations as well."

"You know they sometimes put the builders and sponsors in hospital, right?"

Kingston had indeed read up on that and he wasn't thrilled with the idea, but he shrugged it off as best he could.

"I'm serious," said Rufus. "Last time around everyone from Team Puckle were poisoned. They were also trapped in their workshop for three days, trapped *out* of the workshop for six, their machine was stolen, returned, dismantled, repaired, glued to the ceiling, and then imbued with rotten fish which made everyone so sick that they had to clear the whole building."

"I did hear of that, yes," said Kingston.

"They were also beaten up by teams from Hell, their apartments were ransacked, their heads shaved while they slept, and all of that was because they won their first round. They forfeited in the second round and withdrew from the competition because no one could risk the punishment of winning again."

"Yeah, that's because the Puckles were former referees. They were asking for trouble!"

Rufus shrugged. "Still, it's not something I really want happening to me."

"No one can predict the future with absolute certainty. I've seen the blueprints to your previous contraptions. They're outstanding."

Rufus reeled back in surprise. "You saw them? How? They're supposed to be under lock and key in the vaults beneath our feet!"

"I know," said Kingston. "I used to work here. I still have some access from time to time."

"That's my intellectual property!"

"Yes, and I'm offering to cover the expenses of building a machine. What do you say?" Kingston held out his hand for Rufus to shake, knowing full well that Rufus was coming up with a list of sneaky ways to steal from the team and earn himself some money in the process. Rufus stared at Kingston's open hand carefully.

"I'll do it for a hundred thousand gold pieces," said Rufus.

"Ha!" cried Kingston. "I'll pay you two gold a day from now until the last day of this year's tournament."

"Ten gold a day."

"Two."

"Ten is my final offer."

"Two."

"I'm in more debt than you could possibly imagine!" cried Rufus. "It's ten a day or nothing."

"You're willing to work for nothing?" asked Kingston. "That's very generous of you."

"You know what I mean," sniped Rufus.

Kingston eyed Rufus carefully. "I'll tell you what. If we make it into the last round I'll retroactively pay you six gold a day."

Rufus scoffed and shook his head.

"And if we win we'll make it ten gold."

"There's no hope of winning," said Rufus.

"Are you really telling me that there is no way a team can't cheat and steal their way towards victory? That's very pessimistic of you."

Rufus paused and tried to find a flaw in Kingston's reasoning, and then he shrugged. "We don't have the time to build a proper machine! We also don't have the history of bribing the referees. Other teams have been working on their strategies for years and we have just three months until the tournament begins."

"Plenty of time," said Kingston, and he beamed with a smile. "And I'm glad you said 'we'. Considering I'm covering the financial risk, and the burden, and all of the heartache going along with this, you should remember that you're currently unemployed, in debt, and people are looking for you."

"Oh, so that's how you're going to convince me, is it? Do you want to add breaking my legs as an incentive as well?"

"This is the only way you're going to make any money," said Kingston.

Rufus stared back at Kingston and squinted. "Five gold a day, ten retroactively to make it into the final, twenty if we win."

"Three and a half a day, eight when we're in the final, and twelve if we win."

Rufus bobbed his head as he worked through the various maths of it all, and with a great deal of reluctance he accepted. "Fine. Team Rufus competes again."

"Great!" said Kingston, and he held out his hand to shake Rufus'. "But we should probably come up with a mascot name. 'Team Rufus' doesn't quite cut it anymore."

"Oh, I can't wait to hear this suggestion."

"How about the Dragons?"

Rufus rolled his eyes. "That is beyond lame."

"Teams need a good name with a mascot to them."

"You can call the team whatever you want, but they are all registered under the builders' name. And as far as tournaments go I am, unfortunately, the famous one, the one they all know about."

An hour later, Kingston navigated the team through their first meeting and introduced everyone around.

"Joanna, John, Catalina ... this is Rufus."

Rufus eyed up Catalina and then caught an evil glare of John. Rufus looked up in feigned surprise. "Easy, little fella."

John snorted in surprise. "Little?"

"Your name is Little John, is it not?"

"You can call me *sir*, if you like, but failing that I prefer Nottingham instead of Little."

"Nottingham John?" asked Rufus.

Kingston clapped his hands together. "Okay, let's get the show on the road. We have no assets to speak of, but lots of resources that are available at the right price. Since we're in the bank and surrounded by vaults, Rufus, can we use some of your old machines?"

Rufus shook his head. "I sold the best stuff to the highest bidder ten years ago."

"Then can we buy something from the old teams?"

"Not likely," said Rufus. "Anything that's worthwhile is taken already. There were lots of would-be teams who wanted to compete but couldn't because they couldn't get the machine parts in time."

"Oh, come on, there have to be previous teams that aren't competing with their old contraptions locked away somewhere. Can't we dismantle their entrants and Frankenstein ourselves a complete machine?"

Rufus rolled his eyes at Kingston and shook his head. "Amateur. There would be too much conflict between the enchantments. Every builder has their own style and dependencies, it just wouldn't work. You need to build these things from scratch."

Kingston shook his head in confusion, leading Rufus to groan.

"Do you know anything about industrial trains?" Rufus asked.

"No."

"What about airplanes?"

"Yes, I do know something about airplanes," said Kingston.

"Good, that's something, at least. Imagine trying to build a turbo prop hybrid with a jet engine and a set of propellers, forward facing and rear facing, with a mix of mechanical controls and computer aided, and trying to get them all working at the same time in harmony, while also being capable of vertical take off with helicopter rotors and traditional runway take off, with retractable wheels as well as water skis and snow skis just for fun. That's what it would be like if you mixed machines from multiple builders with differing styles of enchantments. You end up with chaos."

"I'm a little lost," said John.

Rufus dropped his head towards his chest. "Uh ... best way ... dumbed down ... the statues? No ... Ah! Okay!" Rufus raised his head again and pointed at John. "You like drinking, right?"

John beamed with a smile. "As sure as a woodsman likes his axe."

"Imagine a simple cocktail. Vodka, schnapps, pineapple juice."

John gave a sharp nod. "Done."

"Now imagine a second cocktail. Rum, milk, coconut."

"I'm totally enjoying this analogy. Go on."

"Imagine a third drink. Red wine. And a forth. Beer."

"That would be quite an evening," said John, still beaming with a smile.

"Yes, it would be ... quite ... an evening. Four wondrous drinks all by themselves. As long as you stick to one type of drink you're going to have a good time. But if you mix them altogether in the same glass? Disaster."

"It would still get you drunk, though," said John.

"If your goal is just to get drunk, then yes. But you won't enjoy being drunk because it will taste awful and you'll be looking for the nearest toilet to rectify your mistake. The point is: if builders team up, it has to be at the very beginning and they need to agree on how to build their machine, be it a gladiator or a wrecking ball. You can't just slap things together and hope it will work well."

Joanna leaned forward. "But you can still sell parts to other teams?"

"Usually vital parts, the bits that are really hard to duplicate. It either guarantees them that you won't be participating or it gives them ideas on how to bend their enchantments."

"Right," said Kingston. "So according to the inventory, your vault is well stocked. Surely Frankensteining something from only one builder is possible?"

Rufus snorted. "This really is your first rodeo, isn't it?"

John cocked his head to one side. "Rodeo?"

With great reluctance, Rufus led Kingston, Joanna, John, and Catalina to his vault and signed his life away. The vaultier joining them smiled and bobbed his head the whole time, not sure if he was more excited to finally meet Kingston, or to see that Rufus was back in another catastrophe, or even that these two might be pairing up. The vaultier unlocked the vault and the door swung open on creaky hinges, revealing a stack of shelves along three of the walls.

"There," said Rufus. "Everything I've ever built and scrounged together and still have to my name."

Kingston's immediate reaction was that the vault must have been robbed, because the earliest robot sat on the left in a crumpled mass, looking more like a washing machine with two large carriage-like wheels on the side. It was the most complete robot in the vault. Wrapping around the room were the more recent editions, which had been cobbled together from parts of their older versions. There was for another three machines. The paperwork was there, dumped on old wooden chair, but the machines themselves were missing.

"Where'd everything go?" Kingston asked.

"Sold it," said Rufus.

"You sold your last three machines?"

"Yep. I tried selling everything after the last tournament, and this is what no one wanted. Can't blame them, really. Who'd want a robot that's a hundred and twenty years old with rudimentary enchantments?" Rufus looked over Kingston carefully. "You know we're going to lose, right?"

Kingston glanced nervously towards the vaultier, who gave a solemn nod. "Why do you think that?"

Rufus sighed. "The other teams have had ten years to gather materials. Some things are cheaper in the year after the tournament when the buzz has died down. By now, everything is twice as expensive. But it's your money, and you're the genius, so this is what you have to work with." Rufus spread his arms out and waved them at the empty shelves, then he sighed again. "Just to warn you, I could use some cheering up right about now." He then peered at Catalina.

She squinted back at him. "My boyfriend knows a couple of good jokes."

Rufus glanced up at John and found the giant staring down at him as though he was ready to pop Rufus' head off his neck. Rufus looked back to his nearly empty vault.

Kingston smirked at John. "What would Snowflake do?"

Rufus winced again. "Bad idea. Things tend to get a little

electrocuted when I'm nearby."

A little electrocuted, Kingston thought. He tried to find the humour in being a lot electrocuted, but he had experienced that before and had no interest in repeating the displeasure.

"So where do we start?" Joanna asked.

"I'd need a lab," said Rufus.

"You can have access to the janitor areas. There are plenty of rooms."

Rufus shook his head. "No good. We need total privacy and away from other teams, *especially* away from the other teams. One word of where I'm building and they'll be all over me."

"Are you sure?" Kingston asked. "I mean, you do lose quite often. Perhaps they won't bother spying on you."

Rufus rolled his eyes and tutted under his breath. "Amateur. The whole point is to beat the other teams. We'll spy on them, they'll spy on us. You can't have a tournament without spying. And they'll be down here anyway to check on their vaults. They'll find us here, no problem. So no, not here. Not in the bank."

"I think at this point it's wise to introduce a veto policy into our agreement," said Kingston.

"Couldn't agree more."

"Excellent. Then as your bankroller and the owner of the team I will have the power of veto, understand?"

Rufus sighed again and shook his head. "If that's really what you think is best, then I'll build the stupid thing wherever you want. I'll do it in the foyer of Death Incorporated if I must."

Kingston stared off into space for a moment, then he considered that possibility and how viable it was. It would certainly make the other teams paranoid that Rufus was doing everything in the open, as though it was a deliberate attempt to hide something in plain sight. Kingston decided to hold onto that idea for later.

John poked the washing machine and saw it wobble. "This is the worst looking golem I have ever seen."

"We'll need tools," said Rufus.

"Okay," said Kingston. "Do you have a list of tools?"

"I might have to build some of them, but yes, I can come up with a list. I'll need supplies for those as well."

"The sooner you can write a list of everything you need, the sooner we can get started," said Kingston.

"Hold your horses," said Rufus. "I'll also need an assistant."

"Any ideas?"

"Not really. Remember the little electrocuted bit? Yeah. I go through assistants quite quickly. But I need someone who can stir sugar properly. You can't believe how many people give it a single full cup stir and expect the sugar to be evenly distributed. It doesn't work like that. You need at least eight full rotations and two taps on the rim before it's done properly."

"I'll see what I can do," said Kingston.

"And she has to be sexy," said Rufus, grinning into space, and he glanced towards Catalina.

"Ay, for the love of ..." mumbled Catalina.

That prompted Joanna to roll her eyes.

"What?" said Rufus, turning to Joanna. "You look fine."

"Fine?" cried Joanna.

"I'm sure you have a lovely personality."

"HUH!"

Rufus looked back at Kingston with a solemn look. "And if I'm risking my life, again, for this tournament, then I should be able to gawk at some cleavage once in a while and have some playful banter."

"Veto," said Kingston.

"But there has to be cleavage!"

"Veeeeeto," said Kingston.

Rufus glanced over his shoulder and stumbled back in surprise. John had crept forward to stand as close to Rufus' as possible, shielding him from the girls. Rufus looked back to Kingston. "I'll also need a boat load of illegal ingredients."

"That we can do. How soon can we have that list?"

"Ten days."

"How about tomorrow?"

"I don't even have blueprints yet," said Rufus.

"Whatever are the ten most essential items, get them on a list to me by tomorrow. Then we'll look at the next ten."

"You're expecting to enter *this* tournament, right?"

Kingston sighed and felt the strain of dealing with Rufus start to reach a fearful and potentially familiar cliff. "Yes, I expect to enter this tournament."

"We'll need thousands of essential items."

"Good, yes, fine. List. Tomorrow. Okay?"

"Not really," mumbled Rufus.

Kingston sighed again and hoped like hell that this his faith in their builder would be worth it.

IV

The gang spent the night looking for any whirlwind scheme hidden in the back of their minds that would guarantee them victory. Kingston and Joanna went through Rufus' inventory and mass of debt, while John and Catalina read through the rules of the competition. They also went over the previous newspapers to see just how crazy the whole event was going to turn out. John kept imagining giant suits of armour beating each other into oblivion, while Catalina expected them to joust to the death, but the pictures from the newspaper didn't seem to match what they had in mind. Most of the machines looked like carriages with flails spinning around in every direction, or washing machines dropping out of thin air and smashing whatever lay below them.

Kingston hovered over the list of previous entrants. Since the very start of the Games there had been two hundred and sixty three teams from Limbo that had competed. The first tournament was made up of five teams. Rufus came dead last, having his machine smashed to a pulp three times and forcing a forfeit just before the finale. Kingston checked over the paperwork following that event. Three of the teams competed again in the following tournament, the other two sold their machines for scrap to buyers who competed in the second tournament. The losers of the second tournament sold most of their parts to teams who were competing in the third tournament. Despite that, each builder still had a vault in the bank where they stored spare parts, failed parts, and minor details that they were unwilling to sell if the price wasn't to their liking. Some of those vaults still had unsold parts hiding within them. Kingston tapped his pen harder against the stack of paper and glanced up towards the ceiling, putting a plan together.

"That's not helping," mumbled Joanna, as she stared at Rufus' accounts.

"Sorry."

Joanna peered over at the paperwork Kingston had in front of him. She saw that each page had a list of participants from Limbo and Hell, and each page belonged to one tournament, dating back over the previous eighteen Games. All of the Hell entrants were crossed out and Kingston had labelled each of the remaining teams with three options, a tick, a cross, and a question mark. "Figuring out who the competition this year will be?"

"No, figuring out how to cheat." He glanced down at the inventory of Rufus' vault. "There is a bit of shadiness here. There are several obvious items listed here that aren't actually in the vault. The thing is, just about everything in there is the property of the bank, since Rufus used it all as collateral against a loan, and he's had to default on a lot of loans. From what I can tell, the bank tried to sell most of this stuff at an auction, and whatever he still has in his vault never sold. But ..." Kingston flipped over a stack of paperwork and Joanna glanced over.

"Half of his inventory went missing before the bank seized it?"

John and Catalina looked up in surprise.

"Exactly," said Kingston. "I'm willing to bet that Rufus went into his vault, fudged the paperwork, robbed himself, and hid his most prized possessions somewhere else. Considering how easy it is to buy the rights to someone else's vault and keep their name as the owner, I'm sure he has a secret vault somewhere in the bank full of spare parts that he's been itching to cobble together. He just can't do it when the bank is paying that much attention to him, because, technically, none of that belongs to him."

Joanna leaned back and shook her head at Kingston. "Wouldn't it be nice if he had someone covering his expenses so he doesn't have to pay the fines someone receives for using his machine."

"Yeah," said Kingston, and he stared off into space. "Yeah."

"It sure is sneaky. I like it."

"It means if we're going to cheat, we might as well *really* cheat."

Catalina whispered to John. "Don't ever let those two be parents."

The mood was broken when Kingston snorted to himself.

"Something on your mind, dear?" Joanna asked.

"I was just thinking of the easiest, silliest combatant out there.

We build a tiny airship, the size of a balloon, and make it invisible. No one will ever find it. We can build that thing for less than a hundred gold and glide through every round."

"It needs to fight," said Catalina, and she flipped through the big book of rules and regulations. " *'Passive entrants are disqualified from competing.'* It goes on in some detail, but ultimately it has to be capable of defeating another machine."

"Plus, we're looking for sponsors," said Joanna. "No one wants to bet on something they can't see. Plus, they want actual fighting machines to pulverise each other, they don't want cheaters sneaking their way into the finale."

"Fair enough," said Kingston. He looked over to John. "Any advice on gambling?"

John looked up from his set of books and had a bewildered expression on his face. "This betting thing makes less sense the more you look at it. In the last tournament there was a team headed by Louis Sequa, from Hell. There were thirty three teams competing. If you were to bet on his team you would have won the most amount of money, even though he didn't win the tournament. In round one the odds of him winning that match were three to two. He lost. If you were to bet on him not being in the second round, you would have won at six to five ... I don't even know how those odds stack up, but either way he didn't compete in that round. He won the third round by default and that would give you even money, unless you bet that he forced a default, and then that gave you three to one."

"How did he force a default?" Kingston asked.

"He stole his opponent's machine," said John. "Sequa's team was the only one who showed up. But by then he was up against the favourite of the tournament, also from Hell. Sequa said he was going to win, hands down, but it was well known that the Hell teams were bribing each other to better their odds. But the gambling house is onto that, you see, so they only gave the Hell teams even money, meaning that it was pointless to bet on either side. At this stage you might remember that Sequa stole one of his opponent's machines. Well, if you were smart, you would bet that *that* machine was still expected to win its next match. Since it didn't actually compete against Sequa, its next match was ten days later. Sequa's machine dragged the stolen combatant into the arena to, I imagine, thunderous applause. Sequa's machine hurled the stolen one into the opponent, giving you a win of nineteen to one for the little machine, and even money on Sequa. At this point one of Sequa's teammates was knocked out. That could win you four to three gold. His machine also exploded while being repaired. If you saw that coming, and several people did, you would have won yourself eight to one. It failed to enter the arena for its last match, earning another four to one, but only if you bet that it was going to explode before it actually exploded, otherwise if you knew it had already exploded and wasn't going to enter then the odds were even money."

John looked away from his notes, bewildered. "I've read through this thing a dozen times and I still can't make much sense from it. Teams can manipulate the odds for themselves and for everyone else competing. They can bribe, they can even bet that they'll be caught bribing, but they'll also receive a fine for that bribe. Then again, they can also bet on who will take the fall for that bribe which is often another team who desperately need some money, and the whole madness continues. The list of cheats by Sequa is extraordinary. He was sued by four other teams. The odds of him being sued four times is eleven to one. Yeah, you can actually win a bet just by suing someone. He was caught bribing one of Limbo's teams once. That was three to one. He ratted on another team for bribing, that's even money. It took me five pages to write all of these things down, and if you played it right and started with one gold piece, you could have ended up with two hundred and twelve pieces, if you gambled everything perfectly. He didn't, but his team still made the most money, and they didn't win."

Catalina strained her head around. "So actually competing doesn't matter, it's more important to bet correctly?"

"Pretty much," said John.

"And what about Rufus' team?" Joanna asked.

John glanced over his notes again. "Not great. If you thought he was going to lose every single match you would have won even money each time."

Kingston wasn't sure that all added up. "So all we have to do is bet on ourselves losing in every round and we could walk away rich?"

"Not quite," said John, and he flipped to yet another set of notes. "There are four rounds, so you would have to rebuild your machine at least three times, though from what I've seen machines do frequently explode, or are sabotaged, and in the last tournament Rufus competed only in the first and second round. Even then he had to rebuild his machine four times. But every rebuild cost him a lot of money, which he didn't have, so he kept going back to the bank for another loan. The interest rate kept on increasing. By the end he was borrowing thousands of gold pieces and having to pay them back at a rate of fifty percent."

"Right," said Kingston, losing a little steam with his grand idea of cheating. "And yet he kept on playing."

John shrugged. "He's not exactly the brains of any operation."

"And yet he's our master builder," said Joanna, and she stifled a glare at Kingston.

"I see that look," said Kingston.

"It's because you're looking right at me."

Kingston went back to his notes. "We're just going to have to cheat better than anyone else."

Rufus was on his hands and knees rummaging through the various cupboards and closets two floors underground in the Bank of Limbo. He spent the whole time muttering to himself, picking through the random items for anything useful. He wasn't happy with any of it.

"More stupid quills. Paper clips. Bulldog clips. Parchment. Paper." He tried the next room and came across a mountain of spare plates and bowls, knives and forks. "What are we doing, planning for a hurricane? There are more plates down here than people in the entire realm!"

He knew there had to be something that would inspire him, hidden behind a secret door perhaps, or just hiding in plain sight. The problem he found was that he didn't know what that useful item was. He was a builder and an enchanter with nothing to build or enchant. Pretty soon he was sure he would end up making the realm's longest paperclip chain, beating the previous record set fifty years ago by Ernesto Delgordo. Or he would try and stack as many plates on top of each other, reaching a height of seven metres, beating the previous record set eighty years ago by Emille Argent. Rufus slumped back on the floor and stared at the seemingly endless cupboards and realised that the people of Limbo really were a bored lot, and that he knew far too much trivia about their records.

And right now the masses are betting on me losing again, he thought. *At least people know who I am.* Then he remembered that people like Montgomery Stup also knew who he was and they were chasing him down for money. And that the people who knew who he was also knew that he was a colossal failure.

Rufus glanced around the room, number sub-two 92, and froze when he saw a white fluffy cat sitting in the doorway to sub-two 91, staring at Rufus with its tail swishing back and forth.

"So you're real," Rufus mumbled. "A cat in the afterlife. Who'd have thought?"

"His name is Snowflake," said Simon, standing in the doorway to sub-two 93.

Rufus glanced over and was again surprised to see just how frail Simon looked in his overalls. "He's yours?"

"No. He was here when I started work." Simon cocked his head to one side and looked over Rufus, suddenly perplexed by the human facing a set of open cupboards. "Why are you sitting on the floor?"

"I was looking for something useful," said Rufus.

"Ah, well there's lots of that down here. Everything useful ever needed is down here. You'll have to go through the inventory form and have it processed, then a requisition form. You can find them in the filing cabinet in the requisitions department. Then you'll need your supervisor's signature and then you can come down and fill out the acquisitions form to let your supervisor know that you've actually taken the item. They'll need to sign for that as well. Then you staple the two -"

Rufus held up his hand and stopped Simon mid-sentence. "Thanks, but I don't actually know what I'm looking for."

Simon paused and glanced at the cupboard in front of Rufus. "And you think you'll find it among the plates and bowls?"

Rufus sighed and shook his head. "Maybe. Why does your cat keep staring at me?"

"Snowflake is harmless. You could take a few lessons from him, you know."

Rufus looked over to Snowflake, who was still swishing his tail back and forth but was now looking to the side of the room, bored by the two humans talking. Rufus didn't think there were any lessons to be learned from a cat, let alone a cat that hung around the basement of a bank with an absent-minded janitor. "I used to be an apothecary, and now I'm sitting on the floor thinking about plates," Rufus mumbled.

"Hmm. You are probably still an apothecary," said Simon.

"Not without a shop or ingredients."

"A musician is always a musician, with or without their instrument."

Rufus shrugged and knew that might be technically true, and he could probably sympathise with that musician for having lost their purpose in life, but then again sympathising with a long haired smelly guitarist wasn't something that sat well with Rufus, even while looking at a set of plates. "I don't suppose you know where I could find the tail of a meerkat, do you?"

"New born, adolescent, in heat, male or female?" Simon asked.

Rufus looked up at Simon. It felt like a switch had just flicked into place and there was a tantalising moment of hope, that Simon knew what he was talking about and even how to find it. "Let's say ... an adult female, not in heat."

Simon's eyes glazed over for a second. "Fill out the requisition form and have your supervisor sign it. Then -"

"Okay, thank you," said Rufus, slumping back a little. "I don't suppose we actually have any of those items in the bank?"

"No, but you can request them," said Simon.

"Uh huh. So after you request something that isn't here, how do we get it?"

"You need to find the acquisition's form, then -"

"Fill it out, I got it," said Rufus. "But actually getting the meerkat's tail ..."

"Maybe visit an apothecary," said Simon, offering a shrug. "Acquisitions isn't really my department."

Rufus slumped back even farther and rested his hands on the floor behind him to support his weight. "Yeah, that sounds like a bank all right. You've been here a while, haven't you?"

"Since 1804," said Simon, smiling happily.

"Figures."

"I saw you competing in the very first tournament."

Rufus snorted and looked away. "I hope you didn't bet on me."

"Oh, I'm not a gambling man," said Simon. "But I did receive a few bottles of scotch for my efforts."

Rufus glanced up at Simon and found, yet again, another round of mental cobwebs had formed. "Your efforts?"

"My efforts, yes."

Rufus rolled his hand through the air, trying to encourage Simon into elaborating. "Which were?"

"I picked the winner of each round. People gave me scotch to say thank you."

"How much scotch?"

"One bottle per person, per round."

"There were four rounds back then," said Rufus.

"Yes, there were. And eight people said 'thank you'. But that was really only in the last two rounds."

"I don't suppose you have any of that scotch left?"

"Oh, it wouldn't be any good by now," said Simon. "It was already twenty years old when they gave it to me. Hardly worth it."

Rufus arched an eyebrow at Simon. "But, perhaps as an apothecary, I could work some of my skills and make it drinkable?"

Simon shrugged. "Perhaps."

"How many bottles do you have?"

"Hundreds," said Simon.

Rufus' eyes lit up at once. "Where?"

An hour later, Rufus and Simon were drunker than they had ever been in their entire lives.

The following day, a preliminary list of teams from Hell flooded Limbo and caused an onslaught of excitement. There were seventeen teams participating, more than ever before, and most of the names were well known to the gamble-happy residents of the realm. The previous winner, Mai Kwon, was back.

Kingston read over the list and knew that he couldn't rely on just his notes from the previous tournament. He brought the gang over to the basement of the bank for a brain storming session. Of course, Rufus' eyes were bloodshot and his hair was off to one side as a result of sleeping on the sofa. His breath stank of scotch and cheap coffee. He couldn't even manage to look Catalina in the eye.

"This is our genius inventor?" Catalina asked.

"Eccentric," said Kingston. They sat around a small round table while Rufus used his forearm as a pillow and stared at the table top. Simon was snoring from the room just around the corner. Kingston called the meeting to attention. "By now we all know each other. Rufus, I presume you've completed your list of necessary supplies?"

"Not exactly. Have you got me a sexy assistant yet?"

"Vetoed," said Kingston. He knew there was no point in asking about the list of essentials right now and considered calling off the meeting for later, but he decided that Rufus had to work on Kingston's schedule and not the other way around. "What can you tell me about the teams from Hell on this list?"

"I haven't seen it."

"Would you care to see it now?"

"I can't see well right now, to be frank."

Kingston sighed. He could tell that the others wanted to call off the meeting as well, but Kingston shook his head. "How much did you drink?"

Rufus couldn't even lift his head up to answer. "Lots. I couldn't help it. He had a bottle that was two hundred years old. And a bottle that was a hundred and twenty years old. We had to compare them."

"Right. So, the previous winner, Team Kwon. What do we know about them?"

"Korean team. They speak fast. They also speak in codes because they know their language will be translated here. Stupid codes too, like 'Blue one alpha six.' No one has any idea if they're messing with anyone else. Anti-social as hell. They have three builders working for them, each with two assistants. They're going to win."

"Why will they win?" Kingston asked.

"Because no one has ever caught them cheating. We know they're doing it, we just don't know how they do it. Either they're playing perfectly by the rules, and I mean playing *perfectly*, or they're the best cheaters we've ever seen. We can't beat them."

"Fair enough." Kingston and the others each took their own notes, underlining and circling whatever they found most interesting. "Team Sequa. What about them?"

"French husband and wife. They were pilots back in the day. They cheat bigger than anyone else and get caught all the time, but everyone expects it so their cheats don't always work. They spend more time cheating than focussing on their machine. Their machines usually fail. I've beaten them once."

"How?"

"I lost control of my machine and it bumped into theirs. Theirs stopped working. Mine was declared the winner. The crowd were a little let down. I was over the moon. It was my first win in five tournaments. And it's my most recent. My machine kinda exploded after that, but that's because I was up against Horatio. He's Canadian. You can't trust him."

"I don't see Horatio on the list," said Kingston.

"He's one of ours. Real bastard. Avoid him at all costs."

"He's from Limbo?" Kingston asked.

"Yeah. You wouldn't like him. He hides cameras."

"Where?"

"Not sure. It's just a rumour."

Kingston nodded and wrote down Horatio's name. "Back to the list of Hell participants. Lawnston."

"Big on intimidation. He always keeps brutes like your Little John hanging around."

"Hey!" snapped John.

Rufus still stared at the table beneath his arm. "He likes giants, human giants, ones who have fought in wars. Not modern wars, either, but back when there were 'real' men on the battlefield, the kind who, for no reason, will go into a bar and punch anyone at random, steal their drink and then punch them again for not leaving. No reason at all. They go around and kidnap or beat up other teams. They're not officially on his team because they're often ejected from the realm, but it's no coincidence that the team Lawnston is up against next usually suffer a horrendous mishap. If we're on the draw with him we're better off hiding and defaulting."

"I could take care of them," said John, smiling confidently.

"Yeah, except they'll think that we're their equivalent, so they'll target you especially. They don't like that sort of competition."

"Then we'll smash them before they have the chance," said John, and he nodded towards everyone around the table.

Kingston glanced at the next note. "What about Creig?"

"Avoid his machine at all costs. He builds cheap machines that ram into yours and explode. He rebuilds his cheap machine while you can't afford to rebuild your expensive one. He's a crowd pleaser."

"Wayne?"

"Better at enchanting than building. He could enchant a rolling pin to enter the arena and somersault around. Your machine won't ever catch it and the crowd grows tired and leaves. His match usually lasts for days. Your machine will eventually break down trying to chase his, or you'll get so bored that you fall asleep and make a mistake. No one likes going up against him because he drags it out forever. His longest match was twenty eight days and that was just the first round. But since there's only one arena they had all of the other rounds play on the same stage while Wayne was busy avoiding the opposition. The final match came and went while Wayne's machine was still bouncing around."

"They didn't push him off to the side?" Kingston asked.

"The rules say you have to beat the opposition or declare a forfeit," said Rufus. "No one was able to beat Wayne because no one could catch him. Then, the opposition's machine broke down so it was a technical win for Wayne. By then the tournament was over, since he had a technical forfeit on not being available to compete in the second round, because he was still fighting in the first."

Kingston checked the next name on the list. "What about Zamba?"

"Good ideas, bad delivery. Last time he made a suit of armour with a tonne of superglue on the inside. The armour fell on top of the other machine and the glue burst out and smothered the two of them together. Good luck trying to clean that up. The next round took place with those two still stuck in the middle of the arena. Before that he copied the design of another team from Hell to confuse whoever he was fighting against, but he didn't correctly enchant it and the machine never made it into the arena."

"Caffrey?"

"He's pretty good at betting. He comes along more for a holiday from Hell than actually competing. He does well with money and is usually a good guy to talk to for inside dirt on the teams from down South. He's hardly a threat, but there's always a chance that he'll be the long shot. If his odds ever hit forty to one or more to win, you can bet your ass he'll lay everything on the line and beat you."

"We don't have his odds yet," said Kingston.

"We will. He'll definitely compete."

"What about Milliara?"

"One of the devils. He covers his machine in smoke and teleports it on top of yours to smash it. Then he teleports away leaving the smoke behind and you have no idea how bad your machine is. It's the same machine every tournament and is mostly just a great big anvil. Kinda hard to beat an anvil to death. But he has to do whatever Satan tells him to do, which is usually to let someone else win, or he gets called away on assignment."

"Why?"

Rufus shrugged. "Why does Satan do half the things he does? Because it's more interesting than being boring."

They went through the rest of the seventeen names and Rufus knew fifteen of them. He gave them his expected teams from Limbo and gritted his teeth whenever he mentioned Horatio. They wouldn't know who was competing for another few weeks, but it was still possible to find out by going to a couple of the auctions.

"Moving on," said Kingston. "As a former apothecary, how did you get your illegal ingredients?"

"I have my sources. One retired since finding someone she would rather be with and not risking herself dealing with illegal items her whole life. Another got promoted and no longer has access to that world, nor does he want to, since it would look bad if he was caught. Well, badder if he was caught, especially since he's now a judge. Two moved on to Hell. They got caught and so down they went. There isn't much of a police force up here but there is a high honour system and if you piss off your neighbours they might decide not to keep your secret a secret anymore. I told my suppliers ten years ago that I was done and I haven't dealt in anything illegal since. They eventually got the hint and now I don't have any sources left."

"What about the other apothecaries?" Kingston asked.

"Oh, they'll have plenty of illegal items hidden away or already sold. I'm betting on the already sold part. They're all tapped out and the other teams have everything we need. We just need to steal it from them and not get caught."

"Instead of stealing from the other teams, can we just buy what we need from them?" Catalina asked.

Rufus lifted his head off the table and looked at Catalina as though that was the most ridiculous question he had ever heard. "Of course we could buy it from them. Teams usually have a surplus of what's necessary and then sell what they don't need at exorbitant prices because the other teams are desperate. It's one of the few ways of making money in production. But you have to be careful, because price gouging like that can cause some bad blood, and if you rat on someone and they are ejected from Limbo, well, there goes the whole tournament. But everyone has a surplus of something that they're willing to sell."

"Then you're coming with me," said Kingston, clapping Rufus on the shoulder.

"What? But I'm supposed to be here in protective custody!"

"You're also costing me a lot of money and heartache, which you are going to need to work your ass off to make our deal worthwhile."

Rufus bobbed his head and slumped lower into his chair. "I hoped you would wait a little while before bringing that up."

Kingston, Joanna, John, and Catalina all exchanged a look of concern. They were now stuck with Rufus and they had to put on a brave face.

"There, there," said John, and he tapped the table next to Rufus' slumped body.

Rufus lifted his head up. He looked a little less hungover and saw that Catalina was coming back into focus. He smiled at her with a droopy look and still slurred his words. "I need an intelligent girlfriend. I mean assistant! A sexy assistant." He slammed a fist onto the table. "Intelligent! An intelligent ... assistant." He stared at the four people looking at him and groaned. "It was good scotch."

"We've met before," said Catalina.

Rufus looked up and had to close one eye to focus on Catalina properly. "We have? When?"

"You tried to dance with me in a club."

Rufus cocked his head and squinted at Catalina. "I did?"

"Yes. You showed me 'the moves' and then you fell over."

"Oh," mumbled Rufus. "Pity."

John glared at the little man. "And I've seen you staring at her breasts."

Rufus shrugged. "They're nice."

Joanna gave a short sigh and looked away in contempt.

"Sorry," said Rufus. "Yours are nice as well."

Joanna's eyes flared into action and Kingston braced himself for a high pitched squeal. "I wasn't looking for a compliment!"

Rufus did his best to smile, but he breathed another mouthful of cheap coffee and scotch all over them. "I like you. I need an assistant."

"I'll find you one," said Joanna, glaring at Rufus.

"What exactly is this assistant supposed to do?" Kingston asked.

"It takes at least two pairs of hands to build something," said Rufus. "I do expect you all to help out, not just to look pretty. Or big and intimidating. Two people can build this thing in five years. Maybe two years if they get lucky and things don't blow up and they have ready access to materials. We don't have any of that. So we're going to need all five of us, plus an assistant, plus a thief, plus a scout to spy on the other teams."

"I can spy," said Kingston.

"You're rather famous, honey," said Joanna.

Rufus shook his head and stared at the table. "You should've bought into an existing team."

Kingston agreed with him, but for some reason Michelle wanted Kingston to focus on Rufus. He made a mental note to exploit that need as much as possible. He then heard the quiet snoring coming from the other room. He leaned back in his chair and tried to look around the corner. "What about him as an assistant?"

John arched an eyebrow. "Simon?"

"Yeah."

"He's a janitor," said Rufus. "He doesn't exactly reek of qualifications, you know?"

Joanna rolled her eyes again. "You just offered me the position and you don't know the first thing about me."

"Well ... you're a fast learner," said Rufus.

"I'm glad you think so."

"Simon knows his way around here and this is where you'll be building your machine," said Kingston.

Rufus shook his head. "He's all about acquisition forms and requisition forms and something about asking Snowflake what to do. I'm still trying to figure that one out. Frankly, the cat would be a better assistant."

Kingston snorted and rolled his head back. "Rufus, there's no way we're going to win at all. And we're not really trying to win. We're trying to make as much money as possible."

Rufus blinked a few times and looked around the serious faces of Joanna, John, and Catalina, only to realise that they agreed with Kingston. "But you can't make money unless you win!"

"Sure you can," said Kingston. "We're going to cheat our way into making money, because we're certainly not going to be able to cheat our way into winning."

Rufus' jaw dropped open and it took him a moment to recover. "But the others are better at cheating."

Kingston nodded. "Probably better than you, and certainly more experienced than us, but if we work well together I'm sure we can pull this off. First thing's first; do we sabotage the other teams or do we play nice?"

"Play nice," said Catalina.

"For now," said Joanna. "As soon as we know who's competing and what the odds are, then we sabotage."

"By then it might be too late," said John. "We should certainly sabotage this Horatio fellow."

"I like that idea," said Rufus. "But please, I can't have Simon as an assistant. He's not all there, you know?"

"I'll make a note of it," said Kingston, and Rufus noticed that no note was being made. "So we'll delay the sabotage until we know who is competing. We should find out before the official list of names is up. Onto actually building this machine. Rufus, what's your best combat enchantment?"

Rufus shrugged. "John has inspired me towards building a golem. But they're unstable, slow, and easy targets."

"That's not an enchantment," said Kingston.

"Fine. In theory the best one I can come up with is a rapidly extending whip. You aim it at the enemy and it reaches them quicker than they can react. The point then is that it latches on and either electrocutes them or does something else equally nasty. But it requires a chain link and each link needs its own enchantment and that kind of thing gets expensive, especially since you're then running a secondary or tertiary enchantment through it, like the electrocution bit or, say, fire. I've always wanted something like that, where you whip some other machine and drag it towards you while it's being electrocuted and them you stomp it or smash it with a giant war hammer. But in order to be effective at a decent range you're going to need at least fifty links, each at least eight inches long while at rest, and each of which needs to be handmade, but I barely had the money to afford three links in the past. But if you have an unlimited source of money then I say we go with that."

John's eyes lit up in delight, imagining a giant suit of armour with such a whip and war hammer, but Kingston looked a little nervous by the suggestion.

"We don't have an unlimited amount of money," said Kingston.

"I know, but if you did no one would expect it," said Rufus.

"How will that affect our odds?"

Rufus rubbed his chin and looked up at the ceiling. "My odds are already terrible, but we're going to need to win at least once or force someone else into a default. We're almost certain to lose, and those odds are terrible. But our odds to win would be magnificent. If we can actually win one of the rounds we might earn enough money to keep on going. But the gambling house will be on the look out to know what the teams are buying and they'll figure out what we're up to. Luckily we're so far behind that we don't stand a chance. The best odds I've ever had at winning were eight to one. The worst were twenty two to one. We will need an actual chain link whip to scare up the competition. If it looks like we're obviously trying to lose then our odds won't be worth playing."

Kingston hummed to himself and knew that presentation would be everything, but they would have to deliver at least the bare minimum. "You're going to have to start making that today."

"We don't have blueprints to a working machine yet," said Rufus.

"And that would be your fault." Kingston clicked his pen and turned to a fresh sheet of paper on his notepad. "What do you need to make these links a reality?"

Rufus sighed and started shaking his head. "We need a 3K anvil, 5D tongs, a set of NQR pliers, a solid metal box at least ten inches in each direction. We'll need enough sand to fill this box at least a dozen times, that will be hard to get around here. We will need a kiln capable of reaching two thousand degrees.

"Celsius, Fahrenheit?" Kingston asked.

"Celestial. Go to Tom's for that. It'll be expensive. You'll have to flirt with him to make sure you're not getting ripped off."

"I can handle that," said Joanna.

"Not you," said Rufus. "Probably John."

John raised his eyebrows. "Am I supposed to wear something special or braid my hair?"

"Bare chested will probably work," said Rufus. "You'll also want a clay jug with a heating element built into it. Tom can also provide that. It has to hold at least a pint of liquid metal. For the actual metal you'll want Grade 5 Xeno steel, about fifty pounds worth. That will kill your budget right there because it comes from Hell, but you won't find anything stronger in any realm. For the enchantments we'll need a pint of ox blood, twelve ounces of spiced elephant tusk, a pound of opal, ideally from South Australia, a full set of great white shark teeth, a full set of crocodile teeth, and the rags of a mummy that is at least five hundred years old. But, anything older than two thousand years is no good."

Kingston wrote everything down and looked over at Rufus. "Are you making all of this up?"

"No. But that alone will set you back three thousand five hundred gold pieces, that's why you're going to want to steal as much of it as possible."

"And where do I find all of this?" Kingston asked.

"Try filling out a requisition form," said Rufus. "Apparently the bank can get anything you need. Otherwise, find yourself a dedicated thief."

"I should remind you that we're still not trying to win."

"There could be thirty or forty teams competing. If we win every single round the winning pay out will be around eighty to one at worst. Maybe two hundred to one at best. Winning might be the only way to make money."

Kingston groaned and knew that they were aiming blind until the official betting guide was released. It would take a lot of late nights to figure out the best cost to win ratio and still he had to worry about making this whole ordeal worthwhile.

"The golem itself will also cost about eight thousand if we're planning on entering it into every round," said Rufus. "If we had started this years ago it would be about half the price. Since we're already in a bank, I guess you should look into taking out a loan."

V

'*Step one - find any advantage over any team,*' Kingston wrote. He was lying on the sofa in his office, which was one of the few places anyone would expect him to be at this time. The office was still trashed but Kingston had other things on his mind. He was also sure there was a clue lost amongst the rubble about who did the trashing and what they wanted. He would find it soon enough, but for now it was time to start messing with the other teams.

'*Wanted - sponsors and dirt on the other teams,*' he wrote, then he chuckled to himself. He imagined a wanted poster from the Old West, but instead of seeing some hardened criminal there was a golem holding a war hammer and a chain link whip. He scribbled down a few ideas on what he needed to say and how he was going to distribute it across the realm. After an hour he was done.

> *Wanted. Any advantage over any other team.*
> *Will reward handsomely.*

> *Gentiles of Limbo, the Games are upon us again. With team principal Kingston Raine sponsoring master builder Rufus Winston, this year's tournament will be a feast for the senses to indulge.*

> *The kick-off of festivities will include an invitation-only benefit to meet and greet the team.*

Kingston had Rufus work his magic to make the posters sizzle in the electric air, as well as include a coded message behind the fine print to identify who destroyed the posters and who smiled gloriously at them.

"Why?" Rufus asked.

"If the posters are destroyed we will know they are on an enemy team and they want us to lose," said Kingston. "If they smile then they are in favour of us and we can invite them to our party."

Rufus craned his head around. "We're actually having a party?"

"Oh, yes," said Kingston. "We need to be on our best behaviour if we want to get sponsors."

"I thought you were the sponsor."

Kingston nodded. "Of course, but I want their money as well."

It then came time to finalise the details for his hefty loan. Kingston had to put the team assets up as collateral, including the promise that a golem and its weapons would be built. He was willing to set aside fifteen thousand to allow for the cost of building their golem and another ten thousand to gamble with. Given his current allowance from Limbo of one gold eight silver a day, which had to cover renting out the office and his apartment, it would take a hundred and fourteen years to pay off the loan if everything backfired. So, with a deep breath, Kingston followed Sebastian Burrows, the loans manager, down to the vaults to collect his money.

"Nervous?" asked Burrows.

"No, I've this under control," said Kingston. Meanwhile his pulse had skyrocketed. It wasn't just the thought of signing his life away for another century. As ludicrous as it sounded, he kept wondering if he had taken out enough money.

"Either way, I wish you luck," said Burrows.

"Thank you."

Ten thousand gold coins were counted off for deals that didn't require a paper trail, while the remaining fifteen thousand went into Kingston's account for legitimate spending. Burrows pulled out a set of scales and weighed each pouch accordingly. The coins weighed just one gram each and were stamped with 'LIMBO - IN DEATH WE TRUST.' Kingston needed a cart to carry everything to his vault and for a moment he wished he could just throw the coins in the air and dance around among the gold, and then he realised that raining coins would hurt like hell and that he would kill his back if he had to pick them all up again.

An hour later, Kingston, Joanna, and Catalina were setting up posters around Limbo, while John was busy hauling their requirements back from Tom's Metallurgy. He was stubborn enough to move it all in one go, insisting that one hundred kilos worth of tools, kilns, and protective wear was child's play and that he could run with that kind of weight without it bothering him. Tom winked at him and suggested he hire a rickshaw. After an hour spent slowly dragging everything along the ground, John decided that he should have done that from the beginning.

Rufus peered into the canvas bags. "Did he give you any trouble?"

"Some, but then I sandwiched him," said John, trying to hide just how out of breath he was after sneaking everything down the many stairs of the bank.

Rufus glanced up at John and smirked. "You sandwiched him, eh? Well, to each their own." He returned to the bags and picked through them, muttering to himself as he crossed everything off John's checklist. "Which bag are the pliers in?"

John shrugged. "Whatever bag Tom put them in."

"And you brought back eight bags, or nine?"

"Eight," said John. He pointed to them all lying on the ground. "See? One, two, three, four, five, six, seven, eight."

"Right," said Rufus, wearily. "And you definitely saw him put the set of pliers into a bag?"

John grumbled. "Well of course I saw him do it. I asked about everything on the list and he was eager to show everything off to me since they were apparently of the finest quality and his attention to detail was second to none. There was a complete set of pliers like you wrote down. NQR. They were wrapped in a tight leather pouch hand stitched by Lucy from across the road. Tom opened it up and showed me the set of ten pliers, all of different sizes and grades. That was the set you wanted, right?"

"Yes, that is what I wanted," said Rufus. "It's just that they don't seem to be here."

John glared at Rufus and knew that was impossible. He rummaged through each bag, ready to show Rufus just how wrong he was, but the pliers were no where to be found. John then pulled the contents of every bag out onto the ground and laid them all in the order that they appeared on the list. Everything was there, except for a set of NQR pliers. John stared at the empty space, then he checked and re-checked the list, and concentrated with all of his might to remember which bag Tom had put them into.

"It wasn't with the anvil, that had its own bag," John said. "Nor the kiln or the jug. I'm quite sure they were in the same bag as five of the ten empty boxes." John hung his head. Even though he was focussed on the ground he was perfectly capable of seeing Rufus staring back at him.

"They're onto us already," said Rufus, staring off into the distance. "They must have been watching the shop."

"I'll go back to Tom's and see if they're there. Or on the rickshaw."

Rufus arched an eyebrow. "Rickshaw?"

"Well, Tom's is all the way across town," said John. "I gave up halfway along the road and a rickshaw passed me, so of course I hired him." He sighed and thumped his hands onto his hips. He was ready to kick the first thing he saw out of frustration, which would have been the anvil, and he thought the better of it. "Why did you say 'rickshaw' like that? Did someone rob us?"

Rufus nodded. "Probably. Who did you see?"

"Just the driver," said John, with a shrug. "A string bean type. Mousy hair and a unibrow. He said his name was Pete. Very chatty. I was careful, though. I didn't ride in the rickshaw, I followed it to make sure that nothing fell out. I loaded and unloaded it all myself."

"And you never took your eyes off the eight bags?" Rufus asked, peering up at John suspiciously.

John gritted his teeth. "I was very careful."

Rufus bobbed his head from side to side. "Well then, the game is on, it would appear. The extortion will begin soon. We might have some time, since we're still waiting on the sand, powders, and blood. They'll hold onto what we have just to make us sweat."

John clenched his fingers into a fist. "One of the other teams robbed us?"

"Oh, yes," said Rufus. "This kind of thing is quite common, which is why you keep your workshop hidden away. Buying everything at once attracts attention and they are quick to watch everyone. But don't worry, our pliers will turn up. No one will risk holding onto them after the tournament, since by then it's illegal to have stolen from someone and no one wants to be caught with them, so they'll return them or allow them to be found by the rightful owner. It's also a good way of making some extra money. We paid, what, twelve gold pieces for the set? To have them returned we'll be expected to part with at least another five."

John shook his head. "There's no way we were robbed."

Rufus smirked at John and rolled his eyes. "Amateur. This is your first tournament. I assure you, every team robs from every other team as much as possible. These things are necessary."

John threw his hands into the air. "But I didn't even turn my back on the bags!"

"And it makes you paranoid, doesn't it? From now on you'll be checking and re-checking everything you buy. You'll have to make sure that every door is still closed and still locked and that no one managed to find a way in that you didn't think of. It will slow you down because you'll always be on the look out for a thief. Everyone who catches your eye might be there to rob you. If you let it bother you then you'll never sleep. Half of the time I'll be enchanting the doors to remain locked or to open with a specific code, and still we'll be robbed. Just wait until the teams from Hell arrive. Limbo teams play to some kind of a thieving code that rarely gets out of hand, but when you're against another realm your ethics are somewhat freer."

John sighed and started to mentally berate himself. "So what do I tell Kingston?"

"Tell him the bill comes to three thousand five hundred gold. Also, the other teams know that we're competing and that someone has robbed us. It's not fair, but it's expected."

That night, Kingston was alone in his apartment, working through the headache of being robbed, trying to figure out if they should dig into their rapidly decreasing fortune to buy a replacement set or trust Rufus that the pliers would eventually turn up. On the bright side, several of his wanted posters had already been torn down, and Kingston expected the first of many surprise visitors that evening.

Sure enough, there was a tap on his door. Kingston answered and was bemused to see a short man in a long tan trench coat wearing thick bombardier goggles standing in the corridor. He nodded to Kingston and held up a sheet of paper in his hand. "This is dangerous," said Lord Henry Biggins.

"Just a little advertising," said Kingston. "Care to help?"

"No," said Biggins, from under a thick scowl. "I have a brother who is competing and I won't get tangled in anyone else's team."

"Oh, really? Your brother is competing? Which team is that?"

"I'm not at liberty to say," said Biggins, stiffly. "But advertising for this kind of assistance is very, very dangerous. It shows you don't know much about the Games and it sets you up to be taken advantage of. I did you a quick courtesy of removing all of your ads before too many people could see them."

Kingston gave Biggins an award winning smile, but he was still irritated by Biggins removing the posters. "I was trying to advertise a social event."

"I saw the secret message. Others will as well." Biggins looked back at the sheet of paper and cleared his throat. *"Wanted. Any advantage over any other team. Will reward handsomely.'"*

"And it's completely true," said Kingston.

"The other teams can read it, you know."

"So?"

Biggins spluttered. "So? *So?*" He shook his head, trying to gather his thoughts, and when they didn't come he cocked his head to one side and shook his head again. "The other teams have magic at their disposal and they won't like to see this."

"Are they trying to gain an advantage over my team?"

Biggins nodded. "They are."

"And isn't it generally accepted that any team will try to get an advantage over their rivals?"

"Yes, but writing it in an encrypted poster is bad form. They will double their efforts to make sure that no secret of theirs ever gets out," said Biggins.

Kingston smirked, took the poster from Biggins and bowed his head. "Thank you, Biggins. Your insight has been most useful."

Biggins arched an eyebrow and peered carefully at Kingston. "Something just happened."

"Oh, yes," said Kingston. "Something did just happen."

"I'd like to know what," said Biggins.

"I'm afraid I can't tell you, considering your brother is competing. That wouldn't be sporting, would it?"

Biggins looked over Kingston suspiciously, then remembered that Kingston was a master of trickery. "I can keep a secret."

"So can I."

"You won't keep many of them in this competition."

"To the contrary, I plan on releasing as many secrets as possible."

Biggins bobbed his head and thought it through. "You're going to flood the competition with false information?"

"Of course."

"They'll see right through it."

"That's what I'm counting on," said Kingston.

"So ... wait ... huh?" Biggins tried to shake the confusion away but he knew Kingston was simply messing with him.

Kingston smiled at his old friend. "I thought after all we've been through you'd be a little more easy going."

"These are the Games," said Biggins. "The day after they conclude we may each buy a round of drinks and regale one another with the secrets we managed to keep and the subterfuge we employed. Until then ..."

Kingston smirked. "All bets are off?"

"On," corrected Biggins. "Now then, I just hope your plan doesn't backfire on you."

"I have high hopes that it will," said Kingston.

Biggins stared back. "You are tricky, I'll give you that."

"And you reveal more than you care to," said Kingston.

"Perhaps." Biggins bowed his head and stared Kingston in the eye, not the slightest bit pleased to see him again or to be beaten at a game of wits. Biggins raised himself up and popped out of thin air.

The next morning, Kingston made up a second poster to replace the first, this one saying: *'Thank you. Please collect your reward.'* He was sure that would drive the competition insane.

Rufus needed John's help to move all of the heavy equipment into the safest part of the janitorial department. They found a room that had been stuffed with broken filing cabinets and busted chairs. There was fifty years worth of dust covering everything, leading Rufus to hope that no one remembered this room.

Simon stuck his head in the doorway and surprised the life out of Rufus. "You'll need to fix all of them cabinets when you're done."

"They were broken when I got here," said Rufus.

"Aye, but you've moved them from the broken room to the to-be-fixed room. A commitment's a commitment."

Rufus squinted at Simon and knew he was a potential problem.

"I could do with a celebratory nip. Would you care to join me?"

"Oh, aye. I probably still have some scotch left over, unless you're sick of it already."

"No, no, that scotch sounds good," said Rufus.

John dragged the anvil into their new workshop and he looked around his masterpiece of furniture-moving. He was a little miffed that no one was there to congratulate him. "Well done, John. Thank you, John. You did all of this by yourself? I sure did. Didn't Rufus offer to help? Oh, he's a little frail and he complained about his back, but he was nice enough to point out where he wanted everything to be moved. That sounds like it took some effort. Well, it's all for the glory of the team."

John hoped there wasn't any more moving to be done. They had cobbled together a make shift work bench, which was a smooth door with broken hinges sitting on top of two filing cabinets. The room off to one side housed the kiln. Rufus had plans to build a dissipating component that would allow the kiln to reach its two thousand degrees without burning the whole building down. Another room was used as storage for all of the enchantment ingredients, which was still empty, and another room was stuffed full of tools laid out in order. Rufus planned on using the long corridor out in front as a testing ground for the chain link whip. John wondered what Kingston would say about that, considering the ceiling wasn't exceptionally high and the walls were only a couple of metres apart.

John pried open one of the nearly working filing cabinets in the ingredients room and found it was stuffed with machine blueprints and lists of essential ingredients. He checked the dates and knew they were all from previous contraptions, which amused John because he was sure that Rufus had burned everything and left no trace behind. Clearly Rufus had kept a secret stash for some sort of emergency.

It was also clear that Rufus had toyed with the golem concept for a while and had written up a mass of side notes in the margins of his previous blueprints. John rummaged around some more and found old notebooks, each etched with a number on the front. He flipped through and realised that they were Rufus' notes on the opposition from previous tournaments. His notes were rather flimsy in the first couple of years but they improved in detail. He had clearly been spying on the other teams and figured out how they were building their machines, where they were getting their supplies from, and their obvious failures during combat.

Scratch golem, Rufus wrote at the end of the eighth tournament. *Too big, too slow.*

John read over the details and saw that nine other teams had tried to build a walking suit of armour, and none of them had made it far in the tournament.

Scratch whip, Rufus also wrote. *Too many points of failure.*

John glared at the notebook. *He's screwing with us,* he thought. He thumbed through the rest of the stash knowing that the team could use them and yet Rufus had neglected to mention taking such detailed notes on their competition, as well as why he was now building a machine that was doomed to failure. John stuffed the books into one of the leather bags from Tom's and took them straight to Kingston.

Kingston read through the notebooks cover to cover and jotted down the more important details. John paced back and forth and continually interrupted Kingston, demanding to know what was to be done about the situation.

"He's messing with us and we can't let him get away with that," said John.

"A couple of scribbles in the margins isn't enough to punch him out," said Kingston.

"Then maybe I can threaten him a little. Show him who's boss."

"Let's keep our builder as intact as possible," said Kingston.

"I can shout at him. I know a few things that my good lady wife has been teaching me."

"'Intact' also means that he is still emotionally capable of working." Kingston worked through what John had just said and he peered over the top of the notebook. "Good lady wife? Did you propose to Catalina or something?"

John spun around. "What? No. I heard her say that and I thought it was cute."

"Hmm," said Kingston, and he went back to the book. He read over the same sentence three times before realising that he had no idea what it said. "Wait, you heard her say that *she* was your good lady wife?"

John paused and his aggression ebbed away.

"Ah," said Kingston, seeing the look of guilt on his friend's face. "Better not let Joanna hear that you two are calling her that."

"And that's always confused me," said John, stepping forward and using as neutral a tone as possible. "Considering everything you two have been through ..."

"It's not for us," said Kingston, shaking his head and trying to get back to Rufus' book.

"Do you mean it's not for *her*?"

"There's no way I could marry her," said Kingston. "We've been through a lot, yes, and we deserve each other, but still it's not for us."

"That didn't really answer my question."

Kingston sighed and looked up to his friend. "I don't have a good answer. Although, back when everyone was alive and blissfully ignorant of the afterlife, 'forever' meant 'til death do us part.' Now that the actual death has taken place, 'forever' is a little more long term than it was before."

John nodded and stared up at the ceiling, now deep in thought. The silence was broken when he snorted. "So does that mean all of those couples who were 'til death do us part' are officially unmarried when they die?"

"That isn't really my area of expertise," said Kingston, afraid that John might go around and proclaim his new found theory as fact. "But going back to the punching out of our builder, I think we're going to be okay. Yes, he didn't tell us that he had these notes, and yes there is a lot of useful information here, so let's just take the good aspect of your find and treat the actual hiding of it as a miscommunication. We should remember that Rufus did the bulk of his building and enchanting by himself, or with just a single assistant. He's never had to answer to anyone else before and it's clearly taking some time to adapt to that level of trust."

"And if he hides anything else from us in the future?" John asked.

"Then you can use a few choice phrases to straighten him out."

John grinned. "Good, because I came up with a few zingers while on my way over here."

Kingston lowered the notebook and gave John his full attention. "Let's hear them."

"Right." John stood and shook the frustration out of his body, and then he snapped into a crazed look with one finger pointed just above Kingston. "You have a three second head start before my fist meets the top of your head."

Kingston waited for the follow up, then he saw John drop the act and look to Kingston for his assessment. "You think that will work?"

John shrugged. "I imagine his heart will go like the clappers once he sees my stare. At that point he probably won't be able to actually hear what I'm saying, given the hysterical panic. I was thinking of also walking in with an axe. Not a little one, either, but one that's bigger than me. I've used one of those before. Took down a tree in a single swing. I got a little cocky with it though and threw it, to see how far I could hurl that thing. Pulled something in my back. Broke the axe. Broke the tree as well."

"That must have been quite a sight."

John shrugged again. "It would have been if anyone was actually watching."

"You may need to work on your zingers before confronting Rufus," said Kingston, and he went back to the book.

"How about: I'm going to hold you upside down and you're going to read out everything in these books until every book is read and every question we have has been answered."

"Not bad. Can you actually hold someone up for that long?"

"Not sure. I'll get tired eventually, no question there. Maybe I can tie him up to the door frame."

Kingston closed the book he was on. "I'm going to get you, Joanna, and Catalina to read through these as well and take some notes. It'll help to bring us all up to speed."

"I've noticed that this sporting event sure has a lot of prerequisite reading," said John.

"Only for those who want to do well. We have a party coming up in a few days with some guests and if we're going to appear well informed in small talk then we need to know about the previous teams and tournaments. These books will help," Kingston said, tapping the cover with his finger.

"Catalina's been a bit stressed out by that," said John. "Joanna recommended something called a mud bath." John shook his head in confusion. "She said it would relax her."

Kingston arched an eyebrow. "Uh oh."

"Yeah. So they went. They covered her in mud and seaweed and told her to relax. Head to toe. Mud." John shook his head in bewilderment.

"How did Catalina take it?"

"She blamed your good lady wife a few times and thought that covering someone in mud was a little primitive. Between you and me, I kinda want to see that."

Kingston smirked. "Your girlfriend covered in mud?"

"And whatever else happens at the spa. I'm thinking if this tournament doesn't work out for us I should get a job at that place."

Kingston grinned and had to agree with John's fall back plans, though he was sure the fantasy would soon wear off and having a 'real' job would drive him close to madness.

VI

Joanna returned from a tiring day with the news that no business was willing to rent out space for their team party. Rivalries were just too high to risk alienating their regular customers and Rufus had a losing streak of such proportions that no one in their right mind would come to a party where he was the guest of honour. Joanna had begged and pleaded and tried to bribe some venue to accept a booking, but the only way a team party was ever going to happen would be in neutral territory. So, she hired a stretch of parkland in front of the arena and spent the next three days with Catalina by her side setting up a marquee that could house two hundred of Limbo's most influential residents.

Finding musicians to entertain the group was no mere feat. There was a bassist from Stationary who fell to pieces whenever a successful musician died in their prime, the cellist was from Legal, the pianist was one of the winged lion handlers, and the drummer was largely considered to be unemployed. They all came from different musical backgrounds, different eras, and different parts of the world, but they were the only music group in the entire realm who were available on such short notice and who didn't mind performing, though they came along wearing black eye-wraps to hide their identities so that they wouldn't be labelled as pro-Kingston during the tournament. The twelve servers wore the same. Only the two bartenders were willing to show their faces, since they were wearing t-shirts that loudly claimed that they had never bet, never will, and have no interest in any tournament.

It was too dangerous to have every potential donor at the party at the same time. Joanna was sure it would scare most of them away if others knew who were attending, so she split the group of invites into six to encourage some semblance of privacy. Kingston and John were intrigued to see if Joanna and Catalina could pull it off, especially since it meant maintaining a high level of energy across what were effectively six parties spread across three nights.

"Trust me, word of mouth will help us," Joanna said, an hour before the first party was due to start. "You did send all of the invitations, right?"

"Of course," said Kingston. "Anyone who smiled at our poster got an invite."

John walked into the large marquee wheeling a trunk behind him. The trunk was thumping from the inside and there were stifled muffles coming from within. "All clear?" John bellowed.

"All clear," said Kingston.

John set the trunk down on its back, unclipped the hinges and pulled it open, revealing a very disgruntled Rufus.

"What, was the scenic route too fast for you?" Rufus snapped, glaring at John.

"He wouldn't shut up the whole time," John said to Kingston.

"Because I couldn't breathe!" shouted Rufus. He sat up, looked around the enclosed marque and turned his nose up at it all. "The place is dead."

"The party hasn't started yet," said Kingston.

"Yeah, well I can tell you've never worked a crowd of gamblers before." Rufus climbed out of the trunk and dusted himself off. "I'm not afraid of Montgomery, you know."

"You were hiding from him when we first met," said Kingston.

"Still. Not afraid."

"And you have eight others who are after you for unclaimed debts," said Kingston.

"Then I sure hope you didn't invite any of them," said Rufus.

"If I didn't it wouldn't be much of a party." Kingston smirked.

"Oh ha ha." Rufus looked around Kingston's arm and saw Catalina instructing the two bar staff about proper etiquette in being a bar wench. Without even an 'excuse me', Rufus wandered over.

John shook his head. "Next time I *will* take the scenic route." He packed the trunk away and hid it behind the bar, which was looking all the more appealing after the day he'd had.

Kingston found himself without much to do, so he headed over to the entrance of the marquee and checked the invitation list again. He knew the names off by heart but, deep down, he knew that Rufus was right. No one on the team knew how to work a crowd like this and they were all in completely unfamiliar territory. Kingston stared off towards the entrance and heard a couple of the greeters talking excitedly about the previous winners of the tournament, and debating the greatest moment in the arena.

Kingston felt a tap on his shoulder. He turned to find Joanna standing there in a slim red dress. It was strapless and kicked out around her ankles. She held a red purse in one hand and wore gold dangling earrings, a gold and diamond necklace and matching bracelet. She had been wearing something similar on their first date, though at the time she may have tried to poison his drink.

Joanna smiled at him for checking her out. "It's been a while since you did that."

"It's been a while since you wore red," said Kingston.

"A girl rarely has the occasion to glam up like this, especially given that we now live in Limbo."

Kingston smiled and knew she had a point. But then even when they were in Life she stuck to business attire or black evening dresses. "Custom made?"

Joanna nodded. "There's a shop wedged between two restaurants on Valkyrie. Little Welsh girl with a thick accent. It's quite tight around the stomach." Joanna gripped her abdomen and tried to control an exhale. It looked as though she was measuring the tolerance of her waist while wearing that dress.

"I guess you won't be able to eat much," said Kingston.

"I know, and I'm starving. I'll be lucky if I can have just one snack every half an hour, and even then I'm sure I'll burst out of this dress. This has to last me five more parties. I know, it's bad to be seen in the same thing over and over again, but considering how much this thing cost me ..."

Kingston winced, fearing the price tag.

"I have a shawl as well," said Joanna, ignoring her boyfriend's look. "I still can't decide between the red one and the black one. I think the red is a little too much but it might help cover me up if I bend over too quickly and pop out of this thing."

"It would give the crowd something to remember."

"I've got a purse full of safety pins in case this thing does actually fail on me. I might need your help with that kind of emergency."

Kingston tried to contain the imagery of his girlfriend's dress going through a catastrophic failure. "What are you wearing under that?"

"Shoes," said Joanna. She kicked one foot out and pulled her dress up. "You like?"

"I do," said Kingston, aware that 'shoes' was not the answer he was looking for. "I like how they match your purse with the small gold clasp."

Joanna tapped him on the shoulder. "Good boy."

"Thanks. The colour works for you."

"If I pass out you're going to have to catch me," said Joanna.

"It can't be that tight," said Kingston, looking down at her waist.

"Either the designer is on a rival team or she made this dress with centimetres in mind instead of inches. I can't even have any wine in case I spill some all over me."

Kingston cocked his head to one side. "Is this common? Women looking their best and suffering every minute of it?"

Joanna clasped her hand on top of Kingston's shoulder and used him for balance. "It's not my fault. Tonight I'm supposed to make everyone jealous and to do that I have to be confident, and nothing screams confidence like red."

"Like the night we first went out for dinner?"

Joanna smirked. "I had you wrapped around my finger before dawn."

"No, I only let you think that," said Kingston, resting one hand on her waist.

Joanna snorted and shook her head. "You are aware that you and I came from a work of fiction, right?"

"Of course. I was the one who had to tell you. It's not like ..." Kingston drifted off, finally understanding what Joanna was getting at. "You read up on me."

Joanna grinned. "Sure did. I particularly liked the part where it said I had you wrapped around my finger. So there. Joanna one, Kingston zero."

Kingston sighed and shrugged it off.

"See? *See?*" Joanna said, beaming with a smile.

"My good lady wife is crazy," muttered Kingston, and he shook his head.

Joanna's smile disappeared. The colour ran from her face and she stood up straight, now veering towards complete shock. *"Wife?"*

Kingston realised what he had just said and held up his hands in defence. "Sorry. Slip of the tongue. Girlfriend. Not ... you know. *Girlfriend.*"

Joanna looked away and started breathing deeply. The look of panic was still there, which was only exasperated when she realised that panicking would make her sweat, which would ruin her make up, which in turn would run down her dress. She fidgeted to get herself under control but it wasn't helping.

"I didn't mean it," said Kingston. "John has picked up a new phrase, calling you my good lady wife. I just echoed him. And Catalina," he added.

Joanna was still breathing deeply, trying to get her nerves back. She looked everywhere except at Kingston and kept him in the corner of her eye. She tried to blame John for Kingston's slip but she was sure he had picked it up as innocently as everything else he said.

"It's not you," mumbled Joanna.

Kingston nodded to himself. "I'm starting to feel that it's a little bit about me."

Joanna stiffly turned towards Kingston. "No, sorry. Every time someone mentions the whole marriage thing I can't help but remember that I have a habit of screwing things up."

"We both do," said Kingston, with a shrug.

"Yeah, but we *really* do screw things up," said Joanna, and she looked away.

Kingston leaned forward to catch her attention. "Do you need a drink?"

"Yes," said Joanna, while staring across the empty room. "And don't you dare let me spill it."

"I'll get you a straw as well. Are you sure you're okay?"

Joanna snapped her fingers together. "I didn't say I was okay. Go. Now." She waved him towards the bar without meeting his eyes and realised that her shoulders had stiffened. Lowering them was a struggle and even when she thought she had them low enough she was sure she looked more awkward than she had ever been in her life, which may have had some degree of truth to it. "Nice and confident," she told herself. "The crowd will envy you."

Kingston went over to the bar and ordered a glass of pinot and a straw, then decided it was best if one of the servers brought it over to Joanna, to give her some time to compose herself before the guests started to arrive. Kingston checked the time and saw that the first batch of invitees were due in twelve minutes.

Eleven minutes later, Catalina hurried over to Kingston and John with two tumblers and some ice. "They're almost here. Hold these. Look busy."

"Thanks babe," said John. He and Kingston took their drinks and had a sip, then promptly lowered their glasses far from their mouths. "What am I drinking?"

"Faux whiskey," said Catalina.

"Ah," said Kingston, peering into his drink and swirling the ice cubes around. He wondered if it was stale apple juice, but it smelled the same as whiskey. He suspected that Catalina had paid a trip to the apothecary to pick this up.

John stared at Catalina, mortified, as though his life had flashed cruelly before his eyes. "Why am I drinking faux whiskey?"

"So you don't get drunk," said Catalina. She grabbed a serviette and dried her hands and was careful not to ruin her nails.

"Can't I do that without drinking something that tastes this awful?"

"No, you also have to look busy and interesting. Men who stand around without a drink in their hand are boring. Joanna said so. And, coming from years in a drinking house, I agree." She shimmied in her black dress, fitted with a gold chain belt, and looked herself up and down. "Do I have anything on me?"

"You look beautiful," said John.

"No, you have nothing on you," said Kingston as quickly as he could, afraid of irritating two women that night.

"Thank you," Catalina said to Kingston. She turned to John. "And, I know."

They heard a small bell ding from just outside the marquee entrance and knew their first guest had arrived.

"Places!" Catalina cried. She hurried off and had to force herself to slow to a casual walk. She pulled her shoulders back and walked with a strong purpose, even though at that moment she was fighting the urge to itch her shoulder blades.

John glanced down at his drink and looked up at Kingston. "Any chance we can drink real stuff?"

"Yeah, go for it. As egocentric as it sounds, I'm the one who has to stay sharp tonight. I'm the local celebrity. I mean, you helped. You did more than help, you were there every step of the way."

John nodded and clapped a hand on Kingston's back. "I know. You're the one everyone wants to meet. You were the first to arrive and you're the brains behind the operation."

Kingston shied away as best he could. "It's hard hearing that without feeling like an ass."

They looked over to see who the first guest was. It turned out to be a gentleman of around sixty, which was usually deceptive since he may have had more than two hundred years of experience behind those eyes. He wore a black shirt, maroon tie, and a black suit. His hair was slicked back and badly dyed. Kingston appreciated that the gentleman went to some effort, but the suit was cheap and the man arrived alone, suggesting that he didn't have much confidence in the team and that he was also so socially inept that he was unable to rustle up a date.

"Good luck," said John, and he went to the bar to keep an eye on Rufus.

Kingston sighed, considered downing his drink in a single gulp before quickly remembering that it wasn't actually whiskey, and he went to introduce himself.

The night proceeded quietly. There were a total of twenty guests with barely any mingling. Catalina had to walk them hand in hand to others to get the conversation going. Joanna seemed to be back to her usual self and did her best engaging in conversation. The gang tried to keep to the script they had all run through, that this year was their finest year, that after all the experience Rufus had at building he now had a winner, and that he sold his apothecary as a ruse so that no one would be convinced he was competing. Joanna declared that stunt was a complete success, ruined only when Rufus sauntered over to the crowd and corrected her, proclaiming that he had completely retired until Kingston promised to cover the debt of building an entrant. Kingston pulled Rufus away and reminded him of the topics of discussion that were off limits.

"Why?" Rufus asked.

"Because for however many thousands of gold pieces I'm spending, you'll play nice and convince everyone here that you're worth funding. If we don't get their money then we don't have a single gold piece to compete with. No entry? No deal."

"I know you have gold," said Rufus, looking bored and willing to call Kingston's bluff. "And besides, most teams start without even a copper and rely on the banks for loans. You can take out a loan worth a million gold pieces if you like. So we don't actually need these people's money to compete."

Kingston gritted his teeth and smiled across the crowd.

"I don't suppose there's any word on the missing pliers?" Rufus asked.

"Nothing yet," said Kingston, feeling the night getting longer with every passing minute.

"You know, there's only so much setting up I can do before I actually have to start working."

"I understand," said Kingston. "And you're sure they were stolen? You didn't mislay them, did you?"

Rufus stepped back, flabbergasted. "I would never lose such a valuable set of pliers like that. Why, I was the one who sold them to Tom's in the first place!"

"Back when you sold the apothecary?" Kingston asked.

"Yes! Back when I sold the apothecary. I was getting myself as far away from the business of building machines for the tournament as possible, so yes, I sold them to Tom for seven gold pieces."

"And we bought them for twelve," said Kingston.

"No, *you* bought them for twelve."

"So they were definitely stolen?"

Rufus rolled his head to the side. "Yes, they were definitely stolen."

"Then they will turn up. And if they weren't stolen then I can only assume that they were lost, no doubt by accident."

"Then it would've been by that oaf in your employ."

Kingston shook his head in confusion. "You lost me there. Which oaf are you referring to?"

"You know who. John. And you know what I'm getting at as well. You picked him out of the woods from a thousand years ago and plonked him into this day and age. You think he'll just learn everything in one afternoon?"

"He's a quick learner," said Kingston, glaring down at Rufus.

"I don't care. And I know that look of yours. You can't let anything happen to me. You need me to build your machine and I need you to help me with my debts."

"Then you should keep your mouth in check," said Kingston.

"I'll say whatever I want," said Rufus, waving his hand dismissively. He wandered over to the bar and got another drink.

Kingston sighed and turned around. Joanna was standing nearby offering him a sympathetic smile. "You heard that?" Kingston asked.

Joanna nodded. "So did a few others. It won't exactly inspire them to help with donations."

"Neither will a drunken builder," Kingston said, looking over his shoulder at Rufus.

"You know, there is still a way out of this. We can cut and run."

"I know, but you and I are a little too stubborn for our own good, and we need a challenge. Plus, I've seen how bored you've been here. The tournament, for all of its headaches, is probably what we need right now."

Joanna shrugged, knowing that Kingston was right but still unhappy that their lives had been reduced to public relations maestros. "We're in over our heads."

"Then we sink or swim," said Kingston. He stepped forward and gave Joanna a hug, squeezing her tightly. "How are John and Catalina doing?"

Joanna smiled back at Kingston. "They're both like kids in a candy store."

Kingston snorted. That was almost technically true. John had been plucked from *Robin Hood* when he was twenty years old. He was still seven feet tall with a head of dark red hair. He had spent his entire life growing up in the forest, under the stiff northern weather. He looked at least ten years older than he actually was. Catalina was twenty three when Kingston and John rescued her from *Don Quixote*. There were five hundred years difference between their two upbringings and another four hundred years between Kingston's world and Catalina's. He had often tried to imagine what it would be like if someone had brought him forward five hundred years into the future and expected him to cope as though he belonged there. In his opinion, John and Catalina had done far better than he would have. Thus, seeing a modern day party with an open bar and hobnobbing with the elite of the realm was an other-worldly experience for them, and they were both giddy with excitement.

Catalina called out from her crowd of middle-aged men.

"Kingston! Come, tell these gentlemen about the time you rescued John from Hell."

Kingston sighed and put on a brave smile. "It's all about the money," he said quietly, and he headed into the crowd. There were five men, all modestly dressed up. Four of them were in over their heads and even Catalina was able to recognise that, but the fifth gentleman had an air of intelligence about him that caught Kingston's attention. As soon as Kingston joined the group he felt the gentleman's eyes lock onto him and they both acknowledged the other, aware that they were in full detective mode, studying each other. Kingston held out his hand and introduced himself to everyone around him.

"Maurice," said the more intelligent man, in a controlled baritone voice.

The handshake and eye contact told Kingston a good deal about who he was dealing with. *Confident, powerful, used to being in control but not taking it. A side-line observer.* Kingston caught sight of Maurice's cufflinks. *Good attention to detail.*

"A pleasure," said Kingston. He caught a minimalist smile, a look of recognition in Maurice's eye, and the two men knew they were both used to making a lot of money in an unorthodox manner. But, unlike some of Kingston's previous encounters with the elite, Maurice didn't give off the impression that he was a cut-throat money chaser, rather that he preferred a good game of tactics and manoeuvring.

Maurice glanced over to Catalina. "We were just hearing about your experiences in Hell. You battled an army almost single handedly and out-played a revolution."

Kingston slipped into his showcasing mode. While everyone else in the crowd was beaming with curiosity, Maurice was politely flattering Kingston before getting to the crux of the conversation. Kingston indulged him. "It was a harrowing experience, no question there. There was a monstrous serpent creature with the upper body of a man and the lower body of a snake that stretched easily twenty metres." Kingston glanced to the side in a well rehearsed look of trauma, convincing the men that he was back in Hell and reliving the moment. "That thing could move like the wind, darting across the crags and open fissures of the entrance to Hell. Getting the better of that creature was no easy task, I assure you. Then John and I were surrounded by, easily, eighty dour men, zombie-like but still formidable foes. John proved his skills that night, let me tell you. He fought them off with one punch after another, a powerhouse the like of which I have never seen elsewhere. Defeating the coup was easy enough. It was led by one of the Eternals, and we allowed her hubris to get the better of her. We then called upon Death and Satan themselves to guide us out and return us to Limbo. All told, it was an exciting time and I'm grateful that it worked out for us all."

Kingston saw that four of the men were rapt with attention, so he gave them what they wanted. "John? You remember fighting eighty men in Hell?"

John sauntered over, now with a decent glass of whiskey in his hand. "Huh, there could have been eight hundred of them and they still wouldn't have made it past me." He took over the conversation, giving a blow by blow description of the fight, and every other fight he had ever been in, while Kingston and Maurice found a quieter area of the marquee.

"You've made quite an impression in your short time here," said Maurice. "All four of you."

"It wasn't my intention when I first arrived," said Kingston.

"But now you seem to be cashing in on your fame."

"It's time for a new challenge."

"Then you've found one with your builder," said Maurice. "He's spent the evening contradicting everyone and downplaying your chances of success."

Kingston didn't let that faze him. He knew Maurice was likely to push his buttons to see just what kind of a man he was dealing with, and the man Kingston needed to project was that of someone in complete control of himself. "He has his quirks, I'll give you that."

"It's a good strategy. The teams that are united and with an official spokesman are favoured to win. With Rufus out here unsettling everyone, your odds will go through the roof." Maurice raised his glass in salute. "Well played."

"Thank you," said Kingston, and he found an opening to exploit. "It's not something we planned on but I hope we can make it work for us."

"Ah, well played again," said Maurice, this time showing surprise. "Most people would have accepted the compliment, but you were actually honest and humble."

Kingston felt a moment of relief sweep over him. If ever there was a man of equal standing as himself, he was sure he had just found it in Maurice. Then again, he had felt that several times before and had always been disappointed by the end. "So what is your involvement in the Games?"

"I'm one of the directors of the Cascade. We operate only during the tournament and then lead a quiet life for another nine years. We are an investment house. You give us a hundred gold pieces to bet on the games, we place the bets for you, take a commission, and we do our best to see that you come out on top. But as long as we receive a hundred gold pieces or more we don't charge a commission in the event of a loss."

"I like it," said Kingston. "To what extent do you manipulate the odds or the results?"

"As little as possible," said Maurice. "And certainly not towards the beginning of the competition. I like your set up here. Your team has a lot of interesting variables, it will shake the Games around a little. But the Cascade likes to know the ins and outs of every detail and judge for ourselves. We have to anticipate surprises. We're here to make money just as everyone else but we try to do it legitimately."

"I imagine your advice to teams could help to sway your profit margin," said Kingston, with a wry smile.

"From time to time," said Maurice, looking more relaxed as he spoke to an equally minded businessman. "It helps the teams as well. If we find out that your opponent has a well hidden disadvantage, we might be inclined to let you know. Vice versa as well, and your disadvantage can be financially compensated, to a degree."

Kingston smiled and was amused that Maurice's 'as little as possible' in regards to manipulating the odds of the tournament actually meant quite the opposite. "So, you've had a look around and you know our history. What's your honest opinion here?"

Maurice drew in a deep breath and noted the various contenders within the room. He gave a sharp look to the servers and musicians and pulled Kingston aside. "You're under-experienced, under-qualified, and you have a lot of ground to make up. The advantage you have is that you can get a loan from the bank at a reasonable rate of return because it's your first tournament. That's an advantage many teams would love to have, since money makes the team. You're not going to find many investors tonight, but you are building interest in your team, which is good. There are other teams which will try to fly under the radar as much as possible, but you're out here getting noticed without a single component of your machine built yet, am I right?"

"On the money," said Kingston.

"The most advantageous part of your team is your reputation. You have all battled it out in Hell and won, you've all had dealings with Death and Satan and have won, and if rumours are to be believe you kidnapped a dragon and tried to raid the Bank of Limbo. You've over-thrown people much more powerful than yourselves, defeated armies of lawyers and feeble minded paper pushers, and you are a personal favourite of the upper management of Death Inc., including Death himself. What all that boils down to is that people will expect you to know exactly what you're doing, even if the truth is the opposite. If your machine breaks down in the middle of the first battle then the public will assume that it's because you wanted it to and it's all part of some grander scheme. You and I know that you're flying by the seat of your pants and that machine broke down because you have a clumsy builder."

Kingston gave Maurice an amused nod. "I suppose the gambling houses are also aware of this."

"They are prepared for it, yes. But being a gambling house they are prepared for many eventualities."

"How would I catch up to the other teams?" Kingston asked.

"I hear your builder is trying to build a golem."

Kingston wished Rufus would keep his mouth shut.

"It's a smart play by him," said Maurice. "It commits you to actually building the biggest and most expensive contraption out there. Now you know why very few teams actually have sponsors, it's because the builders have wild ambitions that they can't afford, but as soon as they aren't responsible for bankrolling the project they can go crazy with their plans. So, work with it. Build a golem bigger and better than anyone else. Whatever weapons your builder wants to incorporate, double them in size and power. You don't catch up to the other teams by building a flimsy machine, you catch up by blasting away their expectations."

"That's going to be one hell of a price tag," said Kingston, raising his eyebrows and feeling his stomach drop away from him.

"That is why your rate of return on your loan is your strongest asset," said Maurice. "You can afford it, and you can afford to place a few bets on yourself. With your reputation you're going to be the crowd favourite. But your builder is right about one thing. He will certainly need an assistant. Probably several."

Kingston wondered if it really was too late to withdraw from the whole thing. "Do we actually have a chance at winning?"

Maurice smiled and shook his head. "You're still under experienced with a sub-par builder, but this is his moment to shine and prove himself. Then, when you're done, you can sell your machine to the highest bidder and reclaim some of the money you spent on it. If you bet wisely you can see a few extra gold coins come your way. By the time the next tournament comes along you should be in a stronger position to actually make it into the final round."

Kingston rolled his eyes and hoped like hell he wasn't going to have to wait another ten years to pay off whatever bills came his way. "So how do I make more money than anyone else?"

"The bank is the only entity here that will always make money from the tournament. The gambling houses are your next best bet, but you're too late to establish one of your own. You would need at least a ten year heads up to even reasonably compete, and even then you might make only four percent profit. The bigger houses can make up to twenty percent. Next up is the Cascade and we make a healthy living out of it, usually three percent profit for ourselves and eight percent for our clients, without risking much of our own money. Those are the three sure fire ways of making a return on your investment."

Maurice studied Kingston's poker face carefully. "As to how to make money by competing, you're going to need to appear as suicidal as possible while still having a good machine. By this I mean: find whoever is the current leader. As soon as the teams from Hell arrive that is likely to be Team Kwon. Send John over to beat them up. All of them. And then send him over to Lawnston. He has his bodyguards and ruffians. John would probably like that kind of fight. If John takes them all out you can bet that revenge will be the highest priority on their minds. No one will be sure that you'll even make it to the next round, but you're going to have to. Your odds will be sky high. The problem then is that your opponent also wants sky high odds, so they'll let the public know, as quietly as possible, that you've bribed them into taking a fall, so your odds will drop back to normal again. So you're going to need to send John along as close to the time of the match as possible, no sooner than twenty four hours, no later than twelve, to give the odds enough time to change to your favour. You're then going to need to go into hiding because the teams from Hell will rally together and come looking for you. Fake teams even come along and their whole purpose is to be hired for revenge."

Kingston sighed and shook his head. "That's putting a lot of pressure on John and risking his life."

"Yeah, but it will make you a lot of money," said Maurice. "Someone has already started betting on you right now. Twice, actually. Someone actually wagered fifteen gold pieces that you would compete and someone else wagered ten that Rufus would enter again. The Cascade are also taking a lot of requests to focus on you. So you and I may end up as business partners. The more you keep me informed, the more I can help you out."

Kingston arched and eyebrow and gave a cautious nod of agreement. "How do I make twenty five thousand gold pieces?"

Maurice's appearance faltered and his jaw dropped open. He then recovered but took a moment to stare at his drink, working out if he heard Kingston correctly. "You're kidding."

"If I really am shooting for crazy, how do I make that kind of money?"

Maurice looked away with a moment of brain lock. "Well, no one has ever won that much before. Most of the gambling houses have a limit of a thousand gold piece pay out, so you'll have to win twenty five extraordinary bets without a single loss. Perhaps you should focus on something a little more realistic."

"I don't exactly do realistic," said Kingston.

Maurice snorted. "Then brace yourself. Just because you have the bank at your disposal doesn't mean that you can afford to gamble every copper you have. And the gambling houses aren't an entirely legal entity so if they owe you money and they can't pay, then they might decide to cut and run. You can try your luck at the bank by saying these gambling houses owe you money, but because it's an illegal contract the bank doesn't have to chase them for the money, they're going to chase you. So, let's scale back the twenty five thousand and come up with something a little more reasonable."

"We'll see," said Kingston.

"Be careful. None of the gambling houses actually have to honour the bets you place with them, that's why it's safer to use the Cascade. They won't know that it was originally your money, and we can chase these people up to get your money."

"I'll have to look it over," said Kingston. He held his hand out. "It's been a pleasure meeting you, Maurice."

Maurice shook Kingston's hand. "Likewise. I imagine that in a few months, when all of the dust has settled, we'll have a few stories to tell."

"Oh, certainly," said Kingston. "Please help yourself to a drink." They parted. Kingston took a moment to let his conversation with Maurice sink in, while appreciating the music in the background. He quickly realised his knowledge in this area was limited. The score bounced between classical music and contemporary songs. The piece ended and Kingston went back to the crowd of four gentlemen as John was still regaling them with his tales of knocking people out and hurling boulders the size of a bus across the Nottingham countryside. Kingston knew that John was embellishing a little, but he was excited to finally be the centre of attention.

Catalina had moved onto another group and would soon need Kingston's support in dealing with the men and women there. Joanna was talking to a couple who were wearing nice outfits. It looked as though there might be a sponsor among them. Kingston caught sight of the woman's silver bracelet and knew it was a gift, likely from her gentleman friend, but there was a secret attraction there. The gentleman had the hallmark signs of someone who was on a date with his mistress. Kingston wondered where the wife was on such a night and suspected that everyone took a time out from their routine lives once the Games came around.

A light voice whispered behind him. "She looks pretty."

Kingston turned and was surprised to see a young woman in front of him, wearing a wrap around her eyes. She clearly wasn't one of the servers, though her wrap first suggested that she was. Kingston glanced up towards the band and, sure enough, the piano was unattended while the others continued playing, with an obvious look of annoyance on their faces. Kingston looked back down to the girl and smiled towards Joanna. "Yes, she does."

The girl held her purse in her hand but also wore something strapped across her back, holding what would have been a very thin, rectangular backpack. It would have been the right size for ...

The girl popped open her purse and pulled out a small business card. "My services," she said, handing over the card.

'Jezebel,' it said. *'Ninja. Thief. Pianist extraordinaire.'*

Kingston snorted and bobbed his head. "Jezebel," he said.

"The one and only," she said, offering a slight curtsy.

"I presume you have a set of pliers strapped to your back."

Jezebel pulled the rectangular backpack away and swung it around to face Kingston. She pulled the wrapping open to reveal a leather pouch with some weighty pliers inside.

Kingston smirked at her candour. "John said that he never let these things out of his sight."

"John is not as alert as he says," said Jezebel.

"So when did you steal them?"

"There is a secret compartment on the underside of the rickshaw. I just happened to reach into whatever bag was closest to me. I didn't want the square tins, they didn't seem all that valuable. But I know a set of tools can be annoying to misplace so I took those."

"So the driver was in on it," Kingston said to himself. "What about Tom? I presume he alerted you to the purchase?"

Jezebel smiled. "Trade secrets, Mr K."

"Actually it would be Mr R," said Kingston. "And I'll take those pliers back, if you don't mind."

"I don't mind at all," said Jezebel, handing the pouch of pliers to Kingston. "Your team is lacking a thief."

"Right now it's also lacking a pianist," Kingston said, looking over to the band who were shooting poisoned eyes at Jezebel while they played.

Jezebel smiled at Kingston and gave him a slight bow of the head. "You need a thief. I've been listening to what people are saying at this thing. You have barely started building. You need a thief."

Kingston knew she was right, but trusting someone that had already robbed him and knowing that they were going to steal again wasn't the strongest of trust building exercises. "I've always been intrigued by the interview process of hiring someone like you."

Jezebel shrugged. "I'm not. Let's just assume you've already hired me."

She had a spark of Joanna inside her, Kingston was sure of it. He looked her over and tried to figure out her capabilities. She was young, appeared to be twenty, and quite petite. She had brown hair that had been straightened and pulled back into a ponytail. Her fringe hung down towards her eyes. "Let's go easy on the assumptions. If I do need a thief, why are you better than the rest?"

"Oh, I'm not, but I'm the only one here and we've already built a solid rapport."

Kingston glanced down at the weighty set of tools and had to wonder just what a slight girl could manage to carry away and still go unnoticed. "I'll need a lot, and most of it is going to be heavy."

"If it's in Limbo, I can get it," said Jezebel.

"That doesn't sound remotely realistic," said Kingston. "There are going to be quite a few things you won't be able to get."

Jezebel shrugged and quickly checked to make sure no one was listening in on their conversation. "From one professional thief to another, you know that you don't always have to steal something to find a way of getting it. You can romance it out from the owner, blackmail the owner into handing it over, buy it, or even hire someone else to steal it and rob them once they've done all of the hard work. And I agree, there are limits. I mostly hide in small boxes and grab whatever is in reach, but I know the players and the builders. They all have thieves. One of them is in this marquee right now. He hasn't made a move yet, but I'd kept an eye on your girlfriend's jewellery."

Kingston glanced around the room and shook his head. "I know a thief when I see one."

"I've been playing the piano for over an hour and you didn't see me." Jezebel straightened up and pulled her shoulders back. "I'm taking you on as my client, Mr K. I'll be in touch about my bill. In the meantime, I have a badly arranged song from the nineteen eighties to perform. When I'm done I'm going to let your builder hit on me a little. He's not seeing anyone, is he?"

Kingston pulled his head back in mild revulsion. Rufus looked to be at least eighty. Then again, Michelle looked as though she was in her mid-twenties and had been Death's secretary for four hundred years. "He's not seeing anyone, no," said Kingston.

Jezebel smiled. "Glad to hear. And as a welcome to the tournament kind of present I did manage to get a copy of Ernie Sander's blueprints. He's building a drill. If you hire me you can have his plans tomorrow."

Kingston smiled and gave her a nod. "Very well. How do I contact you?"

"You have my name," said Jezebel, nodding to the card. "Write me a note. Later, Mr K." Jezebel turned and headed back to her piano amid the glares and chastisement from her fellow band mates.

Kingston smiled at the girl. She certainly reminded him of Joanna. He slipped Jezebel's card into his pocket and returned to his hosting duties. He took a moment to whisper into John's ear. A moment later one of the guests ran for his life with John bellowing "Thief!" at the top of his lungs. Kingston wasn't sure if the man in question was an actual thief, but he was sure that if there was a real one in the vicinity then it would be foolish to make a move after seeing John's ferocity.

VII

The first edition of *Inside the XIX Games* was out the next day with the headline *'Limbo Celebrity Fails To Garner Interest'*. It was still unusual for Kingston to see his name in the newspaper, but he was quite sure that using such a title as a marketing ploy confirmed the opposite was true. If he really failed to arouse interest then his story would not be the main selling point of the newspaper. John had picked up the copy on his way over to the office and dropped it on Kingston's desk. Aside from a recap of the last tournament, the only point of interest was that two other teams were confirming their status as competitors - one led by Rufus' arch nemesis Horatio, and another by the name of Ernie Sanders.

Rufus had grumbled about Ernie before. He competed by buying previously destroyed machines and entering them as his own. Rufus didn't think it was right, but Kingston appreciated that Ernie wanted to capitalise on the desperation of other builders to sell their scrap while also working towards nostalgia for crowd support.

Kingston read the sixteen page newspaper cover to cover and felt a little defeated by his prospects. The sad truth was that despite holding two parties in the same evening they had not received a single donation for the team. There had been three potential donors but they were still wary of lending any kind of support to a builder that had such a disastrous track record. Another pair of parties were due to take place that evening and Kingston knew it would be a struggle to find something that would inspire the crowd to sponsor them. Worse still was knowing just how out of pocket they were already. It cost eighty seven gold to cover the marquee rental, servers, and musicians for six parties over three nights, and a further fifty to cover drinks and food. Kingston looked over the bills that Rufus was racking up and saw a list of necessary ingredients from the apothecaries that would cost at least two thousand gold.

It called for some desperation. He sent off two letters, the first to Michelle, which informed her that she was invited that evening and that a donation was necessary for the sanity of the team. Kingston decided that was fair play, since she had pushed him in the first place into participating. The second letter was a dicey move. He invited Satan. If nothing else, Satan's arrival would earn a little more promotion and get the people of Limbo talking. Secretly, Kingston hoped that Satan would avoid the party and simply mention the invite to Death, who would arrive in Satan's place and, again, earn some advertisement for the team.

"I'm not sure how many party goers want to be in the same room as Satan," said John.

"We're on protected grounds, we'll be fine," said Kingston.

"Uh huh. You know one day we might find ourselves in Hell again, without your protected ground theory."

The office was still trashed with papers everywhere and the clutter started to blend into the background. The only change to the disaster was that Kingston returned the ash tray to his desk, hoping that someone would eventually steal it. He had gone to a lot of work to have that thing enchanted and, so far, his hard work hadn't paid off. What he needed was someone stupid enough to take it.

An hour later Kingston went down to the basement and met a grumpy looking John standing by the door of Rufus' workshop. There was a handwritten sign in place that said *Bugger Off*. John scowled when he saw Kingston.

"He's really trying my patience," said John.

"I presume it's locked?"

"It is. I was thumping on the door for half an hour and still he ignores me."

"Half an hour?"

"Maybe more," said John, with a shrug.

"Any idea what he's doing in there?" Kingston asked.

"He's whistling."

"Ah, good." Kingston retraced the conversation he had with Jezebel the night before and hoped that she wasn't in there with

Rufus right now. He shuddered at the thought.

"Then he stops half way through a tune, all of a sudden. He waits ten seconds and then continues again. It's driving me nuts. You know he stopped just half a bar before the chorus kicked in? Who does that? Was he dropped on his head as a child? You don't stop whistling before the chorus. If anything, you skip over the verse just so you can get to the chorus quicker."

"Maybe he's working," said Kingston.

"Then don't whistle if you're too busy working!" John thumped on the door. "Rufus! *Rufus!* Kingston is out here. Open this door!"

The door didn't open. Instead, a torn up sheet of paper was flicked out from underneath. John picked it up and glared once again. " *'Genius at work.'* Genius my arse. You want to see a real genius? Open the door."

Kingston held his hand out for the note. "May I?"

"Be my guest," said John.

Kingston looked over the sheet of paper and found a list of key ingredients on the back.

Female squirrel tail - 6 inches
Eye of a blue whale - x 1
Moment of silence from John - x 100
Dead African wasps - x 63
Golem, 9 feet tall, 200 kilos - x 1

Kingston smiled at the list and decided not to show John. He was a little curious about the last entry, though. He gently tapped on the door. "Eh, Rufus? Aren't you supposed to be building me a golem?"

John looked around, convinced that he just misheard Kingston. "What do you mean? You mean he isn't going to build us a golem? What the hell, Rufus? What the *hell?*"

"I'll work on items one, two, and four," said Kingston. "I hope you'll open the door when I return."

"He better," said John. "You know I can just smack this door down, right?"

"He might have it enchanted," said Kingston.

"Then I'll bust open the wall. I bet he didn't enchant that."

"The wall belongs to the bank."

"So? No one likes banks."

"Perhaps Simon knows a better way in?" Kingston said.

John bobbed his head and sulked away. "I'll go find that strange little man and his cat. He better have a key or something."

Kingston went back to the entrance of the janitorial department. He hunted down a sheet of paper and pulled out his fine fountain pen from inside his jacket pocket, then re-wrote the list from Simon and addressed it to Jezebel. He also included the previous items Rufus had requested; the ox blood, spiced elephant tusk, opal, various sets of teeth, and the rags of a mummy. Kingston sealed up the paper inside an envelope, wrote Jezebel's name clearly on the front, and dropped it into the air.

The envelope fell splat onto the ground.

Even though that was logically what was supposed to happen, Kingston knew that what *should* have happened was that the envelope was to disappear and reappear at Jezebel's feet, no matter where she was in the realm. Kingston picked up the envelope and turned it over in his hands, trying to figure out what went wrong. He fished out her business card and considered the possibility that it was a clue to sending her notes, that the usual method wouldn't work for her, especially if *Jezebel* wasn't her real name. Kingston put her business card in with the enveloped, sealed it up again, and dropped it in mid-air.

The envelope fell splat onto the ground.

Kingston picked it up again and added the words *Ninja. Thief. Pianist Extraordinaire,* to the envelope. He dropped it into the air and it snapped out of reality. He snorted, knowing that this kind of trickery was quite advanced to fool Death's laws, and that it forced everyone to acknowledge her skills.

In the meantime, Kingston decided to go out and meet the competition, starting with Horatio, even if he had no idea how to find him. Five minutes later he found that even the statues had an attitude while the tournament was on.

"Why should I tell you where he is?" said the statue of Archimedes.

"Because you're a nice guy," said Kingston, aware that the statue was likely to turn that around on him.

"Oh, you think I'm a guy, is that it? A real guy, like you? With movable limbs and the ability to walk around like a mindless pedestrian? I've got news for you, pal. I'm a statue, okay? I may stand in the same spot all day and act like an information centre to some, but we statues talk, you know? And you know what we talk about? Who is nice to us and who isn't. This guy you're looking for? Horatio? This time of the decade he is not worth locating, so why don't you move along and do your searching somewhere else."

Kingston cocked his head to one side and gave Archimedes a sympathetic look. "What did he do?"

"He blew up Fernando, that's what he did."

Kingston raised his eyebrows as high as they would go. "That's awful."

Archimedes sneered at Kingston. "Do you even know which Fernando I'm talking about?"

Kingston ran through every Fernando, Ferdinand, Fernand, Hernandez, and variations thereof. He couldn't think of any, so he went with the easiest answer he could come up with. "Your friend?"

Archimedes eased up a little with that one. "Yeah, okay, he wasn't my friend in the strictest sense, but I knew the guy and he didn't exactly deserve getting blown up."

"That's rough. How is Fernando now?"

"You know the Humpty Dumpty rhyme? Imagine that with granite. Although, they were able to put him back together, eventually, but that kind of thing changes a person. He's now a little twitchy, and it's all because of that stupid Horatio."

Kingston nodded and gave Archimedes his most sympathetic of looks. "You know, if you want, I might be able to speak to someone about this. Fernando obviously got the rough end of the deal with this one and it sounds like Horatio got away without any hassle."

Archimedes sighed and shook his head. "There's not much point, really, it was twenty years ago."

"Then maybe I can do something nice for him? I've seen people living their lives with that kind of twitch, always jumpy and never as happy as they should be. No one should have to go through that. Maybe if you guys know what Fernando would like I can help him more directly? I could talk to him a little, if he isn't too nervous?"

"I don't know if that would work," said Archimedes, while shaking his head.

"It's worth a shot. Sometimes all someone wants is a stranger to come and show them that the world isn't so bad. A little distraction could help."

Archimedes thought it over and offered Kingston a hint of a

smile. "That is kind of you, but it's not a great time for him. Everyone on the street is talking about the highlights of the previous tournaments and they all look at him and start to whisper. He's going to have to put up with that for another couple of months."

"Then this is the time to do something for him," said Kingston. "Where would he like to go instead?"

Archimedes sighed. "I honestly don't know. I'm not the closest statue he knows."

"I'd certainly like to try. How can I find him?"

Archimedes thought it over for a moment and wasn't sure whether he could trust Kingston or not. "I'll tell you what. I'll point you towards Socrates. He knows Fernando a little better than I do, he'll be better at knowing whether to move him to a safer place or keep him where he is."

"Sounds fair," said Kingston. "Which direction is Socrates?"

Archimedes pointed behind Kingston. "Head along Lower Styx, take a left at Vingólf Boulevard. He's the fifth or sixth statue along."

"Thank you." Kingston nodded a farewell and moved away slowly, giving Archimedes a chance to call him back.

"Before you go ..."

Kingston smiled and turned back. "Yes?"

"Who are you?" asked Archimedes.

Kingston gave a simple nod to the statue and expected something interesting to come from this. "Kingston Raine."

Archimedes raised a granite eyebrow. "Ah. So you're the one everyone talks about."

"Yes, I'm the one."

"I hear your books are pretty good."

"Well, I didn't write them, I'm just in them."

"So, Kingston Raine, why would you help a random statue called Fernando? You obviously don't know him."

Kingston pulled his head up and went into pitch mode, hoping to sway Archimedes into becoming an ally. "I'm competing in this year's tournament against Horatio. But I may be in over my head. I am certainly going to lose every match. I figured the statues are often overlooked and you guys have to get bored once in a while, so as soon as you mentioned Fernando and his accident I thought that if I helped him then maybe some of the statues would help me."

Archimedes looked over Kingston with a mix of suspicion and confusion. "Help you how?"

"No idea," said Kingston. "I don't really know yet what I need to know in order to do well in this tournament, but I certainly want to beat Horatio."

Archimedes looked as though he was thinking it over and he gave Kingston a slow nod, unsure if he trusted him or not. "Go talk to Socrates. He might help you with Fernando."

"I will. Thank you for your time." Kingston walked away, now sure that there was nothing left to say between the two of them. Either way, helping one of the neglected beings in the realm could end up paying dividends, especially since all of the humans were as paranoid and unhelpful as possible.

Socrates listened to what Kingston had to say and advised against talking to Fernando, who turned out to be Fernando de Herrera, a Spanish renaissance writer. It would be too troublesome to move him and it would only draw more attention to his nervous condition. And if Kingston tried to have Horatio punished for blowing him up twenty years after the event then it would seem a little too petty at this time of the decade and wouldn't help any of them.

"Best leave it be," said Socrates, in a slow drawl.

"How did Fernando get blown up anyway?" Kingston asked.

"Oh, he was a little too close to the arena and a thief used Fernando as a shield. Horatio threw a smoke bomb at the girl and hit Fernando instead."

"And that caused him to blow up?" Kingston asked, sure that he was missing something.

"I did say smoke *bomb*, Mr Raine. If the girl hadn't used Fernando as a shield she might not have made it."

Kingston wasn't sure which was worse, the near death tactics used by Limbo teams against Limbo competitors, or the groan that was rising through his chest about who this thief might be. "I don't suppose this girl was a petite brunette who looked to be around twenty years old?"

Socrates shook his head lazily. "She was caught, Mr Raine, and expelled from Limbo. Whoever you think she is, she isn't the girl you're thinking of."

Kingston hung his head, hoping that Socrates would realise that his explanation still didn't rule out Jezebel's involvement.

Socrates read Kingston's look and sighed. "She was Persian, if that helps."

Kingston perked up. "That does, actually. Thank you."

"I'd suggest staying clear of Horatio, Mr Raine. He has a temper."

Kingston left, hurried back to his apartment on Cerberus Avenue and burst inside. Catalina shrieked and scrambled backwards. She was wearing nothing but a black slip.

"I have an idea!" Kingston cried.

Catalina grabbed her dress from the ironing board and she quickly covered herself. "Ay! Don't do that!" she shouted.

"Sorry," said Kingston, as he realised that he had stumbled onto ... in fact, he wasn't sure what he had stumbled onto. "Eh ... what's going on?"

"I'm ironing!" shouted Catalina. She then scampered for the bedroom.

Joanna came out wearing a light blue bathrobe. A towel was wrapped around her head and she pulled her toothbrush out of her mouth. "What the hell was that?"

"I scared Catalina a little." Kingston leaned towards his bedroom door. "I'm sorry!"

Joanna glanced over her shoulder. "So why are we apologising to Catalina?"

"I had an idea," said Kingston. "You know the statues? They're neglected. They know all the secrets of the realm and communicate with each other. Everyone ignores them. We can use them to our advantage."

"I don't ignore them," said Joanna.

"Most people ignore them."

"Why would you ignore them? They're talking statues, not litter. They all have something interesting to talk about. The busts, however, you can take them or leave them."

Kingston nodded quickly and tried to get back to the point. "Right. I'm just saying that a lot of people go about their lives ignoring mostly everyone else and that includes the statues. They are neglected. I was talking to Archimedes today and he said that Horatio, yes the same Horatio, blew up Fernando de Herrera twenty years ago and since then Fernando has been a little twitchy, so if we cheer up Fernando the rest of the statues will talk about it and that might help us with the tournament, since they don't really like Horatio and we can spin that to our advantage. That's why I burst in here like I did and that's when Catalina shrieked and ran off."

Joanna breathed in deeply, giving Kingston a passive look while she considered his supposed masterpiece of an idea. "Are we expecting one of these statues to compete for us?"

"No, they're very slow moving."

"So we're still going to build a golem, which is traditionally a hunk of clay shaped so that it looks like a statue, which is also a very slow moving thing and hard to bring down."

Kingston thought it through and nodded. "Right. We're still going to build a golem."

"Even if we cover a statue in a suit of armour?"

"I like your enthusiasm but I'm still trying to separate the two. Golem in one pile, statue in another."

Joanna shrugged and gave Kingston the benefit of the doubt. "So we cheer up a statue so that every other statue gives us all the inside dirt we'll ever need?"

Kingston nodded. "You know how we're lacking a lot of information right now? Well, they know pretty much everything that goes on around here and they can be our spies. I'm sure they've heard about good bets and bad bets as well." Kingston beamed with a smile and had already run through to the end of his master plan. He even pictured himself standing on a podium with a tournament cup high above his head. He paused and wondered if there even was a tournament cup. Then something caught his attention. "Why was Catalina half naked in our living room?"

"I'm helping her with her hair and make up. She creased her dress last night when she sat down, so she was ironing it."

The bedroom door swung open and Catalina appeared wearing a long yellow bathrobe. "You should give a girl a little privacy, you know? If you say you're going to be home at four then warn her if you're coming back early."

Kingston peered back at Joanna.

"It's nothing kinky," said Joanna, rolling her eyes. "It's not like we can just throw on a suit and ruffle our hair with coconut mousse. There's a whole ordeal to looking better than everyone else."

"I'm aware of the ordeal," said Kingston, nodding politely.

Joanna arched her head to one side and looked at Kingston

suspiciously. "Because you've gone through it yourself?"

Kingston felt himself stepping towards a landmine of trouble and he backed away. "Is there anything I can do to help?"

"You could finish ironing my dress," said Catalina.

"Will do," said Kingston, and he stepped over to the iron board.

"You're not going to burn my dress, are you?"

"No, I have this down to a fine art. See my collars? Pristine."

"That dress is a lot thinner than your collars."

"I know, but I'll be careful."

Catalina became immediately terrified that Kingston was about to get distracted again and burn a hole right through the most expensive thing she's ever warn.

"I do have a favour to ask of you," said Kingston.

Catalina drew in a quick breath and she stared back at her dress.

"Is there any chance you could go down to Xolotl Avenue with a copy of *Kingston Raine and Shanghai Werewolf,* find a statue called Fernando, and read it to him. He wouldn't be hard to miss, he's covered in glue and has been crudely put back together."

Catalina focussed on her dress. "It's six hundred pages long."

"Well, it *is* two hundred and ten thousand words." Kingston realised that he wasn't doing himself any favours with that one. "But maybe you're a little busy right now and I've come at a bad time. It's just, this statue, Fernando, he's really down on his luck and no one pays him much attention."

Catalina gave Kingston a moment to fully reconsider, but he didn't. "We have two different two hour parties to host this evening and I am going to wear a pretty black dress again, and high heels, and I need to do something different with my hair so I don't look like a one trick pony. I'm going to be at the party an hour and a half early to set up, an hour in between to get the change over for food and drinks sorted, and then an hour afterwards to make sure the staff don't run off with the cutlery. This party was your idea."

Kingston felt himself checkmated. "I had a good time."

"We didn't receive any donations."

"But we still threw one hell of a party." He held the iron out in one hand.

Catalina shrieked and reached for the iron. "Just ... gimme that. If I do it wrong I have only myself to blame." Catalina went back to the iron and continued, while Kingston and Joanna gave each other a knowing look.

She's broke, Joanna mouthed.

How much was the dress? Kingston asked.

Thirty gold.

Kingston's eyebrows raised to the top of his head. Then he realised that he had suits which would cost the same, but even then those were excessive and he knew he could afford them. There was no way Catalina could cover thirty gold. Kingston knew it. Catalina knew it.

Joanna lowered her gaze and mouthed again. *She had to take a loan out to buy that dress.*

Then it clicked and Kingston felt a weight drop into his stomach. Catalina needed a dress that equalled Joanna's. She was a girl trying to fit in with two professionals who were used to the millionaire life, and until recently she was a penniless seventeenth century bar maid.

She's scared, Joanna mouthed.

Kingston noticed that the room had fallen deathly quiet. "So did you have a good day?"

Then he mouthed: *She can't afford that dress.*

Joanna nodded. "It was all right. I didn't sleep well. Too much stress."

She thinks she has no choice, Joanna mouthed.

Kingston looked over and saw Catalina work the iron as carefully as possible. He always knew that if he lost everything and fell into a nightmare of debt he would be okay. He had the brains, the knowledge, and the charm to land back on his feet. But Catalina was a different story. She certainly had the brains, and the charm, but she wasn't a gambler. Safety was everything to her, and this tournament had already pushed her far out of her comfort zone.

Kingston leaned in and kissed Joanna on the cheek. "You'll be okay?"

"Always am," said Joanna, and she offered Kingston a smile. "You'll be back at four?"

"Four thirty?"

"I'll make sure you don't scare Catalina while she has the iron in her hand."

"Thanks." Kingston turned and saw the stiff shoulders in Catalina's posture. Even though she was wrapped in a bathrobe, she looked uncomfortable. "Sorry again, Catalina."

"Not your fault. You live here," she said, without turning around.

"I'll see you soon," said Kingston and he left.

Rufus arrived to the party again in a trunk. This time, though, he was less surly. He also held tightly onto a small object wrapped in a strip of cloth. Kingston braced himself, for it looked like a bottle of scotch, but Rufus gleefully shook his head and, for once, he didn't have bloodshot eyes.

"Spectacular party last night!" Rufus said. He paced around the marquee with one finger raised above his head and he stared at the ground. "I was thinking we were missing something. A prototype, something that the punters can actually have a look at. Now, this isn't by any means the final thing, or even something close to what the final thing will look like, but I was able to enchant a little toy soldier into marching around."

Rufus pulled off the wrappings and revealed what looked like a coffee can. He didn't wait for Kingston's approval, instead he lowered the can onto the ground and pushed down on the top. The can shuddered and slowly split apart, folded back, and transformed itself into a short, fat, tin soldier. It had a large head like a can of soda with two glowing purple eyes.

"I haven't named it yet," said Rufus, beaming with pride. "Perhaps one of the punters can, if they donate to our cause."

Kingston smiled at the small gadget. "It is cute."

Rufus prodded it forward with his foot. The little soldier started walking around with its large head bobbing side to side. "That's pretty much all it's going to do today. It can walk and fall over and pick itself up again. If I had a little more time I could get it to do a cartwheel, but those are some tricky physics, changing your centre of gravity like that. Best to keep it simple for a demonstration."

"We're going to build a larger version of this?" Kingston asked.

"That's the plan!" said Rufus. "You know, it's been so long since I actually built something for the enjoyment of it. It really was a good kick up the caboose."

Kingston and John glanced at each other, wondering exactly what, or who, inspired the change in mood. John then pointed at the soldier. "How did you make it?"

"I'm a builder, it's what I do," said Rufus.

"With ox blood?"

Rufus focussed on his robot, which had fallen over and was trying to right itself again. "Well, yeah, a little."

Kingston and John shared another look, this one of equal suspicion.

"And you just happened to have some lying around?" Kingston asked. "That was fortunate."

Rufus continued smiling at his machine, joyfully ignoring Kingston and John. "I should show the girls." Rufus picked up the toy soldier and hurried away.

Kingston and John groaned. "Did he leave the bank last night?" Kingston asked.

"I have no idea," said John. "He's not exactly under lock and key, you know."

"But for his own safety ..."

"I know."

"So he has a secret stash somewhere," said Kingston.

"Maybe. Or maybe your thief pulled through."

"I gave her the list of essentials only after I last saw you today."

John rolled his head with a groan and stared at Rufus, who showed Catalina the cute robot. It seemed to melt her heart. "We don't really know what happened."

An hour and a half later, they knew exactly what happened. Muira, the current owner of Rufus' former apothecary, burst into the marquee while shouting at the two greeters. She stopped, saw the crowd stare at her, and laid eyes upon Rufus. "Thief!" she cried.

Rufus raised his eyes in shock and he quickly backed away while his tin can robot kept falling over itself. Kingston and John glanced at each other and figured it out.

"You broke into my store last night. I know you did! You stole my great white teeth and my ox blood and my scented elephant tusk." She snapped her fingers and a big bellied bearded man followed Muira inside. Kingston had the distinct impression that this man was Muira's husband.

"You will return what you took *and* pay for the damages!" roared Muira. "I am not involved in the tournament and you do not treat me like this. Pay up!"

Kingston stepped forward and smiled. "Muira, please. Come in, don't be shy."

"Who the hell is shy?" Muira roared. "I want my property back and I want the money to compensate me!"

"Pay the woman," glared the bearded man. Kingston altered his opinion away from him being Muira's husband, but he was still someone of close importance and not just a hired thug.

"Who are you?" Kingston asked.

"Someone not to be trifled with," said the man.

"So, because you seem to be unable to tell me your name, I'll just have to assume that it is ..." Kingston narrowed his eyes over the man, trying to come up with the least threatening name he could think of. "... Rebecca."

'Rebecca' sneered and was about to retort when Kingston interrupted him.

"One second, Rebecca, I'm trying to clear this up." Kingston turned to Rufus and lowered his voice. "How much will this cost?"

"Ninety five gold pieces," Rufus whispered.

Kingston arched an eyebrow at his builder and shook his head. "You stole ninety five gold pieces worth of material and thought no one would notice?"

Rufus shrugged. "In my defence, it's not my money that's at risk."

Kingston returned to Muira and Rebecca. "So what are the damages we're talking about?"

Muira nearly shrieked as she spoke. "He stole a hundred and fourteen gold pieces worth of stock and broke twenty seven gold pieces worth of clay pots and urns! He just left them lying on the ground, broken!"

"A hundred and fourteen gold, huh?" Kingston looked back to Rufus, who promptly shook his head, disputing the price. "And broken pots?" Rufus shook his head again. Kingston went back to Muira and Rebecca. "Good news, then. I can swallow the costs of Rufus' indiscretion. You two are now donors to our team. Congratulations."

"I don't want any part of your thieving team!" shouted Muira.

"Think nothing of it, it's our pleasure to welcome you on board," said Kingston, beaming with a smile.

"I want my money back!"

"My friends, please, since you've donated your wares to our good team, there is no need to thank us," said Kingston.

"I wasn't thanking you!"

"No, no, the pleasure is all mine."

Muira turned to Rebecca. "Jeffrey! Get our money back!"

Jeffrey pushed up both of his sleeves. The moment he did that, John stepped forward and locked eyes with him.

"Kindly unroll your sleeves, sir," said John.

"I can beat you," said Jeffrey. "I know jiu-jitsu."

"I know him too," said John. "But he's not here to help you."

"It means I can handle myself in a fight!" said Jeffrey.

John's glare turned into a slow, broad smile. "So you really think you can beat me?"

"Damn straight!" cried Jeffrey. "So give us our money back."

John flexed his shoulders and rolled them around, warming himself up. Kingston seized the moment to address the crowd. "Place your bets here. If you think Rebecca will win I'll give you even money. You won't get fairer odds than that."

Some of the punters started nodding to themselves and fished around their pockets. "Two gold on Jeffrey to win," one man cried.

"Three!" cried another.

John removed his jacket and stared at Jeffrey, while Jeffrey sized up John and prepared his stance.

"Come on punters!" shouted Kingston. "We're all here to bet on a winner and I'm betting on John!"

"Five gold on Jeffrey!" shouted someone in the back.

Jeffrey smiled at the encouragement. John stepped in towards him and the two men began circling each other.

"Last takers!" cried Kingston.

"I love you John!" shouted Catalina.

"I love you too, babe," said John. He stared Jeffrey down and recognised some experience in fighting. "So what is this jiu-jitsu?"

"The most complete fighting style there is," said Jeffrey.

"You know, even if you beat me, you won't get your money back."

Muira glared at Kingston when she heard that. "What? I won't even get my money back?"

"That's right," said Kingston. "Rebecca is fighting John. John doesn't have your money. I don't even have your money. But if Rufus really did rob you of one hundred and fourteen gold's worth of stock and broke, what was it? Twenty seven gold worth of pots and bedpans, then why not wager it against who will win?"

"You already have my stock!"

"And if we beat Rebecca will you go away and not bother us

again?"

"No!" shouted Muira.

"Then why is Rebecca even here?"

"His name is Jeffrey!"

Far in the back of the marquee, Joanna leaned over towards Catalina. "Is this how they always fight?"

"No," said Catalina. "John usually just walks in and punches someone. Something must be wrong."

Joanna agreed. She looked around the crowd and felt the tension in the room. No one was sure how to take the break in the festivities. Even the musicians looked agitated, all three of them. Joanna grimaced when she couldn't see the pianist girl, knowing that she had latched onto Kingston as his thief. More unsettling was that she was now not in the marquee.

"Fight!" shouted one of the punters.

"My pleasure," said John.

"Mine too," said Jeffrey.

"Well, go on then," said John, and he kept his hands out ready to intercept Jeffrey.

"All in good time."

"Now's a good time."

"Then make a move," said Jeffrey.

"I'm making several moves."

"And none of them are any good."

"So you make a good move," said John.

"I'm going to," said Jeffrey.

"You're going to cry like a boy, that's what you're going to do."

"I don't cry."

Kingston looked over to the near-fight and knew that John was looking for help. Kingston knew very little about jiu-jitsu, though he did have some knowledge of karate and boxing. Whatever John did, Jeffrey was likely going to be able to counter it. Even John recognised that. Then it occurred to Kingston. "He knows how to fight only one attack at a time."

"HA!" John lunged forward, swinging both fists down to hammer Jeffrey's sides. Jeffrey froze at the sight of the two simultaneous attacks and took too long in jumping back. Both of John's fists hit their target, knocking the wind out of Jeffrey and sending his senses flying. John followed up with a mighty hammer fist to the top of Jeffrey's head and it was good night to the world.

Jeffrey fell in a heap, unconscious. John stepped back, raised one fist in the air and smiled in victory. "Team Kingston!"

John was met with silence. The awkwardness was broken when Kingston stepped forward to shake his hand.

"Well done! Ladies and gentlemen, I present to you, John! Winner of every brawl and even able to fight off a hundred men in the pits of Hell without so much as breaking a sweat!"

"Rigged," someone in the back of the room said.

John's eyes flared up. "Who said that was rigged? *Who?*"

Kingston looked around the room and caught sight of Joanna, who gestured to get John and Jeffrey out of the marquee quickly. Kingston sighed and knew she was right. The evening hadn't been another lacklustre event but the energy evaporated the moment John won his fight. Kingston looked back to Muira, who stood trembling at the sight of Jeffrey, lying in a heap on the ground.

Kingston pulled John to the side. "Maybe you could help Jeffrey and Muira back to their place."

"Huh? Why?"

"It's the nice thing to do?" said Kingston, though he wasn't sure if that was true.

John sighed. "Fine, I'll take them back."

Jeffrey groaned and was starting to come to his senses. John picked him up as though he weighed no more than a school boy and threw him over his shoulder.

"Where to?" John asked Muira.

Muira trembled at the sudden help from the behemoth that was John, and she shrank away. "Back to the apothecary."

"Very well. Keep up." John bounded out of the marquee, followed by Muira, who struggled to follow at the same pace.

The party didn't seem to recover after that, despite Joanna's best efforts. The musicians were irritated that Jezebel had left them and she still had not returned. Their flourish was off with the lack of a pianist. Kingston collected the bets placed against John and tried to work a positive spin on the evening, but he had the feeling that everyone thought the fight was just for show and that they were being robbed of their hard earned gold.

None of the guests were even impressed with Rufus' toy soldier. They had seen bigger and better, and presenting something that small to inspire their confidence was a joke. They asked him if it could fight, and Rufus admitted that the small thing was limited to just walking around and picking itself up whenever it fell over.

Jezebel returned half an hour later, found Kingston in the crowd and pulled him to the side. "I've got most of your ingredients," she said.

Kingston sighed, afraid of where she had been. "Was it hard to get?"

"No, the apothecary was surprisingly empty," she said, beaming with a smile. "Where do you want the items?"

"In the trunk," said Kingston. He was sure that Muira was going to shriek even louder when she realised that they had been robbed by the same team for the second time in the same twenty four hours.

VIII

According to the newspapers, Kingston's party wasn't even worth a mention. Among the chatter of the people, though, it was all they were talking about. No one knew who Jeffrey was, since he was just a mild mannered cobbler with a lifetime of trying to master his Zen, thwarted in one evening by John. To the locals he was either known as 'the guy with the beard' or 'Rebecca'. By the time the rumour mill had made a full circle, Kingston had a fully working prototype golem, John had stood up for the team's honour against a rival and sent them crying back to their own camps, and Team Rufus was now the favourite to win ... which was news to Kingston, since he wished he had been at the party the locals described. His memory of the events were drowned in disappointment when no one turned up to the second party of the evening and he had to spend the whole two hours listening to She Caught the Katy for the fourth time, because the musicians had only a two hour repertoire at their disposal.

On the third night of partying John was leaning up against the bar reading a book when Rufus sauntered over, looking for a drink. "Brushing up on your betting strategy?"

"No," said John. "I'm reading Sun Tzu's *The Art of War.*"

Rufus dropped his shoulders. "Oh no, we have one of your kind on the team."

"It says here that all warfare is based on deception. Thus, when we attack, we must first seem as though we are unable to do so ..."

"You should try reading Tally Ho's *The Guide to Cowardly Survival.* When in doubt, pass the blame onto someone else."

John grunted and did his best to ignore the little builder.

Twenty minutes before the fifth party started, no one had any energy left. Then, Michelle arrived. She smiled at Kingston and whispered, "You're welcome." She then left immediately.

The fifth party started with more gate crashers than Kingston had ever expected. They had averaged fifteen guests per party so far and now there were two hundred, all clamouring inside, trying to see this fabled golem, the mighty John, and the sneaky Kingston. By the third rendition of the night before, John used a more colourful set of adjectives and knew what the people were looking for, even if it wasn't the truth. He was quick to end the story with his brawl in Hell, since at least that one was true and no one in Limbo could disprove it. Besides, it was far more exciting fighting off eighty people than just one, even if those eighty were as coordinated as a set of socks on an eccentric inventor's feet.

Still, no one put themselves up as a donor. Even though the set of parties ended on a high, the team had only earned nineteen gold pieces, and that was from the betting the night before.

Kingston spent most of the next day filling out the proper paperwork to enter his team into the tournament. He waited in line in a quiet corner of Death Inc. to have it all processed. He paid the ten gold entry fee and hoped like hell his paperwork wasn't about to accidentally disappear. Then, he picked up the last of the ingredients Rufus needed to begin work on the golem. Kingston carried everything into their workshop and organised it all in a neat row along their work bench.

Rufus looked over jars and sacks, checked off the contents from his list, and peered suspiciously at several of the items. Kingston was sure that Rufus was moving exceptionally slowly. He was desperate for him to get a move on. Rufus slowed his pace, glanced at Kingston through the corner of his eye, then reached the end of the ingredients laid out in front of him. Kingston was still standing in the room, watching the builder.

Rufus drummed his fingers on the work bench and sighed loudly.

"Do you have everything?" asked Kingston.

"Yes," said Rufus, and he read over his list.

Kingston moved forward to see what the issue was.

Rufus snapped around. "Do you mind?"

"Not at all," said Kingston. "So where do we begin?"

"Please leave," said Rufus.

Kingston's instincts kicked in, and he had to remind himself that now was not the time to be a smartarse. "You said you needed help."

"Later. This part is for my eyes only."

Kingston peered over and his attention fell onto Rufus' stomach. "It looks like you have a book stuffed down your pants."

Rufus' expression changed to a look of shock. He stepped back, gripped his stomach, and turned away. "I need peace and quiet while I do my enchanting!"

Kingston smirked at his paranoid builder. "Are you secretly reading *the Curse of the Shanghai Werewolf?*"

"What? Please. It's ..." Rufus realised he was about to reveal too much, and he looked back to the door. "I will call you when I need your help."

Kingston felt his suspicions confirmed by just how easily defensive Rufus became. "You have a book of enchantment recipes down there, don't you?"

"Trade secrets!" shouted Rufus. "For my eyes only!"

"Why don't you write them in code?" asked Kingston.

"They are," glared Rufus.

"Then what's the big deal? I'd like to see how this enchantment business works."

"Why? Just in case bounty hunting becomes too dull?"

Kingston glanced to the side, thought it over, and nodded. "That's exactly it."

"No. And just because I wrote them in an incomprehensible scrawl doesn't mean my recipes are immune to being hacked. You could figure out the quantities of this and that while watching me."

"Considering I'm paying for all of this ..."

"No! No spying! Please leave so I can get to work."

"It's just ..."

"Out!" shouted Rufus.

Kingston headed for the door and gave one final look over his shoulder. "How long do you think you'll need?"

"Twice as long as I expect," said Rufus, and he turned again to look over the ingredients laid out in front of him.

Kingston smirked at his paranoid builder and left him in peace.

By the time Rufus actually started work on the golem the list of entrants was released, sending all of Limbo into a frenzy of excited chatter. There were fourteen teams from Limbo up against seventeen from Hell. Almost everyone in the realm had a copy of the list by lunch time, scouring over the details during their breaks and comparing their notes to the tournament from ten years ago.

Kingston was relieved that his team was accepted and officially on the ballot. He looked over everything he had to see what he could learn.

BUILDER	GAMES ENTERED	WINS	DEFEATS
Horatio Vito	2	6	2
Ernie Sanders	2	1	3
Urisha L.	1	0	2
Vincent Denoa	0	N/A	N/A
Rufus Winston	18	4	39
Akira Kazuka	0	N/A	N/A
Booker Newell	1	0	1
Carmen Lucha	0	N/A	N/A
Booker Newell	0	N/A	N/A
Joc Biggins	1	2	2
Chloe Stuyvescent	0	N/A	N/A
Mazoe Redding	1	0	2
Luisa Rose	0	N/A	N/A
Melton Gibbs	0	N/A	N/A
Dan Foster	0	N/A	N/A

John stared at the list. "Mazoe? Someone's name is Mazoe?" He was met by blank stares from everyone around him. "Come on! Mazoe! How is anyone else not laughing hysterically at this?"

Catalina tried to figure it out, but it was lost on her. "Babe?"

"Mazoe!" cried John, as though that answered every question they had. "Oh, wait, you all haven't really met Simon yet." John leaned over. "Simon! You want some ma tea?"

Simon leaned out from his room. "You have ma tea?"

"No, I think Mazoe has ma tea."

Simon peered at John suspiciously, then he retreated back into his room.

John sighed with a smile. "Worth it."

Kingston memorised the list and he couldn't wait to get his hands on the official betting guide.

"We don't have much time before the grand unveiling," said Rufus.

"Sure we do," said Kingston. "The tournament doesn't start for another sixty two days."

Rufus sighed. "You're aware of the grand unveiling, aren't you?"

Kingston looked at his builder as though it was the most obvious question he had ever heard. "Yes. All teams present their machines thirty days before the start of the tournament."

"And if we don't have something by then we'll be penalised."

"How much?"

"That's up to the referees, but at least twenty five gold, maybe even up to a hundred," said Rufus.

"That's not too bad," said Kingston, going back to his notes.

Rufus raised his eyebrows. "Wow, you really don't have any idea how money works, do you?"

"Of course I do. I've made lots of it in the past."

"And a hundred gold fine is just a nuisance to you?" Rufus stared off into space. "Must be nice having that kind of money."

"I'm very careful with the bottom line," said Kingston. "We'll have a machine ready by then and we won't be fined. Trust me."

"Yeah, I've learned a few things about people who say 'trust me.'"

Kingston smiled at that one. "Me too. They then spend the rest of their lives contradicting themselves."

"Good, well, while you're off contradicting yourself ... *We still don't have a working machine and I need parts! I need ingredients!*"

"We have ingredients," said Kingston.

"Not enough!" Rufus started rubbing his hands together as he paced around. "We don't have enough time either. I need a better assistant. Simon's no good. He keeps trying to get me drunk."

"I think it's the other way around, that you're trying to get him drunk."

"Well, I have no choice! I don't have enough parts to continue building the golem!" Rufus rubbed his hands again, working through the tension and stretching his fingers back.

"How's the whip coming along?"

"I almost have one link done."

Kingston arched an eyebrow. "One?"

"These things take time! And as soon as I have some more metal for the golem I'm going to have to stop with the whip and focus on the giant suit of walking armour. It's better to showcase a machine with no weapons than weapons and no machine."

Kingston glanced over his notes. "There's an auction coming up. We can get your suit of armour there."

"We better," said Rufus. "And you better bring a big wallet as well because we're still short on a lot of materials."

Joanna and Catalina came around the corner and they both looked concerned. "Is everything okay out here?"

"Oh, sure," said Rufus. "I mean, the team financier doesn't quite understand money -"

"I understand it just fine," said Kingston.

"- and I don't have the time or resources to actually build anything. And you do know that if you win it's just going to be fifteen thousand gold pieces, right? You're not going to walk away with, say, a million."

"I understand," said Kingston.

Joanna stepped forward. "That's something that has been bugging me. Why is it only fifteen thousand?"

Rufus stared at Joanna blankly. "Because that's how much it is! Seriously, I thought at least one of you was the brains of the operation."

Joanna rolled her eyes. "Fifteen thousand gold is not that much."

Catalina looked away in shock.

"I mean, yes, it's a lot of money, but how many seats are there in the arena?"

"A hundred and twenty thousand," said Kingston.

"And how much do tickets go for?"

Everyone looked to Rufus, and he gave them a shrug. "One gold piece per day, with typically twelve to fifteen days of action."

"Right," said Joanna. "The arena earns one and a half million gold pieces for the whole tournament if it's at maximum capacity …"

"It always is," said Rufus.

"And yet the prize pool is just twenty five thousand gold, with fifteen going to the winner. Why so little money?"

"Simple," said Rufus. "It was supposed to limit corruption and excess spending. Do you know how far fifteen thousand gold would take a team of five people? Spread out evenly, that's a four year salary at a pay grade one level. You can set up your own business, buy a restaurant, or become the hot shot celebrity that every woman in the realm wants to date." A faint smile crept across his mouth, but it faded when he realised his moment of glory was likely never going to come.

"So the idea is to make the reward something to shoot for, but low enough so that you have to be careful on what you spend. For the first few Games no one really spent more than a thousand gold pieces. But then people started getting more and more competitive. The previous winners were now willing to spend five or ten thousand gold, so everyone else had to spend the same amount just to realistically compete. But still the reward remained the same so that someone would eventually win having spent just a thousand gold pieces and everyone around them would realise that it's not how much you spend that guarantees your victory, it's being so ingenious in your creation that you don't need to spend a fortune. But it turns out no one is actually that smart, so we spend everything we have just so we have a fighting chance against every other team." Rufus looked from Joanna and Kingston and glared. "You two should really study a little accounting because your knowledge in this department is baffling even to me. I can only assume you lot are exceptionally gifted bounty hunters."

Kingston and Joanna shared a nervous look.

Rufus caught them. "Oh, boy. You two are going to have serious problems with your reputation after this."

"We know," said Kingston.

"What's the problem?" asked Catalina.

Kingston gave it his best. "We receive a bounty hunting salary from Death Inc. only if we take on a certain number of cases. The less jobs we work on the less money we earn."

Catalina wheezed as she realised that her only source of income was in jeopardy.

John leaned forward. "And what happens if we earn nothing?"

"After three months of no cases they would revoke our license and re-test us for jobs that we are actually qualified for, and they will assign us to those positions."

"Well, that's ... not so bad," said John.

Rufus snorted. "Oh yeah, because right now you four can work the hours you want, sit around and chat all day on Death's money, and claim every meal as a work expense. Sure, that's much better than spending eight hours a day filing hundred year old documents and taking orders from a boss that no one likes, working with people who have lost the will to live, while listening to a radio with the worst selection of music imaginable. Much better. It's called rock bottom for a reason, and you'll be there for a hundred years. Separately."

"But everything will be okay," said Joanna. "I'll be working that angle with the sponsors as well so that if they ever need a private matter handled then we are their go-to bounty hunters."

Rufus shook his head. "Do you know how many bounty hunters compete in the games? Zero. And this is why."

A week later, Kingston and a heavily disguised Rufus were at the open air auction in Docklands. There was no actual dock, but there was a replica sailboat that looked to be shipwrecked in the middle of Limbo. It was in truth a piece of art, commissioned by one of the British unions two hundred years ago, since they had conquered the world through the seas and decided that everyone needed reminding of the fact. Satan had laughed himself stupid at the grand unveiling of the three masted schooner and Death accepted it as one of the quirks of running a republic.

It wasn't easy disguising Rufus. No matter what he did he always looked like a ten year old in an Albert Einstein costume. He moved slowly along the rows of tables and benches, trying to find spare parts for his machine. He walked with his hands clasped behind his back, since Kingston told him that would show he was confident, and he wore a large grey fedora with a black band, hoping that someone would recognise him and call him out of his ridiculous costume. Rufus was sure it was pointless disguising himself since he was always within reach of Kingston, John, Joanna, and Catalina.

The auction was the time of the decade when hopeful teams decided against entering, paid the fine, and offloaded their wares for some financial return. It was also the time when the bank emptied everything in the vaults from their closed accounts, meaning anyone who no longer lived in Limbo and wasn't expected back. The auction brought out a mass of bargain hunters, all looking for a new sofa, nightstand, or nine foot tall suit of armour.

Joanna had spent the week researching every builder from Limbo and learning everything she could about them, but there was only so much she could learn without the use of a computer. She passed on the information and Catalina shuddered when she realised there might be a dozen teams out there who had spied on her and John without their knowledge.

Rufus strolled through the aisles looking over what was on sale. After doing a full lap of the auction house he leaned in towards Kingston and held out a copy of his auction guide, folded back to page 111. "We need this thing," he whispered. "And whatever else I've dog eared."

Kingston looked down at the main point of interest and nearly dismissed it out right. Rufus wanted a set of hanging ornaments, like a street mobile of spinning metal shards that some nitwit considered 'deep and meaningful art'. Then Kingston saw the size of the beast and realised it was ten metres high. There were enough thick metal sheets in that thing to build Rufus' golem.

"I can break the spinning enchantments," said Rufus. "Shouldn't be hard. I enchanted them in the first place."

Kingston flipped through to the other pages Rufus had selected a set of perfume bottles in the shape of horses, a collection of glass beer steins, and a comb. Rufus explained that the perfume could be broken down into basic elements and would be useful in the making of the whip. The glass could be melted down and used as the irises to the golem's eyes, unless by some miracle they could find an ancient film projector, and the comb was to hold finicky things apart from each other while he was soldering everything together.

"Can't you just buy a comb?" Kingston asked.

Rufus shot him a look of the obvious. "If you want to pay full price for a comb be my guest, but this is an auction and things can be purchased cheaply here." Rufus rolled his head and went back to looking through the stalls.

Aside from being a bargain for most of the residents in Limbo, it was also an excellent hunting ground to stalk out the rival teams in the tournament. After three hours of walking around Rufus finally came to a halt and nudged Kingston. He nodded towards one of the rows of tables at a thin man of eastern European descent.

"Horatio," Rufus said.

Kingston smiled and took that as his cue to misbehave. He looked over to John to make sure that Rufus was protected. Joanna caught the signal as well and stepped around to the side of Horatio's row of tables, flanking him. Kingston crept away, keeping an eye on Horatio for ten minutes, figuring out who his people were and what he was looking at. He caught the bored look in the man's eye and the constant glances around, but he always looked at the same three people. Horatio had brought his team along and they were the scouts. They had also seen Kingston and Joanna.

Kingston recognised the scout. He had been at the fifth party and tried to blend in with the other two hundred guests, but had completely avoided Kingston, John, Joanna, and Catalina. Kingston made his move. He headed forward, side stepped the man intentionally blocking him, and stuck his hand out to the thin and lightly bearded Horatio.

"Kingston Raine. It's a pleasure," said Kingston.

He caught Horatio by surprise, though Horatio quickly dropped back and knew it was inevitable for teams to pounce on each other during the auction. "So you're the loquacious one," Horatio said.

"Moderately erudite, yes. And somewhat famous. Not quite screaming fan famous, but I'm getting there."

"Well, give it a few months. By then your team will be drowning in humiliation that you'll wish for this level of notoriety once again."

"Cute. I heard you're a little reckless with your builds," said Kingston.

"I've done far better than your builder has and trash talking won't make me fear you, Kingston."

"Ah, confident and intelligent, I get it."

"You should," said Horatio. "I have three degrees, from Oxford and Harvard, all before I was twenty five. I speak eight languages. I revolutionised mathematics for forty years. There are countless people on Earth who still wish they could meet me."

"Impressive. I myself graduated from Oxford. I also went to

Cambridge and Harvard. They were both nice days. And I was too busy making money and getting laid to revolutionise mathematics but, you know, some people aim to find a proof for Goldbach's Conjecture while others like to solve horrendous corporate fraud and celebrate by hosting a drunken orgy with supermodels. And not just ordinary models. *Super.*"

Horatio glared at Kingston and flared his nostrils. "My achievements are real. Yours are fictional."

Kingston pulled back, faking an injury to his chest. "Ah, oh no, the stab of reality." He laughed and shook it off, coming closer to Horatio and towering over him. "Three degrees when you were alive, eight languages when you were alive, revolutionised mathematics when you were alive. You've been dead for eighty years and yet you've done nothing of significance since then. I on the other hand have been dead for a year and a half and have had more success than in your entire existence." He beamed at Horatio and gave him a slight nod. "Death was right about you. You do sound like a weasel." Kingston stepped away and went back to John and Rufus.

"Looks like you made a friend," said John.

Kingston nodded. "Yeah. He's a genius all right and he knows it. He's going to be tough to beat."

"But not impossible, right?" Rufus asked.

"Nothing's impossible," said Kingston.

"Horatio is whispering to his bodyguards," said John, peering over the crowd.

"Excellent," said Kingston. "Let's go find more competitors and trash talk them."

"You don't think we could use an ally?" Rufus asked.

"Tomorrow, maybe. Right now we have to try and bankrupt the other teams while at an auction. Pick a few more things on the brochure, things that look like we could genuinely use. We'll see how desperate they are to bid us out of the game."

"That sounds a little risky," said Rufus.

"You seem overly concerned about my money," said Kingston.

"Because it's supposed to buy me a lot of junk and if you run out then I don't have a golem to compete with."

"One of the bodyguards is heading this way, trying to blend in," said John, peering through the crowd.

"Let's get Rufus out of here," said Kingston, and they slipped past one table and headed as close to the stage as possible. They were met by dozens of people all pushing their way through, bumping into everyone else and all eager to see what people were selling. Kingston glanced over his shoulder to see where Horatio's man was and he felt Rufus fall back and bump into him.

"Hey!" cried Rufus, turning around quickly. "That guy! He stole my auction guide!"

Kingston looked at Rufus' empty hands and felt his stomach tighten. He had been played by Horatio's team into heading straight for their thief.

Rufus slapped Kingston on the shoulder. "Don't just stand there. Get it back!"

"What did he look like?" Kingston asked.

"He's wearing a beret," said Rufus.

Kingston signalled to Joanna and nodded towards where the thief was heading, hoping he was still in the area. Kingston hurried through the crowd, scanning the tops of every head and every pair of eyes that met him, trying to find the signs of a thief desperate to escape. Out of the corner of his eye he saw a short, thin man jump up from the underside of a set of tables, surprising the two women on either side of him who were hoping to sell tea pots and fine china. He was also wearing a navy blue beret.

That's him.

Kingston locked on and memorised the thief's appearance - five foot seven, forty years old, pale skin and covered in freckles, hunched shoulders, a thick scarf hiding his chin, a blonde goatee and blonde hair, capped with a beret. Joanna saw him as well and she edged around the row of sellers to intercept him. Kingston ducked under the tables, surprising the two women again. He apologised quickly before dodging through another crowd. The thief was heading towards one of Horatio's bodyguards. Kingston was locked onto his target and he forgot all about his surroundings, which was another amateur mistake that he realised the moment he felt someone's fist slam into his solar plexus.

Kingston gasped as the air ran out of him in an instant. He fell to his knees and raised one hand high to block a second attack, but it never came. He saw a pair of feet scamper away from him, in the opposite direction to the thief, and before he could blame himself for making so many stupid mistakes in under a minute he saw the face of an old lady peering down at him.

"You okay there, sonny?"

Kingston tried to speak and the words failed him. He tried again and found he could only manage a gasp. "Who hit me?"

"Take it easy now, that was quite a fall. How are your knees? Your knees okay?"

"Someone hit me," said Kingston. He quickly patted himself down, sure that he must have also been robbed, but his wallet was still there, which wasn't much of a victory since he wasn't carrying much in the way of cash. For a moment he expected John to appear, or Joanna, or even Catalina, but they all had their roles to play and none of them included rescuing Kingston. He staggered to his feet and caught sight of John not too far away. They exchanged a look and John figured out what had just happened, but the rage within him was kept under tight control when he remembered that his priority was to not let Rufus out of his sight.

It took several minutes before Kingston had the strength to move properly. There was no point in heading back to John and Rufus. All that was missing was the auction guide and Kingston knew that Horatio was determined to see what Rufus was bidding on, and then to screw things over for Kingston's team.

As long as Horatio knows I'm watching him he won't dare use Rufus' guide.

It was Kingston's only plan to stop their opponent from reading everything were trying to buy. It wasn't a great plan, but it was all he had at such short notice. Unfortunately, not everyone was aware of Kingston's plan.

"Kingston, glad to see you again," said Maurice, stepping through the crowd to shake Kingston's hand.

"Likewise, Maurice. Is there any chance we could do this later?"

Maurice snorted. "I'm not here to interfere, merely to observe the proceedings and tally things up for the Cascade. You look a little pale. Are you feeling okay?"

"I've just been robbed and assaulted," said Kingston.

"Oh. Well, at least you're still walking," said Maurice.

Kingston peered around him to lock eyes with Horatio. The two men glared at each other. Horatio knew what Kingston was up to, and Kingston saw his chances of getting the booklet back slip away.

"I take it you'll be an active bidder today," said Maurice.

"Somewhat active," said Kingston, with his attention never

leaving Horatio.

"Well, you won't be the only one. Just about every team from Limbo is here today. Be careful about what you bid on and be prepared to lose every single time. No team wants any other team to succeed today. In fact, today is often more important than the final match in the arena."

"Lovely to know," said Kingston. "Will you excuse me?" Kingston didn't wait for a response. Instead, he headed straight for Horatio. One of Horatio's bodyguards saw Kingston getting closer and he raised the alarm. Horatio looked up and quickly whispered to a man by his side.

That man has the guide, not Horatio, Kingston told himself. He saw Joanna step up behind Horatio and his men, and she moved into position.

Kingston marched up to the guide holder and snatched it out of the man's hands. "The day won't be over until Little John knocks you out," said Kingston. He glanced down to the dog-eared booklet and was relieved that he had reclaimed Rufus' guide.

"You will watch yourself," said Horatio. "I don't like being embarrassed in public."

Joanna winked at Kingston and let out an ear piercing shriek. Horatio stumbled around and snapped his hands up to his ears as quickly as he could, but he wasn't fast enough. Joanna slapped him across the face hard enough to make her hand sting. "I saw what you did!" she screamed, and stormed off.

Kingston felt a flow of pride engulf him as he saw Horatio's face turn the shade of a ripe tomato. Kingston stepped away, held onto the booklet as tightly as he could, and returned to John, Rufus, and Catalina.

Randolph Hunch, accountant first class of the Union of Numerology, was the appointed auctioneer for the day, as he had been for the last eighty three years. He wore half-moon spectacles, maintained an impeccable pencil thin moustache, and his cheeks were pocketed with a bad case of scars from acne. His voice was as nasal as they came. He took to the stage and addressed the crowd.

"Madams and gentlemen, good afternoon." He gave the audience the slightest of bows. "I am Randolph Hunch." He glanced over the crowd, though no one applauded or gave him anything other than a blank look on their faces. "We shall begin shortly. If all interested parties could ensure that they are registered with my colleague, Gloria Seschwin, we may proceed sooner rather than later."

Rufus leaned over to Kingston. "You have to sign your name and details on the items you wish to bid on."

"And if we try to keep this whole thing a secret?" Kingston asked.

"Not with Hunch running the show. If you bid without registering he will stop and make you call out your exact details in front of everyone. He's a stickler for procedure," said Rufus.

Kingston went forward to mark his name on the nine items he wanted to bid on. There was a sizeable line building. Gloria Seschwin, who looked to be all of twenty two years old, appeared to be overwhelmed with everyone's requests, especially since some of them included a few weirdoes asking if they could bid on her.

"You couldn't afford me," she mumbled a few times, but diligently took their details.

An hour later, eighty participants were ready to bid on three hundred and twenty items. Kingston groaned at the idea of such a long wait, expecting this to take at least six hours. According to everyone around him, this was the largest auction Limbo had ever held, and they were not renowned for being prompt. Most of the final items were left without much competition simply because the prospective bidders had to abandon the auction to go to work.

The first item that Rufus wanted was number 80, the set of fine china. No one else was interested and Kingston was asked to meet the reserve price of four gold pieces, which he agreed to. He earned a few interested looks for that as the rival builders tried to figure out what he and Rufus were up to.

The next item was a set of cutlery, which Rufus hoped to melt down. It was the first time Horatio and Kingston were up against each other and Rufus kept muttering that Horatio was only doing it to drive up the price. It reached seven gold pieces with Horatio as the highest bidder.

"How much is a regular set of knives and forks?" Kingston asked.

"About two gold," said Rufus.

"And we can buy them locally?" Kingston asked.

"Sure can."

Kingston smiled and shook his head at Hunch, refusing to bid any further.

"Sold for seven gold pieces,"said Hunch, nodding towards Horatio. Horatio didn't look too pleased with himself, especially when he realised that he had just paid more than three times the price for a regular set of cutlery.

"Yeah, I hope that stings," Rufus said, looking over. "That should make him back off a little."

The hunk of scrap metal took four more hours to come up, and by then the crowd had dwindled to ninety three people. Joanna and Kingston took turns in counting the number of bidders and making sure they remembered each of the faces. Kingston recognised Montgomery Stup, who spent his whole time glaring at Rufus and didn't lay a single bid. Still in the crowd was Maurice, nodding away at the progress of the builders, all of whom he knew on a first name basis. He was eager to see how it would play out for the Cascade.

By the time the scrap metal come up, Rufus was nearly falling over from being on his feet for the entire day. He hoped this would play out well, especially since he needed to reshape the metal and turn it into the body of the golem. Without that, they had no entry.

Randolph Hunch didn't seem the slightest bit fazed that he had been speaking for so long in a monotone. "This next piece, item 232, comes from the artist Vincent Denoa. It was commissioned by the Retier Council and was completed 2013. It was retired six months later and the starting bid is set at forty gold pieces, increasing by five gold." Hunch checked his paperwork and saw that there were six people interested in bidding on the item, and he was unsurprised to see that they were all entrants in the tournament. "Do I hear forty gold pieces?"

Horatio raised his hand and gave the auctioneer a nod. Kingston looked over and made a note of who bid at what price.

"Forty five?"

Another hand was raised. Kingston nudged Rufus. "Who's that?"

"Denoa," Rufus whispered.

"The artist?"

"Yeah. Clever bugger. He was hired by the union to build that piece, only it became a folly and the union has been trying to get rid of it to earn back some money. So not only was Denoa paid to build that thing, he might be able to buy it for less than what the union spent on it. I should remember that for next time."

"Is that legal?"

Rufus shrugged. "I admire his ingenuity. He's a terrible artist, though. He'll definitely want this piece, since he's probably enchanted it with whatever he could get away with."

"And we definitely need it?" Kingston asked.

"We definitely need it, so we're either going to buy it today or steal it tomorrow. Buying is easier, especially when we walk out into the arena and everyone recognises the metal work as Denoa's."

"Fifty?" Hunch called.

Horatio raised his hand again.

"Fifty five?"

Denoa and a new face bid this time.

"Ernie Sanders. Another builder."

"Sixty?"

Kingston raised his hand. By the time the price reached one hundred gold pieces, all six bidders had tried their luck, the final two additions being Booker Newell and Akira Kazuka.

"Both strong contenders," Rufus told him. "The Kazuka team always bid at the auctions, ready for the following tournament. They've already built their machine. Booker is just a moron. He's here to raise the price as much as he can. It stings him from time to time but he'll know who is interested and he can sell it back to the team who really wants it, usually to trade some item that we would have that he wants."

"That's not the hallmark of a moron," said Kingston.

"Have you noticed his toupee?" Rufus asked.

"Sure have."

"If he thinks something like that blends in well with his head and is undetectable, then he's a moron." Rufus peered through the crowd and saw one of Denoa's men moving closer to Akira Kazuka. "Get ready for a fight."

Kingston checked over his shoulder and saw a brute take a swing at Akira, punching him in the stomach as hard as he could. Akira dropped to the ground.

"Hopefully that's him out of the auction," said Rufus.

Kingston's jaw dropped open, stunned at such a brazen act in the open. "Is Akira going to be okay?"

"Probably," said Rufus.

"That can't be legal," said Kingston.

"And yet it happened. Keep bidding."

Kingston raised his hand at one hundred and twenty gold pieces.

Rufus tapped his stomach and it was clearly padded with some kind of armour. "I always hope I don't need this. Akira should have known better."

"Is competing really worth all of this hassle?" Kingston asked.

"Of course not, but most people think they're pot committed. When you put so much time, effort, and money into seeing this through you get tunnel vision. All that matters is making it to the first day of the tournament."

The bid climbed to one hundred and fifty.

"Just so you know, we're about to spend maybe a year's worth of salary on this hunk of metal," said Kingston.

"Don't chicken out now," said Rufus.

John leaned in and whispered to the two of them. "We should move to the front of the group, in the open. Some of the heavy weights are starting to circle us."

Kingston nodded and moved Rufus to the front of the crowd, making it as awkward as possible for anyone to try and start a fight.

"Two hundred?" Hunch called out.

Kingston raised his hand.

"Two hundred and five?"

Horatio raised his hand.

"Two hundred and ten?"

Kingston and Denoa raised their hands. Denoa looked as though he was about to have a heart attack. He was pale with sweat and he kept looking around nervously, terrified that so many builders had picked his contraption to bid on.

"Two hundred and fifteen?"

Horatio raised his hand again.

Rufus pulled Kingston in close to whisper. "You're going to have to stop them from bidding!"

Kingston called out to Hunch. "Three hundred!"

Hunch paused and looked over to Kingston, bored with the outburst. "Sir, the bid is at two hundred and twenty, not three hundred. Do I hear two hundred and twenty?"

Kingston sighed and raised his hand. "Now what?"

"Tell John to go and punch someone," said Rufus.

"As much as I would like him to, I don't think we would get away with it. They'll out bid us in spite."

"Oh, well, it's only your money. Don't give up on it."

By the time the bid reached three hundred and twenty, it was down to just Denoa, Horatio, and Kingston. Denoa shrieked when it reached four hundred and it was clearly far beyond his limit, and he bowed out at four hundred and twenty. When Kingston bid six hundred, Horatio bowed out. He did so with a victorious smile and a chuckle, knowing that he had successfully pushed Kingston far beyond the expenditure of reason.

Joanna looked back at Kingston and saw him turn pale. He smiled weakly at her, and she returned the look.

"You know, even three hundred was pushing it," said Rufus, and he shook his head at the auction guide.

"Could we have bought that much metal from anywhere else?" Kingston asked.

"Maybe from Hell, but it wouldn't be available for quite some time. At least now we can actually start building. Besides, we did better than I was expecting."

"Well, that's something, I suppose," said Kingston. "Are they going to deliver all of this to the bank?"

Rufus stared at Kingston as though he had just grown an extra head. "This is an auction house, not a delivery company. We'll be lucky if they even help us load everything onto the rickshaw."

John glared as soon as he heard the word 'rickshaw'. "We're going to trust those thieving bastards again?"

"Unless you want to buy your own rickshaw," said Rufus. "And even then we won't know if there's a thief already hiding inside, or some kind of enchantment to make our goods suddenly disappear. The safest way to go about this is to get a big rug, lie it on the base of the rickshaw and dump everything on top. That will help stop those thieving little fingers. But remember I did say 'help stop' and not 'it is one hundred percent fool proof.'"

"I understand," said Kingston.

"Good, because I seem to get a lot of blame for you not knowing some of the more basic features of a tournament. But it is your first time so of course you're going to be in over your head until the final gong. It's to be expected. When you're old and bitter, that's when you're ready to actually compete."

Catalina and John went to find a rickshaw. Catalina used her charm to keep the driver, Manuel, enthralled, while John climbed onto the back and inspected the cart for any secret door. Manuel assured them that he wasn't party to a thief, though goods were carried at the owner's risk. They backed the cart up to the rear of the auction stage and pushed the great metal sculpture onto the cart. The colour started to drain from Manuel's face as he realised that he was going to have to pull several tonnes worth of goods in a single trip. Rufus sat in the back of the cart while the others walked behind, where they all kept an eye on anyone watching them or getting too close. Rufus started testing the enchantments already on the items and spent the whole trip muttering to himself and shaking his head.

"There are some tricks here," Rufus said. "Another team has already intercepted this sculpture. It looks like Urisha's work. Tricky little thing as well."

"Problem?" Kingston asked.

"It's booby trapped. I'll have to be careful in breaking the enchantments."

"Will it take long?"

"It will, yeah. We're going to need some more ingredients to help break everything down. Better call your thief again. And tell your giant to smack anyone who comes near the rickshaw."

IX

Rufus was on a constant supply of coffee while trying to break all of the enchantments and booby traps. The most difficult took thirty eight hours straight of potion making, invoking, and turning the hunk of metal over several times to confuse the magicks which kept it primed to explode. The main problem Rufus had and tried to explain was that there was little way of knowing how long it would take to break a single enchantment until he started, and by then there was no going back. There were a few explosions and mild burns in the workshop, and several blasts with the fire extinguisher.

Kingston received a letter in mid-air one afternoon while in his office. *'Come to Xolotl Avenue at 2 o'clock, if you like. John.'* Kingston was grateful for the distraction, but he was concerned that John asked to meet him on the same street as where Fernando stood.

He headed out across Limbo and caught sight of John hiding in an alley. "Psst. Over here."

Kingston looked over and edged forward, wondering if someone had managed to disguise themselves as John. "Everything okay?"

"Yeah. It's Catalina."

"Is *she* okay?"

"She's fine," said John. "Come on."

"You're acting a little strange," said Kingston.

John sighed and stepped out from the alley. "We're near that statue you were talking about. The one blown up by Horatio."

Kingston looked around the landmarks and knew that John was right. "And?"

"And Catalina is reading to him," said John.

"Oh." It took a moment for Kingston to process, but it still felt strange for John to be acting like this. "So everything else is okay?"

John sighed again. "Everything is fine. I just didn't want to spook Catalina or the statue. She's been sneaking off to read to him for several days now."

Kingston cocked his head to one side. "I didn't know that."

"Well, you don't know everything that's going on around here. Not even Death knows everything. Come on, it's something you should see." John led Kingston along the road. They reached the far end without incident and John ducked into another alley. Standing in front of Fernando was Catalina, wearing an emerald shawl over her head to help disguise her, with a thick copy of a *Kingston Raine* book open in front of her. She was reading aloud while Fernando looked down at her, unmoving.

"She's been doing this for about two hours a day for the past week," said John. "She keeps it quiet. She didn't even tell me, I had to follow her to figure it out. That kinda bugs me. I don't have a problem with her reading to a statue, it's just that she wanted to do it in secret, even though you asked her to do it."

It was an unusual sight and Kingston tried to figure it out, but the Catalina he first met and the Catalina he now knew weren't the same. He knew she had been a little more distant than usual lately, but he wasn't one for prying into John's love life. He was sure that it would open the door for John to ask about Joanna, and that was another mess that Kingston was trying to avoid.

"Any ideas?" John asked.

Kingston withheld a sigh and plunged in as carefully as possible. "You remember her black dress from the party?"

"Sure do," said John.

"It cost her a fortune."

John bobbed his head, almost understanding the problem but not quite getting there. "That's quite common though, isn't it?"

"Well, yeah. Joanna told me that Catalina is scared about money and how much she has to spend to be around us."

John looked back to Catalina and seemed a little heart broken over the news. "She didn't say any of that to me."

"Well, Joanna is guessing. I don't think Catalina has told anyone about it."

"That's unlike her," said John. "Do you know of anything else she probably hasn't told anyone?"

"Couldn't begin to tell you. But with the dress, you two have a different attitude to receiving gifts, loans, and money in general," said Kingston. "You're quite happy to get a suit for free, right?"

"If you want me to pay for the suits, I can," said John.

"I don't mean it like that, I'm just trying to show you the difference. And no, you don't need to pay for the suits. They're gifts. But you're happy to get a suit for free, you understand it's an act of generosity, that I'm not throwing it into your face. Catalina, though, is a little awkward when she gets things for free. I don't think she understands fully that it's free with no further implication. Instead she might feel that she owes the giver a favour equal to the gift."

"Who doesn't like gifts?" John asked.

"Some people just don't," said Kingston. "I've noticed that Catalina tries to invite us out for dinner every now and then and she insists on paying, but when she does she also orders two bottles of the cheaper wine instead of what Joanna and I would normally order. And when she offers to pay, that's when we usually split the bill. Whether it's a free dress or a free meal, she feels awkward about it and wants to remain even."

John looked up to the dark sky and started to nod again. "I have seen that. If I give her a compliment, she gives me a compliment. If I surprise her with a drink, she'll surprise me later with a tea. So why is she reading to a statue in secret?"

Kingston shook his head. "That could be unrelated to the expensive dress story."

"So why did she have to buy an expensive dress instead of a regular one?" John asked.

"For the party, Joanna's dress cost thirty four gold. Your suit was twenty eight gold, mine was thirty two gold. Catalina didn't want to stand out as being poor."

"How did she get that kind of money?"

"She took out a loan."

John arched his eyebrows and stared off at Catalina, halfway through the book. "For a dress?"

"I know," said Kingston.

John thought it over for a moment, then he turned back to Kingston. "Wait, I was wearing a suit that cost twenty eight gold?"

"Yep. Your whole wardrobe is worth about two hundred gold."

John shook his head. "Now you're making me paranoid."

"Back in Life, or rather Fiction, I had a wardrobe worth half a million pounds. Hell, I had a couple of watches worth twenty five thousand." Kingston smiled happily at John, and then he noticed that John held an incredulous look that didn't fade even when he tried to shake off his surprise. "I didn't *pay* half a million pounds for it all. I used to target crooks who had my build. I'd break into their apartment and go back a couple of times until I had cleaned them out. Some of them had a decent wine collection. But it got to the point where I had two spare rooms full of suits."

John thought it over and shrugged. "Did it make you happy?"

Kingston smirked. "Gloriously happy. Until Joanna broke in and cleaned me out. That was a bit rude, so I did the same to her."

They fell into silence and watched Catalina for a few minutes. She was animated enough to give a few gestures as she read and didn't seem to be speaking in a monotone. They saw Fernando tilt his head a few times in curiosity and even nod when Catalina reached the cliff hanger of one chapter.

John shook his head again. "Why won't she tell anyone that she's reading to a statue? Even when you asked her to?"

"I think Joanna is more in tune with this than I am," said Kingston. "Maybe she just likes a little privacy."

"She's standing in the middle of the street," said John.

"Hardly anyone uses this street, that's why they put Fernando here."

John cocked his head to one side and tried to put two and two together. "Where does Fernando come from?"

"Spain."

"What era?"

"Catalina's," said Kingston. "Maybe that's it. They both miss Spain."

"There's not much we can do about that, is there?" John asked.

"Not really," said Kingston.

"I don't suppose we could go back to our own books for a while," said John. It was one of the few sentences that Kingston feared.

"It's possible. You've thought about going back to Nottingham?"

John shrugged and stared off into the distance. "It would be nice to see the old gang again, tell them a few stories."

"You know the four of us have possibly the most advantageous positions in the whole of creation? When people come to Limbo they are almost never able to go back to their world again, but we can."

"We might also get stuck there," said John. "We're allowed to stay in Limbo even if we don't really belong here, but if Catalina came with me to Nottingham and we were stuck there she would hate it. I could probably handle being in Spain but there's coffee here just a five minute walk from my apartment. And there's a copy of every book ever published. There are almost a million people living here compared to a couple of thousand living in Catalina's town. And then there's a nearly endless supply of music."

"The Beatles," mumbled Kingston.

"Black Sabbath," said John.

"Pink Floyd."

"Led Zeppelin."

"And you couldn't leave that behind?" Kingston asked.

John glanced up to the sky and considered it for a moment, then he shook his head. "I broke up with my first girlfriend and had only beer and manly competitions to cheer myself up with. Now I have music, movies, and those fruity little cocktails with the weird straws in them. I know if Catalina went back home I could soldier on. I don't want to, and you better believe that I would pull out all of the stops in trying to keep us together, but ... if she's miserably homesick then there's only so much I can do. I would have to let her go."

Kingston clapped John on the back. "You two will be okay."

John wasn't so sure about that. "It's a little troubling that she wants to have a secret readathon with a socially fragile statue who needs saving, and that she can relate to that. Maybe I should just go over there and give her a hug."

"No, no no no no no noooo. She's doing this in secret and you've been following her. If you interrupt her now you'll scare the crap out of her. Let her come to you about this when she's ready."

John looked over to Catalina and the statue and hoped that Kingston was right.

Kingston received a second message that day, this one from Jezebel. *Kazuka's machine just exploded. They're bringing it to the bank to get another loan.*

Kingston leapt to his feet in victory and threw his fist into the air. His was no longer the worst team. Then he paused and realised that someone could have been seriously hurt in the explosion. He slunk back into his chair, ashamed of himself, and he knew he had to get to the bank quickly to stop anyone from stumbling onto Rufus.

A crowd had already formed out the front of the bank, eager for the first taste of carnage. They were talking excitedly about what had happened, even if it was nothing but conjecture.

"There was smoke coming from the back of the restaurant," one young man said. "Blue smoke as well, so you know they were trying something tricky."

Kingston still had no idea where people were able to build these machines. He suspected that the teams all had friends who had some spare room for tinkering, but the back of a restaurant was a dangerous place to dabble with enchantments and constructs. Then Kingston caught sight of Montgomery Stup and his brother, the lawyer. The two Stups glared at Kingston, while Kingston smiled joyfully at them, all the while wondering what they were doing at the foot of the steps to the bank.

Maybe they know that Rufus is hidden away in there, Kingston thought. *Or they have a vested interest in Kazuka's machine.*

It turned out, most of the spectators were interested in Kazuka's machine. Kazuka needed another loan to repair his machine and the bank needed to hold onto it for the night so that it could be evaluated. A loan would be issued the following day that reflected the value of the machine. Kingston learned that this was common throughout the games. He also learned that several teams had managed to break into Kazuka's restaurant hideaway and steal whatever they could.

Akira Kazuka was left with a mostly damaged machine, no tools or spare parts, and a hefty loan to repay. Kingston also learned that he shouldn't celebrate other teams failures quite so soon.

As Kingston headed home he kept to himself with his head down, thinking about everything that still needed to be done and trying to work out a winning strategy with the gambling house. He glanced up only when one of the statues turned as he walked by, but the statue didn't say anything. Kingston kept moving, sure that it was only because he was famous. He walked a little farther when he passed another statue and heard a familiar voice.

"Kingston Raine," said Archimedes.

Kingston paused and looked up, surprised that he had walked so far with his head in the clouds. "Archimedes. How are you today?"

"I am well. And you?"

"Surviving," said Kingston. He then remembered that Catalina had been reading to Fernando, but that was supposed to be a secret on his end. "How are the statues?"

"Appreciative," said Archimedes. "I have some news. Montgomery Stup and his brother Edgar have been trying to locate your apartment. We statues try not to reveal that kind of information, only where you might be found."

Kingston nodded. "I saw them at the front of the bank."

"Which is where you can often be found," said Archimedes. "In other news, several of the teams from Hell have come and gone from Limbo, scouting the area and ensuring that it is safe for them to travel around. They have not come with their machines."

"I expect that will be in a few days time."

Archimedes nodded. "At the grand unveiling."

"And the great big book of betting will be updated a few days later."

Archimedes nodded again. "The teams from Hell are renowned for cheating. I suggest keeping your machine in a blast proof chamber during the unveiling."

"I will try." Kingston smiled at Archimedes and he hoped there was more information to come, but the statue simply smiled and bowed his head slightly.

"That is all the news I have."

Kingston thanked him and continued on his way, hoping that he could use some of that information to his advantage, although he was sure that every other team in Limbo would have known about the arrival of the teams from Hell. Kingston reached the next statue along the way and it pointed at him.

"Are you Kingston Raine?"

Kingston glanced down to the base of the statue and saw that it was Magellan. "I am, yes."

Magellan winced. "Your friend, the big one, is looking for you."

Kingston saw that look and knew that something bad had just happened. "Where is he?"

"Last I heard, he's in the bank."

"Thanks," said Kingston. He turned and hurried back along the way he came, past Archimedes who also said "Your friend is looking for you," and stopped only when an envelope fell out of the air and landed at his feet. Kingston pried it open and saw John's frantic scribble.

'One of the enchantments blew up. Rufus is okay. Says we don't have enough parts for a golem any more. Plan B.'

Kingston felt his stomach drop away and he walked towards the bank at a casual pace, knowing that people were watching him for any signs of unusual behaviour. He was also equally sure that he needed as much time to process just how bad this was going to be.

In a word: catastrophic. One of Denoa's enchantments was booby trapped by Urisha. Rufus was able to release one enchantment but another became unstable. He had all of five seconds to get to another room before the entire section of metal blew itself apart. It also took out the kiln and most of the ingredients that Jezebel had managed to locate.

John had burst into the debris-strewn room, rescued Rufus, went back in to pull Simon out, and then spent a few minutes on his hands and knees looking for the terrified white ball of fluff known as Snowflake, who hissed when John carried him through the smoke-filled room.

Kingston finally made it home, realising that he was on the verge of digging into the ten thousand gold he had set aside for gambling. The kiln would be expensive to replace, the ingredients would be even harder to locate, and they would need to buy two hundred kilograms of metal from Hell, which would take forever to deliver.

He looked around the apartment and was surprised that he was the only one home. The sofa called to him and he kicked off his shoes, laid down and closed his eyes. Half an hour later he heard a mild tapping at the door. Realising that he had just been caught asleep, and that he might be close to being attacked by a rival team, Kingston sprang into defensive mode and looked around for a club, or a bat, or something easier to wield than a chair.

Nothing sporting came to hand, so he went for the chair.

"Who is it?" Kingston asked.

"It's Michelle, sweetie. Open the door."

Kingston released his grip on the chair, pushed it back under the table, and opened the door for Michelle.

She caught one sight of his frazzled appearance and knew.

"Were you taking a nap?"

Kingston snorted and shook his head. "No. I haven't had a nap in years. And aren't you a sight for sore eyes? I sure hope you've come to cheer me up."

"If our history says otherwise, then yes." She came in and Kingston offered her the sofa. She sat down and laid her purse next to her. "I heard about your machine blowing up."

Kingston shook his head. "How did you hear about that?"

Michelle smiled cautiously. "Your builder is in a bar getting hammered, telling everyone he can that it's hopeless, that he nearly died, and that he's going to take up yoga."

"You saw him?" Kingston asked.

"No. Biggins did. He likes to keep tabs on the teams and we chat from time to time. How are you holding up?"

Kingston sighed and slumped down next to her. "Ever get the feeling that you're being stretched out in every direction with no hope in sight?"

"Frequently."

"Good, then you can stay and help me through this mess."

"Because I got you into this?" Michelle asked.

"Mostly that. A little because you're feeling guilty about throwing me to the wolves."

Michelle smiled and shook her head. "Oh Kingston, if you think it's bad now, wait until the middle of the tournament. *That* is when things get crazy."

Her words of comfort did little to ease the lines on Kingston's face. "I've over burdened myself."

"Well, I've never competed so I don't know what that's like. But I have come with a present."

"Is it twenty five thousand gold pieces?" Kingston asked, though judging by the size of Michelle's purse he was only going to be disappointed.

"It's the great big book of betting." Michelle leaned down and pulled a paperback book from her purse. It contained five hundred pages and the binding was on the narrower side, making it readable in a landscape orientation. She handed it over. On the cover it read *The Official XIX Betting Guide.*

Kingston felt his mind stretch a little further. "That looks like five hundred pages of madness."

"It is. This is the first copy for release. Death always gets it. Or, rather, the gambling house gives their first copy to Death just so they don't irritate him. And he also gets ten percent of the sale price."

Kingston took it and was surprised by the hefty weight. "How much does this thing sell for?"

"One gold piece."

Kingston nodded, knowing that it was worth a day's wage for the poorest of employees. Then he remembered that there were eight hundred thousand people in Limbo and most of them were gamblers. "How many copies are sold?"

"Half a million. It's the one time in the decade when everyone goes all out and a little crazy. There aren't really any vacations here, or the need to buy a car. I mean, there's time off, but no real holiday spots. Expenses are limited to food, rent or a mortgage, clothes, and furniture. So people need a way to spend money and the Games are a perfect opportunity to let your hair down."

"So who gets the half a million gold pieces?" Kingston asked.

"The gambling house gets fifty percent, but they have a lot of expenses as well. They have to pay off the right people for accurate information. The rest goes to printing costs."

Kingston stared off into the cover of the book and his imagination ran wild.

"Maybe next time you can buy your way in," said Michelle. "Anyway, I did kind of throw you into the deep end, so I'm giving you an advance copy of the betting guide. It's magicked and will update itself accordingly."

"I was hoping for something a little extra," said Kingston.

"I'm sure you were. The book itself won't be released for another two days, they're still printing them. You can be sure that the other teams have a copy by now. It's hard to print half a million books without some slipping through the cracks. There's no point letting you fall behind while the other teams have spent ten years working on their contacts."

Kingston flipped through the pages and felt his world start to desert him. The first section profiled each of the teams, and their members, giving a list of strengths and weaknesses. He was sure to find a good deal of weaknesses within his team. The second section covered the rules and regulations of the games, then the rules and regulations of betting. The third section was four hundred pages of various bets and odds.

"The easiest way to play is to set up an account with the house, keep a certain amount of money with them, and just mark on the book what you want to bet. Most of the people in Limbo have existing accounts so setting one up for yourself won't take long."

"Death has already read through this, hasn't he?" Kingston asked.

Michelle nodded. "He sure has."

"And you?"

"I have a copy in the office."

Kingston drummed his fingers on the cover. "Death gambles, doesn't he?"

"He'll wager ten or twenty gold."

"And he wins?"

"Nine out of ten times, I think."

"Good," said Kingston. "Then I could do with some pointers."

"I'm pretty sure Denoa is going to forfeit," said Michelle. "He hasn't done so yet, but he's spent a lot of money and the auction didn't work out well for him. His odds of competing are very low. Now, someone else might be able to fund him. If they get him into the arena then he could target a specific enemy team or even sabotage them behind the scenes."

Kingston cocked his head to one side. "How much would this fund have to be?"

"Equal to whatever he has spent to build his machine. That could be a thousand, five thousand, even ten thousand gold."

"That doesn't sound like forfeiting," said Kingston.

"All his machine has to do is grab onto one of Hell's machines and blow up."

"From what I've heard, that's actually a legitimate form of competing."

"I know. If his machine blows up someone else's then he wins. His may have been obliterated in the explosion, but he defeated an opponent, and that counts as a win for him and a loss for whoever he ran into."

"Huh," said Kingston. Then he wondered just how many opponents were going to try that strategy against him.

"There are thirty one teams. Half of them think they have a chance but only six or seven might actually make it."

Kingston glanced back down to the book and knew that somewhere in there were his odds of winning, and losing, and he wasn't sure which would be more terrifying to read. "I'd like to make twenty five thousand gold pieces once all of this is done."

Michelle snorted and quickly raised her hand to her mouth. "You didn't hear me do that."

"You should hear what my girlfriend does that I'm not supposed to be able to hear."

"I'm sure I can imagine," said Michelle. "Twenty five thousand gold is not remotely realistic. Fifteen thousand is a stretch, even for a winning team, because that's how much they would have spent just to compete. But twenty five thousand? To guarantee that amount you would have to bet with at least ten times that much gold, and there's no way you could handle all of that no matter how brilliant you think you are."

"I don't know, I am quite brilliant," said Kingston.

"Says the man who -"

Kingston held his hand up, interrupting Michelle. "Yes, thank you."

"I was going to say -"

"Yes, I'm sure it was witty and scathing."

"One might say 'devastating'. I do rehearse these things before coming to see you, you know."

Kingston nodded and tapped on the betting guide. "I have figured out several ways of winning twenty five thousand, based on the last ten betting books. I've read them cover to cover. I'm nothing if not thorough. Of course, predicting the outcome well in advance is the tricky part, but all I was doing was figuring out if twenty five thousand is possible, and it is."

"Well, of course it is, there are thousands of ways to bet," said Michelle. "You just have to be sure that they'll have the money to pay you at the end."

Kingston leaned forward. "You asked me to ensure that Rufus wins, and you said you've saved up for two years to win some money. So help us out."

Michelle leaned back in the sofa and sighed. "I don't have any great idea that will help you win."

"But I'm sure you know something," said Kingston.

Michelle curled her lips, thinking through the potential problem of revealing too much. "Biggins is quietly complaining about one of Hell's teams, and he's trying to get them fined or disqualified. Milliara. He's a devil. He has a muse and a psychic working for him."

Kingston raised his eyebrows in surprise. "A muse *and* a psychic?"

"Yeah," said Michelle. "The psychics don't have any real sway over predicting the results of the tournament, because it is so open to chance and accidents. Their speciality is in letting the builder know if something is going to blow up or fail during construction. And, the muse ensures that the team is fed nothing but good ideas. They will be a serious problem when they actually get into the arena, because the muse will figure out a good strategy against the opposition and the psychic will be able to see into the future. If they're any good they will see your attacks coming."

Kingston's confidence dropped away. "I kinda wish I had thought of that."

"Just about every bet is in their favour with terrible odds, so it isn't worth gambling on them, but they are more likely to win the whole thing."

"What else can you tell me?" Kingston asked.

Michelle sighed and patted Kingston on the knee. "You don't have much chance of winning. Please try to win, and please aim to win. But what you will be very good at is still cheating. Cheat better than everyone else. Cheat so brazenly that their heads spin around. Cheat towards victory."

Kingston smiled at Michelle and was grateful for the pep talk, regardless of how insignificant it felt.

X

Late one night the three masted schooner located at Docklands, commissioned by a British union two hundred years ago and regarded as one of the quirks of the realm, was ransacked for parts by Kingston, Rufus, John, Jezebel, and Joanna. Catalina waited nearby with three hired rickshaws and no drivers. She also made Kingston promise that the metal would be returned and the ship restored once the tournament was over. Kingston was perfectly fine with that until Catalina specified that 'once the tournament was over' had a finite deadline. It took several days for Rufus to de-enchant the ship and strip it for useful parts, and all of the sneaking around started to fray his nerves, but soon the team had their metal and Kingston managed to stave off losing another fortune.

Kingston was forced to hire Jezebel on a full time basis as Rufus' assistant, in addition to usurping Simon from his usual duties of pattering around the basement. John found himself particularly useful in smashing together great hunks of metal, while Catalina and Joanna both found some success in charming the other teams out of their extra ingredients, though it was still at a heavy price inflation.

Kingston listened to the clanging of Rufus' machine around the clock, all the while trying out one system of gambling against another, testing it on previous tournaments and finding several that were good, but nothing that was great. So far, he couldn't find a guaranteed winner. He knew he likely wouldn't, but it became a game of Wall Street proportions when he realised the odds would change automatically and he could set up buy-in and sell points.

No one knew who was against who yet, and that information wouldn't be released until three days before the first game. Right now it was all speculative, and this was where most of the punters had a crack at figuring out the line up, even if it was randomly selected. The gambling house offered odds of 850:1 for whoever picked the right opening line up. Kingston had several goes at that after studying the previous tournaments and figuring out if there was actually any element of randomness involved.

"You can sometimes provoke a challenge," Rufus said. "And someone can always be bribed. All you have to do is have John slap one of the teams from Hell and you'll probably find yourself up against that team by some sort of strange coincidence."

Kingston made a note that John was going to have to slap someone big and mean. He then tried to figure out the winners of the first round for his predicted line up. That offered additional odds of 1,100:1.

Then Kingston broke the bets down into less long shot odds. He paired each team up against another and used a lot of contingency bets. Most people played it safe with, *'If Denoa is against Sequa, Sequa will win.' 'If Kazuka is against Horatio, Horatio will win.'* However, there was an extra level of complication that appealed to Kingston where he could manage the expected odds and only bet if the odds were favourable. *'If Denoa is against Sequa, and if Sequa has odds of 2:1 or greater to win, play for Sequa to win.'*

Kingston tapped his pen against the betting guide and stared up to the ceiling. There was a small *pop* of an explosion from Rufus' workshop and the door swung open. A thick cloud of yellow smoke billowed into the corridor and John stepped out, waving his hand to clear the air and holding back a cough.

"Was that supposed to happen?" Kingston asked.

"I'm told it was expected," said John, his eyes red and his hair frazzled.

"It was expected!" Rufus called out. That was followed by a slight thump.

John looked back into the room and marched back inside. "Oy! This is no time for a nap!" He emerged a moment later carrying Jezebel and Rufus to safety. Kingston climbed out of the sofa and made room for them to lie down and regather their thoughts.

"Was the smoke golden?" Rufus asked, through a fit of coughing.

"Yellow," said John.

"There was some gold in there," said Kingston.

"I didn't see any," said John.

"You didn't have the greatest of views," said Kingston.

John raised himself up and put both of his hands on his hips. "I had a pretty good view considering it exploded in my face!"

"But I got the bigger picture. There was some gold in there."

"How much gold?" whispered Rufus.

"How much are you looking for?"

"Lots."

"There was some."

"Damn."

John looked down at Rufus. "Is gold smoke good?"

"Yes. We'll have to try again."

"Does that mean it's going to explode again?"

"It's to be expected," said Rufus.

"If it's to be expected then how about the next time you don't say, *John, can you stick your head in there and tell me what colour the smoke is?*"

"It was for science," said Rufus.

"Science, my butt. An explosion in the face is not something that everyone needs to experience."

"He has a point," said Jezebel, finally sitting up. "And if someone has to carry me out, let's go easy on the commentary about who weighs what, okay?"

"I wasn't referring to you," said John.

Jezebel leaned forward and stuck her head between her knees. "And, next time, maybe we could help poor Jezebel to her feet and walk her out, instead of scooping her up like a damsel in distress?"

John patted Jezebel's back. "Poor thing. The smoke must have scrambled her noggin." He knelt down so that he could get closer to her face. "You are Jezebel, okay? You."

Jezebel glanced up at John as though she was caught mid-sneeze, then looked over to Kingston. "What's he doing?"

"You were speaking in the third person," said Kingston.

"And they don't do that in Nottingham?"

"They do," said John, rising to his feet, "if they've abandoned all sense of grammar."

"Fine, I'll try the hoity toity way of speaking, if it pleases you."

"It may resolve some unnecessary miscommunication," said John, while barely hiding a glare in his eye.

Jezebel grimaced. "Then let's resolve this. The next time you drag me out of a smoke filled room, help me walk out instead of picking me up like I can't stand on my own two feet. And if you do have to carry me, please don't say *'bloody hell'* when you lift me up, okay? It makes a girl a little self conscious." Jezebel thought over what she just said and corrected herself. "It makes *me* a little self conscious."

"Consider it done."

"And I'm not that heavy."

"Is this really necessary?" Rufus asked, looking around the group.

"I'm less than fifty kilos!" Jezebel said. "I'm lighter than all of you!" She got to her feet and stormed off towards the kitchen.

John waited until she was gone. "I bet she used to be fat."

"Easy, John," said Kingston. "You don't want to piss off a ninja."

"I don't see what the big deal is," said John. "Catalina likes it when I scoop her up and carry her around, or even throw her over my shoulder. She giggles and can't stop laughing. She says it's sexy. And the sex is amazing."

Both Kingston and Rufus looked up at John with a look of awe and wonder.

John shrugged it off. "We only do that once in a while, and Catalina's a lot heavier than Jezebel, let me tell you. Catalina has hips and bazoombas. Jezebel is just a stick, which I guess is good for a ninja. I think I better go sandwich her." John headed down the corridor after Jezebel.

It took a moment for Rufus to process everything that John had just said. "Is he about to go use her as a sandwich?"

Kingston shook his head. "No, he's going to compliment her, give her some advice to work on, and then compliment her again."

"Oh." Rufus looked down the corridor and was curious to see how John was going to handle that situation. Then he thought back to what he said about Catalina. "Lucky bastard."

Catalina received some strange looks when she delivered the last of the powdered tusk. "All done. You guys need some help with the golem or the whip?"

"The golem," Kingston said. "Things twitch, usually randomly, but there's not much in the way of coordination."

"That's because it doesn't have a brain yet," said Rufus. "So, really, the twitching isn't a great sign."

"Do we have a brain made already?" Kingston asked.

"I sold my last one to Booker at the end of the last tournament. He might still have it. But it'll be expensive and we're running out of time."

Kingston went back to the table to check his paperwork, and he looked over their ideal schedule. Their progress on that front was a disaster, so he checked the expected schedule. That, too, now appeared as a flight of fancy in a far off whimsical land. He then checked their worst case scenario schedule. They were failing that as well. Kingston dropped his head and, not for the first time in recent memory, had no idea what to do. There was the official unveiling in twelve days, and he was haemorrhaging money every second.

Kingston laid back on the sofa in the tea room next to his office and closed his eyes. He hoped the world would just fade away for a moment, allowing him to regain some clarity without all of the clutter rampaging through his mind. Then, just as he was about to doze off, a piercing shriek at a hundred decibels ripped through the office, lifting Kingston off the sofa like an electric shock and sending him into something akin to a heart attack. The shriek faded and Kingston remembered that it was the sound of his security system. Someone was breaking into his office.

Kingston scrambled to the doorway and peered around the corner. His front door swung open on its own, creaking as it went. Kingston stepped out and saw Jezebel pressed up against the far side of the corridor, her eyes wide with fright and her chest heaving in shock. Their eyes met and she looked as though she was about to break into a cold sweat from the nasty surprise.

"Right," she panted. "That ... that was ... what the hell was that?"

"The alarm," said Kingston, and it took a moment for his nerves to settle down as well. "I didn't expect you to break in." He looked up and down the corridor and felt a moment of sympathy for his poor neighbours.

"I wasn't trying to break in," said Jezebel. "I was just going to walk through the front door because I knew you were inside." She gasped and regained her composure.

"You can come in now if you like," offered Kingston.

"Sure," said Jezebel, though she was convinced the shrieking in her ears would never fade completely. "Nearly blown up, a face full of smoke, and now screamed at," she muttered. "Can't wait to tell my folks about this."

Kingston looked back in surprise. "You keep in contact with your parents?"

Jezebel shrugged. "Yeah. Not all parents are evil, you know. Some are actually quite loving."

"Are they in Limbo?"

"If they were do you really think I would get as many care packages from Hell as I do?" She rolled her eyes at Kingston and shook her head. "By the way, we have a problem. We're out of ox blood. And by 'we' I mean Limbo." She pulled out a folded sheet of paper and handed it across to Kingston. "And we're not going to be able to get the rest of these items. Now, even though I have plenty of contacts in Limbo and Hell, most of these things still come from Life, and getting them from Life through to Hell is the safest option, but it's also the most expensive. What I was thinking, and this might sound a little radical, but what if you sign me up to your bounty hunting guild? That would grant me access to teleport, and I could even teleport into Life, after a visit or two from an apothecary to get some Nekirin's Fire to help guide me. Then I can get everything we need and be back in just a couple of days." Jezebel beamed a smile at Kingston and, for a moment, did her best and sweetest impersonation of an innocent princess asking for a new pony.

Kingston looked over his thief with a good deal of suspicion. "You want to travel freely to Life?"

Jezebel shrugged. "Freely, but not for free. We're running out of time, Mr K, and even getting everything through Hell legitimately will be pushing it, and they're already jacking up the prices. It will cost at least two thousand gold pieces to buy all of this stuff. If I nip over to Life I can probably pick it all up for, say, fifty gold? Plus expenses, of course."

"Hmm," murmured Kingston. He looked over the list and saw it had grown considerably.

50 kilograms of dead vulture
10 kilograms of ocean salt

12 kilograms of fresh seaweed
1 shell of a giant female tortoise, minimum 26 kilograms
15 kilograms of fresh birch
14 kilograms of fresh pine
13 kilograms of fresh oak
80 kilograms of Botswanan meerkat
3 litres of Ox blood

The list went on.

"There's no way you can carry all of this," said Kingston.

Jezebel shrugged. "Not all at once, no."

"You're going to struggle with the fifty kilograms of dead vulture."

"I only need to be able to hold it, Mr K. I can then teleport back here and no one else will notice. Besides, it will save you two thousand gold pieces."

Kingston considered his options quickly. If there really was a potential saving worth that much, he had to take it. But he was also sure that Jezebel could have fudged some of the details on the list. "Are you in contact with any of the other teams?" Kingston asked.

Jezebel feigned shock and surprise. "What?"

"Okay, you are," said Kingston. "That's fine, we're all here to make some cash."

Jezebel spluttered. "I ..."

"You're not that offended, and it's okay to talk to the people in your trade," said Kingston. "But I'm thinking we can gain an advantage here."

Jezebel leaned to one side and stared at Kingston suspiciously. "I'm listening."

"The other teams need last minute supplies as well, don't they?"

"Of course."

"And if we sell it to them?"

Jezebel drew in a sharp breath. "That'll be risky if you get caught. The apothecaries might cut you off completely. And not just for the rest of the Games, but for the rest of your time in Limbo."

"Because the other teams will confess?" Kingston asked.

"Yeah. They might do it out of spite."

"So what about the teams from Hell?" Kingston asked.

Jezebel considered that for a moment. "We get our supplies

from Life and sell the excess to Hell?"

"Something like that," said Kingston.

Jezebel shook her head. "They will rat us out as well."

"Hmm," said Kingston. He turned and headed over to his desk, trying to figure this all out. An idea was forming, but it was just out of sight. He knew there was an opportunity here, as risky as it was, but if there was a way to earn more money on the side then he would have to take it, since he had already started to dip into his ten grand gambling pool just to cover the team's expenses.

Then the idea came from Jezebel. "There's another possibility," she said, glancing to the side while she gathered her thoughts. Then she stood up straight and snapped to attention. Her eyes lit up in wonder and she began clicking her fingers rapidly. "I have it! It's not great, but ... if we had an excess of material then we can use it as collateral in another loan from the bank. Say, we have an excess worth a thousand gold pieces. The bank will value it at a thousand and give you a loan equal to that. But you got it for far less. Far, far less. If you default on the loan then the bank gets to keep whatever it was that was worth a thousand gold and you're, what, fifty gold poorer? That's certainly better than being a thousand gold poorer." Jezebel beamed with what she thought was the idea of the century.

Kingston gave her an admiring nod. "I like it."

"Like it? You should love it! I mean, how brilliant am I?"

"Quite brilliant," said Kingston, as a smile crept over his face.

"Damn straight!" She clicked her fingers together and bobbed her head. "Jezebel and Mr K, both with the big ideas. Oh, and I should mention that is very, very illegal, but only if we get caught."

The steam in Kingston dissipated for a moment. "Ah. How illegal are we talking about?"

"Stealing from Life is kind of a big deal around here, that's why we go through Hell to get our supplies."

Kingston perked up again. "And you're willing to take on this challenge?"

Jezebel faltered for a moment. "Well, no. I was going to hire someone. He doesn't mind, his contract in Limbo is up at the end of the year anyway, it's okay if he gets booted off to Hell."

"And you still wanted to sign up so you could teleport?"

Jezebel shrugged. "Well ... yeah. I'm sick of running around everywhere. I just figured, if you sign me up to the guild then I can pull a few strings and get someone to hunt down however much vulture skin or ox blood you need."

The cogs in Kingston's plan started to come together. "But it's only illegal if someone robs Life?"

Jezebel shrugged. "It's very illegal to rob Life, certainly, it's only slightly illegal if you rob Hell. But I can call my guy and see what we can do about it."

Kingston smirked and felt a moment of pride bristle through his veins. "No need to call your guy. I'll pay you your finder's fee for the idea, and for your secrecy in the matter, but I can handle this with my own people while you help Rufus when he's at work."

Jezebel's jaw hung open as she was trying to figure out what had just happened. She knew she had missed something obvious, but she couldn't quite figure out what that might be. "Care to explain?"

Kingston smirked. "I'll tell you at the end of the tournament."

"Oh come on!" cried Jezebel. "After I gave you that brainwave about the bank and the loan and the excess stock?"

"Yes, which is why I'm paying you a finder's fee."

Jezebel sighed and looked away. "How much is this finder's fee?"

"Fifty gold pieces," said Kingston.

Jezebel grumbled, battled out an argument in her head, and almost refused.

"And I'll get you one item extra that you can sell for yourself," said Kingston.

Jezebel paused at the sound of that, then she raised herself up and considered the offer carefully. "Anything on this list?"

"Yep. Name it."

Jezebel took back the sheet of paper and glanced over the details. "It calls for five kilograms of amber. I would like the same."

Kingston smiled at Jezebel. "Done."

She bounced up on her tiptoes, giddy with excitement. "Really?"

"Sure. How much does that stuff usually go for, anyway?"

"It retails for one hundred gold a kilo," said Jezebel.

Kingston rolled his head back in surprise. "What?"

"I know! So if I can sell it for even three quarters of the price then I'll be rich for the rest of the year!"

Kingston looked over the list and couldn't believe how easy it was to spend money during the Games. And, the only way to guarantee a decent loan was to put up for collateral twice as many components that were on this list. Any more and the bank would become suspicious. Any less and it wouldn't be worth while. Then, when the Games were done, he could sell the golem and the components to recoup a lot of expenses. Kingston smiled and looked back to Jezebel. She didn't know it, but she had just saved his ass from oblivion.

"You're sure you'll tell me when this is all over?" Jezebel asked.

"I'll think about it," said Kingston.

"Just remember, it's very illegal to get this stuff from Life."

"I believe you," said Kingston.

And I'm not going to Life, he thought. *I'm going to raid Fiction for all it's worth.*

XI

Rufus groaned at the list and shook his head. "It should be perfectly obvious. I need fifty kilos of dead vulture like I specified."

"Male or female?" Kingston asked.

"It doesn't matter," said Rufus.

"Young, middle aged, old?"

"It doesn't matter."

"Held in captivity or free?"

"It – doesn't – matter."

"So any vulture will do?"

"Yes!" cried Rufus. "And the thief and the apothecary will know this. They already know all of this." He stared through Kingston as though they were both using the same words and yet speaking a completely different language. "It's simple ... to a professional!"

"I'm not using either of those two options," said Kingston.

"Clearly," said Rufus, and he rolled his eyes.

"I mean -"

"I know what you mean," said Rufus.

Kingston sighed and made a note on the list. "Is there anything on here that requires something so exact that if I get it wrong then it will blow everything up?"

Rufus looked over the list. "The amber is quite particular."

"I've been hearing a lot about that."

"Our people in Hell have a hard time getting it in one piece, considering they usually burst into flames when they teleport. But, uh ... we will definitely need at least five kilograms of the stuff. Per round of the tournament."

Kingston arched an eyebrow. "Oh, do we?"

"Yes," said Rufus, and he wished he could control his eyes from darting side to side.

"Five kilos?"

"Yes."

"Per round?"

"To be safe," said Rufus.

"And not to sell to anyone else?"

Rufus froze and was stuck trying to find a way out of this mess. "Perhaps we can get just eight kilograms. That should keep us going for a while."

Kingston stared down at Rufus. "I see. I'm starting to understand now why very few teams get official sponsors."

Rufus snorted and faked a laugh. "And with these restrictions you can see why many builders refuse to take on a sponsor."

"Right," said Kingston. "So I'm looking for your ordinary orange coloured amber?"

Now Rufus completely froze and went into a full brain lock. It was broken ten seconds later when he was finally able to get a word out. "Well ..."

Kingston felt a groan coming on and he knew this was about to get complicated. "Let's hear it."

Rufus glanced away. "The orange amber is essential, yes. But ... if you come across any blue amber ... get it. Get all of it you can."

"Because it's worth a lot of money?" Kingston asked.

Rufus grinned. "You might be able to sell a kilo of amber to a dealer for, say, fifty gold pieces?"

"Really?" said Kingston, bobbing his head enthusiastically, knowing full well that Jezebel was hopeful to sell a kilo for seventy five. "Fifty?"

"If your buyer is desperate, yes," said Rufus. "But blue amber is exceptionally rare. It's also exceptionally difficult to find a buyer for. It's like trying to sell the Mona Lisa. You can't exactly show it off to anyone without drawing suspicion, and very few people have that kind of money."

"How much per kilo does it go for?" Kingston asked.

Rufus raised his eyes in shock. "Per kilo? No, we're talking about grams here. You get one gram of blue amber and that will retail for thirty five, maybe forty gold."

Kingston's jaw dropped open. "Get the hell out of here."

"I know! It retails at four hundred times that of the orange amber!" Then Rufus fell quiet, looked over his shoulder, and he leaned in closer to Kingston. "But listen, if you're able to get five or six grams of the stuff, we could make quite a killing."

"And the thousands of gold pieces that I'm sinking into this project will make me feel better about a couple of grams of amber?" Kingston asked.

Rufus leaned back and sighed. "Okay, fine. But if you do come across any of that stuff it would actually be useful. I'm serious. If you coat, say, a war hammer with enough blue amber, and if you're able to smash that into an enemy, then bam! That poor guy is going to get walloped so hard into the grandstands that the opposing teams won't have any choice but to run for cover." A devilish grin crossed over Rufus' face as he pictured the chance of actually beating someone in combat.

Kingston quickly worked through the logistics of it all. "And if we get this we'll win the fight?"

"Hopefully," said Rufus. "We would certainly have a much better chance of winning than without it."

Kingston thought through everything he had read on Rufus and his previous entries into the tournament. The best odds he had received in the last ten games were 4:1 in a single fight. The worst were 16:1. But there were other bets to consider as well; going from last place to first in terms of popularity after the first round, going from first to last, forcing a complete re-build of your enemy's entrant, forcing your enemy to forfeit, forcing an investigation into your own team, being the first team to be beaten up by your opponent ... it all added up.

Kingston stared off into space and quickly crunched the numbers. If that blue amber really was as good as Rufus said it was then their team could climb the leader board and win anywhere from seventeen gold to twenty eight, per single gold piece that Kingston bet. He grinned and looked back to Rufus.

"Will any of the other teams use this stuff?"

"Not likely," said Rufus. "It is ridiculously hard to come by. But, you know, if you have your own contacts then ... well, most likely that will spark an investigation into the team. The officials will need to see if you're cheating or doing anything *too* illegal, which is why we can only use a little blue amber and not a lot."

"Right," said Kingston. "I'll see what I can do."

Half an hour later, Kingston ran through his plan with Joanna.

"I suppose you'll be taking John with you?" she asked.

"Actually, I was hoping you could come with me instead."

Joanna sat up higher and her lips curled towards a smile. "Me?"

"Of course," said Kingston. "Things tend to go more to plan when I listen to you."

Joanna smirked at her boyfriend. "So I'm your good luck charm?"

"That, and if we get caught doing something illegal you and I will be okay, and John and Catalina will be okay, but if John and I get caught doing something illegal that would leave you two girls picking up the pieces from our disaster."

Joanna nodded. "You two do have a habit of needing to be rescued."

"So you're in?" Kingston asked.

"Sure. Where are we going?"

"How about back to the *Kingston Raine* series? We're rich there and we can buy almost everything on this list."

Joanna nearly spluttered in surprise. "We're going to buy dead vultures in Florence?"

"Probably not. But we can teleport to wherever they live and be back in a few hours."

Joanna looked over her shoes and sighed. "This is a jeans and t-shirt day, isn't it?"

"Yeah. And maybe while we're out we can pick up a pretty necklace or something. It's for John."

"Oh, really?"

"Well, it's for John to give to Catalina."

"Aren't you sweet," said Joanna.

Kingston left a message for John, saying that they were picking up some supplies, and half an hour later Kingston and Joanna left Limbo and arrived in *Kingston Raine and the Curse of the Shanghai Werewolf.* They expected to be back within six hours. It took three days. And even then they could only manage to get half of the items on the list.

"Wow," said John, seeing Kingston and Joanna teleport back into their office, loaded with sacks, bags, and backpacks full of gear. "Wow," John said again. "You two look awful."

Kingston and Joanna groaned at John, dumped their gear, and staggered to the side. They were both soaking wet and covered in mud that had clumped together in their hair. Kingston had a bruised jaw and a black eye, Joanna's left wrist was held tightly in a splint, and they weren't even wearing the same clothes they set off in.

"What the hell happened to you two?" John asked.

"Just ... about ... everything ..." said Kingston. "It takes a long time to bleed out a vulture."

"And we didn't have scales with us," said Joanna.

"So we had to guess the weight."

"And we had to over guess to make sure."

"And the vultures didn't like to be hunted," said Kingston.

"So we had to set a trap."

"And that was just the first item on the list," mumbled Kingston.

"The meerkats were more difficult," said Joanna.

Kingston groaned and nodded. "And we haven't slept in ..." He looked over to Joanna.

"Three days?"

"Yeah," said Kingston. "Three days. I think. Unless it was more."

John nodded. "You were gone for three days. It's almost dinner time."

"Oh," said Joanna. "And we haven't eaten in a while."

"I'm getting that starving shaking feeling in my chest," said Kingston.

"I have it in my legs," said Joanna. "And people tried to kill us."

"What?" cried John. "Who?"

"They *weren't* trying to kill us," said Kingston.

"They chased us," said Joanna.

John shook his head in confusion. "And you didn't teleport away?"

"We did," said Kingston. "Except I teleported to our rendezvous point in Paris and Joanna didn't show up."

Joanna sighed and shook her head. "I dropped the pearls."

"She went back for them," said Kingston.

Joanna stared off into the distance and finally shivered. "It's going to be quite obvious that we've been up to no good if we trundle through Limbo this wet, and this muddy."

"Yeah," said Kingston, and he too was starting to space out.

John stepped forward, climbed over the sacks of dead animals, and gripped onto Kingston and Joanna's arms. "Workaholics," he muttered, and he teleported them back to the entry of their apartment building. There were a couple of people coming out of the building who noticed Kingston and Joanna. John simply smiled at his neighbours, assumed that they would believe that something catastrophic had happened to their golem, and John left it at that. He led his friends upstairs and stopped at their front door.

"So where are your keys?" John asked.

Kingston and Joanna blinked a few times. "Uh ..."

Joanna turned to Kingston. "Were they in your jeans?"

"My other jeans, yeah."

"Where are they now?"

"Somewhere in the Sahara, I think."

Joanna sighed and shook her head at John. "I dropped the pearls, he dropped the keys."

"Wait here," said John. "I'll get the spare set." John headed down the corridor, down two flights of stairs, and he returned with the extra set of keys. He also came along with a tub of paella that Catalina had made the night before. He found Kingston and Joanna leaning up against the wall, spaced out, and barely able to stand. John opened up their apartment and helped them both inside.

"Don't get mud on the floor," Joanna mumbled.

"And don't sit on anything," Kingston warned.

Joanna reached down and struggled to pull off her soaked top, which clung to her abdomen and wouldn't release its grip.

"Okay!" said John, and he hurried through the apartment. "Clearly you two have no idea how to take off wet and cold clothes. First you get into the hot shower, fully dressed, and *then* you strip. You do a quick shampoo and body wash, get out, blow dry yourself into a frizz, wrap yourself in your bathrobe, then come out here for some food, which I will heat up in a moment, along with some hot soup." He glanced over their kitchen and saw a sink full of rinsed but unwashed dishes. "You two do have soup, don't you?"

"Not sure," mumbled Kingston, and he stifled a yawn.

"Never mind then. Eat up. Go to bed. Do you have an alarm?"

Joanna opened her eyes wide. "Yep. Pretty sure that thing has been ringing everyday that we've been gone."

"Ah well," said John. "I'll turn it off for you two. Do all that, go to bed, and I'll see you tomorrow."

Kingston slowly blinked to John. "Okay. Thank you."

"Not a problem," said John.

Joanna again tried to peel off her top.

"I said do that in the shower!" cried John, and he pushed them both into the bathroom.

"Never again," mumbled Kingston.

"I'll hold you to that," said Joanna.

John headed back to the bank with the last sack of dead vultures and dumped them on the ground.

"That's it," he said, and he stretched his arms out to the ceiling to release the tension.

Catalina looked up from her study notes and closed them over. She smiled at her boyfriend and held out one hand. John took her hand and sat down on the sofa next to her.

John peered over Catalina's notepad. "You're eager."

"My classes are on hold for three months. Considering I've forgotten half of what I learned last semester I really can't afford to lose any more."

John kissed her forehead.

"Are you disappointed you didn't get to go into Fiction?"

"Nah," said John.

Catalina arched an eyebrow at him.

"Maybe a little. Hey, I was thinking, after this whole tournament is over, you and I can find somewhere to travel to. Maybe find a beach, have a few cocktails and let people massage our feet."

Catalina smiled and gave him a non-committal shrug. "I have class to go to."

"Not all the time," said John.

"It's going to take me ten years to become a lawyer at the rate I'm going," said Catalina. "Especially with how spaced out I seem to be going over the last month."

"Either way, I'm proud of you, babe. And the others are as well."

Catalina rolled her eyes and didn't seem so sure about that one.

"I'm serious! You're doing an awesome job."

"Yeah, well those two could probably become lawyers overnight."

"But not very good ones," said John.

"I think by the end of it you're going to end up a lawyer as well."

John cocked his head to one side. "Hey?"

Catalina nodded. "You're my study buddy."

"That's because you're my girlfriend."

"So you know pretty much everything in those textbooks."

"That's because you like to be spot tested and I'm the only one around," said John.

Catalina turned to face John, then she climbed onto his lap. "You know, one day you might end up being the president of Limbo."

John rolled his eyes. "Have you been drinking?"

"I haven't had a drop in days! And you could, you know. You have the strength, you have the connections with Death and the Devil, Michelle likes you, and you'll have a sexy lawyer on your arm at all times."

"I hear the workload can kill people," said John.

"I saw how you mingled at the parties. Everyone wanted to hear your stories, your adventures, how you didn't take any crap from anyone. They envied you. They've lived a quiet life, a safe life, and you go out and make an adventure out of it." Catalina's smile faltered. She looked away and John leaned around to face her.

"What's wrong?" John asked.

Catalina pulled away again. She tried to figure out how to tell John what was on her mind, but it took a few attempts before she had the words lined up in order. Then she gave up. "It's just something stupid Rufus said."

"What was it?" When Catalina didn't respond John poked her. "Hey!"

"Tell me what's bothering you or I'll poke you again."

"He was looking at Joanna and he mumbled to himself, saying that there was a woman who's life didn't go according to plan."

John blinked a few times and shook his head. "And that bothered you?"

Catalina rolled her shoulders and forced herself to shrug. "It was the exact same thing my mamá said a few times in her life about most of the women in town. She may have even said it about herself. I'm pretty sure she said it about me after I arrived in La Mancha. But Joanna should be the exception, right? She's the smartest woman I know. She is more successful than any other I've heard of. She did everything by the age of twenty nine and then this little pig comes along and says *there's a woman who's life didn't go according to plan.*' Then ... *then* he looked over to Kingston, who's five years older, and everything turned out perfectly for him. There's no second guessing. Kingston is living the dream and Joanna must have had a life that fell to pieces."

John nodded in sympathy. "But you know that's not true."

"I know," said Catalina. "It's just ... I look around Limbo and I see everyone has had some kind of disaster in their life. Probably several of them. No one's life ended up being what they expected and that just left me feeling scrambled."

John could feel Catalina start to tear up and he pulled her in for a hug.

"I see all of the heart-break everywhere I go," said Catalina. "People talk about the love of their lives and they may have last seen that person a hundred years ago. I was talking to the statues, and I know they're not the actual person but they do have some of their memories and personalities, and so many of them lost their wives and moved on, found someone else, had another family, and all I could think of was the misery of the first wives waiting patiently in the afterlife for their husbands to come along, only to realise that ten or twenty years later their husbands have married someone else and it's not the first wife they are hoping to see in the afterlife, it's whoever they died next to." Catalina pulled back and looked up at John. "And I know it's the same for men who died before their wives, it's just that no one's life went according to plan, but some people get away with it and others are looked upon with pity."

John smiled at Catalina and tucked a loose strand of hair back behind her ear. "Is there something in particular you want to tell me?"

Catalina shook her head.

"No secret desire that is ready to burst out of you if you don't tell someone?"

Catalina peered at John suspiciously.

"It's okay if you don't. And my life turned out better than I expected." He tapped Catalina on her nose. "You are more interesting than any woman I know. You read people better than anyone else I know, better than Kingston and Joanna. And if your dream was to be a bar maid then we can always open up a bar and live that life, if you want. But instead of doing that, this morning you were studying *An Introduction to The History of Law in Limbo*, while I worked on my painting, *Girl Studying An Introduction to The History of Law in Limbo*. You already know that life is whatever you want to make of it. Everyday we get to decide who we are. I'm glad you've decided to be remarkable."

Catalina gave him a weak smile. "I'm never going to see my family or friends again."

John glanced over his shoulder to make sure no one was creeping up on them, and he leaned forward. "You can, you know. We can teleport back into *Don Quixote* and see them as often as you want."

Catalina shook her head. "I ran off with a foreigner, have survived several cities in Hell, and flew on a dragon. My family will think I've gone insane. I can't lie to them, nor can I tell them the truth."

"What if you told them you became a lawyer?" John asked.

Catalina sniffed back a tear. "That might help."

"What if you told them you found the love of your life and you are blissfully happy?"

She smiled and leaned into John. "My mamá will ask why I don't have any children."

"Tell her we've adopted two grumpy men who try to out drink each other, and two over achievers who race each other to finish the crossword."

"It's not the same as having a little girl of your own," said Catalina. John pulled her in and hugged her tightly, and they didn't say a word for several minutes. "Don't tell the others," said Catalina.

John kissed Catalina on the forehead and swore to remain silent.

Despite their promises, Kingston and Joanna waited just one more day before they went back into Fiction to get the rest of their supplies, plus a surprise for Rufus.

"What the hell is in that?" asked Rufus, staring at a barrel that

John was struggling to guide through the corridor.

Kingston beamed with a grin. "That, my friend, holds a unique war hammer named Titan."

Rufus leaned back in confusion. "You bought a war hammer?"

"Borrowed, yes."

"And it's bloody heavy," said John. He stood the barrel up and pried open the lid. "And if it wasn't so heavy I could simply walk through Limbo without attracting so much attention."

"Then people would know that we had a war hammer," said Kingston.

"Instead of a bloody big barrel," said John. He reached inside and pulled Titan to the surface. It looked like a granite anvil with a long, thick handle, and it came up to John's waist.

Rufus' eyes went wide with surprise. "Just how heavy is that?"

John sighed and shook his head. "Fifty, maybe sixty kilos?"

"About that," said Kingston.

"And it's fine if you want to just walk around with it, but the moment you try and take a swing?"

"Yeah, don't do that," Kingston said to Rufus.

John shrugged. "Momentum kinda got the better of me."

"And now I need a new desk," said Kingston.

Rufus stared at Titan and he was sure it was about to drop through the floor based on its weight alone. "Where did you get it?"

"Uh ... I'll tell you after the tournament," said Kingston. "And I might have to return it before it lands us in trouble."

Rufus seemed very unsure about accepting something that was so noticeable as a Titan. "If it's already magicked I can't use it."

"Don't worry, it's just a solid piece of metal."

"It's made from one piece of metal?" Rufus asked.

"Of course," said Kingston. "And I did take into consideration the need to have the purest of metal, and made by the best smith in the land. It was also forged with the aid of dragon's breath." Kingston smirked, hoping that would buy him some favour with Rufus.

The builder peered at Kingston suspiciously. "You got this from Fiction, didn't you?"

"I'd better not say," said Kingston.

Rufus cocked his head to one side as the weight of the situation dawned on him. "And everything else you've been dragging along is also from Fiction?"

"Again, it's better that we maintain some sort of plausible deniability."

"And what the hell does that mean?"

"It means I'm not going to tell you where I got any of this stuff from," said Kingston.

"But none of this is real? I am a specialist with *real* materials, not fictional ones. I have no idea if any of this will react correctly. I'll even have to mix real materials with fictional ones!"

"Rufus?" said Kingston. "Just make it happen."

Rufus spluttered, reached up to his head and almost pulled his hair out, and then he stared from Kingston to John as a fit of insanity nearly got the better of him. "This is madness!"

Kingston stepped in closer and lowered his voice. "I also have five grams of blue amber."

All of a sudden, Rufus' near panic attack eased away, and his jaw dropped open in surprise. "Five grams ..."

Kingston nodded. "Of blue amber."

"Well then ..." mumbled Rufus, and he built himself up into a series of shrugs. "I suppose something could work out in our favour."

"So we're best of friends again?" Kingston asked.

Rufus shrugged. "It's possible."

"Good. How long until the grand unveiling?"

"Eight days."

"Do you think you can get or golem ready in that time?"

"No," said Rufus. "No chance at all. But we can get *something* ready. He might not be able to walk, or even stand, but we can certainly get a contender into the arena. Assuming, of course, that we all work around the clock and everyone follows my instructions to the letter."

"And everything will be ready by the opening round?"

"Well, now that I don't have to build a war hammer that certainly speeds things up a little. I'll still have to enchant it and put it through its paces, but I'm feeling a little more optimistic now than before."

There was a flash of light and a letter dropped to the floor right in front of Kingston.

"Secret admirer?" asked Rufus.

Kingston glanced over the note. "Business associate." It was from Maurice, saying that he had some information for the team.

Two hours later, Kingston returned to his apartment and found Joanna at the stove working on their dinner.

"Hey, babe!" cried Kingston.

"Someone's in a good mood," said Joanna.

"Of course. I just had a meeting with Maurice."

"Oh, so that's where you hurried off to."

"Yep. He showed me two sheets of useful information." Kingston pulled out a page of folded over gibberish from his pocket.

"He showed you or gave you?" asked Joanna.

"Showed me. I wrote down everything I could remember while walking back. Are you ready?"

"For ...?"

Kingston cleared his throat and read over his notes. "'Horatio - Cannon. 87.'" He looked back to Joanna. "From what I understood, the eighty seven is out of one hundred and represents the expected odds of that machine making through the first round." He went back to his notes. "'Biggins - Tornado. 81. Sanders - Drill. 78. Rufus - Golem. 64.'"

"Sixty four?" Joanna asked. "We have a sixty four percent chance of making it through the first round?"

"Yep. Considering that Chloe Stuyvescent, who has Rufus' old machine, stands at 27, that's pretty good."

"Let me see," said Joanna. Kingston handed over the list of unconfirmed machines. "And you think this is accurate?"

"Very," said Kingston. "Maurice is doing what he can to build trust so that we deal with him and help him make a lot of money. He needs to prove that his information can be trusted."

"And you know he's shown this to every other team."

"Of course," said Kingston. "And we knew a lot of this information already, but what we didn't have were the odds of success. Now we have an obvious front runner, being Horatio and his cannon, and that gives us something to work towards."

"But this list only shows the teams from Limbo."

Kingston grinned and pulled out a second list from his pocket.

"That's more like it."

"It's incomplete, but the Cascade deal with a gambling house in

Hell, and so they share information wherever they can.

Joanna read over the details. "'Aurelius. 94.' It doesn't say what kind of machine he's participating with."

"Whatever it is, he's beaten the Kwons as the clear favourite."

"'Kwon - Scorpion. 91. Milliara - Anvil. 90.' So far the teams from Limbo don't have good odds compared to Hell." He looked around the kitchen and peered into the saucepan. "What are we having?"

"John made some pasta so I decided to make up some ragu."

"Excellent!" He looked over to his bedroom door and felt the urge to step into the shower. "Well, I should -"

"You should help by doing some of the dishes," said Joanna.

Kingston thought it over quickly and nodded. "I will do exactly that." As he walked by he pinched Joanna's bum, making her yelp in surprise.

Several days later, Kingston was tasked with breaking down an old cinema projector from the Art House, and Rufus gave him explicit instructions to keep the lens as intact as possible. Meanwhile, John went down to Rufus' vault and picked up an old brain unit that Rufus had built a hundred years ago.

"There's no way this thing will still work," said John, as he dumped it on the work bench.

"Nothing will work if that's your attitude," mumbled Rufus. He looked over the tin can head and noticed a smell coming from within. "Hmm."

John arched an eyebrow at Rufus. "Problem?"

"There's a leak," said Rufus.

In the adjoining room, Joanna was carefully mixing together the ingredients that Rufus had specified, down to one hundredths of a gram while stirring as carefully as possible. Catalina and Jezebel worked on the junior version of the golem as it tried to focus on several moving targets, but the cute little toy soldier had a hard time figuring out where his target was.

While Rufus tried to repair all of the brain units from his previous entries and cobble them together, Kingston was stabbed with a moment of panic when a hundred gold piece lens rolled off the table. He shot his foot out to catch it and, miraculously, stopped it from shattering on the ground. He looked up to the evil eye of Rufus.

"Dodged a bullet there," Kingston said, smiling in relief.

"Hmm," mumbled Rufus. "This would be quicker if Booker was able to sell my old brain back."

Kingston did his best not to fire back with a smartarse comment, and he simply shrugged. "Booker said it wasn't for sale."

"We have a thief, you know," said Rufus.

"We also have four brain units from the vault."

Rufus shrugged and tried to upgrade what he had. John was forever going back and forth to the vault to bring up something that could be used as an arm, or at least as a finger, but Rufus had a dozen different machines to cannibalise and he admitted that most of the enchantments were starting to fail due to old age.

At last, Rufus had a workable head. He fixed the projector's lens into helmet and fastened most of the enchanted steam-punk projector into the body of the golem. Rufus snapped his fingers in front of his creation and smiled in delight as the golem was able to focus on Rufus's fingers. By the end of the week, the golem was able to stand under its own weight.

XII

It was the day of the grand unveiling. The arrivals from Hell began to appear at 14:00 in the large teleportation circle to the north of Limbo, where large teams could land safely without bumping into anyone else. They were then processed by Maggie, the immigration officer who last year had the shock of her unlife when an unauthorised dragon burst into Limbo right in front of her. The seventeen teams from Hell came in ten minute delays, and they all carried their contraption in a secured wooden box to avoid anyone tampering with what lay inside. The teams then made their way south to Mictlan Parklands.

The grand unveiling would take place within the arena, which was packed with 120,000 spectators around the circular floor below. Tickets were, officially, one gold piece, but bartering and trading for better seats was the norm. From there the audience could see the teams gathered all at once, greasing each other off, while the referees and gaming commissioners wandered about to make sure each entrant met all of the basic safety and legal policies.

"I can't do this," said Rufus, as he stumbled towards the arena.

Kingston rolled his eyes towards Joanna, but he could see that she was just as nervous as their builder. They had hired a rickshaw, which was pulled along by John, and Jezebel kept a safe distance behind to keep an eye on anyone who might tamper with their ride.

"No, really, I can't do this," said Rufus, and he came to a stop.

Kingston fell into a sarcastic tone. "No, please, don't stop, tell me what's bothering you, don't be nervous ..." he sighed and clapped Rufus on the back. "You're going in there and you're going to make us rich."

"This is my nineteenth tournament!" Rufus cried.

"So you're a seasoned pro."

"I've been humiliated eighteen times before. And the golem isn't even finished. He can barely stand, let alone walk. We're going to be a laughing stock."

"Well, now that we've accepted that, we can move forward." Kingston grabbed Rufus and dragged him along.

The competitor's entrance was located between gates twelve and one, and were marked by a large black marquee. There were signs everywhere to guide everyone their respective points of entry, and there were even more signs advising the locals and tourists of the penalties involved in fighting and other such breaches of the peace.

"Nope!" cried Rufus, and he came to a stop. "I can't go in there!"

Kingston stopped and shook his head. "John?"

John reeled around. *"Do you want to see how close my hand will get to your face?"*

Rufus grumbled, and Catalina came over to tap his hand.

"It's okay, Rufus. We're all nervous about going in there."

Kingston rolled his eyes. "Put him in the rickshaw."

Rufus climbed in, crossed his arms in a huff, and allowed John to pull him into the arena. When they reached the main gate Jezebel peeled away and gave Kingston a quick nod to confirm that she was staying out of sight. The team were then met by several officials who took their names and the name of their entrant.

"Mortimer," said Rufus.

Kingston shrugged and thought it was as good as any other name. The team then proceeded out onto the battlefield and were met with a great deal of indifference from the crowd, who were chatting amongst themselves. Kingston glanced around at the competition and he could see a clear difference between the Limbo teams and the ones from Hell. Those from Limbo brought along the barest number of team members, keeping their reserve mechanics out of sight, whereas Hell brought everyone they could find. The typical size of a Limbo team was six members. At a minimum Hell brought fourteen. Team Kwon had twenty eight.

The combatants were all assigned to a specific numbered square marked on the ground. As Kingston and the team wheeled Mortimer to square twenty nine they had a chance to finally see what everyone else was competing with.

The Kazuka team, whose combatant exploded just a few weeks ago, had cobbled together enough spare parts to build something that could move, but it looked like a steel barrel. Kingston wondered if the machine was inside the barrel, or if the barrel was the actual machine, allowing it to speed into the opposition and smash them with nothing more than momentum. Kazuka and his engineers were still making last minute modifications.

The Kwon's had built a giant scorpion, the size of a minivan. The legs were gold in colour, the tail was purple, and the body was silver.

Horatio had built a cannon. The top was fitted with several cylindrical compartments, and Kingston presumed that each one held a different weapon inside. He expected one to be a net, another to be a grappling hook, and another to actually fire off cannon balls.

It was easy to pick out Milliara's team. The team principal was a devil, with long pointed ears and even longer fingers. Near by stood a spaced out psychic swaying in the breeze, and next to her was an old woman with wild, frizzy hair, who was no doubt the team's muse.

Wayne, renowned for the longest match in tournament history, had built a dozen large balls that could fight independently or as a team. Kingston sighed when he saw them and realised that in order to defeat Wayne someone would have to destroy all twelve balls.

The most surprising team, though, was Stuyvescent, from Limbo. Kingston recognised the features from Rufus' old blueprints. Joanna saw it as well and shot Kingston a look of concern. "Rufus?" asked Kingston. "You didn't happen to sell your past creations to that team over there, did you?"

Rufus peered out of the rickshaw. "Yep. Got a good deal for them as well. A thousand gold pieces."

Kingston had to take the bad news with a grain of salt. "I guess you'll know some of her weaknesses and how to best defeat them."

"Not exactly," said Rufus. "I sold everything I could to Stuyvescent the day after the last tournament. She's had ten years to figure out where I went wrong."

Kingston and Joanna exchanged another look. They knew that Rufus had sold most of his gear after the previous Games, but they didn't know that he had sold it all to just one team. Thankfully, it looked as though Stuyvescent was giving Rufus the evil eye, so clearly she didn't want him participating in this year's tournament, which gave Kingston some hope. Maybe she hadn't changed many of Rufus' enchantments and he would know how to break them mid-match if they came face to face with each other.

The team stopped at square twenty nine and John sighed when he was finally able to stop pulling the rickshaw. He rubbed his hands and stretched his arms, and it was no wonder why he was exhausted. Mortimer weighed three hundred kilos. His whip and hammer were secured in hiding under the rickshaw in case a thief decided to break into the bank and rob the team of their weapons. The whip and hammer were still incomplete, but all up John was pulling four hundred kilos using nothing but brute strength.

Kingston pulled off the canvas sheet protecting Mortimer from the stares of onlookers, and the crowd had their first look at what Rufus had thrown together in just a few weeks of mayhem. There were some nods of admiration, as well as some puzzled expressions, and most of the crowd agreed that it was quite a departure from Rufus' usual brand of foolishness.

"Right, let's get him down," said Kingston.

Rufus tapped Mortimer on the forehead and shouted, "Stand!"

Nothing happened. Kingston looked over to John and sighed. "Let's give him a hand."

"Righto," said John. He and Kingston dragged Mortimer's legs out so that they dangled into the air, and Rufus tried again.

"Stand!"

In that moment, the rickshaw lost its balance. Mortimer's feet landed on the ground, but the rest of him flipped over and he face planted the arena floor. Then the rickshaw fell on top of him. Joanna and Catalina stepped back and covered their mouths as everyone scrambled out of the way. The crowd tittered in delight.

Rufus sighed and muttered to himself. "Nineteen tournaments now. Nineteen humiliating moments."

John pulled the rickshaw off Mortimer, but it was a struggle with the war hammer and whip hidden in the compartment below. With some effort he was able to set the rickshaw back on its wheels and, again, he stretched the tension out of his arms. Mortimer was still lying face down on the ground.

"Stand!" commanded Rufus.

"Is he turned on?" Joanna asked.

Rufus rummaged around the base of Mortimer's helmet and

saw a blue glow emanating from within. "He's on."

"And he can hear?" Catalina asked.

Kingston grumbled as Rufus tried to figure out what had happened between their successful walk that morning and the failure of not even being able to stand by the afternoon. He pulled Joanna, John, and Catalina in for a quick meeting. "We still need to get some of the odds in our favour. Maybe this isn't a complete disaster."

"It is if we get fined," said Catalina.

"She's right," said Joanna. "Even a hundred gold piece fine will be hard to make back from the bookies."

"Unless we're the only ones who are fined and that's what we bet on," said John. "Two to one that we're the only ones."

Kingston looked over at the other combatants and shook his head. "Kazuka's team doesn't look too hopeful. We shouldn't risk betting on us getting a fine."

"Stand!" shouted Rufus. Mortimer remained on his front.

"I'm kinda liking that team with the muse," said Joanna. "Sure might help us right now figure out how to get Mortimer on his feet."

"They're from Hell, honey," said Kingston.

"Stand you worthless piece of -"

"Maybe they'll be nice enough to help us out," said Joanna.

"Or, more likely, they could sabotage us."

"That's no guarantee, just because they're from Hell."

"I said stand!"

"I mean, we're not going to sabotage any other team, are we?" asked Joanna.

"We haven't yet," said Kingston.

Catalina arched an eyebrow at Kingston.

"And that doesn't mean that we're going to," said Kingston. "Just ... you know ... it's a possibility."

"That's unsporting," said Catalina.

"Only if we get caught," said Kingston.

Rufus slipped to the back of the rickshaw and muttered to himself. "A hundred years I've been planning this thing, and the moment I get him to the arena he has a heart attack."

"So what do the judges do here?" asked Catalina.

"Look important without contributing to anything, is my guess," said Kingston.

"Honey, this isn't football," said Joanna.

Rufus picked at his collection of tools and went back to Mortimer with a set of pliers. "This is what happens when you get inferior dead vultures," he muttered.

Kingston clapped his hands together and smiled at the team. "Right, this is where we win over more sponsors and contributors. We need to sell t-shirts, calendars, socks, key chains ... whatever we have, we need to sell."

"We don't have calendars," said John.

"We should get cheerleaders and feature them in a calendar," said Kingston.

"Big, hunky cheerleaders," said Joanna.

Kingston mumbled and shrugged it off. "Maybe we should have two sets of calendars."

"Oh, one for Limbo and one for Hell?" asked Joanna, with a smirk.

"Four sets of calendars," said Kingston. He looked over to John and dropped to a whisper. "We may need to start a fight."

John arched an eyebrow at Kingston. "We, huh?"

"Okay, maybe not *we*, exactly."

"You mean me?"

"More or less," said Kingston.

"Well, is it more or less?"

Catalina moved over in a stiff walk. "I don't want John starting a fight just so you can win a bet."

John smiled and wrapped his arm around Catalina. "And the lady has spoken. Plus, there's quite a lot of people watching. We'd never get away with it."

Kingston grimaced. "I wish you told me that earlier. I have ten gold on you to win a fight against another team today."

John arched an eyebrow and smiled at Kingston. "You did?" Then he looked puzzled. "Wait, why only ten?"

"First bets are always a bit risky and I wanted to stake out the competition before putting up more money."

"Oh," said John. "What else did you bet on?"

Kingston glanced around the arena. "That two teams and only two teams would be fined by the referees, that Creig's machine would blow up ..."

"His always blows up," said Joanna.

"That's why the odds were terrible," said Kingston. "Also that

Kazuka would make it into the unveiling ..."

"That was dicey," said John.

"That was a last minute call, and Jezebel helped me out with that. I only spent one gold piece on it, though."

"What else?" John asked.

"That we would end up in the top ten of crowd favourites."

Everyone stared at Mortimer and they didn't look so sure.

"That one may have been a stretch," said Kingston.

Rufus pulled the pliers free from Mortimer's neck, dusted off his hands, and got to his feet. "Stand!"

Mortimer shuddered.

Rufus looked back to Kingston. "The fall knocked a few things loose. And I don't think he was ever able to stand up from this position. He just doesn't know how to."

Kingston nodded and looked over to John. "We're going to have to stand him up."

John shrugged, moved over to one of Mortimer's shoulders, and together the whole team were able to lift the three hundred kilo hunk of metal onto its feet. When Mortimer stood upright there were some unenthusiastic cheers from the crowd, and several of the teams were smirking to themselves.

Rufus stepped over to Kingston. "Just so you know, a bipedal machine is much less stable than, say, a scorpion."

"Then you better figure out how to get him back onto his feet whenever he falls over," said Kingston.

John sighed and looked around. "So now what happens?"

Rufus looked over. "Now we wait until a referee comes and qualifies Mortimer."

"How long will that take?"

"They don't start until 18:00. And we're twenty ninth on the list, so we're going to be near the end of the list."

"Shouldn't Limbo entrants have the priority?" Joanna asked.

Rufus shrugged. "We were the twenty ninth team to register."

Kingston checked the time. It was 17:30. They had half an hour of waiting around.

John saw something in the distance and he raised himself up onto his tiptoes. "Oooo, I see a fight over there." Everyone turned and, sure enough, two teams had swarmed in on each other.

"That has to be Lawnston," said Rufus. "He's always a trouble maker."

"And the other team?" asked Kingston.

"Sanders, from the looks of things."

One of the brutes from Lawnston's team punched one of Sanders' teammates in the face. A sharp whistle blew and several referees hurried over.

"Isn't fighting like that illegal?" asked Catalina.

"Very much so," said Rufus. "And yet it happened."

"What happens to them now?" asked Joanna.

"Well, there's a chance that neither team will confess to what actually happened, because if someone gets fined then there will be bad blood. They'll be given a warning. But it's good to see that the referees are actually trying to get there as quickly as possible. With most fights the referees don't seem to notice, which is all nonsense, they've just been bribed to look away. Or not. Maybe someone legitimately distracted them."

The referees hurried into the Lawnston / Sanders melee and both teams started to back away. A puff of black smoke from team twenty six, Creig from Hell, caught Kingston's attention. It looked like a lumbering and oddly proportioned tank. Presumably it was designed to ram into the opposition and topple them over.

Joanna saw it too. "Isn't that the team that usually explodes on purpose?"

"Yeah," said Kingston. He looked back to Rufus. "My instincts are telling me that spiral of smoke isn't normal."

The crowd near to Creig's team started to back away. Creig and his engineers ran quickly to their machine, one of them with tools, another with a bucket to douse the flames.

"It's just a publicity stunt," said Rufus. "It will get people talking about his team."

Kingston stepped behind Mortimer and used him as a shield. Several of the other teams began to quickly erect solid doors and sheets of canvas. "Yeah, those are blast curtains," said Kingston. "I'm kinda wishing we had brought some along."

"I said we'll be fine," said Rufus. "I've done this before."

Joanna pulled John and Catalina away. "We should get to a safe distance."

Rufus shook his head. "Black smoke is a ruse. I've seen him do this a hundred times already. It's only when the smoke is blue should you be worried."

The black smoke settled down from Creig's machine. Two of

the engineers backed away in relief, but they were quickly shouted at by Creig and his second in command.

"See?" said Rufus.

The other teams kept their blast curtains up in place.

"Now can you see why the Games are as stressful as they are?" asked Rufus. "Everyone cheats, steals, fights, explodes, and paranoia is as high as ever."

Joanna kept her eye on Creig's team, determined not to be distracted. "I'm just going to keep a safe distance from that thing."

"Good call," said Kingston.

The second to last team pulled into the arena. They were from Hell, and they dragged in a large trailer with a mound of engineering hidden under a thick, black canvas sheet. Kingston checked his paperwork to figure out who they were, and all he found was the name of the team builder. Aurelius. Kingston nudged Rufus.

"Do you recognise anyone on his team?" asked Kingston.

Rufus glanced over and instantly took several steps back in fear. His eyes lit up as wide as they could and he quickly turned away so that no one could see him.

John saw Rufus' reaction and groaned. "That doesn't bode well."

"Who are they?" asked Kingston.

"That's Fernando," muttered Catalina, her eyes wide as well and staring in utter shock. She leaned over to see if Fernando took any notice of her, and then she shook her head as her senses returned.

"Fernando?" Kingston asked. "Fernando de Herrera?"

Joanna craned her head around. "The statue?"

"Well, obviously he's not the statue," said Catalina. "He's human."

"I recognise a couple of them as well," said John, as he peered over their heads and picked them out one by one.

Kingston turned back to Rufus. "Who are they?"

Rufus ducked away from their sight. "Those people made half of the statues in Limbo."

Kingston looked over to Team Aurelius and nodded with admiration. "So they're sculpting enchanters?"

"Six of them are," said Rufus. "The rest would be assistants, mechanics, engineers, or whoever. But six of them are the real deal."

"So why does that guy look like Fernando the statue?" asked Catalina. "Is he really Fernando de Herrera?"

"No," said Rufus. "I mean, it's unlikely. There used to be a union of sculptors here who would make statues and busts of famous people. But they didn't always know what the famous person looked like. Or, they were just vindictive. Every so often one of them would build a replica of himself and say it was Fernando de Herrera."

"So they're good?" asked Kingston.

"For the last fifty years I heard rumours that they were trying to enter," said Rufus. "Now they've finally done it."

John peered over. "I wonder what's under that sheet."

"Whatever it is, it's huge," said Joanna. "Certainly bigger than Mortimer."

"Yep," said Rufus. "And they're going to be the favourite. Six builders working together. Six! Do you know how stressful it is working with just one other builder?"

"Yes," said Kingston.

"But they've been working together for hundreds of years, building statues, and the statues actually work."

"Do they walk?" asked John.

"They can move," said Rufus. "Some move quicker than others, but mostly they have a role to do, so they prefer not to walk away, but they can. I heard one of the first statues went mad and just walked off. She headed in a straight line out of Limbo and kept walking. No one has seen her in a couple of thousand years."

Catalina looked over, now concerned. "What was her name?"

"I don't know, it was just a story," said Rufus. "But someone in that team might have actually built her."

Team Aurelius pulled the canvas cover off from their large trailer, and the crowd of a hundred and twenty thousand people fell quiet. All at once, Kingston felt the strength in his legs fade away and he had a sickening feeling in the pit of his stomach. Aurelius had built a dragon. The body alone was three metres long and was the size of a large pick up truck. The dragon unfurled its tail, its wings, and extended out its head, and now the creature was twice as long and three times as wide.

"A dragon," muttered Kingston. "We almost called ourselves the Dragons and built a golem, while Team Aurelius actually has a dragon."

Rufus looked over and shrugged. "I don't care either way."

Kingston looked back over to Aurelius' dragon. It looked like a sandstone skeleton, but Kingston was sure it was made with some of the hardest materials known to Hell. He could see the row of thin spikes along its spine, and the head was excessively large compared to the size of the body, but it was, without a doubt, the most impressive entrant in the arena. And it was standing right next to Kingston's team.

Rufus looked back over to Creig's team in lot twenty six. He held a puzzled expression on his face and tried to think through some kind of strategy.

"What is it?" asked Kingston.

"It looked like Creig was sneering at one of Aurelius' builders."

Kingston looked over and exchanged a quick look with Joanna. Joanna nodded towards Aurelius' team and shot Kingston a concerned look. Her instincts had flared, but Kingston wasn't sure exactly what she had picked up on. He looked from one team to the next and tried to work through everything as logically as possible.

Aurelius' team stole something from Creig? Sabotaged him? Conned him? Or ... wait, Joanna picked up on something personal.

Kingston took a second look between the teams and looked to Joanna for confirmation. She blew a kiss in the air and Kingston figured it out.

There's an ex-boyfriend or girlfriend in that team, and it looks like it was a bitter break up.

Kingston reached into his pocket and pulled out a sheet of parchment with Jezebel's details written on the front. He quickly scribbled in: *'Find out if there is bad blood between Aurelius and Creig's team, specifically if someone dated someone else.'* He dropped the letter to the ground and saw it disappear in a flash.

It was now 17:50. The referees were starting to gather at the far end of the arena, ready to start their assessment. Teams twenty seven and twenty eight were standing on the far side from Creig's team, concerned about another plume of smoke.

"We only run when it turns blue," said Rufus.

"I don't like how those two teams automatically assume that it's going to explode," said John.

At 18:00 the crowd began chanting and clapping, building themselves into a frenzy, and broke into thunderous applause when the referees marched across the arena with their clipboards and forms and began to officially welcome each entrant into the tournament.

"There's a benefit in signing up first," said Rufus. "It means you can pack up and leave when the last couple of teams break into a fight."

"So there will definitely be a fight?" asked John.

"Definitely? No. But there will be something."

"Something like an exploding machine from Creig?" asked Catalina.

"That would be my guess," said Rufus. "But don't worry, they won't do anything until after they get certified, otherwise they have to pay a fine. After that, though, we're standing on borrowed time, because they can explode with no financial repercussions at all."

"Great," said Kingston. "Time to buy some blast curtains."

"We'll be fine," said Rufus.

Joanna looked over to Horatio's team. "If someone could keep an eye on that cannon and make sure it isn't pointing at us, that would be great."

Several groups of referees moved from one team to the next, judged the paperwork carefully and inspected the machines. Each combatant was expected to make some kind of movement so as to not appear as a lifeless cannon, or a lifeless barrel, so that they wouldn't be wasting anyone's time. Some machines were able to move quite freely. Others still needed some fine tuning to their basic mechanics. By the time the referees reached Creig's team all eyes in the arena watched with glee. The black smoke coming out of Creig's tank drew a few concerns from the referees.

"Hurry up," said Kingston, willing one set of referees to stay at Creig's side for the duration of the unveiling, and begging for the rest of the referees to saunter over to Mortimer and give him an official entry. "Any time now."

Joanna glanced at him. "Kingston, honey?"

"Yes dear?"

"Easy, does it."

Kingston nearly yelped in surprise when an envelope burst into existence right in front of him. Someone had scribbled out Jezebel's name and wrote Kingston's in its place. Kingston knelt down and scooped up the letter.

'Danicka from Aurelius' team used to date Achim, Creig's

brother, also from Creig's team. She defected to Aurelius' team and is now dating Aurelius himself. Achim claims that Danicka used him and has ruined his life. Lots of bad blood.'

Kingston showed Jezebel's letter to the rest of the team. "So the chances of Creig's tank exploding is a little higher than it was before," said Kingston. He looked back over to the referees and willed them to hurry up, but some of them were still concerned about the amount of smoke still coming Creig's machine. Creig finally doused it with a bucket of water and the smoke disappeared.

"That will fix the problem for a couple of minutes," said Rufus. "When we leave we're going to want to go in the other direction."

One of the referees stopped in front of team twenty seven and sized them up.

"Come on," said Kingston. He could see the crowd were building in excitement, waiting to see exactly when Creig's tank would explode.

There were sudden shrieks as everyone's attention turned to the far side of the arena. Lawnston's team had also built a golem, though this one was in the shape of a minotaur. It roared into life and the team scrambled out of the way as though they were no longer in control of their machine. The minotaur charged across the arena, heading straight for Kingston and Mortimer. John stepped into the way and faced off against the two metre high hunk of slag rock.

"John!" screamed Catalina. Kingston ran forward and pulled on John's arm.

Rufus locked eyes with Mortimer and pointed quickly to the minotaur. "FIGHT!"

John realised the minotaur would surely crush him and he jumped to the side. Mortimer took one step towards the minotaur, lost his footing, and face planted the arena floor. The minotaur didn't seem to notice and continued running at full speed, whereupon it tripped over Mortimer's shoulder and fell straight into the rickshaw. The weight of the machine shattered the rickshaw into oblivion. Kingston grabbed Joanna and pulled her away.

"Stand!" cried Rufus, but Mortimer remained on his front.

The minotaur looked as though it was trying to get back to its feet. "OH NO YOU DON'T!" roared John. The fifty kilo war hammer had broken free from its hiding place in the rickshaw.

John scooped it up, swung it around in a mighty arc, and slammed it into the back of the minotaur. A sudden blast of light threw everyone backwards, causing the team to land flat on their backs.

Kingston coughed and sat up. "Is everyone okay?"

Joanna gripped her wounded wrist and winced in pain. Catalina had ripped her outfit, and Rufus remained lying on the ground, blinking in surprise. John, though, remained on his feet, still holding onto the war hammer, which was wedged in the minotaur's armour. His hands were wrapped so tightly around the handle that even the blast from the minotaur hadn't been able to shake him.

A silence fell over the arena as they realised what had just happened. Then, in an instant, they burst into cheers of joy as the illegality of the Games were now underway. Team Lawnston glared at John, staring him down. Several of the brutes marched over, ready for a fight. When John heaved the war hammer out of the minotaur's back and stared across at the approaching onslaught, the brutes finally paused. John stared them down with the war hammer in one hand and flared his nostrils. He turned to his girlfriend. "I love you."

"I know," said Catalina, as a grin of pride crept over her face.

Joanna got up and stared at the minotaur in surprise. "I don't think I've ever actually seen John in a fight."

John scoffed at her. "You're saying you didn't believe that I took on eighty men in Hell with my fists, or a dozen men in New York with a table?"

Joanna spluttered as the shock of inhuman strength got the better of her. "Uh ..."

John smirked, then he raised his hand to the cheering arena. Lawnston's brutes wavered about how best to approach the situation, but since the minotaur looked done and dusted there didn't seem to be any hurry in approaching the giant with the war hammer.

One of the referees finally came over to Kingston's team and stared at the mess. "Which one is your entrant?" he asked.

The team pointed at Mortimer. "This one."

The referee looked over to the minotaur. "And who's is this?"

"Lawnston's, I believe," said Kingston.

The referee sighed. "As you know, there is a fine for illegal competition between entrants."

"But only if the two entrants actually engage each other," said Kingston. "Our's did not engage Lawnston's, nor was it actually involved in any combat. The minotaur tripped and fell. My human friend then smashed it to pieces, and since he's not an entrant, and doesn't appear on any paperwork, no rules were broken."

The referee arched an eyebrow, then consulted his clipboard. "I will have to bring this up with the governors of the Games. You will have to state your case to them."

"With pleasure," said Kingston, giving the referee a simple nod.

"Now then, I assume your machine is supposed to stand up," said the referee.

Rufus scrambled to the back of Mortimer, trying to reconnect whatever cable had just come loose. "Stall him!" he shouted.

The referee rolled his eyes. "He has two minutes to get to his feet before you receive a fine."

Joanna smirked at the referee. "You're very handsome."

The referee stared back at Joanna and he didn't look impressed.

Catalina hid behind John, then she saw the state of her dress. "Ay! I liked this one."

"It's okay babe, we'll get it fixed."

"It's silk. You can't fix silk."

"We live in a world where clumps of metal can walk and smack each other down. I'm sure we live in a world where rips in silk can be fixed."

Rufus jumped back to his feet. "Stand!"

Mortimer shuddered, pushed one hand to the ground, and slowly climbed to one knee.

"How come he couldn't do that before?" asked John.

Kingston grunted and cleared his throat at John, willing him to remain quiet on the matter.

"Never mind," said John, and he looked over to Lawnston's brutes, who were still unsure about whether it was safe to approach.

Mortimer stopped while resting on one knee.

Rufus leaned in towards Kingston. "This might be the best we can get for today."

Kingston reeled around to the referee. "This is his preferred stance," said Kingston. "But as you can see he can move on his own."

The referee arched another eyebrow at Kingston. "Your builder did say *stand*, and he is not standing."

"He said *stance*, not *stand*."

The referee sighed and scribbled a note on his clipboard. "What weapons will he be using?"

"This," said Kingston, pointing to the war hammer.

"Are there any explosives hidden on his person?"

Kingston looked over to Rufus, and Rufus shook his head. "No," said Kingston.

"Is the primary source of combat bludgeoning damage, then?" asked the referee.

"Yes."

"No shrapnel?"

"None."

"We ask for the safety of the crowd," said the referee.

"No shrapnel," said Kingston. "Just good old fashioned smackage with a war hammer."

"And a whip," mumbled Rufus.

The referee made a note of that as well. "And you have your official entry documentation?"

"We do," said Kingston. He pulled the paperwork from his pocket, all eighteen pages of it folded over, and he handed it across.

The referee made sure everything was signed and that Kingston was aware of the rules and regulations, the penalties and warnings, and the whole process took ten minutes. The referee finally ticked his paperwork and nodded to Kingston. "Your team is approved."

"Thank you," said Kingston, and he beamed with a smile to the rest of the group.

Rufus happily patted Mortimer on the shoulder. Mortimer rose to his feet and stood to attention.

"Ah, there you go," said Kingston.

The referee rolled his eyes. "I hope for your team's sake that he can do more on the day."

"He will," said Kingston.

The referee moved on. Joanna ran in and hugged Kingston.

"How's your wrist?" Kingston asked.

"Sore." She then caught sight of Creig's team. "Blue smoke!" she cried. The crowd saw it as well and everyone scrambled out of the way. Even Creig and his builders ran for cover.

"DUCK!" cried Kingston.

Everyone dove out of the way just as Creig's tank exploded, sending a plume of blue flames roaring into the air. Kingston looked over to Joanna and saw her still breathing, but there was a grin spreading across her face. Kingston felt himself laugh as well and he wasn't exactly sure why. He hoped it was some nervous reaction to almost dying, and he quickly regained control over himself.

A second later, Creig's tank, in one piece, landed straight on top of Aurelius' dragon.

"Oh, that's a pity," said Achim, Creig's brother, and he greased off Danicka, his ex-girlfriend.

Kingston snorted and climbed to his feet. Mortimer was undamaged.

"I think it's time to go back home," said Rufus.

"We'll need to get another rickshaw," said John, as he looked over what would now best be described as kindling.

Kingston leaned over to Joanna and whispered. "It's time to make a lot of souvenir war hammers."

Joanna nodded. "And host a party."

"Absolutely."

XIII

While Rufus was working frantically on getting Mortimer to do more than just stand and fall over, Kingston, Joanna, John, Catalina, Jezebel, and Snowflake were all gathered in the basement of the Bank of Limbo.

"The unveiling went well," said Jezebel, smiling happily. "The crowd were entertained, bets were made, won and lost, and the rivalries between teams is higher now than it has been in decades."

John beamed with a smile and turned to Kingston. "How much money did we make?"

"Well, thanks to you smacking that minotaur to oblivion, I made three to one on my ten gold bet."

"Nice!" said John.

"Oh, yes. That qualified as a fight against another team. I lost a couple of bets, but nothing serious. Three teams were fined instead of two, and Kazuka's machine didn't exactly explode, it just fell apart. And we did not make it into the top ten of crowd favourites."

Joanna turned her head in surprise. "What? After John smashing the minotaur to pieces we still didn't make it into the top ten?"

Kingston shrugged with a nod. "The thing is, if it was the team as a whole, then yes, we probably would have been up with the best of them, but it was John versus the minotaur. Since Mortimer didn't do much except fall over ..."

"Right," said Joanna, nodding in near defeat.

"Which, still, is no bad thing," said Kingston. "The odds are still in our favour. And if we get in now our chances of winning the first round are four to one, the second round seven to one, the third is eleven to one, and the fourth is twenty to one."

Catalina shook her head. "But we don't know who we are up against."

"I know, it's a blind gamble right now," said Kingston. "They just looked into our history, and only the strongest of teams manage to make it through to the end. And if we win the tournament with no defeats that's a hundred and thirty to one to us."

"I wouldn't count on that," said Joanna.

"I know, which is why I only bet one gold piece," said Kingston.

Catalina raised her eyes in surprise. "That's most of a day's wage."

Kingston then remembered just how scared Catalina was of losing a fortune, and he decided to tone down the excess spending to something a little more reasonable. "I know, but it costs a lot to compete, and we have to make that money back somehow."

Jezebel sat up and smiled at the group. "I'm keeping my ears open to see if any of the teams need some of our excess stock. They probably have their own supplies right now, but they should start to become desperate at the end of the first round."

"I've got some fake blueprints for Mortimer," said Joanna.

John peered over at her. "You what?"

"It's in case we get robbed, they'll have the wrong designs."

Rufus sneered at Joanna. "How exactly did you come up with these designs?"

"They are incomplete drawings of your original ideas."

"Excellent," said Kingston, and he clapped his hands together. "So, let's get to it. We have sponsors to find and merchandise to sell."

It was party time again. Once more the marquee was hired, the musicians were masked, and the drinks were free. The difference now was that the marquee was packed with a hundred enthusiasts. Kingston wined and dined his way towards the donations, but everyone wanted to see the might of Little John. Sensing another opportunity to make some money, Kingston had spent the last few days making war hammer key rings, and he sold them for one silver piece each. He also made a giant version of Titan for John to walk around with. It was carved out of a solid piece of black coral that Kingston had acquired through Fiction, which was enchanted by Rufus to be as light as a feather whenever it came into contact with a specially designed ring, which John was presently wearing. The fake hammer was twice the size of Titan, but it would shatter if it was actually used during combat. That said, it did allow John to walk around the party with it slung over his shoulder, and whenever he handed it to someone who wasn't wearing the ring they would see just how heavy it seemed to be.

"This is the one," said John, to a group of potential sponsors. He lifted the hammer off the ground and held it out as if inspecting the perfect symmetry of it all. "The minotaur never stood a chance. I was kinda hoping that dragon would have a go at me as well, but he wisely chose to remain where he was. Anyway, this is what Mortimer will be wielding, and when he's done with it I'm perfectly fine with going hammer to skull against Lawnston and his sissy men."

The crowd gasped at John's handling of the hammer, as though it was nothing more than a toy, and they kept having to duck away as John swung it around to show off a better angle.

"None of the teams stand a chance, really. We have the best weapons, the most experienced builder, the smartest of team bosses, and a proven record of none of us ever giving up."

Kingston heard a pompous voice come from behind. "So this is your idea of competition?" He turned to find Horatio standing there, looking around the party with a great deal of disdain. "You certainly have a desideratum for the lowest common denominator."

Kingston smiled at his competitor. "Come in, stay for vodka, drink yourself stupid. I'd watch out for the giant with the war hammer, though."

Horatio rolled his eyes. "Any nitwit could see that John is simply swinging around a hunk of black coral. Go on, hit something with it. Your credibility will be shattered like the brittle club he wields."

Kingston's face took in a deep grin. "Your trash talking could use some work."

Horatio sneered back at Kingston. "Your maladroit charms won't win over everyone."

Kingston continued to smile. "Then let me offer you my most sincere contrafibularities to the participation of what is the afterlife's grandest measuring contest."

Horatio arched a suspicious eyebrow at Kingston, turned, and walked away.

Joanna stepped up behind Kingston. "Needing a thesaurus, dear?"

"Nah. He's not the first to try and out-word me."

"If the next word out of your mouth is pericomo -"

"Pericombobulation," said Kingston, nodding happily.

"That's not a real word," said Joanna.

"And yet when I say it with enough authority no one ever questions its meaning," said Kingston.

Joanna rolled her eyes and went back to the crowd. Kingston looked around and was pleased to see Horatio storm off in a huff. He was also pleased to see Maurice again.

"He's getting better," said Maurice, looking over towards John.

"He is," said Kingston. "When I first met him he had something of a gruff exterior. He didn't really know how to work a crowd without getting aggressive. Now ..."

"Now he could run for office and actually have a chance," said Maurice, bobbing his head with a smile.

Kingston arched an eyebrow at Maurice. "Is that what they're betting on these days?"

"Oh, no," said Maurice. "There isn't an election for another nine years, and even if he ran then John would no doubt get creamed."

"What if he had a law degree?" asked Kingston.

Maurice shrugged. "It would certainly help, but I think it's too early to see if the man has the chops to deal with an entire realm." One of the waiters came by with a tray of drinks. Maurice and Kingston both took a martini. "Is that line of work something you've ever considered?" Maurice asked.

Kingston snorted. "I think being president is a little too legitimate for my tastes."

Maurice took a sip. "Not even in the back of your mind?"

"Well, sure, who hasn't thought about ruling an empire? But I would be terrible with that much power. Not useless, but terrible."

Maurice nodded in surprise. "You think so?"

Kingston gave him a diplomatic nod. "I'm a little too sneaky for my own good. I'd find a way to beat the opposition by any means possible, legal or not." Kingston looked back towards John, with

Catalina keeping on eye on the wild swings of the hammer. "So how's the Cascade working out?"

"Very well, actually," said Maurice. "The moment your name appeared as a contender people started to take an interest. Thanks to you we were able to meet our pre-unveiling quota."

"That sounds like you were struggling beforehand."

Maurice shrugged. "Hardly struggling, but there are more financial houses this year to compete with. They're all small enterprises, right now. The Cascade is still the largest. But the people were a little weary of supporting a team from Limbo, to be honest. The teams from Hell have a habit of winning, so Limbo was suffering from a little tournament fatigue. After the unveiling we are actually twelve percent up from the last set of Games."

"Maybe I should receive a commission," said Kingston, looking back to John.

"I can give you good odds," said Maurice. "Better than the official betting guide, that's for sure."

Kingston craned his head around. "You what?"

"Yeah," said Maurice. He looked over his shoulder and, when he felt it was safe to continue, he dropped to a whisper. "We have a deal with the gambling houses. Because we place a lot of bets with a lot of money we often get more favourable odds. Nothing excessive, of course, just seven to one instead of six to one, for example. It's how we make our money."

Kingston thought it through and knew he would have to meet with Maurice on a more frequent occasion. "Any idea who we're up against in the first round?"

"No clue," said Maurice. "It's all done randomly. Your name is written onto a ball, the balls get mixed together, and then they are drawn in secret."

"Secret, huh? So, really, it could be engineered and not at all by random?" asked Kingston.

Maurice shrugged. "Could be, but does it really matter?"

"It matters a great deal," said Kingston. "I'd prefer to face a losing team on the first round and another losing team on the second."

"Yeah, and there's quite a few of those. But at least half the field have the potential to win."

Kingston looked to Maurice with a hopeful smile.

"Yes, your team is one of them," said Maurice.

"Glad to hear," said Kingston.

Again, Maurice glanced over his shoulder. "I can tell you one thing, though. Lawnston is gunning for you. Even though you have thirty possible contenders to face in the opening round, the odds of you getting Lawnston are, officially, four to one."

Kingston grinned. He was delighted to have made a nemesis that early in the tournament.

"But I wouldn't go gambling away every penny you have," said Maurice. "Lawnston is also quite smart, and if you gamble everything on a four to one chance he might be trying to bankrupt you by the start of the tournament by bribing someone to make sure you two don't compete against each other at all."

"And if I bribe the right officials?" asked Kingston.

Maurice peered at Kingston carefully. "I'll tell you what. If you allow the Cascade to place some bets for you then I might be able to pull a few strings here or there."

Kingston knew that Maurice had led him into that moment of temptation quite well. "How much would I have to invest?"

"A thousand gold pieces," said Maurice.

Kingston raised his eyes in surprise. "A thousand?"

Maurice nodded. "As someone who wants to make twenty five times that, a mere one thousand isn't too much of a surprise."

Kingston looked away for a moment and instantly felt the same sting that Catalina had felt since the tournament was first announced. A thousand gold pieces was what Catalina earned in three years. "Four to one odds, huh?" said Kingston.

Maurice nodded and took a sip from his martini.

"And you can guarantee that I'll be up against Lawnston in the first round?"

"No," said Maurice. "But I can guarantee that the Cascade will do their best at making you a return on your investment." Maurice finished his martini and smacked his lips. "I enjoyed that."

"It comes highly recommended," said Kingston.

"It's not from Limbo, is it?"

Kingston smirked at Maurice and shook his head. The drinks were fictional and they saved Kingston a hundred gold pieces in expenses. He had also picked up several crates of fine wine, scotch, and vodka, so that he could raffle them off at the end of the night to anyone who sponsored the team.

It wasn't the only freebie that Kingston and Joanna had brought back with them from Fiction. They came armed with a collection of new outfits for the group, which they hoped would save Catalina from taking out another loan for a dress, but she smiled weakly at Joanna and mentally clocked up another IOU that she had no hope of repaying.

Kingston looked over the crowd and knew he would have to host a party at the end of every round just to make some money out of it. "I'll tell you what. However much we make tonight from sponsors, donations, and purchases, that's what I'll put towards the Cascade. So I'd appreciate it if you could stir up some generosity."

Maurice smirked and nodded. "I'll see what I can do."

By the end of the evening, Kingston auctioned off the last of the scotch, vodka, and rum. The gang also signed as many copies of the *Kingston Raine* series as they could and sold them off through a raffle, but they still didn't raise a thousand gold pieces. Kingston dug into his private fund and made up the difference to Maurice, who walked away with forty more customers and quite a few bribes to ensure that Mortimer and the minotaur faced each other in the opening round.

The next day, Kingston placed a hundred gold pieces on a Mortimer v. Minotaur confrontation in the first round, and another hundred that if they did compete then Mortimer would win.

It was three days until the start of the tournament. Kingston teleported to the main circle in front of the bank and climbed the stairs to head inside. Out of the corner of his eye he saw someone run towards to him. Kingston flinched away, fearing for a moment that it was one of Lawnston's brutes, then he saw the man slow and looked excitedly to the celebrity of the hour. Kingston ran through every face he knew, from the opposing team builders to the sponsors, but couldn't place this new fella.

"Mr Raine!" the man called out, eagerly. "Mr Raine! Please!" He reached Kingston halfway up the steps to the bank and puffed in relief. "Hi there. My name's Roger."

Kingston held his hand out for politeness sake, but he wasn't sure why Roger was so eager for them to meet. "How are you?"

"Great! Thank you!" cried Roger. "So listen, my buddies and I have our own little tournament going, based on this year's Games, and I have your team. The golem guy. The stats had been a little shaky until the unveiling but even so I was hoping for some help."

"Hang on," said Kingston, and he shook the cobwebs of confusion out of his mind. "You're playing a fantasy tournament based on the actual teams competing right now?"

Roger nodded. "Yeah! We pit each team against another in different scenarios to see who will come out on top. We play the combo a few times and, well, your team is quite strong. But I think you have a couple of tricks up your sleeve and we haven't seen the full potential of this golem. There's talk of a whip. Can that be charged with fire damage, or electricity, or is it only whip damage?"

Kingston squinted at Roger with nothing more than a vague idea of what was happening. "Do you play these combinations so you can make a more educated bet?"

"Oh no, we just do this for fun," said Roger.

"And there's no money involved?" asked Kingston.

Roger glanced to the side, looking as though what happens at a night of fantasy gaming should already be common knowledge to everyone in the realm. "Money? Not quite, but we do bring over some chips and beer, throw in a couple of copper pieces every now and then, but it's all friendly, you know?"

The full weight of Kingston being the main man in a fantasy tournament started to sink in, and he wasn't sure if he should be flattered or paranoid.

"So, the whip. Can it shoot fire damage?" asked Roger.

"Not ... yet," said Kingston, and then an idea came to him. "Do you have all these stats off the top of your head?"

Roger stared back, blankly. "Uh ... not all of them, no."

"Okay. Who's likely to win in a fight between, say, us and Lawnston's team?"

Roger blank stare faded away and was replaced with a beaming grin. "We actually tried that scenario last night because it now seems like a sure thing, you know? Chris ... I mean Lawnston ... I mean, Chris was playing Lawnston, but ... his team was fined for cheating. He tried to introduce a block of slime that oozed out and covered half of the arena floor, so that it would help tire out the golem and put me into a corner, and even though it isn't technically cheating in the fantasy tournament, because Lawnston did that last year and made it a precedent, we had to invoke the anti-cheese law -"

Kingston held his hand up to stop Roger from babbling away. "Who won?"

"Rufus," said Roger. "I mean you. Your team. Tonight I have you pitted against Biggins, which should be one hell of a fight, because it's a tornado, and Dave worked with Biggins and got quite the coup with some inside stats. I mean, most of them are probably made up, but I'm sure with a little finagling I can get your team up on top of Limbo's leader board, that's why I had to ask about the whip. Even the war hammer you're using. I just hope I do better than in the last tournament because I couldn't roll for crap."

Kingston arched an eyebrow at Roger. "Roll?"

"The dice," said Roger. "Got a couple of ones. Pulled off a twenty, though. That came just as I was dying, but by then it didn't do me much good."

Kingston sighed and had little choice but to hope for the best. "I'll tell you what. If you guys run these games, and keep playing all of those different strategies until your team wins, and then you tell me *how* your team wins, I'll supply you guys with the beer for the whole night."

Roger leaned back in surprise and grinned. "That's ... thank you!"

"My pleasure," said Kingston, though he felt as though he was now sending perfectly good beer to waste.

"So ... the stats on the whip ..."

"Let's go with electricity," said Kingston.

"Will do. Is there anything else you can help me with? Can you use the spike on the back of the war hammer?"

"We can."

"Okay." Roger checked his notes. "And what's the golem's full run speed? I've got him down at twenty five kilometres an hour."

Kingston thought it over for a moment. "He can cover the length of the arena in fifteen seconds."

Roger nodded. "That's about right. Okay, thank you. I'll let the guys know about the beer."

"Of course. I have to go," said Kingston, now more desperate than ever to get inside that bank. "It was nice meeting you Roger."

"Thank you, Mr Raine. Uh, can I call on you again? I can let you know how the team went."

"Sure," said Kingston.

"Okay, thank you!" Roger stayed where he was and smiled at

Kingston, forcing Kingston to turn and head up the stairs.

Kingston headed into the bank as casually as he could, but he couldn't help but feel a little strange in knowing that there was a fantasy league tournament and he was one of the playable characters. He stopped in the janitorial department and shook the weirdness from his body.

Jezebel came bounding down and wore a large grin on her face as she walked with a pocket watch in her hand.

"T-Minus two minutes, Mr K!"

Kingston turned around. "What's this?"

"They're about to release the line up," said Jezebel.

Kingston checked his own watch. "That's not supposed to happen until the end of the day."

Jezebel smirked at Kingston. "This is why you hire a thief, Mr K. You pay off the officials so you can get an advantage. Don't worry, all the teams do it. We get to know the line up three hours before the rest of the realm do. That's when everyone can buy their tickets and get the best seat in the house." She checked her pocket watch again. "One minute forty to go. Do you have your line up sheet?"

Kingston rummaged around and found a nearly blank sheet of parchment. It had the title *The XIX Games* and nothing more.

"I should warn you of something else," said Jezebel. "I asked one of the officials if it was a straight one on one opening round and he winked at me. He also said, *'That will cost you extra'*. So a heads up: it might be free for all, considering how many teams there are."

Kingston raised his eyebrows in surprise and he looked over his shoulder. "Joanna!"

Joanna leaned out into the corridor. "The love of my life?"

"We're going to see the line up in a literal minute. And Jezebel is suggesting that there might be a surprise in store for us."

"And potentially a heart attack," said Jezebel.

Joanna checked her watch. "Isn't -"

"Yes," said Kingston. "But Jezebel says we're getting the line up now."

"In sixty seconds," said Jezebel, and she bounced up and down on her feet in excitement.

"Hang on," said Kingston, and he turned slowly to Jezebel. "I've placed a lot of money in guessing the line up, and now you're telling me that all of that will be blown to hell?"

Jezebel shrugged. "It was a gamble, wasn't it? Besides, if you bet you were up against Aurelius, and that the Sequa's were up against Horatio, then that might still come true, only that the four of us might be against each other at the same time instead of one on one. Personally, this whole mix up might have something to do with you being the strategic genius that you are, and the gaming houses paid off enough officials to jazz it up a little. Or, maybe thirty one teams is just too much for the audience to sit through unless it's a great big mash up of flying debris." She glanced at her pocket watch again, and Joanna joined them. "Twenty seconds."

"Any last words?" asked Joanna as she came down the corridor.

"Yeah," said Kingston. "Don't pit us up against Wayne or we'll never finish the match."

"I would've thought going up against Aurelius would have been the worst," said Joanna.

"Nah," said Jezebel. "Milliara is the team to fear. They have that muse and the psychic. And who's going to cheat better than a devil?" She glanced at her watch and squealed. "This is it! This is the best, and worst, part of the tournament!"

They all turned to stare at the sheet of parchment. A set of names and numbers appeared and, just like Jezebel had said, it was not a one on one fight. Kingston did a quick count and saw that there were four battles with four combatants, and five battles with three combatants. He scanned over the names as quickly as he could, looking for his own. Then, his heart fell.

"We're up against Lawnston, Kazuka, and Milliara in the fifth match," said Kingston, and he felt a groan slip out of his soul.

"Ooooo," said Jezebel. "I don't want to jinx it, but I just won three gold."

Joanna turned to Jezebel. "You did?"

"I thought we would be up against Lawnston. The way John smashed their minotaur to pieces I was pretty sure one of them would pay off an official and get us paired up."

Kingston shrugged as well. "Yeah, I bet on that as well. But I also bet on a couple of other line ups, not just our own."

Kingston laid the draw out on the table and studied it carefully. There were nine battles in the first round, fought over three days.

Scamp v. Horatio v. Urisha v. Kwon

Gibbs v. Nocht v. Puck
Denoa v. Sanders v. Redding v. Jones

Foster v. Carver v. Wayne
Lawnston v. Rufus v. Kazuka v. Milliara
Cove v. Lucha v. Rose

Stuyvescent v. Aurelius v. Bonaparte v. Creig
Zamba v. Biggins v. Newell
Sequa v. Semper v. Caffrey

Jezebel stared in surprise. "Ooooh, I am definitely getting a ticket for the seventh battle. Aurelius up against Creig? Those two are going to murder each other! *And* they're up against all of Rufus' old designs. They're like our sister team up against that damn dragon! Ooooh, definitely getting a ticket."

Joanna pointed to the first battle. "Horatio is up against Kwon. He'll hate to see that."

"And Scamp is a bit of a light weight," said Kingston. He looked up to Joanna and they both shook away the shock of facing multiple opponents. "Okay, we need gambling strategies. Lawnston will definitely come after us in the arena, Kazuka has a steam rolling barrel that blew up not long ago, and Milliara will have the best of ideas. So, what do we do?"

"Lawnston is at a major disadvantage," said Joanna. "He'll be rebuilding his minotaur right now. And Kazuka will be lucky to survive just one round before it gets too expensive."

"Pay off Kazuka," said Jezebel. "Get him to take out Milliara while Morty goes up against Lawnston."

"It's not a bad idea," said Kingston.

Jezebel grinned with the compliment. "I can tell you the good news is that Morty is now at a considerable advantage. A lot of these teams were hoping for a one on one battle, and they're going to be a one shot kind of deal. The teams are going to be overwhelmed, so your inexperience is levelled because they too have an inexperience in dealing with multiple fighters. I mean, there are battle royales every now and then, but even those have very little strategy. If Rufus can get the hammer and whip working then Morty can take on two teams at the same time."

They were distracted by a mild explosion coming from the lab.

The door swung open and another billow of smoke flooded the hallway. John emerged with Catalina scooped up in one of his arms as he dragged Rufus by the foot.

"All good?" Kingston asked.

"Oh, sure, sure," said John, as he walked forward. "From what I gathered in that split second of horror in the look of Rufus' eyes, something didn't go entirely to plan with the fifty seventh link in the whip. So now we're back to zero links in the whip."

Kingston raised his eyes in surprise. "We lost the whip?"

John lowered Catalina to the ground and she stepped away, trying to regain her composure while reeking of smoke. "He mentioned something about a stability issue when you push past a dozen like-minded enchantments, and he said something about diminishing returns and point of utter failure. But he was determined to get to sixty links. Fifty six apparently isn't good enough, it has to be a round number like sixty." John looked down at Rufus' squirming body on the floor and he shook his head. "Pillock." He shuddered and looked back to Kingston, then noticed that he, Joanna, and Jezebel were standing around a sheet of parchment. "What are we doing?"

"Looking over the line up," said Kingston. "We're up against Kazuka, Milliara, and Lawnston. All at the same time."

A broad grin spread across John's face. "Nice."

"Lawnston no doubt has it in for us," said Kingston.

"Yeah, but his little mouse of a machine is useless, Kazuka's blew up not too long ago, so the only real competition is Milliara. He'll know how Lawnston's build is going while we're left in the dark, but with a psychic he'll have a pretty good idea about how we and Kazuka are doing. We'll know in the first ten seconds who the real threat is, because Milliara is the powerhouse and he'll take out the strongest team first, which, hopefully, will mean us."

Kingston nodded admiringly at John and was glad to see that he had given it some meticulous thought. Joanna, meanwhile, rummaged around and pulled out the betting guide, which was in the process of being updated. She flipped it open to *Round One*.

"Well, that's a surprise," said Joanna. "Everyone in our draw is two to one. The others actually have some decent odds, like Horatio is three to one, and Aurelius is even money. So how come there are four of us competing and we're all two to one?"

Kingston felt his good will drop a little and suspected the truth.

"It's probably because Milliara is renowned for cheating and winning, Lawnston will have bribed an official to engineer the line up, Kazuka might win by default if he's able to take out the last fighter, and we are the wild card here. We know how to cheat, we have access to a lot of money, and John proved that our team can lay the smack down when we have to. Thus, it's anyone's game."

John grinned. "But we're still betting on ourselves to win?"

"Of course," said Kingston. "And our previous odds of four to one in the first round are still good. It's only if we were to bet now would we receive two to one. So we're doing okay."

Rufus spluttered with a lungful of smoke and rolled to his side.

"Stand!" shouted Rufus.

Mortimer pushed himself off the ground, rose to his feet, and stared down at Rufus.

"Good," said Rufus. "Arm yourself!"

Mortimer looked down to his side, picked up Titan, and grabbed the whip that was only ten links long.

"Good." Rufus looked over his shoulder at Kingston, who was in control of three toy cars. "Ready?"

"Ready," said Kingston.

Rufus backed away and went to check his monitor, which showed him exactly what Mortimer was looking at. "Focus on the three machines." He was pleased to see that Mortimer was able to follow his instructions. It also pleased Joanna and Catalina because they had spent the last ten days teaching Mortimer's head how to focus on moving objects.

"Fight!"

Mortimer took a shaky step forward, raised Titan into the air, and hurled it down the corridor.

"STOP!" shouted everyone at the same time.

Titan flew twenty metres, bounced off the floor, and slammed into the far wall, which then cracked into a wild spider web.

Rufus sighed and stepped forward. "I'm glad no one else was here to see that."

Kingston glanced around to make sure everyone was still okay. Joanna and Catalina had covered their ears from the noise, and no one knew if the damage was enough to bring the whole building down on top of them. Titan was still wedged firmly in the wall, surrounded by dust and falling bits of broken plaster. Kingston glared at Rufus.

"Admittedly, that was a good idea of his," said Rufus.

Kingston shook his head. "Losing a weapon is *not* a good idea."

"Well ..."

"No," said Kingston. "He could have killed someone! Can you make sure he doesn't do that again?"

"I can try," said Rufus. It took an hour of reprogramming and practice with a broom handle until Mortimer was able to be trusted again. John pulled Titan out of the wall and returned it to the golem.

"I'm getting out of the way," said Catalina.

"Me too," said Joanna, and they spent the next round of trials in the tea room.

Kingston felt another near death experience coming along, but he had no other choice. "Let's try again."

"Fight!" shouted Rufus.

Thump.

Mortimer had taken one step forward, lost his balance, and he fell onto his knees.

Rufus shook his head. "We had that sorted out days ago."

They tried again, this time focussing on the whip. It worked like a charm. Mortimer pulled his arm back and shot the whip out, where it stretched to three times its length and zapped the closest toy car.

"Good," said Rufus. "Now imagine that, but with sixty links instead of just ten."

They all had to take it in turns to get Mortimer up to speed. While Rufus slept, John, Catalina, and Jezebel walked Mortimer through his paces. John gave basic instructions on how to get up, walk, squat, and pounce, leaving Catalina to focus on picking out all of the different distractions that Mortimer would face in an arena with more than a hundred thousand people screaming at once. The pair then wrote up their notes so Rufus had something to work on when he wasn't asleep. Since Jezebel was the only other person to have witnessed a tournament, she was able to tinker with some of the basic reactions that Mortimer would have to be prepared with, such as ducking out of the way, keeping an eye on what was above him, and how to operate in a cloud of thick smoke.

While those three slept, Kingston, Joanna, and Rufus worked

on the improvements, built the whip, fine tuned Mortimer's reflexes, and had him in somewhat of a working condition. There were only three minor explosions, and only five occasions when Rufus stormed off, threatening to quit.

John decided that he could fix the wall in the bank by placing a couple of filing cabinets there, believing that Simon was not likely to notice the change in furniture.

Kingston and Joanna returned from another round of dealing with potential sponsors, and they both looked defeated.

"That's not a happy camper," said Jezebel.

"It turns out, we're very unpopular."

"That's no surprise. You're going to have a public relations nightmare after robbing Muira's apothecary."

"Which you did," said Kingston.

Jezebel grinned and nodded. "But she knows that Rufus robbed her, and she'll be shouting so much about that like you wouldn't believe. So what we need to do is balance everything out. We need the other teams from Limbo to be caught stealing from the apothecaries. And restaurants."

"Restaurants?" asked Joanna.

"A chef's apothecary is very important in the afterlife," said Jezebel. "And very secretive. There's big money to be made there, if you do it right, but that guild is as closely guarded as the vaults of the bank. In fact, rumour has it, some of the chef's *run* an apothecary from the vaults in the bank. Others try to build these things in some storage unit or unused room somewhere in the realm. And a big expenditure of the restaurants is just to gain access to these ingredients."

"Woah, hang on," said Joanna, and she pushed her hands out to steady her thoughts. "All this time I've been eating out at restaurants what have I actually been served?"

Kingston leaned forward. "Is this a time when ignorance is bliss?"

"Yes," said Jezebel.

Joanna groaned and looked away, then she quickly turned to Kingston. "Hang on, we did five different cooking courses and no one told us what we were using?"

Rufus looked on in confusion. "There are five cooking courses?"

"There are hundreds," said Jezebel. "And these two were the best cooks in everything they entered."

Rufus bobbed his head. "In that case I'd like one of you to make me a sandwich."

"Joanna was also the best at flower arranging," said Jezebel.

"You heard about that?" asked Joanna.

"Yeah. You were also the best at knitting. And Kingston was bumped up to advanced archery after just one lesson as a beginner."

Rufus stared back at the illustrious couple. "So, what, you two do everything well?"

"No, noooo," said Kingston and Joanna.

"They do everything damn near perfectly," said Jezebel.

"Then why are we not winning?" asked Rufus.

"It beats the hell out of me," said Kingston.

Rufus sighed and shook his head.

Jezebel continued. "We'll need to have the other teams caught raiding the apothecaries so that the heat isn't completely on us. But we have to make it look like they aren't sabotaged because of us."

"That seems a little underhanded," said Kingston.

Jezebel cocked her head to one side. "If you wanted to play fair you shouldn't have bought a sports team. Besides, you want sponsors? No one is going to sponsor you if you're the only one caught doing something wrong."

"So in order to appear innocent I have to rob every apothecary in town and let someone else take the blame?" Kingston asked.

"Exactly," said Jezebel.

Kingston leaned over to Joanna and whispered: "We're not going to tell Catalina about this."

"No, we are not," said Joanna. "And when we're done we should reimburse Muira."

"Or make her the official supplier of the team shawls." Kingston looked to Jezebel. "So how do we make the other teams look guilty?"

Later that night, Kingston ran through every previous entrant in the Games and consulted with Rufus on the main ingredients that each of the teams required to make their machines run. Rufus also knew the style of every other builder and he knew what they liked to work with. Then, mysteriously, each of the apothecary's were broken into with specific items stolen to make certain teams appear as though they were behind the ruse.

Then Jezebel came in with a newspaper. "Bad news. It looks as though our thievery has backfired."

Kingston took the newspaper and read through the article. "The teams are professing their innocence."

"Well, of course they would," said Joanna. "Especially because they didn't do it."

"Well ... they did," said Jezebel. "Most of them did, anyway."

Joanna squinted in suspicion. "The other teams robbed the apothecaries?"

"Yes," said Jezebel.

"You're not lying to us, are you?"

"No, I'm being quite honest," said Jezebel.

"Quite honest or one hundred percent honest?"

"Ninety nine percent," said Jezebel. "See, us robbing the apothecaries is a good idea, and using robbing them to make it look like someone else robbed them is also a good idea. And forcing the other teams under suspicion is a doubly good idea."

"Uh huh," said Kingston. "So what happened?"

"What actually happened was that the other teams robbed the apothecaries."

Joanna arched an eyebrow at Jezebel and was still suspicious. "You had nothing to do with this?"

"No."

"So what's this one percent that you're holding out on?"

"I robbed one of the other teams," said Jezebel. "It was nothing major. I just took a vial of goat's spit from Booker. Then I snuck into Madam Brax's and put the vial back on her shelf. I knew Booker would eventually go to Madam Brax's to see if he could buy some more of it. I also knew that he would find his vial there and wonder if she stole it from him, thus inspiring him to steal it back. But I also made sure that he would be caught doing it."

"That's pretty smart," said Joanna.

"Well, I was inspired by *Kingston Raine and the Dungeon of the Shanghai Werewolf.* You and Kingston did something very similar."

"So how did this plan backfire?" Kingston asked.

"I'm not sure if this is technically what you would call a double bluff, but yesterday each of the apothecaries announced that they had been robbed. Now, Joc Biggins requires lots of oil. Lots of oil was stolen, but he's been steadily buying the stuff for the last five years. He has plenty of it, enough to last the entire tournament. So when lots of oil was stolen he was the prime suspect, except that he has so much of it that he doesn't need to steal any more. It's the same story with everyone else. They already have an excess supply so they don't need to take the risk in stealing anything. Except ... they did steal it, only not recently. I'll wager a gold piece that they did."

"They stole something they didn't need?" asked Joanna.

"Yeah, that does make sense," said Kingston.

"It's a good move," said Jezebel. "The builders can argue they had no need to steal whatever it was that was stolen because they already had an excess supply of it. And they could complain quite loudly that whoever did the thieving was just trying to set them up. They'll make it sound like whoever did the thievery was an amateur because clearly they don't know the intricacies of running a team, and that you need as much time as possible to gather your materials together."

"But you still think they robbed the apothecaries?"

"Well, I didn't rob them," said Jezebel. "Aside from that vial of goat's spit, nothing else was taken. I'm pretty sure the other teams figured out what we were planning to do, probably because Booker found the vial at Madam Brax's and knew he was being set up, so he did the only sensible thing he could think of – he convinced the other teams to rob the apothecaries and steal something that was vital, and then proclaim their innocence and turn the attention onto us."

"You're sure of this?" asked Joanna.

"Yes. I went by Madam Brax's today. The vial of goat spit is gone. Booker would have stolen it back. So someone on his team robbed Brax, and now we're the prime suspect."

Kingston groaned and he ran a hand across his face. "So how do we recover?"

"Beats me," said Jezebel.

Kingston looked to Joanna. "Please tell me you have a brilliant solution to all of this."

"Yeah," said Joanna. "We do nothing."

Jezebel looked from Joanna, to Kingston, and then back to Joanna. "As far as plans go that is the easiest."

"I'm serious," said Joanna. "The other teams are forcing us to retaliate. They'll expect us to be just as dirty as they are, but the longer we do nothing the more they'll believe that we're up to something even more diabolical. And then, slowly, the apothecaries will realise that we didn't rob them at all, because we aren't using goat's spit or oil or whatever it was that was taken. The other teams will figure out that they are holding onto a lot of stolen property and they can't get rid of it."

"It's as good a plan as any," said Kingston. "I guess I'll go and make a statement to the newspapers and claim our innocence."

"But they will ask about Muira," said Joanna. "We did rob her."

"We didn't. We had no idea."

"Rufus robbed her."

"Nonsense. We have plausible deniability."

"And Jezebel robbed her."

"Then I'll pay her off," said Kingston. "She'll be the team supplier of shawls and whatever else and we can tell the newspaper that she's on our side."

"How much do you think that's going to cost?" asked Joanna.

"A lot, but we need all of the goodwill we can get."

XIV

Jezebel rattled on the door to Rufus' workshop.

"Come on, Mr K! Round one begins in forty five minutes!"

Kingston pulled open the door and looked as though he had tried his best to dress down for the occasion. He wore jeans and a black shirt, which caught Jezebel by surprise.

"Well, colour me purple," she spluttered.

Kingston smiled at her. "Thanks. This is about as incognito as I can hope to achieve."

"You look like you've put on some weight."

Kingston tapped his stomach and a dull thud bounced back. "Body armour. Just in case someone wants to cause some trouble."

Jezebel looked him up and down and smirked. "Are you armoured anywhere else?"

"Not that I want anyone to find out, but yes. Full body."

"Oh. Even your -"

"Yes, especially there," said Kingston. He looked back into the workshop. "Everyone ready?"

Joanna stepped out, also in jeans, a t-shirt, and a leather jacket. "How do I look?" she asked Kingston.

"Radiant," he said, beaming with a smile.

"Yeah, well, it's like I've been poured into a cat suit with no give."

"It will keep you safe," said Kingston.

"Do you have any idea how difficult it's going to be when I have to go to the bathroom?"

"I suggest going now, then."

"Trust me, I'm on top of the situation. I haven't had anything to drink in the last hour, I'm about to have a single sip of water, and then that's it until we get back here. I can tell a guy designed my outfit because it's stupidly impractical."

"Maybe you should design the next range of body armour cat suits. The Yorkshire Tights!"

"Don't tempt me. If I do it will be with your money."

John and Catalina were the next out. They were walking freely and without anything encumbering them. Jezebel was about to ask why when Kingston quickly shook his head at her. Jezebel guessed that Catalina couldn't quite fit into her suit. Not that it mattered, since she knew that John would beat even the Hounds of Hell into oblivion if anyone messed with Catalina.

John swung the giant cousin to Titan over his shoulder and he gave a quick nod to the group. "Are we ready?"

Jezebel craned her head over their shoulders to peer into the lab. "Is, uh, Rufus coming along?"

"He doesn't want to," said Kingston.

Rufus cried out from the lab. "I have a tonne of work to do!"

John nodded at Jezebel. "He's in something of an overly cautious mood today."

"Because people get hurt at these things!" Rufus shouted.

Jezebel fell back, disappointed, then her disappointment turned towards sorrow. "He won't even see any of the Games?"

"He has a screen," said Kingston. "And Simon is lending a hand in the lab, so he'll have company."

"He's working on a drinking game as well," said John.

Kingston peered over. "I didn't know that."

John nodded. "The first match is two of Limbo's against two of Hell's. One sip every time someone from Hell hits someone from Limbo, one sip every time someone from Limbo hits someone from Hell, and one shot if the teams hit someone from the same realm."

Joanna raised her eyebrows in horror. "It's a good thing he's already dead."

"Ah, he'll be fine," said John. "He has a litre of coconut shavings. I'm not sure what that will do exactly, but every time I offered some advice on taking it easy he said, *No need to worry, I have a litre of coconut shavings.*"

Jezebel nodded to John. "It cures a hangover in half an hour."

"And all of the alcohol poisoning leading up to that?" Joanna asked.

"The same," said Jezebel. "When you start to get blurry vision you take two tablespoons of the stuff. And before you go to bed, take another two tablespoons. The problem is, most people are too sloshphisticated at that point to remember about the coconut shavings."

John bobbed his head. "Sloshphisticated, huh?"

Kingston checked the time. "We should go."

Jezebel called out to the dark workshop. "Bye, Rufus!"

"Yeah," he mumbled, and he got back to work on enchanting the links to the whip.

Kingston and the gang headed over to Mictlan Gardens, home to the arena. There were rows of villas and marquees lining the far side, where teams gathered to cheer their opponents into defeat. Inside the arena were a hundred and twenty thousand spectators, chatting to themselves, but even the dull whispers cascaded over the walls, electrifying the air throughout the realm. Crowds gathered near the gardens, where large screens had been erected to broadcast the tournament from several simultaneous angles. In countless restaurants, bars, and offices across the two realms, millions of viewers were keeping a close eye, waiting for the Games to commence. Almost two million gold pieces were wagered on the first round alone, and thousands of people were still going through the betting guide trying to find a winning system that would make them rich within the next few hours.

Kingston invited all of the sponsors to watch in his marquee while they were being served drinks and nibbles. The intrepid team moved about, entertaining their guests. Five minutes before the first match began, the trumpets from the arena sounded. The crowd screamed in delight and a countdown timer began. The teams of Scamp, from Hell, Horatio, from Limbo, Urisha, from Limbo, and Kwon, from Hell, moved into position. They guided their machines onto the arena floor, and each waited in their own allotted corner. The crowd got to see a close up of each team going through their final preparations, and last minute bets were placed.

John leaned over to Kingston. "Who are we betting on?"

"Kwon to win," said Kingston.

"Because we don't like Horatio?"

"Horatio is a fine builder," said Kingston. "But Kwon has a history of winning. I also have Scamp going out first, then Urisha."

John looked over the betting guide. "That seems like the obvious choice." He then looked back to the screens, which had focussed on Urisha. "I have no idea what she's built there."

Jezebel smirked at the screen. "It's like a spinning top with a flail. The base rolls into place while spinning around and the flail smacks into anything that comes in its way. Quite simple, really."

"As long as it keeps spinning, yeah," said Joanna.

John then squinted at Scamp's machine. "Looks like he's built himself a car."

"He did," said Jezebel. "It's modelled after an Alfa Romeo 159."

"Looks like a bullet with wheels," said John.

"That's the point," said Jezebel.

"So a spinning top against a speeding bullet ..."

"Yeah. Urisha's going down," said Jezebel.

"That's not what it says in the betting guide. It says Scamp will go out first."

"That's just because his has a lot of moving parts," said Jezebel.

John glanced over to Kingston. "How tall is that car thing?"

"Exactly one metre," said Kingston.

"And how high does that flail work off the ground?"

"It's movable," said Kingston. "But I like how you're thinking about it."

"Those things have no chance against Horatio's cannon," said John.

"Nor Kwon's scorpion," said Kingston.

Catalina glanced at the crowd in the marquee and tugged on John's arm. "We should mingle."

"Good idea, babe," John said, and he sauntered off with the mighty war hammer over his shoulder.

Kingston and Joanna made the rounds as well. When one of the drunken sponsors came over with a spare drink for Jezebel, she simply looked him up and down, asked if they had already dated, and then she took three steps to the right. The sponsor followed.

"No, you don't," Jezebel said, and she moved back to her original place in front of the large screen. The sponsor decided to try his luck somewhere else.

The pitch in the arena reached a crescendo when the one minute trumpets blared, and most of the team members pulled back to a safer location. The team principals remained next to their machines, on watch for any last minute attempt at sabotage.

The tension started to get to Kingston and he felt the excitement and bloodlust run through the realm. Even the crowd looked as though they were about to tear their hair out at the first moment of mayhem in a decade.

Ten seconds to go. The crowd started counting down, and the team principals hurried back to their booths where they could monitor and, to some degree, control their combatant.

Three seconds.

Two.

One.

The siren blasted through the realm and the crowd burst into thunderous cheers and drunken screams. The four machines shot off in all directions, following some kind of game plan that, in an instant, went horribly wrong. Horatio's cannon first blasted at Scamp's car but missed, then realised that Kwon's scorpion was racing towards it. Urisha's spinning top shot towards the scorpion, and Scamp's bullet on wheels sped towards the cannon. The cannon blasted a charge of smoke at the scorpion, the scorpion jumped out of the way then zigzagged across the arena floor towards Horatio's cumbersome cannon. At the last second, the cannon spun itself down, fired into the ground, and flew into the air. Scamp's car, racing towards where the cannon had just stood, didn't slow down quickly enough and slammed head on into the wall. Urisha's spinning top followed after Kwon's scorpion, but it couldn't keep up. The scorpion backed away and waited for the cannon to land, which it did, at which point the cannon promptly shot itself off at an angle to land closer to the centre of the arena.

The car backed out of the wall, crumpled but not quite defeated, and the crowd roared in delight at the first sign of carnage. Even Kingston felt himself grin beyond control. He stood next to John and kept an eye on the war hammer, in case they were both surprised and John started swinging without knowing where everyone was. He watched the cannon take aim on the scorpion. It fired again.

"Stupid," said John. "He should've taken out that car."

"The car is wounded and can provide a good distraction against the scorpion," said Kingston.

"But they're both from Hell, they're not going to turn on each other. Take out the car and let Urisha and Horatio gang up on Kwon."

The scorpion charged after the cannon, ignoring the spinning top that was desperately trying to catch up to it. Then, just like

John wanted, the cannon turned away, focussed on the car again and fired, scoring a direct hit. It had just enough time to turn back on the scorpion, release the brakes, and fired, allowing the recoil to push it back to safety. That became the strategy of choice from then on, lifting the brakes and firing, turning ever so slightly, while the scorpion dodged as many of the blasts as it could, until one charge ripped through a set of legs, knocking the scorpion down. Urisha's spinning top finally caught up to the scorpion and belted it a dozen times a second. The scorpion kicked back, knocked the spinning top onto its side, and the momentum from its flail launched it into the air in an uncontrolled arc.

The crowd screamed in delight, and somewhere nearby Urisha and Scamp were feeling the agony of losing thousands of gold pieces in necessary repairs.

Sensing a potential ganging up from the Hell teams, the cannon turned on the car, fired again, then resumed trying to blast the scorpion while pushing itself farther away. The constant moving hurt each blast's accuracy, and soon the scorpion was back onto its feet and racing after the cannon once more.

The spinning top, deciding that it couldn't possibly take on the scorpion, lumbered towards the car. The car backed away, turned, charged in reverse, and rammed the spinning top with its undamaged side. The collision of the flail against the hard surface again forced the top to fly into the air as it lost control, but the car was relatively undamaged. When the top landed, though, it raced after the car's damaged side, forcing Scamp's machine to speed away as quickly as possible. Then, one of Horatio's cannon blasts found its mark, and the car flipped onto its side. The spinning top sped in and smashed its way through the damaged end of the car.

The scorpion zigzagged across the arena, dodging cannon blasts, and forcing Horatio's machine in a circle until it came across the carnage of Scamp versus Urisha, and the cannon's escape options became grim. It had to dodge out of the way of Scamp's wreckage, costing it valuable time, and the scorpion pounced, landed, and swiped at the cannon. It connected with the very tip of the barrel. The shot spun off trajectory and was caught in the blast screen before hitting the crowd. Several spectators leapt back and grabbed their chests, convinced they were about to endure a heart attack in their unlives, before they eventually settled back into their seats.

"Come on!" roared several of Kingston's sponsors.

Even John got in on the chanting. "Go my good son!"

Joanna burst into laughter and she patted Kingston on the shoulder. "Did you teach him that?"

"No!" laughed Kingston. "I swear!"

The scorpion jumped again, landed on top of the cannon and gripped it tightly with its legs. It then pushed back with its tail and tried to knock one of the wheels free. The spinning top, still under command from Urisha in her team booth, pulled back from attacking the car and hurried over to take on the scorpion. The flail smashed its way through the legs and landed several direct hits to its face. The cannon spun downwards, trying to knock the scorpion off while also giving the spinning top a better angle to strike, and it blasted itself into the air. It spun around so the scorpion was now between the cannon and the arena floor, and the pair slammed into the ground. The scorpion's legs shuddered and released their grip. The cannon fired again to break free, launched itself into the air, and fired from ten metres up into the stomach of Kwon's scorpion.

The scorpion was hit once, scrambled back onto its feet, and snapped one claw at the spinning top. It caught the chain connected to the flail and refused to let go. The top shuddered and tried to break free, but it was now rendered useless. The cannon landed and the scorpion launched after it.

"This is one of the longer ones," said a grey haired sponsor. "It really was a good idea pitting them all against each other like this."

Kingston bobbed his head, but he could see the look of concern in Joanna's face as they both tried to place Mortimer in the melee to figure out how he would fair against the speed of the cannon and scorpion. Mortimer was slower, clumsier, and had more things that could go wrong with him. Kingston mentally checked over his betting notes. He knew that Horatio taking out Scamp's machine had odds of three to one, and Horatio taking out the first opponent was four to one. But looking back to before the line up was announced, Horatio being the first to take out an opponent was fifty to one, and taking out Scamp's machine in the first round held odds of seventy three to one. Kingston guessed that Horatio had wagered on himself, as the cannon focussed on taking out what was left of Scamp's car. After two more blasts, the car collapsed onto its back, shuddered, and burst into smoke. The screens displayed the first casualty of the tournament, and the crowd screamed in delight.

The scorpion reached up to the flail's chain and with two arms it broke it apart, rendering Urisha's contraption useless. It then released its grip and charged after the cannon. Thirty seconds later, the screen was updated with Urisha's voluntary defeat, no doubt in the hope that she could avoid any more damage and she rebuild her machine at a cheaper penalty.

The cannon limped backwards with one wheel at an angle, and the scorpion quickly attacked. It flew into the air, attached itself to the top of the cannon, and spun them both around so that the cannon's muzzle pointed straight up. The scorpion tore into the cannon's wheels and mechanics, fighting furiously while the cannon rocked back and forth from one blast to another, trying to break itself free. The scorpion ripped both wheels free, and the cannon collapsed onto the ground, unable to move. The crowd cheered, and Kingston felt the first glorious moment of winning four bets all at once. The scorpion staggered back towards Scamp's car, then dragged it across the arena, no doubt to the screams of pleading agony from Scamp and his builders in one of the team booths, who couldn't face the thought of further annihilation. Then the scorpion used the broken car as a mace and slammed it repeatedly into the cannon, until the muzzle broke and the base exploded. The scorpion stepped away in glorious victory.

The arena erupted into mixed screams of bloodlust and agony, as many made a small fortune and many more lost just as much. The marquee was almost lifted off the ground by the jubilation, and Kingston quickly called for more drinks. Everyone began talking excitedly amongst themselves, reliving the best moments, complete with sound effects and mimed explosions.

One hour later, Gibbs, Nocht, and Puck squared off in the second battle of the day. They each took a more evasive approach, and the fight lasted half an hour, with Puck claiming victory.

An hour after that battle, the next and final one of the day pitted Denoa, Sanders, Redding, and Jones against each other. Denoa crashed out first, having been forced to cobble together something utterly useless after Kingston and Rufus had walked away with his prized metal sculpture. Sanders won, crushing his three opponents single handedly. As far as the crowd in the marquee were concerned, it was the best day of combat they had ever seen.

Kingston and Joanna waited until the last of their sponsors had left, which took two more hours as it was difficult to tear people away from free drinks, and they finally had a quiet moment together.

"Tomorrow's going to be mayhem," Joanna said.

"You're telling me," said Kingston. "I doubt Rufus will be in much state to finish even half of the whip."

Joanna shrugged and rolled her eyes. "At least we have Titan, and a sluggish Mortimer."

"Yeah," sighed Kingston. "After the frenzy of today I'm starting to think that we're doomed."

"I got that too," said Joanna. She held onto a distant look, realising how much they had both invested in the team. She then went in for a hug.

"Huh," mumbled Kingston.

"What?"

"First time hugging a girl in full body armour."

She looked up. "And?"

"It's not remotely comfortable," Kingston said.

Joanna shrugged and she looked back to the entrance. "Come on, I need some water before my insides dry up."

They returned to the bank. Sure enough, Rufus was sleeping off half a bottle of gin. Jezebel wrapped a blanket over him. "I'm hiding the coconut shavings," she said. "That might teach him a lesson."

"Uh, you know, he *is* expected to help guide Mortimer into combat tomorrow," said Kingston.

"He'll be fine by then, but in the meantime he's going to learn a thing or two about drinking on the job."

Kingston and Joanna shrugged and went back to their apartment. They each carried back a special edition of the local newspaper reliving the highlights of Day One with various statistics, winners and losers, brawls between the teams, and rumours of teams being robbed, trapped, and bribed. He read through the featured section of Aurelius' team, but it made no mention of why Fernando the poet was actually Fernando the enchanter.

Kingston woke up three hours earlier than usual with a nervous knot in his stomach. He looked over and saw Joanna blink at him.

"You too?" she asked.

"Yeah," said Kingston. "It's going to be an expensive day."

"Don't worry. They're only going to target us because we need to be made an example of."

Kingston rolled his eyes at her. "You're not helping."

"Well, darling, I'm in this as much as you are, and I'm starting to think we should sell the team and run off with the money."

Kingston jutted his jaw out and thought it over. "We could certainly recoup a lot of money."

"And sell the extra junk we have in the vault."

Kingston got out of bed and made breakfast while Joanna had a shower. When she came out, Kingston surprised her with lemon crepes and a white omelette. On the side was a fruit platter.

"What's all this for?" Joanna asked.

"This is probably the last day for the next hundred years that we're going to be rich, so we might as well make the most of it."

An hour later, they were ready to head over to the bank to check on Rufus. Unfortunately, their apartment door wouldn't open.

"Help!" cried Joanna.

"Anyone?" cried Kingston.

"We should try the window."

"We'd need a grappling hook and we don't have one."

Joanna closed her eyes and tried with all of her might to teleport out of there, but it didn't work. Personal spaces were locked against such a thing in an effort to protect privacy and theft. The only spot in the whole building that allowed them to teleport was the lobby.

The superintendent eventually came up and was able to call an apothecary to unenchant the door, which took several hours that Kingston and Joanna couldn't afford.

"Yep, Skunk Breath," said the superintendent. "Nasty stuff. Good thing we got you out in time!"

"Very good," said Kingston, and he and Joanna hurried over to the bank to check on Rufus. He was awake, standing over Mortimer like a near blind coroner, and from the look of things Rufus was suffering through an awful hangover. His hair was a mess, his eyes bulged and had bags under them, and he looked pale and sweaty.

"Morning!" cried Joanna, to make him suffer as much as possible.

Rufus slowly glanced over at her, slow blinked, and he turned back to Mortimer. "I uh ..." He paused, surprised at his sudden baritone voice, then he cleared his throat and was returned to normal. "I have a question for you two."

"Fire away," said Kingston.

Rufus pulled out two glass jars, both containing what appeared to be blood. "You see this? This is what comes out of a buzzard's liver when you soak it for long enough." He popped open the two jars and pulled out a small pinch of purple powder. "And this is Helix's Gambit," he said. He dropped a pinch into one of the jars, and it fizzled. "Quite impressive, isn't it?"

Kingston and Joanna had the distinct impression that Rufus wasn't in a good mood.

"Now if I do the same thing with the other jar ..." Rufus dropped a pinch of powder into that one, and it blasted to the ceiling, filling the room with smoke, which promptly turned into sparkles of gold and silver. Rufus stared back at Kingston and Joanna. "I hoped like hell that you two hadn't actually gone to Fiction to get this stuff. I wanted to believe that you had gone to Life and only told me you went to Fiction because raiding Life is quite illegal. But no. Fiction, am I right?"

Kingston and Joanna held their stares and didn't give anything away.

"Wonderful," mumbled Rufus. "So here's the problem. A lot of the ingredients you got me weren't working properly. I have a shell of metal that we stole from a ship, built hundreds of years ago by British sailors, purchased from a metal smith from Hell, who acquired it from Life, and I'm trying to figure out why half of the enchantments aren't working the way they're supposed to. Some are dull, some are sparkly and over powered. All of the enchantments I installed before you two went off on your treasure hunt work fine, and they work perfectly together. All of the enchantments I have from your treasure hunt also, kinda, work fine. But do they all work fine together? No. In unison? Not even close. I started to wonder why the chain whip kept exploding, and then it dawned on me. Half of the links came from Life, through Hell, were tainted, came to Limbo, and were acquired legitimately. The other half came not from Life, not through Hell, are untainted, and hate every fibre in my being because they will not behave with the other links!"

Kingston and Joanna held their best look of nonchalance and knew there was nothing they could do about it now.

Rufus sighed. "So we won't be fighting with a whip today. And Mortimer will be unusually sluggish. That's because his chest is racing through a caffeine rush while his legs are numb. The moment someone hits him he's probably going to collapse. Hopefully he'll explode. If he explodes we can forfeit and start again, because we can either build him exclusively from Hell's supplies or from wherever it was that you picked everything up. But if he does explode you might as well find yourself another builder, because knowing where you got everything a month ago would have saved me seven hundred headaches, and it would have saved you several thousand gold pieces in expenses the moment Lawnston comes at us." Rufus grumbled and closed his eyes. "Seven hundred headaches."

"But he'll be ready to fight today?" Kingston asked, undeterred.

Rufus shrugged. "He can stand, walk, and swing his arm about, but I honestly have no idea what will happen when a fictional war hammer comes into contact with a real minotaur from Hell."

Joanna smirked. "Hopefully, what happened last time will repeat itself," said Joanna.

Rufus paused and cocked his head to one side. "You what?"

"Well, a fictional character picked up a fictional war hammer enchanted with fictional ingredients, and he smashed that minotaur in a single blow. Everyone was surprised by it, as though he was much more powerful than anyone expected. So hopefully little Mortimer will do the same."

Rufus stuck his lips out as he thought it over, and he looked back to the golem. "We'll see. In the mean time, neither of you two are in my best books. You weren't honest with me and it's going to cost us all a lot of stress, headaches, and money. Especially with this," and Rufus pulled out a headset with a microphone. "I'm not going to be standing next to him in the arena, so when he goes out there all he's going to have to listen to is me, through this, and if those enchantments don't work because of your trickery then he's going to keep walking around until someone goes out there to physically stop him. And speaking of money, how are we doing with our winnings?"

Kingston shrugged. "We made thirty gold from yesterday's results."

Rufus stared back in surprise. "Only?"

"The teams I'm not competing against aren't really my focus," said Kingston.

Rufus snorted. "Well, just so you know, I made eight silver and three copper. I plan on blowing all of that in a restaurant with all of the booze I can handle."

"After the tournament," said Kingston.

"Nope. After the first round," said Rufus. "And today I have five silver on us, so I'm feeling lucky. Now go. Leave me alone. I have six hours to figure out how to get Mortimer to live up to his name, and not to his reputation."

Kingston and Joanna left Rufus in peace.

XV

Jezebel called down the corridor of the janitorial department. "Two minutes, Mr K!"

Kingston looked over to Joanna and Rufus. Even though he beamed with a smile, Joanna could see that he was terrified.

"Good luck," she whispered to Kingston.

"Ta," said Rufus. He reached into the base of Mortimer's neck and powered him up. "Stand!"

Mortimer sat up on the work bench, pivoted, lowered his legs to the ground, and stood.

"Well, that went better than last time. Arm yourself!"

Mortimer looked down to the ground, where Titan was resting. He bent down, gripped the handle tightly, and stood back upright. He then looked to his left and searched back and forth.

"We're not using the whip today," said Rufus, and then he peered at Kingston. "Because someone got me components from two different realms."

Kingston shrugged it off. "Now you know."

"Yes, now I know," said Rufus. He turned back to Mortimer. "Follow him," he said, pointing to Kingston. Kingston led the way, left the workshop, and headed down the corridor. Mortimer followed, thumping his steps as he walked, while Rufus and Joanna took the rear.

It was quite a sight to see a two and a half metre tall iron golem walking through the Bank of Limbo, especially one carrying a fifty kilo hammer in one hand. It was impossible to go unnoticed, so Kingston simply walked as though he owned the place, while Rufus followed as the most paranoid builder ever to grace the realm. Jezebel was somewhere nearby, keeping an eye on anyone who might run in and attack the team.

There were gasps from the crowd, all staring at the unique sight of Mortimer. Kingston and his team left the bank. They headed along Upper Styx Boulevard towards the arena, and the walk took them half an hour. Already the ticket holders were making their way forward, eager to see the second day's events of the first round. John and Catalina were waiting at the front of the team's marquee, watching the crowd, while trying to settle their own nerves. When they saw the golem approach John hugged Catalina tightly, kissed her forehead, and joined Kingston. Joanna peeled off and went inside the marquee with Catalina to entertain the sponsors, and she fired off one last look of hope to Kingston, as he, John, Rufus, and Mortimer headed to the combatant's entrance of the arena.

The tunnel was excessively large, no doubt to accommodate even the most ridiculous of entrants, and one of the referees guided Kingston to their player's booth.

"How long do we have?" Kingston asked.

"There's been a delay with one of the first teams," said the referee. "If they're not here in half an hour, you'll be up first. You'll have a ten minute warning."

Rufus spluttered. "We're not supposed to be on for another hour and a half!"

The referee stared back at Rufus. "Be prepared to fight in forty minutes. We may have to bump the teams in the first round of the day to the last round of the day." The referee smiled weakly at Rufus, then he beamed a grin at Kingston. "Good luck." He lingered for a moment, hopeful for what may have been a tip, and Kingston knew the guy was looking for any advice to help place a bet for himself, which was no doubt illegal.

Kingston gave his thanks as the referee walked away, and he looked around their player's booth. It was a small room with a Tuscan painted wall and a large glass window where they could see out into the arena. John peered through the window and saw the other teams preparing themselves in their booths.

Kingston looked back to Rufus and John. "Right! Let's assume we're on in forty minutes. Is Mortimer going to be ready?"

"Well, that's the thing," said Rufus. "It takes twenty minutes to charge him up to full power, into a berserker frenzy, if you will. But we only have enough Helix's Gambit for a single charge. So how do you like your gambles, *Mr K*?" Rufus smirked.

"You can call me Kingston," said Kingston.

"Glad to hear. So what happens? Do we start to power up Mortimer in twenty minutes, or do we hope that the tardy team actually arrives on time?"

Kingston pulled out a sheet of parchment and quickly scribbled a note to Jezebel, and one to Joanna, trying to find out who the delayed team was and if they could be stalled. He dropped the letters into the air and they shot into the ether.

"That's not going to work when we're fighting. There will be a lock on us to prevent anyone from dropping, say, a smoke bomb into our booth."

John arched an eyebrow at Rufus. "They do that?"

"They'll try," said Rufus.

"Then Joanna better get back to me quickly," said Kingston.

John pulled out his copy of *The Art of War* and flipped to one of the highlighted pages.

"Any more pearls of wisdom?" asked Rufus.

"Yes," said John. "Bait the enemy to lure them away from their strong position. Feign disorder, then crush him."

"And how would you do that against, say, a teleporting anvil?"

John smacked his lips together and thought that one over. "Punch him."

"Punch him?"

"Punch him," said John.

Rufus shook his head. "According to Tally Ho you would set up a decoy. Let the anvil destroy that while your real machine is hiding somewhere else."

"How do you hide in the arena?"

Rufus shrugged. "Makes about as much sense as punching him when there's half an arena worth of locked doors between us."

Ten minutes later, the first note bounced back, and it was from Joanna.

'Every team today has already arrived. There doesn't seem to be a delay.'

"Crap," said Kingston. He hurried out of the room and went to find someone who knew what was going on, and he caught sight of that referee. "Hey! So, what's going on? Who's holding us up?"

The referee looked up, panicked. "No one. I mean ... the Wayne team aren't here yet. They're making an appeal."

Kingston squinted at the referee and knew there was something else happening. "I need to speak with your boss."

The referee pulled his shoulders back and in a squeaky voice he called out: "All team members must wait in their designated player's booths until such as time as -"

"Yeah, yeah, I can't keep my builder sane without knowing when we're actually going to be out there."

The referee tried again. "Sir, all team members must wait -"

"In their designated player's booth, I get it," said Kingston. "Are we actually competing in half an hour or not?"

The referee looked around nervously and dropped into a whisper. "No official decision has been made."

Kingston sighed and shook his head. "Will you let me know when one has been made?"

"I can in twenty minutes," said the referee.

"Lovely," said Kingston, and he walked back to their booth. "We're being dicked around," said Kingston.

"Oh, great," said Rufus. "Our referee is on the job. Figures."

John grimaced. "We should scare him into telling us the truth."

Kingston thought it over for a second and wondered if John was on to something. "Hang on," said Kingston, and he hunted down the referee again.

"Please, sir ..." begged the referee.

"Easy does it," said Kingston, calmly. "I'm wondering something. Are you actually telling me the truth, but acting as though it's a lie?" He studied the referee closely, and within a blink he had him.

"Sir, I ..."

"It's okay," said Kingston, with a smile. "I'll take your words at face value."

"I haven't lied," said the referee.

"I actually believe you," said Kingston. There was a sudden blast from just outside the arena, and Kingston's heart stopped in an instant. Then he looked back and realised it couldn't have come from Mortimer, but instead came from the combatant's entrance. There were shouts and cries of sabotage. The referee's jaw dropped open and he turned slowly towards Kingston, now suspicious.

"I'll let you get back to your job," said Kingston, and he hurried to his booth. The moment he burst into the room he spun and slammed the door shut.

"Was that you?" John asked.

"No, I -" A letter burst into the air right in front of Kingston and landed at his feet. "I was afraid of exactly that happening while standing in front of a referee." He bent down and picked up the letter. It was written in Jezebel's scrawl.

'Wayne's team will be somewhat delayed.'

Kingston beamed a smile at Rufus. "Get ready to fire up Mortimer!"

"If you like," said Rufus.

Soon enough, the senior referee knocked on the door and stepped into the room. "There has been a change of plan in today's schedule. You and the other teams in your division will compete first. You have ten minutes." He left, and Rufus sighed with relief.

A moment later, another letter appeared from Joanna.

'They've announced that you're going first. Not all of our sponsors are here yet.'

'Get ready to cheer us on!' wrote Kingston.

The young referee returned. "Gentlemen, in four minutes I will need you to move out into the main corridor and take your position on the arena floor. You will have five minutes there for final preparations."

The burst of adrenaline started to hit Kingston. He looked over and saw John beaming with a grin. Rufus still looked uncertain.

"Oh, come on you little man!" cried John. "This is it! This is when your greatest creation will prove itself to the world!"

Rufus patted Mortimer gently. "He's going to get smooshed."

John rolled his eyes. "The words of a pessimist, ladies and gentlemen."

When the referee returned, he nodded nervously towards Kingston. "It's time. Please take your place in the arena."

Rufus looked up to Mortimer. "Follow me." Mortimer glanced down at his maker, and lumbered into the corridor.

Kingston led the way and could feel the tremors through the building as more than a hundred thousand spectators moved, talked, and chanted their way to a spectacle. There was a final pair of doors down a short flight of stairs, and Kingston came to a stop. Rufus did as well, and Mortimer stood tall, with the giant hammer in his fist. John stepped around and took one last look at the golem.

"Make us proud, Pinky."

Rufus gritted his teeth. "He's not called Pinky."

John shrugged with a smile. "I'm trying to inspire some aggression into him."

Rufus checked his watch. "In four and a half minutes he won't need any inspiring."

"Just how berserk will he go?" Kingston asked.

"Hard to say, given the unusual mix of enchantments and ingredients from differing realms," said Rufus, while he glared at Kingston. "Right now the best he can do is walk. *Maybe* even jog. But from what we saw yesterday he would have no chance of out-running a cannon, car, or scorpion. And the whole point of the chain whip was so that he could drag the opposition towards himself and smash it like a watermelon. But with what he's got in him right now? Who the hell knows?"

Mortimer jerked and his two hands began to tremble.

That caught Kingston by surprise and it did little to steady his nerves. "He's not going to explode, will he?"

Rufus shook his head. "Nah, that's Helix's Gambit kicking in. Besides, we all have to follow the safety guidelines and place some fail safes in there. The moment you see blue flames coming from him, leg it, because that's when he *will* explode."

Mortimer trembled again, looked up at the pair of doors in front of him, and stepped forward.

"STOP!" cried Rufus, but Mortimer ignored him and swung both arms out to push the doors open. Since he was also wielding a mighty war hammer, the doors simply blew off their hinges, and Mortimer stepped out into the arena.

"I said stop!" shouted Rufus.

The moment the crowd of a hundred and twenty thousand spectators saw Mortimer smash his way into the arena they roared in excitement.

"It's not time!" shouted Rufus. He turned back to Kingston. "He's not ready. If we go out too early we'll be fined."

Kingston laughed at the state of the doors and knew there was nothing he could do. He looked out and saw Mortimer stop three metres from the door, where he would have to wait for another five minutes. He was the first one into the arena and the crowd loved every second of it.

The young referee hurried forward and saw the state of the doors. "Hey! What ... what's going on? It's not time yet!"

"Our golem thought it was," said John. "And what's the use in waiting?"

The referee spluttered. "I'll have to write this one up."

Kingston turned on the charm and smiled at the referee. "What's your name?"

The referee blinked nervously, now wondering if he was about to get in trouble. "Kenneth."

"Well Kenneth, have you ever met Joanna York?"

Kenneth turned his head, now confused. "No."

"Would you like to?"

Kenneth was still confused. "Uh ... sure?"

"I'll see what I can do," said Kingston. He dug into his pocket and wrote a note to Joanna, dropped it into the air, and a moment later received his reply. "Read this, if you will," said Kingston.

Kenneth unfolded the note and spluttered in surprise. Kingston had written: *'Kenneth, our referee, would like to meet you sometime.'* To which Joanna responded with: *'Damn it Kingston, you know how I love those uniforms!'*

Kenneth grinned dopily.

The trumpets sounded and a buzz came from the hinges of the doors, which would presumably open them to the arena. Sure enough Kingston could now see Lawnston, Milliara, and Kazuka heading out in the arena.

"Five minutes," said Kenneth, and he stepped away.

Kingston went out and joined Mortimer, then he waved to the crowd of thousands. John headed out as well and the cheers erupted even higher, as the man who destroyed the minotaur was once again in front of his people. Rufus remained in the corridor, hiding. He pulled out his headset with a microphone and stared at his portable panel of buttons.

Kingston looked across at the other teams and saw the two from Hell death staring him. There was no mistaking who they were gunning for. The countdown timer started, and everyone could see Mortimer tremble with energy. He took one step forward and Rufus had to run out to stop him.

"Wait! Wait! Not until I say so!" He hurried to place his headphones on and get everything set up.

Mortimer stopped, but he looked as though he wanted to charge into the fray immediately.

"Wait!" Rufus shouted again.

Kingston looked up to the crowd and saw everyone with their

eyes fixed in his direction. He never had that many people paying such close attention to him before, and it was still a new experience to get used to. But they loved seeing Mortimer as something of a rabid animal, uncontrolled and anti-authoritarian.

Rufus clicked a button on his headset. "Wait!" he shouted, and Mortimer paused, rose up, and ... waited. "Step back," Rufus said, and Mortimer stepped back to his original spot. "Good."

Kenneth peered out into the arena. "I advise you all to step back inside, please, and take your places in the player's booth."

John nodded to Kingston. "That's my cue." John ducked inside to make sure no one was going to sneak in and ambush them.

"Rufus? Time to hide," said Kingston.

Rufus was caught staring at Mortimer, and he knew it would be the last time he would ever see the golem undamaged. "He's about to hit full on berserker, you know."

"If he's anything like John then we're in for quite the show."

Kingston and Rufus followed John into the competitor's booth and closed the door. The large timer counted away the seconds.

Rufus covered his microphone. "Do we have any particular opponent to go after, money wise?"

"Milliara," said Kingston. "Avoid Lawnston at all costs so that he becomes enraged."

"What about Kazuka?"

"Don't hassle him. Focus on Milliara."

Rufus clicked a button and went back to talking to Mortimer. "Focus on Milliara." Mortimer turned in the right direction, and Rufus saw through his screen that Mortimer was looking at the right team. "Good. Focus on that one."

John watched the timer tick towards the ten second mark and he beamed a smile at Kingston. "This is going to be awesome!"

The trumpets sounded and the crowd erupted.

"NOW!" Rufus shouted.

Mortimer broke into a jog, which was far from the berserker-like sprint that Kingston was hoping for, but he had to remember that Mortimer now weighed three hundred and fifty kilos, so perhaps that was as fast as he was capable of going. Meanwhile, Milliara had the foresight that Mortimer was going after his team first, and his machine – an enchanted anvil – teleported away ... and appeared right above Kazuka's barrel. The barrel was already charging towards Lawnston's minotaur, and the anvil thudded into the ground. The minotaur, to no one's surprise, raced across the arena to take on Mortimer. The anvil continued to teleport in and out of the arena, trying to predict where Kazuka's barrel was going to be, but the barrel zigzagged about and jumped into the air to change direction.

Rufus looked back to Kingston for guidance.

"Stay on the anvil," said Kingston.

"We'll never catch him," said Rufus.

"Stay – on – the – anvil."

It was obvious that Milliara and Lawnston were united in not taking on each other. All the while, Mortimer got closer to the barrel, which was getting closer to the minotaur, which was getting closer to Mortimer, and the anvil kept dropping in and out of the air.

"Smash the minotaur," said John. He gave Kingston a serious nod. "We won't be able to get to the anvil until that barrel is gone, and that barrel won't stay in one place until the minotaur is dusted."

"This is where the whip would come in handy," said Rufus.

Mortimer continued chasing after the barrel and he swiped the air above it. As soon as Kazuka realised that Mortimer was not trying to smash his barrel to pieces, Kazuka took a gamble, and Kingston saw it.

"He's pausing," said Kingston. "Get ready to smash!"

"Smash the barrel!" shouted Rufus.

"NO! The anvil!"

"PULL BACK!" shouted Rufus quickly. "Hit the anvil!"

Mortimer jerked back and forth. The minotaur ducked its head down and bull rushed Mortimer. At the last second, the anvil appeared above the barrel just as Mortimer swung his mighty war hammer, and connected. The anvil shot off at an angle, teleported to safety, and reappeared over the barrel once more.

The minotaur slammed into Mortimer and the two crashed to the ground in a heap.

"Punch him!" shouted John.

Mortimer swung his arm around and hit the minotaur in the side of the head.

"Again!" shouted John.

"Stand!" shouted Rufus.

In a brief second Kingston saw everything turn to disaster.

Kazuka's barrel sped in and the moment it reached the tangled mess of Mortimer and the minotaur it exploded in a burst of fiery light.

Kaboom!

Black and blue smoke billowed out from the centre of the arena, and a hundred thousand people jerked out of the way as metal legs and arms skidded across the floor. There was a single flash of light from within the smoke, and the anvil dropped down into the wreckage. It disappeared again and continued teleporting in and out, striking the same spot over and over again.

Kingston's jaw dropped open. John's eyes were as wide as ever. Only Rufus maintained a look of expectant resignation. He glanced down at his control panel and a single blue light was showing.

"Well ... yeah," said Rufus.

John blinked in utter shock. "What the hell just happened?"

Rufus flicked a couple of switches, but nothing worked. "We've lost him."

"Wha ...?" cried Kingston, and he turned around in disbelief. "Just like that?"

Rufus shrugged. "I gotta hand it to Kazuka. He took out two teams at once. Well technically three, because it looks as though his is gone as well, but that will count as two solid victories towards him, and a definite loss for us."

The anvil kept teleporting in and out, trying to finish whatever remained of the debris in the middle of the arena.

"Is there something we can do?" John asked.

Rufus shook his head.

"Can you make him stand?" John asked.

Rufus sighed and spoke into his microphone. "Mortimer? Stand."

The three of them looked out the window, but all they could see was the plume of smoke from three destroyed machines, and an anvil continuing to smack the remains into obscurity.

"Nothing," said Rufus.

"The whole thing was over in just thirty seconds!" cried John.

"Yep," said Rufus.

Kingston glanced over to one of the screens showing the results. It flashed with an update, with three team names scratched out.

~~Rufus~~ - *Kazuka*

~~Lawnston~~ - *Kazuka*

~~Kazuka~~ – *critical failure*

"What?" cried Kingston. "No!"

"Yep," said Rufus.

"But ..."

"Nope."

"Isn't there ..."

"No."

"Why the hell not?"

Rufus sighed and shook his head. "Nineteen tournaments. Nineteen stupid tournaments."

Kingston stared up at the screen. "Why are we first when Kazuka blew himself up?"

"Because he did the wrecking, and we were the ones who got wrecked," said Rufus.

"And we're out first?"

"It appears so," said Rufus. "If we had gone after the minotaur we could have crushed him and allowed the other two to fight it out, or wait for an opportunity to take out that anvil."

Kingston stared back into the wreckage and felt his heart sink. There went an eight thousand gold piece investment. He had also just lost a thousand gold pieces in gambling.

The screen updated itself and Milliara was declared the winner. The anvil stopped attacking the ruins of three teams and the crowd clapped in disgruntled applause.

Kenneth reappeared. "If you gentlemen could wait here please, we need to make sure the arena is safe before you retrieve your combatant."

Kingston mumbled in quiet defeat and he couldn't take his eyes off the wreckage.

"Cheer up," said Rufus. "We have three more rounds to go, and we have sponsors who will want to see you. Maybe now's a good time to sell a few t-shirts."

Kingston shook his head in disbelief.

Rufus peered back at Kingston. "I thought you would now be in your element. Don't the English feed off disappointment?"

"Shut up," said Kingston.

XVI

John hauled the remains of Mortimer back to the bank in a rickshaw, and Rufus was finally able to assess the damage. He picked through the disjointed scraps of metal and shook his head, then consulted his list of enchantments and marked off everything that was broken or salvageable. Two hours later, Rufus returned to Kingston, Joanna, John, Catalina, and Jezebel.

"How bad is it?" asked Kingston.

"Dire," said Rufus. "The war hammer is undamaged. Everything else is pretty much smashed beyond recognition. The enchantments holding the armour together didn't fail, it was the armour itself. I can fix that, but the joints will need to be remade from scratch. That's going to take some time, about a month, actually."

Joanna raised her eyebrows. "Round two begins in five days."

"Yep," said Rufus. "So it's time to pull out all of the stops. Whatever trickery you lot usually get up to, it's time to do it." He glanced over Jezebel and wasn't sure if she knew that Kingston and the others had acquired most of their goods from Fiction, so he kept his conversation as nondescript as possible. "I'll get working on the second half of the whip while you lot get busy. You know, the half of the whip that I expect will actually work with whatever you have hiding in the vault."

Kingston and Joanna nodded and knew what he was talking about. Jezebel squinted suspiciously at the pair.

"We need to find an open door," said John.

The crowd slow turned to stare at him.

John nodded enthusiastically and pulled out his mangled copy of *The Art of War.* "Probably metaphorically speaking, but if the enemy leaves a door open you must rush in. So, we need to find that opportunity. If everyone has a common weakness then we can exploit that."

Rufus shook his head. "Couldn't you just close the door and keep it safely between you, instead of rushing in?"

"That kind of strategy doesn't win a fight," said John.

Catalina gently patted John on the hand. "Can I read that book when you're done?"

"Of course!"

"We better get going then," said Kingston.

"Wait," said Rufus. "You'll need to get a loan from the bank."

Kingston glanced over to Jezebel and smiled weakly at her.

She sighed and shook her head in resignation. "Fine, I'll leave you lot to have your private conversations. But I do follow people and find things out for myself you know, and we are all on the same team." She headed out the door.

Kingston turned back to Rufus. "Why do I need a loan?"

Rufus stared back at Kingston as though it was the most obvious answer in the world. "If you go through the next three rounds without needing a single loan from the bank people will become suspicious. They'll know you're cheating."

"Everyone's already cheating," said Kingston.

"Yes, but you have to appear as though you are *not* cheating, that's the point."

Joanna nodded at Kingston. "You can always funnel it into the sponsor's haul and claim that you've received thousands of gold pieces already. That might inspire more people to our side of the tournament."

Rufus shrugged. "And either way you can gamble that money away. I doubt you'll be able to sell anything fictional, though."

Kingston gave it some thought and he didn't like how much this was costing him. "Can you strip all of the real material from Mortimer and leave the fictional behind?"

Rufus rolled his eyes. "Amateur. I have a brain unit in there that's a hundred years old and took months to build. I have the eye piece and internal mechanics from a projector built in Limbo. I have the shell of a ship fashioned into the armour for the body, and you think I can strip all of that away and have a working fighter on my hands?"

"Yeah," said Kingston. "Because we could probably get you an entire robot."

"I don't need an entire robot, I need something that actually works in this realm."

"Kingston might be onto something," said Joanna. "The other teams will need spare parts. If we sell what we have from Mortimer that we don't need and get you an actual robot, or even an actual golem from some other story, then we'll have something that will work and we can recoup a little money on the side."

Rufus glared at the both of them. "I don't want an entire robot, because it won't work properly."

"We're supposed to cheat, aren't we?" asked Kingston.

"Yes, but -"

"And this will show that we are cheating better than the rest."

"Maybe, but -"

"Then it's settled," said Kingston. "We'll get you everything you need, you strip out everything that's real, I'll get a loan and fake the money trail, and in five days we'll have a new and improved Mortimer ready for the arena."

Rufus shook his head and held his hands out to stop Kingston and Joanna from hurrying off. "The other teams will know something is going on. They know I have only just started building Mortimer, so to come along with a brand new Mortimer with only the supplies to build one, then they'll know. If I had ten years to plan this, then yes, it's possible that no one would raise too many suspicions, but this? This is madness."

"Oh pish," said Joanna. "If you're going to cheat, you might as well *really* cheat."

"Exactly," said Kingston.

"Then he has to look identical to old Mortimer," said Rufus.

"We'll find something."

"In just five days?"

"We are *very* good at stealing," said Kingston. He then beamed a smile at Joanna. "My darling, care to raid Fiction one more time?"

"Anything for you, dear," she said, and they headed back to the surface of Limbo, leaving Rufus to almost tear his hair out.

Word soon spread that Kingston had been forced to take out another ten thousand gold loan, and that he spent it frivolously on parties and functions. The truth was that instead of lavish get-togethers he had funnelled the money through the Cascade to help make some kind of return on their investment. Then while Kingston and Joanna were, again, fighting meerkats and vultures in Fiction, Rufus was stripping back all that he could from Mortimer.

After another gruelling session of hunting down the strangest of shopping lists, Kingston returned and dumped a chest of goods for Rufus to rummage through. Rufus went straight to the joints, fashioned from the finest of graphene, and he turned them over in his hands.

"Well?" asked Kingston.

"They look good, but do they actually work?" asked Rufus.

"Of course they work! You have two complete feet and ankles, two knees right there, a pelvis, shoulders, elbows, wrists, and a neck."

"But will they work with my enchantments?" Rufus asked.

"No idea," said Kingston. "But we don't have long to find out."

"In that case maybe we shouldn't sell the old Mortimer just yet, in case what you have here is nothing but a complete waste of time. And what about this new fandangled projector?"

"We're working on it," said Kingston.

Pop.

Kingston and Joanna reappeared in their office on Anubis, dumped the chest of machine parts, and heaved with a resounding sigh. They stared at each other for a moment, looked over their soaked clothes, and burst into laughter.

"Okay," said Joanna. "Science fiction from 1920 was kinda messed up."

"You're telling me, but if there was any other way of getting a brand new hundred year old film projector I'm sure it would have been more difficult."

"You didn't even haggle with the guy," said Joanna.

Kingston stared at Joanna as though she had grown a second head. "We're *never* going to see him again!"

Joanna crossed her arms. "You could've haggled."

"We didn't even pay him! We just stole it!"

Joanna shrugged and looked away. "He was into me. We could've bargained a little."

"Well, everyone loves the charm of Joanna York," muttered Kingston.

Joanna grinned at Kingston. "Oooo, you're mad at me. You only use my last name when you're in a mood."

"The hell? I used to call you 'York' all the time."

"Yeah, and then you fell in love and started calling me Joanna."

Kingston stepped in closer, so that his nose was almost touching Joanna's forehead. "So, Miss Joanna Charlotte Deveraux York, what's on my mind right now?"

Joanna looked into Kingston's eyes and winked at him. "Would it have something to do with a one track mind?"

"Well, you are my good lady wife."

Joanna reeled back and her eyes almost shot out of her head. "WHAT?"

Kingston smirked at her. "You heard me."

They were interrupted by a slight tap on their office door.

"We are by no means done," said Joanna.

Kingston stepped to the front door and called out. "Who is it?"

"Montgomery," came the voice.

Kingston sighed and shook his head. "Now is not a good time."

The door flew off its hinges, bounced against Kingston's shoulder, and the piercing shriek from the alarm nearly deafened everyone in the building. Kingston scrambled back and nearly tripped over the trunk. Two large men stepped inside and glared at Kingston and Joanna.

"That's some alarm you have there," muttered one of the brutes.

Montgomery Stup nervously followed them inside. He caught sight of Kingston and Joanna and hung his head. "I'm sorry," he mumbled.

Kingston stood up and composed himself. "You okay?"

"Shut it!" shouted one of the goons.

Kingston didn't take his eyes off Montgomery. "Seriously, are you okay?"

"They forced me to," said Montgomery.

"Oi!" shouted the other brute. "We're not here so you two can catch up."

"No, you're here to accept a bribe," said Kingston, smiling at the two men. "I recognise you from Lawnston's team."

"Oh, do you now?" He looked around the office and his eyes fell over the trunk. "Nice office."

"Actually you've caught us in the middle of renovating. We were just having a word about where best to rearrange the furniture. See, I think the desk is best when it's lying on one side at a weird angle against that wall over there, but my stylist here thinks it would be better thrown out the window."

Joanna nodded. "I really do. The desk is tacky and carries bad karma with it."

"I'm starting to see that too," said Kingston. "But I did like your suggestion of the sofa being used to barricade the door."

"Yes, that would have been useful to try out a few minutes ago," said Joanna.

"Shut up! Both of you!" shouted one of the brutes.

Kingston and Joanna obliged and stared at Lawnston's men.

The more talkative brute stepped forward and grinned at them. "Just so you know, we're here to rough you up a little bit." He smiled at his prey, then grew a little perturbed when Kingston and Joanna simply stared back at him. "This is usually when you lot start to beg, or try to reason with us."

Kingston and Joanna bobbed their heads in tandem and remained silent.

"You told them to shut up," whispered Montgomery.

The other goon spun around at Montgomery. "Hey! No one invited you into this conversation."

The first brute grinned at Kingston. "And we know your little friend's hammer is just going to shatter the moment he uses it. We know a thing or two about these things."

Kingston and Joanna rolled their eyes at each other.

"A thing or two about these things?" said Joanna. "Man alive, am I judging you right now."

"Yeah," grinned the brute. "I like it when people get all smartassy with me. Get's me fired up."

Kingston leaned to one side and glared at the brute. "Did you just threaten to hit my girlfriend?"

"I'm working my way to it, yeah," said the brute.

"You're seriously going to hit a woman?"

"It's an equal world," said the brute. "You can't hit a man and then hold back against a woman. That isn't right."

Joanna edged her hand towards Kingston's and gripped onto one his fingers. Kingston smiled and readied himself for another retort. Then Joanna's expression dropped.

"Ah, good, she's starting to figure it out," said the brute, and he looked over to his friend.

"She was willing to run sooner than I expected," said the goon.

"We've put a lock on the room. No teleporting in or out," said the brute.

Kingston glanced over to Joanna and sighed. Their quick and painless escape had just been crushed. He looked back to the brute. "Just so you know, there's no point in stealing the chest. You'll never get it open."

"Oh, I think we could manage that," said the brute.

"I'm not so sure. You need a key to open it."

The brute snorted. "We have magic at our disposal, we can get around some stupid lock."

"But this one came with a guarantee," said Kingston. "It was made by Houdini himself."

Montgomery Stup looked around in surprise. "Really?"

"No, you idiot, I'm making this up as a way to distract this moron," said Kingston. He rolled his eyes and grunted. "For crying out loud. I mean, you two have done this before, right? You've threatened people, you've beaten them up?"

The goons snorted. "Oh yeah, it's kind of our thing."

"And Charlotte Deveraux here has seen a few of them as well, so we're all seasoned professionals here except for your guide over there. So really, did either of you think that I was telling the truth about the chest?"

The brute shrugged. "I don't really care."

Kingston looked over to the other goon. "What about you? Was I at all convincing?"

"Against a lock? No."

"And then Montgomery Stup has to go and ruin the whole charade. Bravo."

The brute arched his eyebrow at Kingston. "You sure talk a lot."

"It's my thing," said Kingston. "I can not, however, take any responsibility for the misfortune you three find yourselves in when our giant comes along with his war hammer."

The brute shrugged. "Honestly, I'm looking forward to that."

Joanna glanced over to Kingston. "Do I have a thing?"

"You're the eye candy."

"*What?* I've *crippled* companies before. Big ones."

"Yeah, you did," grinned Kingston.

The brute stepped forward and thumped Kingston in the chest with one mighty finger. "I don't think you're taking this seriously."

"I can bribe you," said Kingston.

"No, you couldn't," said the brute.

"Sure I could. I can bribe anyone. Everyone has their price. And even though you're about to go back to Hell, and Limbo has no real worth to you, I'm sure I have something you could use. Maybe a new suit? New pants at least." Kingston looked the brute up and down. "You're standing really close to me."

"All the better to hit you with my d -"

Before he could finish the sentence, Joanna shot her foot out and kicked the brute in the shins with the front of her boot. Kingston saw the cue and did the same, taking out the brute's other shin. The brute cried out in pain, realised he was under attack and swung his arms out, but the moment he backed away the shock in his shins got the better of him and he stumbled backwards.

Joanna reached out, grabbed onto Kingston's hand, and tried to teleport them away, but it didn't work. Kingston reached back, picked up the ashtray sitting on his desk and hurled it into the face of the stumbling brute. The other one jumped the chest and charged across the room. As he landed one foot onto the ground, Joanna struck out again and kicked him in the shins as hard as she could. The sudden agony rushed up his leg and knocked him off course. He swung at Joanna but she ducked away. The moment she saw her opening she kicked him again in the same spot. Kingston did the same and hit the other leg, then he pulled one of John's framed paintings from off the wall and clobbered the goon over the head.

Kingston and Joanna scrambled out of the way but they were still pinned against the far wall. Montgomery stood in the doorway, realised he was in over his head, and ran for it.

Joanna glanced out the window. "We need a grappling hook."

"No kidding," said Kingston.

The two brutes stood themselves up, checked over their injuries, and stared at Kingston and Joanna with undulating hate.

Kingston threw his hands into the air in defence. "Believe it or not, I can still talk my way out of this."

The goon wasn't having any of it so he lunged at Kingston. Once again, Kingston and Joanna kicked him in the shins as hard as they could. The goon did get one decent punch against

Kingston's jaw, but the sudden kicks threw him off balance and he fell against the window, and for the briefest of moments he was stunned. Joanna kicked him again in the shins. Kingston did the same. Finally the agony was too much and the goon wasn't able to get to his feet again.

Kingston and Joanna scrambled behind the desk then hurried into the tea room. They pushed the sofa against the door to barricade it and swung the far end of the sofa around so that it was now pinned up against the far wall. They were met with violent thumps against the door as brute number two sounded like he was trying to break it down with first his fists, then with the trunk. Kingston and Joanna panted and braced themselves for another fight.

Joanna looked over to Kingston. "I don't want to say that we're trapped ..."

"Do you want to use the word 'inconvenienced' at all?"

"No," glared Joanna. She sighed and felt her pulse start to level out. "How's your jaw?"

"It hurts," said Kingston, and he winced as he assessed the damage. "I don't suppose we have an ice pack in here?"

"No," said Joanna. The thumping against the door continued. She rummaged around the small kitchenette and grabbed one of the tea towels, soaked it in cold water, and held it against Kingston's jaw. "Thank you for not letting me get hit," said Joanna.

Kingston smiled and shrugged it off. "I expected our retirement to be a little safer than this."

"Well, if I was in any more danger, I was about to drop them with the whole 'I'm pregnant' thing."

Kingston nodded for a moment then, as the words sunk in, he glanced over to Joanna.

Joanna met his reaction, but it wasn't what she expected. "What's that look?"

The banging against the door continued. "I was just wondering if that was possible in Limbo. I mean, we went to Fiction for a few days, back to our own world even, and ... you remember."

Joanna smirked at Kingston. "I'm not."

"I was just wondering if it was possible," said Kingston.

"And if I was?"

Kingston felt a thump in his chest that was well timed with the two goons banging against the door. "Are you?"

"No!" cried Joanna. "But if I was, what would you do?"

"You're kinda giving me mixed signals here, honey," said Kingston. He held out one hand and brought Joanna over to the far end of the room where it would safer in case that door suddenly broke open.

"And with any luck that alarm will get someone to rescue us in a hurry."

"Here's hoping." Kingston said, and the pain in his jaw started to spread.

Joanna squeezed Kingston's hand. "I'm not pregnant. It was just a line I was going to use on those two to distract them for half a second before I nailed them in the shins. But you just said we're retired, and you used to say that kids weren't in our future unless we retired. So ..."

"Ah," said Kingston. "Then I support this imaginary pregnancy whole heartedly."

"Good, because I'm -"

"Don't mess with me, York," said Kingston.

She smiled and kissed him on the lips.

"My good lady wife," said Kingston.

Joanna turned away and stiffened. "Well that was uncalled for."

Kingston snorted and glanced back to the doorway. The banging had stopped, and it was now replaced by the unmistakable sound of their office being completely trashed. When the goons got tired of that, they started pushing the furniture around and they heaved everything in front of the door.

"Sounds like we're being barricaded inside," said Joanna.

"Yep," said Kingston.

"Do they realise that as soon as they leave the block leaves with them and we can teleport out of here?"

"Well, they are kinda dumb," said Kingston. He then raised his eyes in surprise, hoping that they *would* leave, instead of forcing Kingston and Joanna to wait it out in that dinky little room. He looked over and saw that Joanna had the same unsettling thought. "Yeah," mumbled Kingston.

Joanna sighed and they fell into silence. After another minute of listening to their office being trashed, she looked over to Kingston. "How come you never call me Charlotte Deveraux any more?"

"Today was a slip of the tongue," he said. "Won't happen

again."

"Why not? I miss it."

Kingston ran his hand over his face and he felt the adrenaline fade away. "I had a whole speech prepared for you, once upon a time. A few days after getting the wording *just* right your full name became synonymous with a crushing level of heartbreak. Joanna York I could handle. The Charlotte Deveraux part of it was ..." he looked up to the ceiling to find the words, and gave up. "It was too much."

He found Joanna was staring at the ground, keeping an ear on the trashing going on in their office, but mostly she was doing her best not to break down in front of Kingston. She forced it all away and smiled back at her boyfriend. "So what happened today?"

Kingston shrugged. "Slip of the tongue."

"Are you sure? You slip those two names into it and the very next sentence you're calling me your good lady ... you know."

Kingston smiled back at her. "We just spent two days on our own, like good old times. We were chasing down information, breaking into places, trying to find all the bits and pieces needed for this stupid golem, and I got nostalgic. A couple of weeks ago when we did it for the first time, we hadn't done that together in years."

Joanna reached around and hugged Kingston tightly. "Are those two ever going to leave us in peace?"

"Well, you know as soon as they're gone we're going to have to steal another projector again."

"Remember to haggle."

Half an hour later, Kingston and Joanna heard the thundering boom of John's voice.

"Are you two in here?" John called out.

"Yes!" shouted Kingston. "We're okay."

"How's the office?" asked Joanna.

John paused, and finally found the right words. "You remember that rickshaw of ours? The one that was blown to smithereens?"

"Yeah?" grumbled Joanna.

"Well, the filing cabinet has been blown to smithereens. The desk? Smithereens. My paintings? Smithereens. And they've used one door to barricade the other. Hang on." John pushed the front door away and kicked over the pile of rubble pressed up against the interior door.

Kingston and Joanna pushed their sofa out of the way and they finally saw the state of their office. John caught sight of Kingston's face and whistled. "You feeling okay?"

"Sure," said Kingston. "We kicked them pretty hard."

John bobbed his head. "In the balls?"

"Shins."

"I would've kicked them in the balls."

"The shins are easier to kick, and most thugs try to swing with their fists, forgetting completely about decent footwork."

John shrugged. "Still ..."

Kingston looked across the debris and shook his head. "We're going to need to go and get another projector."

Joanna winced. "They're going to figure out that it's fictional."

John turned in surprise. "Oh, I should tell you, two other teams from Limbo have been beaten up."

Joanna shook her head at Kingston. "So what now? Get another projector or are you two going to seek your revenge?"

Kingston rummaged through the clutter on the floor. "They broke the ashtray."

John rolled his eyes. "Man, that's a relief."

"I was hoping they would steal it," said Kingston.

"Why?"

"It has a tracking agent on it. I could also listen in on what they were talking about," said Kingston.

John grinned and stretched out his arms. "Want me to bring Titan's cousin?"

"We need a projector," said Joanna.

Kingston looked back to his girlfriend and nodded. "Okay, battle plan. Joanna and I will go back to 1920, get another projector, potentially haggle or at the very least steal it, we'll come back here and meet in, say, half an hour. In that time, John? Go and get Titan."

"Not his cousin?" asked John.

"No, we better go with the real thing. Meet us here and then we'll go and see who broke our ashtray."

Half an hour later, John grinned as Kingston and Joanna popped back into existence. He picked up the mighty war hammer and swung it over his shoulder. "Ready?"

"We need to drop this off," said Kingston, and he pointed to the large chest at his feet.

"Tut tut," mumbled Jezebel. She poked her head into their office. "There's a better way to do things," she said.

John glanced over. "How long have you been standing there?"

She shrugged. "I followed you in. You were humming to yourself."

"What was I humming?"

"*Gonna smack some people, doo dee doo DOO doo.*"

John shrugged. "Yeah, that sounds like me."

Joanna looked over to Jezebel. "What's your way?"

"I know a guy. He has an anvil. It's not Milliara, but it's the same principle. For a hundred gold pieces he'll teleport his anvil onto Lawnston's minotaur during the final ten second countdown during the next round. Lawnston won't see it coming. It will look like Milliara broke the rules. The anvil will teleport away, Lawnston's minotaur will be pulverised, and Milliara will take the blame. No one will know it was us. All for a hundred gold pieces. Oh, and feel free to make a bet on Lawnston going out first in that round, and an investigation into Milliara. It also means that we don't get fined because, right now, Lawnston's team is surrounded by officials."

Kingston glanced over to Joanna and smiled at her.

"It's sneaky," said Joanna.

"Let's do it," said Kingston.

"Are there any drawbacks?" asked Joanna.

"Not really," said Jezebel. "But for another fifty gold he'll teleport the anvil and the minotaur away at the same time, but while the anvil goes back to him the minotaur will simply reappear a couple of hundred metres in the air and crash back onto the arena floor. Double dusted. What do you say?"

John snapped his fingers together. "That! I like that!"

"Me too," said Kingston.

"All for only one hundred and fifty gold pieces," said Jezebel.

"Haggle," whispered Joanna.

"There's no haggling here," said Jezebel. "Trust me. It's a straight up one fifty or nothing that all."

Kingston held a quick telepathic conversation with Joanna. Then he looked back to Jezebel. "What's your cut in all of this?"

"Ten percent," said Jezebel. "Plus whatever I make from the gambling house."

"I'll get you twenty gold worth of amber if you cut the price down by fifteen gold pieces," said Kingston.

Jezebel arched an eyebrow. "I can't sell fictional amber for real gold."

"Twenty two gold pieces worth," said Kingston.

"Is it still fictional?"

"Yes."

"No."

Joanna stepped forward. "How about twenty five gold pieces worth of clothes and dresses? And shoes?"

"Maybe even jewellery," said John.

Jezebel thought it over for a moment. "I want to swim with dolphins."

Kingston and Joanna glanced at each other for a moment and they shook their heads in confusion. "You what?"

Jezebel nodded. "I will drop my fee if you take me into Fiction so I can swim with dolphins. And I'd like a case of hundred year old scotch."

"We can do that," said Joanna.

"Then we have a deal," said Jezebel.

"Is there any chance your anvil friend would be willing to drop his price as well, also for a case of scotch?" asked Kingston.

"Perhaps," said Jezebel. "But if I make that offer I'm putting myself at risk of exposing some of our team secrets."

Kingston smirked. "And what would compensate this risk?"

"How about if we moved the dolphins over to this risk, and put something else in place of where the dolphins used to be?"

Kingston smiled at his devious little thief. "Such as?"

"I want to see the Earth from space."

Kingston snorted and couldn't believe the ridiculous idea that Jezebel presented, and then the reality of it sunk in.

John looked over. "Can I get in on that? Maybe even walk on the moon?"

Joanna glanced over to Kingston. "So, instead of saving ourselves fifteen gold pieces, we're now getting two cases of premium scotch, a swim with the dolphins, and a very complicated trip to space?"

Kingston sighed. "We can do two cases of scotch, a full wardrobe, and some jewellery."

"No dolphins?" asked Jezebel.

"Can we hold that for later?"

"And the space thing?"

"We have a situation where time is of the essence, and figuring out how to get us all into space, or swimming with dolphins, is a little too impractical when we need to cram as many minutes into the day as possible."

"But I'll still get a new wardrobe and scotch?" asked Jezebel.

"Yes. That is far less of a hassle than going into space where we might all die."

John quickly jumped in. "And can you find out why Fernando de Herrera is working on Aurelius' team?"

Jezebel slowly bobbed her head. "Sure. And, we have a deal."

XVII

The team were gathered around the blank sheet of parchment, waiting for the line up for the second round.

"Who are we betting on?" asked John.

"I have a hundred gold on another multiple melee, paying at three to two," said Kingston.

"So we don't want one team up against one other team?"

"Realistically we do, but betting wise? No."

John lowered his head and shook the nonsense away.

"I know," said Kingston. "We're betting on something that we don't want to actually happen."

"Meh," mumbled Rufus. "At least you'll be happy either way."

Jezebel stared at the parchment intently and sat up with glee. "Here it comes!"

The words slowly materialised into view.

Round Two
Kazuka v. Carver v. Scamp
Stuyvescent v. Foster v. Creig
Redding v. Urisha v. Semper

Puck v. Cove v. Horatio
Sequa v. Biggins v. Zamba
Jones v. Newell v. Sanders

Lawnston v. Caffrey v. Milliara
Aurelius v. Kwon v. Lucha
Bonaparte v. Rufus v. Wayne

"Huh," said John. "We're in the last match. That's good, right? That will buy us some more time to tinker with Mortimer?"

Rufus sighed. "We're up against Wayne and his twelve balls, presuming he comes in with twelve balls. He might have a hundred by then. Or one. Either way, that's going to take some time, and the turn around between round two and three isn't long."

Jezebel nodded. "Wayne took the approach, again, of evasion. He was able to tire out the other two teams and he made only periodic attempts to attack."

"Great," mumbled Kingston. "His strategy is to force the opponent to the point of exhaustion."

Joanna looked over her notes. "How did Bonaparte do in the last round?"

"Pretty good, actually," said Jezebel. "He came in with a wall of spinning spikes. Well, it was more like a barrel of spinning spikes. He's a miner down in Hell, so, go figure, he came in with a machine that digs tunnels. Probably stole it as well. He was up against Aurelius with the dragon, Creig with the tank who tried to take out the dragon at the unveiling, and Stuyvescent with Rufus' former machines. *That* was an epic match. Since none of them had any projectile components, Bonaparte just sat his machine down, spun the spikes around, and waited for people to come to him. Meanwhile, Aurelius, Creig, and Stuyvescent all fought each other. Stuyvescent got knocked sideways with the dragon's tail, was picked up and dropped onto Bonaparte's drum of spikes and was shredded, leaving Creig's tank and the dragon to smash it out for fifteen minutes. The dragon kept trying to do the same trick with the tank by picking it up and dropping it on the drum of spikes, but every time it tried the tank shuddered and the dragon lost its grip. Eventually the tank hit the ground so many times that it got damaged. By then the dragon lost use of one of its wings. Then, out of no-where, the barrel of spikes chased after the dragon. It couldn't catch up, and turned against the tank, and boy did it rip that thing to shreds. Bits of tank went flying in every direction, and while it was busy with that the dragon jumped up and smashed the barrel with its tail and shot it towards Bonaparte's team box. Smacked straight into the glass. Probably gave them all one hell of a scare in case that glass broke, and for a moment the barrel stopped spinning. The dragon ran after it, grabbed onto the spikes with its claws, and as the drum tried to speed up against the dragon resisted. The motor must have failed because two of the rows of spikes fizzled and blew. After another few whacks the dragon was able to get hold of the other two rows of spikes, and that killed the machine completely. The dragon was in pretty bad shape by the end of it. Its tail was lying in the middle of the arena, its wings were busted, and it lost the use of most of its claws, but it still won." She then looked over to John. "I did some digging into Aurelius' builders."

John flared his eyes as a telepathic signal to stop Jezebel from revealing too much in front of Catalina. Jezebel reacted to that look, which caused Catalina to see everything. She rolled her eyes.

"Really?" asked Catalina, and she shook her head.

John dropped his shoulders.

Jezebel grimaced. "I was just going to say that most of Aurelius' builders were trained in Limbo, and a lot of the trainers were former writers and artists, and they'd all meet together. When your contract is close to expiring sometimes you take on a job just to give yourself some options so that you're not just a one trick pony."

Kingston looked over the team and could feel the tension nearly burst. "So we have a wall of spikes that will wait for someone to attack it and a team of bouncy balls that avoids combat at all times."

"They won't expect the whip," said Rufus, though it was barely above a mumble.

"Does it work yet?" asked Kingston.

"We're getting there," said Rufus. "We should be up and running by the time we reach the arena."

"What's the hold up?" asked Joanna.

"Well, now that Lawnston knows about the projector I've had to work on a few fail safes against the gaming commission."

The team silently glanced at each other and then stared back at Rufus. John shook his head. "Huh?"

"Don't worry. If I give the signal, duck. In the meantime, new Mortimer has to be put through his paces."

"I kinda liked the old Mortimer," said Jezebel.

"It's still the same concept."

"But a completely different machine."

"It will look and act similar," said Rufus. "It still has the same enchantments, and most of the same internal mechanics. It's just the shell doesn't come from an old ship. It comes from ..." He turned to Kingston. "Where did it come from?"

"Norway," said Kingston.

John read over the line up and snorted. "Lawnston and Milliara are up against each other again."

"Ah," said Kingston. He felt their good fortune turn against them. "We have an anvil scheduled for Lawnston with the hope that Milliara was going to take the blame."

"Hmm," said Jezebel, and she realised it as well.

"Yeah," said Kingston. "So we have an anvil that is going to drop onto Lawnston's minotaur, in full view of the entire arena, and they're going to see that Milliara was not behind it."

John shrugged. "On the bright side, Lawnston still gets screwed."

"There is that, but I did also lay a fifty gold bet on Milliara being investigated for the anvil surprise."

Catalina shuddered. "You've just lost six weeks' worth of earnings?"

"Pretty much," said Kingston.

"At least he's doomed," said Jezebel. "And we have our revenge."

Joanna shrugged. "Let's hope no one tries the same trick on us."

"Don't worry," said Jezebel. "As soon as the referees realise what happened they'll put a teleport lock over the arena until it's game time, and since we're last we're going to be okay. Besides, Lawnston's brutes have terrorised half the teams in Limbo, so no one will know that it was us. We'll be doing everyone a favour." She looked over the rest of the line up. "Aurelius up against Kwon. I'm definitely watching that."

"They're just before us," said Kingston.

"Then we should get to the arena early," said Jezebel, and she beamed with a smile.

Kingston turned to the betting guide and consulted his notes. "Any ideas?"

"Aurelius to win, certainly," said Rufus. "He has the money to pull it off."

"And in our match?" asked Kingston.

"We're going to have a problem with Mortimer as a berserker," said Rufus. "Going after a dozen balls is going to be really confusing and it will tire him out."

"Then don't let him go berserk," said John.

"It's just ... when he's enraged that might actually draw out a few more sponsors, otherwise it would be boring."

Kingston thought it over and knew he was going to have to trust his builder more than ever right now. "Are you absolutely sure that you can get the whip up and working by the time we're in the arena?"

"I think so," said Rufus. "Either way, I'll know one hour before we have to leave. Ideally you could have hired me a year ago and we would have avoided most of this mess with a little more preparation."

"Well, we didn't know each other a year ago," said Kingston.

"And there went a beautiful friendship," mumbled Rufus.

The gossip was rife through the realm. So far Rose and Gibbs had both of their machines sabotaged beyond repair and they were forced into forfeiting for the rest of the tournament. They had even sold their machines to the rivals to recoup some of their money. Booker Newell's thief had been arrested for breaking into Horatio's workshop. Foster had been punched out several times by Lawnston's brutes, even though those two teams were never directly competing against each other. All of the teams from Hell were under investigation for cheating. Puck had been fined for trying to bribe one of the gaming officials. Carmen Lucha and Urisha, both from Limbo, had been fined for match fixing, then for accepting a bribe, then for not reporting an attempted bribe.

The news from Roger and his fantasy tournament league wasn't all that encouraging either. Even Kingston could see that the only strategy in defeating Bonaparte and Wayne was to be the aggressive one while the other two would remain as defensive as possible. Apparently all Kingston had to do was roll a whole lotta twenties on the dice, but that was hardly going to help him win the actual match in the real arena.

The team worked around the clock to ensure that Mortimer would be back up and running by the start of round two, but as the hours tumbled towards their match Kingston knew that he and Joanna had to get back into the real world to earn a little more gold. That left John and Catalina to help the increasingly grumpy Rufus, who had the worst luck of being locked in the bathroom.

"Help! Someone's enchanted the door and I can't get out!"

That led to a desperate need for revenge, and Jezebel was sent out to stink-bomb several of the other builders at random.

Then one day it rained in Rufus' workshop.

"I don't think this is normal," said John, as he stared up at the ceiling.

"Clearly you haven't played in a tournament before," said Rufus, and he tried to work in the rain. He glanced around the work bench. "Where did you put the pliers?"

"I didn't touch them."

"They were right there."

John looked over to where Rufus was pointing. "I didn't move them."

Rufus stared back in horror. "Seal the bank! We have a thief on the loose!" Rufus ran to the door and expected to charge straight into the corridor, but the door was locked and enchanted, causing Rufus to slam into it at full speed.

"That was unexpected," said John.

"Break the door open!"

After getting rid of the rain and drying himself off, Rufus refused to get back to work until he had a few shots of whiskey in him to relieve the stress of being back in the Games. Then he had to put up with a very drunk Simon who was determined to argue the merits of the traditional rendition of *Auld Lang Syne*.

"Ma Simon! Will you stop with ma singing so I can drink ma drink in ma peace and you can go back to that stupid ma cat and keep an eye on anyone who comes down here who wants to sabotage ma stuff!"

"Ah can try," muttered Simon.

Catalina grimaced at the two and she looked over to John. "You're just lucky my classes were put on hold during the Games, otherwise I'd be too busy to help you lot."

"We're very lucky, babe," said John. "How about, no matter what happens, you and I celebrate the end of round two?"

Catalina bobbed up and down as she toyed with the idea. "Can we go dancing?"

"Of course!" John then took a moment to think that one through. "We may need to ask someone where we can go dancing, though."

Catalina slumped a little in her posture, sure that John had just deflated her great idea. "Okay."

John saw that look and knew he had to act fast, but no matter what he considered he kept thinking back to Catalina hiding the fact that she was secretly talking to Fernando the statue, although that secret was now likely blown out of the water. For once John started to appreciate how secrets between couples could build, and he just couldn't figure out a way to tell Catalina he knew without sounding like he had been spying on her.

Rufus stumbled out of the workshop with an old mug and a plate full of crumbs. "Less chat, more work," he said, and he headed into the small kitchen.

John swept Catalina into his arms and planted an enormous kiss right on her forehead.

She squealed in shock. "Ew! Right on my forehead?"

"Yep! Right on your dainty little forehead."

They were interrupted by a cry of frustration coming from the room nearby. Rufus stepped out into the corridor, stared back at John and Catalina, and grumbled. "Well, our morning tea has been disrupted because Mr Singalot decided to be a bit cavalier with the margarine."

John stared back at Rufus. "I did what?"

"Simon. Not you."

"Oh. Then you may carry on."

Rufus shuddered and went back to the kitchen. "Where is that requisition form? Maybe we can hire a janitor who actually does some work around here!"

John looked back to Catalina. "Maybe in the next Games we'll build a catapult and insist that there is only one proper way for a builder to test it."

Catalina arched her eyebrows in surprise. "You mean we're going to enter the next Games as well?"

John did a quick check of Catalina's reaction and knew that he was dicing his way towards disaster. "Well, no one has talked about it yet ... it was just a joke."

Catalina looked away in shock. "Are those two serious?"

"By 'those two', do you mean Kingston and Joanna?"

"Yes," said Catalina.

"Well, like I said, no one has talked about it."

"You also said 'yet.'"

John nodded. "I feel like there's no right answer here."

"Promise me that you and I will not be involved in the next

Games."

"Babe, come on."

"Promise me," said Catalina, and her eyes spoke with years of pleading. "Please? I love those two, but they're insane! They get caught up in these crazy ideas and everything in their past ended up working out for the best ... but that was before they actually lived in reality. Does no one else see they are running head first into disaster?"

"I see it," said John.

"And you can't stop them?"

John wasn't able to offer more than a shrug. "There's a chance it might actually work out."

They heard Simon singing to himself again, at which point Rufus nearly screamed from the other room. "Simon! Please ... singing is not something you are remotely good at!"

Catalina looked back to John, then stepped away. "When do they come back?"

John checked the time. "They have another hour of rounding up donations and talking to sponsors."

"Okay." She ducked into the kitchen and clapped her hands together. "Let's go Rufus! That whip isn't going to finish itself!"

An hour later, Kingston and Joanna stared at their dismal fortune.

Joanna smiled weakly at Kingston. "I guess, really, twenty two gold pieces is a good haul."

"It might help if we had some cheerleaders."

"I've met cheerleaders. We're better off without them."

Kingston peered at Joanna with surprise. "Jeez, what kind of school did you go to?"

"A bitchy one," said Joanna. "And by now they're all fat and pregnant."

The third day of round two was upon them and Rufus had spent the night scrambling to get everything ready. Jezebel had kept him going with coffee while Simon was able to lend some kind of support by not appearing at all, which suited Rufus just fine.

Kingston and Joanna had spent the previous bouts in their marquee, entertaining their sponsors and picking up some advice on how to handle their opponents, and everyone was eager to see a little more from Mortimer this time, compared to the last round when he exploded spectacularly as a result of Lawnston and Kazuka getting close enough to do some actual damage.

They all watched the large screen as Lawnston, Caffrey, and Milliara guided their teams into the arena. Kingston did his best to keep his smile at bay. He knew that at any moment an illegal anvil would drop onto Lawnston's minotaur and crush it beyond recognition. The chatter in the marquee was at a minimum as no one had any particular preference for the three teams from Hell. It seemed like a sure thing that Milliara's teleporting anvil was going to win, especially with the help from Kingston's side of things, and Caffrey only participated in the tournament as an excuse to get up to Limbo and avoid Hell for a few hours.

The teams did their final checks and with one minute remaining they all hurried into their player booths, leaving their combatants alone in the arena.

"How long do you think it will last?" one of the sponsors asked another.

"Three minutes, tops."

Kingston had ten gold on the match lasting less than thirty seconds. He would have bet more but he was sure that Caffrey was trying to drag the match out for as long as possible. Being an incompetent builder had a few drawbacks, but he was certainly devious with his plans. He came along with a cluster of landmines. In order to beat him, the opponent would have to smash one of the landmines, which would trigger the explosion. In theory, Milliara was the only team that could win, but Caffrey was playing a long and simple game and had no need to update his strategy mid-fight.

With thirty seconds to go, Kingston paid close attention to the minotaur. Any second now an anvil would smash into its skull.

Ten seconds to go.

"I love you," whispered Joanna.

"My Charlotte Deveraux," Kingston whispered back. He saw her bite her lower lip in response.

Five. Four. Three. Two.

SMACK!

One.

All at once, millions of spectators between the realms leaned in closer at the sudden, and blatant, cheating that occurred, as an anvil very similar to Milliara's dropped out of thin air and landed straight on top of Lawnston's minotaur.

The trumpets blared and the match began. In an instant, the anvil teleported away, taking the minotaur with it. The minotaur reappeared three hundred metres in the air and plummeted to the arena floor. It slammed into the ground with enough force to shatter it into a hundred pieces.

The crowd cheered as the tournament bully got what was coming to him. The joy that ran through Kingston told him that the hassle in getting the clothes, booze, and money to Jezebel's contact was worth it. Caffrey's landmines flipped themselves into the air and landed throughout the arena floor. Milliara's teleporting anvil proceeded to slam into each of the bombs. The anvil came away unscathed, and Milliara was victorious.

It took thirty two seconds.

Damn it, Kingston thought, and he knew he had just lost the chance of making eighty gold pieces. On the bright side, he did just win a hundred and twenty knowing that Milliara was going to waltz into the third round, and another sixty that Lawnston would be the first to go out.

Joanna leaned over. "You better get yourself into the arena before Lawnston comes looking for you."

"I'll send John over as protection."

"Good idea."

Kingston walked as nonchalantly as possible over to the arena, hoping to get there before anyone from Lawnston's team was able to greet him, while also hoping that no one saw him acting suspiciously, then lo and behold he saw the two brutes standing guard at the player's entrance. Kingston came to a stop and shook his head.

"Just what I need."

The brutes saw Kingston and they assumed a look of bristling vengeance. They left their post and walked towards Kingston. Feeling as though it was best to leave those two alone, Kingston turned towards gate twelve and dug his hand into his pocket. When the brutes realised that he was about to head into the grandstands they hurried after him. Kingston flashed his team pass to one of the attendants and joined the hundred and twenty thousand spectators, who were mostly heading to the stalls for a snack.

Kingston slipped through the crowd as people pushed past him.

He managed to squeeze through the masses to get himself around to gate one. He had kept an eye out for anyone that would seem like they were on Lawnston's team, but somewhere his attention had slipped. A middle aged woman with long blonde hair stepped out in front and glared at him.

"You and Rufus are lying sacks of crap, you know that?"

It took a moment for Kingston to register what she was talking about, and then he recognised her. Chloe Stuyvescent. She had bought Rufus' old parts under the proviso that Rufus wasn't going to compete again.

Kingston bobbed his head sympathetically. "I do apologise, but now is not the best time for me."

"It's not the best time for me, either," said Stuyvescent. "He broke a promise and now I'm humiliated with his dinky little contraptions while you come out with the pièce de la résistance of the whole tournament."

Kingston was surprised by the compliment.

"Oh, please," said Stuyvescent, and she rolled her eyes at him. "Every team now has it in for you."

"I have no doubt," said Kingston, and he stepped around her. "I must run. I'm competing in an hour."

Stuyvescent snorted with a grin. "We'll see. Word among the builders is that you're about to be disqualified."

Kingston paused with that unsettling remark, regathered himself, and he slipped out through gate one. Sure enough, the brutes from Lawnston's team had returned to their position and were making sure that Kingston met as much opposition in getting into the arena as possible.

Still, there was another way inside. Kingston went back in to the arena, headed down to the first row, and slipped over the railing. He landed on the arena floor in front of a dozen referees who were busy cleaning up the remains of Lawnston's minotaur and ensuring that Caffrey's landmines were fully disabled. One of the trumpets blared and Kingston saw himself flash up on the large screens above the grandstands, and an unsettling feeling popped up in his gut. He was pretty sure that what he had just done would prompt a fine within the hour.

Sure enough, one of the young referees looked up and hurried over to him. "Sir! It is not time for you to enter the arena!"

"I'm completely turned around," muttered Kingston. "Where is my player's booth?"

The referee grumbled and stared at one of the three open doors while trying to figure out which would be the quickest way to get Kingston off the arena floor. "This way," the referee said, and Kingston was then escorted back underground, around a few twists and turns, and he was pointed to booth eight.

Kingston waltzed inside and saw Mortimer surrounded by four referees and one gaming commissioner. The unsettling feeling in Kingston's stomach didn't go away. Standing at the side of the room was a sour looking John and Rufus. The gaming commissioner, Hubert Stance, glanced up at Kingston.

"Mr Raine?"

"Mr Stance," said Kingston. "To what do we owe the pleasure?"

Stance didn't seem all that eager to be entertained. "What can you tell me about your machine, here?"

Kingston looked over to John and Rufus and knew they were in trouble. "That's a loaded question with thousands of possible answers. What exactly did you want to know?"

"It looks different to the model you previously entered with."

"You're absolutely right," said Kingston. "Every machine is a work in progress, and this one is more refined. The metal work is second to none. Still, at its heart it's the same old Mortimer. Still clumsy. Still a golem. Only he looks a little better for the cameras."

Stance rocked back on his heels and peered at Kingston suspiciously. "Where did the materials come from?"

Kingston smiled and shook his head. "It would be a disadvantage to all competing teams if I gave you the name of every supplier I've met with."

Stance looked as though he had spent the morning sucking on a lemon and had yet to find a way to relax his face from the ordeal. "We believe that you have illegal components in your machine."

"Oh, do you?" said Kingston. "No doubt one of the teams has filed a complaint."

"They have," said Stance.

Kingston was sure it was Lawnston, after figuring out the hundred year old projector that contributed to Mortimer's head didn't come from Life. "And have you found any illegal components?" asked Kingston.

"We're still investigating," said Stance. "We'll need to take possession of your machine."

"That's not going to happen," said Kingston, with a quick shake of his head. "Not now, not ever."

Stance glared back at Kingston. "Your team is under investigation, Mr Raine. We do have the power to disqualify you."

"Do you have any idea how much paperwork you would have to go through if you did that? The amount of appeals we would send your way, investigations into your conduct, even looking to see if anyone on your staff has taken a bribe?"

Stance drew in a sharp breath and was about to shout back at Kingston, and he was then interrupted.

"Can you guarantee that your staff is perfectly innocent?" asked Kingston. "And I mean *perfectly*, because we'll dig through every last correspondence and we'll find any bribe or back door deal that has gone on through your office. I have my suspicions already about who is not entirely honest, and who may have looked the other way while something illegal happened just outside of their line of sight. My instincts tell me that corruption has been running rife since the very first tournament, and since you hired these people with your best judgement it would show that your judgement isn't all that accurate. Could you really ensure the thirty other teams would maintain a noble conduct of honour while the gaming commission is exposed for being not only corruptible, but under the influence of one of the teams from Hell?" Kingston held his attention on Stance, forcing the man to back down and reconsider how he handled his opponent.

"There is something unusual about your machine," said Stance, now in a huff.

"There is something unusual about every machine competing today," said Kingston. "But 'unusual' is not grounds for taking mine away an hour before combat. Now, this is the player's booth, not the gaming commission's, and we need to prepare ourselves. The referees are allowed in here but you are not."

Hubert Stance shook his head. "We're taking your machine away now, Mr Raine. It's under official investigation."

Kingston looked over to Rufus. "Is this the first time this has happened to you?"

"Yep," said Rufus.

"You can have it after we compete," said Kingston.

"That's not actually how it works," said Stance. "You know the rules. You agreed to them among the eighteen page entry form, allowing us to seize any machine suspected of illegal components. We're taking your combatant now so that you can't cheat your way into victory."

"I will be filing an immediate appeal," said Kingston.

Stance reached into his jacket pocket and pulled out some paperwork. "By all means. I have the appeal right here and we should be able to conduct our review quickly."

"And will we be able to compete today?"

"If everything passes, then yes," said Stance.

Kingston squinted back at Stance and he did his best not to double check with Rufus, but he saw a slight shake of the head and knew he had to act quickly. "And if your investigators are delayed will we be wild-carded into the third round?"

"I really can't say," said Stance. He looked over to Rufus and held out one hand. "The controls to your machine, please."

Rufus held back a sneer, but he did glare at Kingston as he handed the control panel over to Stance. "Now be careful there. I want him back in perfect working order."

Stance took the control panel and handed it to one of the referees. "Let's get the machine out of here."

The strength in Mortimer's knees gave way and he started to tip forward at a precarious angle. The referees all scrambled out of the way, and ...

SLAM!

Mortimer fell flat on his face.

"I said be careful!" shouted Rufus.

Stance recovered from the near heart attack and glared at the young referee holding the control panel. "We weren't ready yet."

"I didn't touch anything!" said the referee.

"You powered him down," said Rufus.

"So power him back up," said Stance.

There was a slight whining sound coming from Mortimer and one of his legs twitched. Blue flames began shooting out from his joints and an odour settled into the room.

"What's it doing?" asked Stance.

Rufus glanced back to Kingston and darted his eyes to the ground. Rufus dropped to his knees, Kingston did the same, but no one else in the room caught the signal in time. A flash of purple burst through the room, bounced off the walls, and shot back inwards again. John, Stance, and the four referees all fell to the ground, unconscious.

Rufus sighed and climbed back to his feet. "Are you okay?" he asked Kingston.

Kingston remained lying on the ground, but from what he saw of the others he considered himself lucky. "What just happened?"

"We cheated. And quite epically, I must say."

Kingston rolled over to check John.

"He'll be out cold for an hour," said Rufus. He went to check on Mortimer, and the golem slowly stood up again. "Good, he's not damaged. I figured I needed a fail safe against the commission after Lawnston stole our projector. They were going to tell on us, that much was certain. This will buy us some time. We'll do the match, swap Mortimer over with the previous shell, send that one to the commission, get passed with flying colours, and in the meantime these numbskulls will work off a hangover the likes of which you wouldn't believe. And, by the way, we're going to need to fake that as well, otherwise it will look like we planned on knocking out the senior gaming commissioner."

Kingston tapped John on the chin. "I kinda need him to keep the girls company, now that Lawnston has it in for us."

"Well, don't do anything rash, because we have to lay low for the next hour until we can get into the arena. And we need them to prepare the other Mortimer."

"How are they going to prepare the other Mortimer if they're in the marquee entertaining our sponsors?"

Rufus shrugged. "Either we get fined and risk disqualification, or we earn a few silver pieces from drunken fools. Your choice."

Kingston fired off a quick note to Joanna, updating her on the situation, and he hoped like hell she would be able to work some kind of miracle. Then, Kingston did his best to wait patiently, but he was surrounded by five unconscious officials and he was supposed to be in full damage control. He and Rufus carried John, the commissioner, and the referees over to the door, and made sure that the commissioner's head was going to come into contact with the door the moment someone opened it. Half an hour later, they were still left alone. They watched the match between Aurelius, Kwon, and Lucha, and were unsurprised when Aurelius and his dragon won. The match took half an hour as Kwon's scorpion and the dragon ripped each other apart, but it was a decisive victory when the dragon shot the scorpion across the arena and forced it to slam into one of the far walls.

"We're up next," said Kingston, and he looked back to the unconscious men in the room. He quickly wrote up a note to John, giving him instructions on what to do when he woke up, and Kingston hid it in one of John's pockets.

"Stop pacing around, you're putting me off," said Rufus.

"Then don't look at me," said Kingston.

"Just sit still and be ready for one of the referees to come in and spoil our fun."

Sure enough, twenty minutes later, the door swung open and banged into Stance's head.

"Careful!" shouted Kingston.

The young referee glanced down at the floor and realised that he had just smacked into his boss' head.

"Get a stretcher in here, the commissioner has taken ill!" shouted Kingston. The referee froze, trying to process what had just happened, and Kingston hurried after him. "Go! We need medics! Stretchers! These men need to be treated immediately!" Kingston coughed and feigned a sour look, as though he was about to be sick.

Rufus quickly dropped to the ground and groaned. When the referee came back he and a friend tried to make sense of the situation.

"What happened here?" asked the referee.

Kingston snapped back. "Either we were sabotaged by another team or one of your morons caused an accident. It damn near killed him as well."

Rufus groaned and staggered to his feet. "We need an apothecary," he mumbled.

Kingston hurried over to Rufus and feigned an emergency. "An apothecary? Why?"

"Rhubarb," said Rufus. "We need it. Lots of it."

"Oooo, that's expensive," said the referee.

"Don't just stand there!" shouted Kingston. "Get your boss to an apothecary!"

The referees scrambled to get help, and they ended up carrying every unconscious man to the medical centre. It took half an hour. At that point, Kingston and Rufus hurried Mortimer into the arena.

"We're going to be in quite a lot of trouble after this," said

Rufus.

"Will we be disqualified?" asked Kingston.

"Probably. But at least Stance won't come and bother us directly again. He'll probably go into convulsions just looking at Mortimer. Which is good, I guess. It will also make everyone investigating us as paranoid as ever."

They looked over and saw that Wayne had come armed with eleven bowling balls that could roll in any direction and bounce at will. Bonaparte's drum of spinning spikes greeted them at the other end of the arena.

Rufus didn't like the look of Bonaparte's team. "If those things grab onto Mortimer they'll rip him to pieces. And I'm not sure if we can get him repaired in time for the next round."

"We will," said Kingston. "I have twenty five thousand gold at stake. So come Heaven or Hell we're going to make it through to the last round."

"Easier said than done," mumbled Rufus.

"With the amount of thieving I have at my disposal I expect to enter every tournament from now until I'm expelled, and I can do it without spending a single penny."

"Copper," mumbled Rufus.

Kingston turned to his builder. "You what?"

"No pennies here. Just coppers. So you hope to compete without spending a single copper."

Kingston shrugged and looked away. "That wasn't the focus of my point."

"We need a fast match," said Rufus. "We need to swap this Mortimer out for the old one and mimic the damage he receives."

Kingston rolled his eyes and stared at Wayne's team. "We're up against the one guy who will probably take the longest and you want a fast match?"

"The longer it takes the more trouble we'll be in," said Rufus. He fixed his headset into place and stared up at his golem. "Mortimer? Turn your head to the left."

Mortimer did so.

"Good. He can hear me."

With one minute to go they hurried back to their player's booth.

"Rise and shine, Mortimer," said Rufus. He looked over to Kingston. "Any particular strategy?"

"Avoid the spinning spikes and work as quickly as possible."

"Whip the balls," Rufus said into his microphone.

The ten second timer ticked down and the crowd rumbled to a roar, but they all knew they were in for a dull match. One team was going to sit still and wait for trouble to come to it, while another would avoid trouble at all costs, leaving Mortimer as the only aggressive element.

The trumpets sounded again and the match began. Bonaparte's machine stayed where it was and fired up the spinning spikes. Wayne's eleven bowling balls rolled in all directions, aiming for the outer edge of the arena, in such a lackadaisical speed that the crowd could see that the conclusion to this match rested squarely on Mortimer's shoulders.

Mortimer released his chain whip, took aim on the closest of Wayne's balls, and fired. The crowd snapped back in surprise as the whip shot out across the entire arena.

"Woah!" said Kingston.

Rufus smirked. "I've been trying to build that thing for a hundred years. Only cost four thousand gold."

The whip missed, and Wayne's balls started moving quickly now, reluctant to be caught by surprise again.

"Forward," commanded Rufus, and Mortimer stepped into the middle of the arena. He continued to fire the whip at whichever ball was closest, but the balls kept bouncing out of the way. Until, at last, Mortimer finally latched onto one. An electric charge fired through the chain and the ball fizzled. The crowd applauded, then rescinded their praise when they saw the ball shudder around the arena again.

"Great," mumbled Rufus. "It's going to take more than one hit to take them out."

"Bring the ball to Titan," said Kingston. "And please hurry." It had taken two minutes just to hit the first ball. It took another three minutes for Mortimer to get lucky again. He latched onto a distant ball and retracted the whip, causing it to fly towards him. In a mighty smash the ball was obliterated by Titan, and the crowd finally had their carnage.

At this point, Bonaparte's drum fired into life. Mortimer had his back to it and the drum sped into the arena, hoping to take Mortimer by surprise.

"Bonaparte!" shouted Rufus.

Mortimer turned, fired the whip at the drum, and saw it fling off to the side as the speed of the spikes knocked it away. Mortimer raised Titan into the air and charged into the drum.

"Careful!" shouted Rufus.

"It's going to rip him up," said Kingston.

"Throw it!"

Mortimer hurled Titan into the drum of spikes, a move that was clearly unexpected by Bonaparte's team. Titan smashed into the machine, causing it to fly backwards and topple over. Several of the spikes broke off, making the machine vulnerable. It bounced back upright and Titan skidded off to the side.

"Get the hammer!" shouted Rufus.

Mortimer hurried after Titan while being chased by the drum of spikes. As soon as Mortimer reached the hammer, Bonaparte's machine backed away and retreated to the far side of the arena, much to the groans of the audience. Once again it seemed as though it was Mortimer against the ten bowling balls.

None of the balls attempted to attack Mortimer, they all remained on the edge of the arena, and they got better at dodging the whip whenever it shot at them. Bonaparte's machine did make another move on Mortimer, but Mortimer fired his whip at the drum, halting the attack.

"He's just toying with us, hoping that we'll break down before he does," said Rufus.

"He's annoying the hell out of me."

"And this won't inspire a lot of sponsors," said Rufus.

Mortimer lumbered after the balls and he was able to smack one with Titan, but not even that was enough to earn an applause from the audience.

"It's been half an hour already," said Kingston, and he could feel the panic building within him. He looked over to the door and knew that John and Stance would be awake by now. "Are they going to disqualify us?"

"Not right now they're not," said Rufus. "No one is allowed in while we're at combat. Not even referees. It's the only way they can limit cheating. And we're under lock while we're at combat. Stops people from sabotaging us."

Kingston wondered just what kind of hell John would be putting everyone through, then he hoped that John would head back to the marquee and realise that the girls had run back to the bank to get old Mortimer up and running. With any luck, John would read Kingston's message in time and know what to do.

Mortimer lumbered after every ball in the arena for another half an hour. It wasn't until he stepped into Bonaparte's starting square did the audience finally get some action. Out of thin air a sack of bricks landed on top of Mortimer, and he crumpled to the ground. The crowd howled in laughter, while Kingston's jaw dropped open.

"What? *What?* What the hell just happened?"

Rufus smacked his lips together. "Someone cheated."

Mortimer did his best to climb out from the rubble, as brick upon brick tumbled to the ground. The moment he stood up, a second sack of bricks landed on top of him.

"WHAT?" screamed Kingston.

"Yup, definitely cheating. I bet it's Lawnston."

Then, just for good measure, a third sack of bricks full onto Mortimer. Rufus checked his monitor and pulled his headset off.

"I thought there was going to be a teleport lock to protect us!" cried Kingston.

"Looks like there wasn't," said Rufus. He checked his panel and shook his head. "We're done. No more signal from Mortimer. And you know what the really annoying part is? We have to pulverise the remains of old Mortimer and cover him in brick dust."

The audience began drifting away as the drum of spikes chased after the balls to little effect, and an hour later a thirty minute countdown timer showed up on the screens. Kingston was barely paying attention, as he had spent the entire time pacing around the player's booth.

We can't afford this anymore, he told himself.

"This is new," said Rufus, and he pointed out into the arena.

Kingston looked over and saw the timer. "So if that reaches zero, who would be declared the winner?"

Rufus shrugged. "Whoever is the most aggressive of those two teams."

They had their answer. Wayne's balls spun up and started to engage the drum of spikes, but kept from actually getting in contact with them. Bonaparte was forced to send his machine charging into action while Wayne was able to lead him into a trap and attack from all sides. Two of Wayne's balls struck ... and were destroyed. From then on Wayne maintained a safe distance and Bonaparte's machine wheeled after the balls to little effect. The timer reached zero, the trumpets blared, and the crowd had dwindled by half.

Rufus looked around to Kingston. "Better get your game face on, because Stance is about to shout at us."

The moment the arena was clear for the teams to reclaim their machines, Kingston and Rufus hurried to the arena door. They were blocked by Stance and his team of sour looking referees. Kingston feigned another stomach ache but he knew they weren't going to get out of this one quickly.

"Mr Raine," grunted Stance.

"Mr Stance, how are you feeling? Better, I hope."

"Somewhat," muttered Stance. "We're here to seize your machine."

Kingston handed over his letter of appeal. "Here you go. If you could tell me what you are looking for, maybe we could help."

"Oh, you're finally willing to cooperate?" asked Stance, though it was clear he didn't believe a word of what Kingston was saying.

"It depends. On what grounds are you hassling us?" asked Kingston.

"On the suspicion of violating regulation 19, paragraph 1, that components used in their combatants must originate from the realm of their builder."

"Which is flawed, because most teams use parts that come from Life. Although I suppose most of the builders were originally alive, so there is a little wriggle room in the wording of 19, paragraph 1. I expect to see an equal penalty written up against every other team out there. Maybe even a few disqualifications. Particularly Milliara and Horatio."

"We have no reason to suspect the others of cheating," said Stance.

Kingston looked over Stance's head and saw that there were several referees carrying the broken remains of Mortimer off to the side. He glanced back to Rufus and the look on the builder's face told him that they were screwed. "How long will this take?" asked Kingston.

"Twenty four hours is standard," said Stance. He turned to the youngest of referees. "Kenneth? You may show Mr Raine and his builder to the front door."

Kenneth nodded nervously and waved his hand out into the corridor. "Gentlemen, if you could please follow me."

XVIII

Back in the bank, Kingston spent the next few hours pacing about with his hands clamped behind his back. "There's nothing illegal about Mortimer."

"There's nothing legal about him either," said Joanna, while sitting as calmly as she could on the sofa and keeping Snowflake company.

"I know you're just playing devil's advocate, but the rules never say that using anything from Fiction is illegal."

"They might enforce it by this time tomorrow."

"Then we can delay it with appeals and ... more appeals, and ..." Kingston stopped walking and stared off into the distance. "What if we do one final raid on Fiction, transport everything to Hell, and then bring it back here? Everything will appear to have the taint from Hell and will cover us from any wrong doing."

Joanna shrugged. "It might work. In the meantime, I'm on full damage control with the sponsors. We've lost our first two rounds. No one is interested in throwing money at a losing team."

Kingston stared off to the side, held his eyes closed for ten seconds, and tried to regain some kind of focus. "At least our odds at the gaming house will be more favourable."

"Honey? We lost the first two rounds. We didn't want to, it just happened. Our odds could be even money or a hundred to one, but if you have a look at the last couple of weeks you'll see that we still haven't won a single round. Chances are we're not going to win the next round either."

"We need to get better at cheating," said Kingston. He looked around and his temper started to settle down. "Where's John?"

"He and Catalina went out," said Joanna. "You know, on a

date."

"Huh," said Kingston, and for a moment he was caught in a distant thought. Then he snapped back to reality and looked to his girlfriend. "Sorry, we haven't had a lot of free time lately," he said.

Joanna toyed with a smile. "If I wanted a date I would take you out on one. I'm not some damsel in hopeful distress."

"It's been a while since you were in that kind of position."

"I tend to rescue you more than you rescue me," said Joanna.

Rufus slumped into the corridor with his head down and he came to a stop in front of Kingston. "Quick update. Old Mortimer is now dearly departed Mortimer." He looked up and sighed at Joanna.

"Sorry," she said.

"Me too. You did a good job on him. It really did look like he had been hit by a tonne of bricks."

"We used a couple of sledgehammers," said Joanna. "And John walloped him with the work bench."

"He certainly did," said Rufus. He sighed, looked back to Kingston, and almost collapsed in defeat. "We've had our combatant confiscated, our back-up is destroyed, and we're eight days away from round three. There's nothing to fix, nothing to work on, nothing to do, but I hear a bottle of gin calling to me."

Kingston saw that look of despair and he braced himself for the worst. "Go easy on that, okay?"

"I always go easy on the gin. It's the vermouth that kills me." Rufus shuffled off and drank his miseries away.

Kingston looked back to Joanna. "We're not as good at this as we thought we would be."

"Maybe we're just not cheating well enough," said Joanna, offering the slightest bit of hope.

Kingston could barely manage a shrug, and he slumped down on the sofa next to Joanna. "Still, raiding Fiction for all it's worth is a pretty good idea."

"Yeah, but getting down to Hell and back again is going to be chaotic." She could hear Rufus pulling out the glass bottles from down the corridor as he mixed himself a drink, and she considered going over to join him. "Just how much have we spent so far?"

"Thirty three thousand seven hundred and twenty gold."

Joanna leaned back as her neck and shoulders tensed up.

"Of that, we've spent seventeen thousand two hundred and

eighty gold on gambling, and have earned back eighteen thousand and sixty gold."

The only word that Joanna had at her disposal was a vacant, "Wow."

"Yeah," said Kingston. "When I say it like that, it feels a lot more real."

"You're telling me," said Joanna. "It was easy thinking about millions of euros, dollars, and pounds, because it seemed so astronomical that it never even mattered if we lost it all, but so far we've gambled ... what, twenty five years' worth of your salary?"

"Yeah," said Kingston. "The walk back from the arena was a long one and it gave me time to figure out that if we're in this mess together, then we're left to survive on your salary alone."

Joanna smirked at Kingston. "I'm glad my earnings covers the practical side of things and yours is reserved for these insane ideas."

A flash of light appeared in front of Kingston's eyes, and a letter dropped to his feet. He could tell right away that it was from the gaming commission. "Let's hope this tells us we can collect Mortimer." He read it over and groaned.

"Is it a fine?" asked Joanna.

"Yep. Climbing into the arena from the seating area is a ten gold fine. And we're being investigated for dropping an anvil on Lawnston's minotaur."

"At least we haven't yet been fined for building a fictional golem."

There was another burst of light. A newspaper landed on the ground with the highlights of the day's events. Kingston flipped it open and read up on his blunder through the arena, and how his team now risked disqualification.

Later that night, Kingston and Joanna were onto their eighth drink. She stared at the bottle of vermouth and squinted at the lettering.

"Too much for Miss York?" asked Kingston.

"I'm just looking at the picture. It looks like a woman in a dress." She then turned to Kingston. "Do they do weddings in Limbo?"

Kingston held back a splutter and stared in shock at his girlfriend. "I haven't looked into it. Why?"

"Just ... Catalina and John."

"Oh. You want to be her maid of honour?"

"It would be nice," said Joanna.

"But weddings are still stupid?"

"Very stupid."

"And expensive?"

Joanna stared drunkenly at her glass and nodded.

"But you would still go."

"If I was the maid of honour I would have to go." She then looked over what she had just said and stared up at the ceiling, now lost in thought. "If I *were* the maid of honour ... was ...?"

"When was the last time we actually went out on a date?" asked Kingston.

Joanna snorted and shook her head. "You mean out for a movie and a show?"

Kingston smirked at Joanna. "Yeah, a movie *and* a show. And dinner."

"It's been a while."

Kingston tapped the last drop of gin into his glass and realised that he couldn't quite take a gulp. "I think John would sing at his own wedding."

Joanna started leaning to one side, and it looked as though she was slowly falling over. "You know, if we end up making money out of this thing we should start our own business."

"We have a business. We're bounty hunters."

"But ... a proper business."

"This is a proper business and it's not really working out for us."

"No, I mean like a karaoke bar. You know, something real."

Kingston smiled at Joanna. "A karaoke bar?"

"Everyone we know likes to sing! And John would be our best customer. And they could get married in our karaoke bar! Write that down." She reached out to the table to pour herself another drink, but the bottle was empty. She shook it in front of Kingston and nodded at him.

"Maybe you could open up a bridal shop."

"No." She tapped the bottle again.

"No?"

Joanna *dinged* the bottle with her nails.

"Fine, I'll go find some more." He got to his feet and went to hassle Rufus for another bottle.

"Be careful what you drink in that room," Joanna called out.

"Yeah, yeah," said Kingston, and he headed towards their lab. Rufus was inside, lying on the sofa, snoring gently. Kingston crept in, rummaged through the cupboards for some more gin, and he glanced over to Rufus' hand, hoping that he had a bottle nearby. Instead, Kingston caught sight of a shadow underneath the sofa.

Kingston climbed down to his knees and saw a thin leather-bound book lying on the ground, hidden under the sofa. Kingston glanced back to the sleeping Rufus and took a gamble. He pried the book out to freedom, and Kingston knew this had to be the coded book of recipes Rufus used to make his enchantments. As carefully as he could Kingston peeled open one of the pages. As he suspected it was written in code.

.rasetbhsle.

18.534 wi cmher oll ret
ahen dywa
13.4 eht
3. yer psnouo 63
x.
dleabt nit lilst w op
gnacau tosmwob re o hre rthi

The rest of the pages were similar. Kingston closed the book and admired Rufus' ability to write up a code that defied the laws of Limbo, where everything written could be read at a glance. Then again, Kingston knew that codes and gibberish could exist even in plain sight. He left Rufus to sleep and returned to Joanna on the sofa.

"We're out of luck," said Kingston.

"That's too bad."

Kingston sat next to her and they fell quiet for a few minutes.

Joanna finally looked over. "You know what's weird? When John took Catalina out tonight he carried her off in his arms. You know, like the whole Sir Lancelot thing."

"That's not exactly weird, my dear," said Kingston.

Joanna glanced back up to the ceiling. "Was it actually Lancelot who did that?"

"Clarke Gable did."

"And I know I sound very much like a teenage girl when I say this, but it made me jealous."

Kingston leaned back in surprise. "What? *What?* I will carry you anywhere you want!"

"No, I mean ... not the carrying bit ..."

"You weigh as much as a Chihuahua," said Kingston.

Joanna glanced off to the side and thought over what she had just said. "That may have been a case of verbal diarrhoea."

"You think so?"

"I wasn't jealous of you not carrying me off to dinner. I was jealous, for the tiniest of seconds, of Catalina. John scooped her up! That could have been me!"

Kingston leaned forward and shook his head. "I do love you, but you're really digging yourself into a hole with this one."

"It was romantic!"

Kingston looked to one side. "Help me out here, are you looking for flowers? Or a necklace? Chocolate mints?"

"No, I'm just telling you what I saw today."

"And it made you jealous."

"You and I are the ones heavily in debt and she's not."

"I'm sure Catalina has her own insecurities," said Kingston.

"I don't have insecurities!" snapped Joanna.

Kingston arched an eyebrow and pointed his finger at her. "So you're fine if I call you poor?"

Joanna reeled back in shock. "I - AM - NOT -"

"Well, look at this," said Kingston.

Joanna pulled all of her anger inside, bottled it up, pushed it down, and reclaimed her sanity. She then bounced back into as sincere a smile as she could manage, and she held out her hand for Kingston to shake. "Friends?"

Kingston took her hand and held onto it. "Always."

"Good."

"I'm sorry."

"Me too." Joanna tucked her legs up onto the sofa and curled up next to Kingston.

"So why were you jealous?"

Joanna shrugged. "Because."

"Because of a karaoke bar?"

Joanna stared back at Kingston "No! Because you and I spent years trying not to fall in love. Years. And we were bad at that. But them ... they ... those two ... they did it so effortlessly. Plus, we're in over our heads with debt and they're not. Believe it or not, those two have done everything right and we've done everything as inconveniently as possible, which is dumb." She sighed and stared at the empty bottle of gin. "We're in a lot of trouble, aren't we?"

"Yep," said Kingston.

A burst of light shot into the air and another note from the gaming commission landed in front of them. Kingston reached out and broke the official seal.

"Well ... crap," said Kingston.

"What is it?" asked Joanna.

"We're being fined a thousand gold for using illegal material."

Joanna sat up. "What?"

"Yeah, right here," said Kingston. He handed the sheet across and Joanna studied it, though she had to close one eye to focus properly.

"So we're not disqualified?"

"I suppose the commission realised that they would have to disqualify every team for using illegal components, so we're being fined instead. Don't worry, we'll file an appeal," said Kingston.

Joanna read through to the next page. "At least we can pick him up now."

"I'm a little too drunk for that, and we'll need John to pull him along in a rickshaw."

"Looks like we're also being investigated for sabotaging Lawnston's machine in the second round."

Kingston snorted. "And what about our sacks of bricks?"

"Those are being investigated as well."

"I suppose that means we're doing something right. From what Jezebel tells me, if we're not being investigated then we're doing it wrong."

"Then we're doing very well for ourselves," said Joanna.

Kingston leaned back in the sofa and wished he had found another bottle of gin. "We need a lawyer."

"Catalina's working on that. And these fines seem like the type of thing we should talk about when we're sober, and not when we've demolished most of the gin and vermouth."

"Give me that coconut shavings," mumbled Kingston.

Rufus passed the container. "Strong stuff, was it?"

Kingston didn't answer. He was so stiff from sleeping on the sofa that he could barely move his neck. He poured himself a glass of shavings with some water, then tried to guzzle it all in one go. He spluttered, coughed most of it back into the glass, and then stared into the mixture when he realised what he would have to do next.

"Yeeeeaaaah," said Rufus, with a broad grin. "Back down the hatch it goes."

Kingston hesitated with the glass resting against his lips.

"Come on, they're only your germs."

Kingston took a couple of deep breaths, then sunk the last of the water. He gasped, winced, and shuddered as the mixture dropped into his stomach and fought against the acid built up inside. He looked over to Joanna, who was curled up asleep on the other sofa, cradling Snowflake. She had managed to take one glass of coconut shavings before she went to bed, but she was still sleeping through what was about to become an incredible headache.

"Like I said, it's the vermouth that kills ya," said Rufus.

"Was it really vermouth?"

"One of Hell's finest." Rufus poured a glass of coconut for Joanna and laid it on the coffee table next to her. Then he picked over the paperwork they had gathered during the night and looked over the various sheets of official paperwork. "Looks like we can collect Mortimer after paying the fine."

"Off you go then," said Kingston, and he was finally able to get to his feet.

Rufus shook his head at Kingston. "Did you know that Stalactite Vermouth is made by one of the oldest cartels down South? It's supposed to be drunk at near freezing temperatures. That way it mixes with whatever else is in the glass and gives you one hell of a good taste to it. If you drink it at room temperature it tastes just like regular garbage bin Vermouth from Hell, except it purposely punishes you in the morning. The idea is, only those who know how to drink it properly will dare order it in a bar. The amateurs will avoid it at all costs for fear of a nasty experience. Therefore, it's reserved for only the most distinguished of drinkers. You, my friend, are paying the price of not knowing your Vermouths from Hell."

Kingston did his best to ignore Rufus. He stumbled over to

Joanna to wake her up, and he rocked her hips back and forth. "Honey?"

Joanna groaned.

"We have work to do."

Joanna made no attempt to get up.

"You're going to want to drink something soon," said Kingston.

But, after years of knowing Joanna, he knew there was no way of getting her out of bed if she refused to move.

"John and Catalina will be down here soon. And Jezebel. And Simon. They're all going to see you lying here." He held the glass of water out for Joanna and she finally opened one eye. "Drink this and I'll let you go back to sleep."

Joanna groaned, sat up slightly, took one sip, and pulled a face.

"You have to drink all of it," said Kingston.

"No," said Joanna, and she tried to lie back down.

"At least drink half of it," said Kingston, and it took half an hour before Joanna was coherent enough to finish the glass. Then came another half an hour of sweeping declarations that she was never going to drink that much again.

Two hours later, John and Kingston unloaded the last of the satchels containing the broken Mortimer, and Rufus hung his head in defeat.

"We can't fix all of this in eight days," said Rufus.

"It's time to pull out every last miracle," said Kingston.

"This is going to go beyond miracles," said Rufus. "We're talking about an actual breaking of reality just to get this done."

John grunted. "That sounds exactly like a miracle."

Rufus glared at John. "Then you two better work on your rain dances, because this is going to take some divine intervention."

They jolted back in surprise as the door to the workshop burst open. Jezebel ran inside. "Did no one hear me?" She was met by three blank faces, and she shook her head in despair. "The line up to round three is being revealed in thirty seconds! Come on!" She ran back out into the corridor, and Kingston, John, and Rufus quietly followed.

They found Jezebel, Joanna, and Catalina huddled around the coffee table, having taken up their spots on the sofa. The guys joined the girls and waited for something to happen.

John looked over to Kingston. "What are we hoping for?"

"Hopefully that we're in the last fight of the round, to give us enough time to repair Mortimer."

"It still won't be enough," said Rufus.

They all stared at the sheet of parchment as the writing materialised, and for a moment none of it made any sense. All it had was a date and time.

Round Three
18:00 10 October – 18:00 15 October

Everyone glanced over to Rufus and Jezebel to see if they knew what was going on.

"No idea," mumbled Rufus.

"My gut is telling me something painful is coming our way," said Kingston.

The parchment was updated.

Last Man Standing

"Uh oh," mumbled Kingston.

Division One
Horatio v. Sequa v. Kwon v. Milliara v. Semper v. Cove v. Bonaparte v. Aurelius

Rufus dropped his head onto the table. "It's a battle royale."

Division Two
Rufus v. Sanders v. Lucha v. Biggins v. Wayne v. Carver v. Creig v. Kazuka

"I think it's worse than that," said Joanna. "It's several battles royale at the same times."

Division Three
Newell v. Stuyvescent v. Redding v. Lawnston v. Caffrey v. Puck v. Scamp v. Foster

Division Four

Urisha v. Denoa v. Rose v. Gibbs v. Zamba v. Nocht v. Jones

Then, at the very bottom, was the final update.

Round Four
31 October
Winner of Division One v. Winner of Division Two v. Winner of Division Three v. Winner of Division Four.

Everyone's jaws dropped open.

"That's one hell of a free for all," said John.

"Yeah, last man standing," said Kingston. He looked up to Rufus and Jezebel. "Has this ever happened before?"

"I've seen two battles royale," said Rufus, still with his head on the table.

"And thirty years ago we had a last man standing," said Jezebel.

"So what happens?" asked Kingston.

"It's five days of carnage," said Jezebel. "The last time it was during the finale. Everyone turns up at, in our case, 18:00 on the tenth of October. Whoever is still standing five days later will go into the finale."

Joanna almost stopped breathing. "Five days later?"

"They have lock-outs," said Jezebel. "We'll all be out there at the starting time and none of the combatants can leave for the first hour, or however long they decide. Sometimes you're allowed to leave the arena for repairs, sometimes you're not. Sometimes you're allowed back in, sometimes you're not. But whoever is the last team remaining in each round, they get to face off against each other in the finale two weeks later."

Kingston looked over the divisions again. "It seems as though the weakest teams are in division four."

"Yeah," said Jezebel. "And the strongest are in the first."

"So we're second," said John. "That isn't too bad."

"There's only one team from Limbo in division one," said Kingston. "Horatio and his cannon."

"He'll be pleased with that," said Jezebel. "Of course, he's up against the most badass teams from Hell who will pick him off. And we're all fighting at the same time, so there's no reason why anyone from another division can't pick a fight with us."

"Exactly," mumbled Rufus, still with his forehead on the table.

"And it isn't so much that we're up against thirty other teams at the same time. It's the five days of constant repairs and endless fighting. Someone has to be awake to keep an eye on Mortimer and do repairs on him, and since there's only one builder here I'm going to spend five days without sleep trying to fix this guy back together."

"We're up against Wayne again and his balls of boredom," said Kingston, looking over who else was in their division.

"Strangely, he can take on half of the field at the same time," said Joanna.

"And we're up against exploding Kazuka," said Kingston. "Let's see if we can avoid him."

"There are going to be bribes across the divisions," mumbled Rufus. He lifted his head off the table and finally stared across at his team mates. "Most of the division four teams can't even compete because they've already been taken out of the competition."

"Then they forfeit," said Jezebel.

"Or they turn up because they've been hired by the richer teams and given a helping hand. Two teams make an alliance to take out the competition. We may need a sister team," said Rufus.

Kingston spluttered a laugh and shook his head. "And who did you have in mind?"

"Chloe Stuyvescent," said Rufus. "I built most of her machines."

"She's in division three and we're in division two," said Joanna.

"Yeah," said Rufus. "But Mortimer is strong enough to fight everyone in division three, so she'll want us on her side as some kind of protection, and when it comes time to fighting everyone else in division two we'll have her help."

"She doesn't like you, though," said Jezebel.

Rufus shrugged. "She doesn't need to. She just needs to like Kingston's money. And maybe if we get Denoa as well the three of us can team up and take on every other threat out there."

Kingston reeled around in surprise. "You want me to buy *two* other teams?"

Rufus shrugged. "You don't have to buy them, you just need to bribe them into working for us."

"Except for Denoa," said Jezebel. "He forfeited at the end of the first round. He'll need to be bought back into the tournament and he needs a repaired machine." She looked across the room as though she could hear a fly buzzing nearby.

"Okay, so you will have to buy him back in," said Rufus. "Then, if we and Stuyvescent all team up and take out everyone else in the fourth division, you'll have Denoa's team in the finale. Then we work on destroying the other teams in division three and that will put Stuyvescent into the finale as well. Then we all work together to clear out the rest of division two and you'll have three teams in the finale under your control, all against whoever wins division one, which will probably be Aurelius. With the three of us against the one of him we'll stand a decent chance at winning. As soon as his machine is blown to pieces we'll make Denoa and Stuyvescent forfeit, and we'll win."

Jezebel clapped her hands together and held a petrified look on her face. She then pointed to a mug sitting on the counter. Kingston stared at it while Rufus crept forward muttered under his breath.

"Well, well. Good spot, Jezebel."

"What is it?" asked John.

"A bug," said Rufus. He tapped the mug and saw the handle swivel slightly towards him. He picked it up, went into the tea room, and dropped it in the sink. "There, that should drown things out for a while."

Kingston glanced nervously from one person to the next. "So ... how screwed are we?"

"That's just harmless spying," said Rufus, and he saw Jezebel grimace. "No big deal."

Kingston sighed. "Right. So let's not get carried away with buying or bribing multiple teams. They can always turn against us if they accept multiple bribes."

Rufus sighed and slumped back into the sofa. "Getting Stuyvescent on board is still a good idea."

"Then maybe we can talk to her about teaming up," said Joanna.

Rufus shrugged in some kind of acceptance, and fell quiet.

John finally leaned forward. "The whole idea is to cheat as best we can, right?"

"Sure," said Joanna.

"So what's the craziest way we can cheat?"

The table fell quiet again as everyone considered the most ludicrous idea possible.

"Can we just not turn up until the last hour?" asked Catalina.

Jezebel shook her head. "All teams must be there at the start of combat to qualify. If we don't make it there we're completely out of the tournament."

Joanna looked over John and turned back to face Kingston. "Put John in a telemetry suit."

Kingston lit up in delight. "Yes!"

"Put me in a what?" John asked.

"A telemetry suit," said Joanna. "You move around and Mortimer copies your actions. It would be like you're inside him but from the safety of the player's booth."

John grinned. "You mean, in some way, I would actually be in the arena fighting all these things with a war hammer in one hand and a chain whip in the other?"

"Yeah," said Joanna.

John slammed his hand down on the table. "I'm doing that."

"That is especially complicated," said Rufus. "And easy to tamper with. This is actually the first tournament where no one has been caught using one of those, because it always seems like the most straight forward way to win, but the link is easy to sabotage and you lose contact with your machine half way through combat."

John sighed and stared at Rufus. "You're really harshing my buzz on this one."

"Just bringing you back to reality," said Rufus.

"Even if the machine and telemetry suit are fictional?" asked Kingston.

Rufus paused and thought it over. "It might work."

"Would it be more likely to work than anything built in Limbo? It might make it harder to be tampered with."

Rufus shrugged. "We can try, but we would need to build that as well, and I don't have the supplies or manpower for that."

Kingston and Joanna glanced at each other and knew they would have to build this thing in Fiction and sneak it across to Limbo.

Catalina leaned forward. "Is there any chance that we are all over complicating this thing?"

Rufus shook his head. "I don't see how, not when it's their money at risk."

"Isn't there an easier way to beat the competition?"

"I'm open to all ideas," said Kingston.

Catalina readied herself, paused, and finally gave up. "I have nothing."

Kingston looked over to Jezebel. "How about you? Any idea how we can cheat our way to victory?"

"I do know a guy," she said.

Kingston smirked. "Let's hear it."

"For twenty gold he will irritate the hell out of one team with this high pitched whining noise hidden in the player's room. Apparently it sounds like a mosquito when you're trying to sleep, and just when you think it's gone away the sound sneaks up on you and buzzes right behind your ear. Whoever is controlling their machine will go insane. Twenty gold per team, and I suggest annoying the hell out of them all."

Catalina blew out a lungful of air and shook her head. "That sounds mean."

"It's five days of brutal combat and repairs. A mosquito buzzing next to them will have them making mistakes in a matter of hours. Failing that, I know another guy."

"What does this one do?" asked Kingston.

"He imports coffee from Hell. Have you ever tried to stay awake for five days straight on decaf?"

Catalina shuddered. "Or, just not drink coffee."

Rufus raised his hand. "By the way, Satan is likely to be at one of these matches. Probably this one, because he can't get enough of the battles royale, but he'll certainly be at the finale."

"Ay," cried Catalina, and she looked away.

"I do like the decaf idea," said Kingston.

"Me too," said Joanna.

"I have a feeling Milliara is going to be the hardest team to beat," said Kingston. "We know when the lock-outs take place, right?"

"Yeah," said Jezebel. "Usually there's a timer for everyone to see, but you've seen what it's like trying to survive for ten minutes against three opponents. Imagine trying to survive five days against the entire competition."

Kingston shook his head. "Milliara is almost guaranteed to waltz into the finale. All he has to do is arrive at the start of the tournament, and the moment we're under way he teleports himself to safety and reappears just before any of the lock-outs begin. Hell, he could just pay the fine and avoid them completely. He'll disappear two seconds after the battle begins and reappears moments before the end, five days later."

"It's possible," said Jezebel. "But at the same time, Aurelius' team might just break down Milliara's team door and remind them of just how unsporting that is, if you catch my drift. Then Milliara won't be able to teleport his anvil back in time."

"Doesn't he have a muse and psychic?" asked Joanna.

"Yeah. And?"

"And the psychic will know when someone is about to break down their door, and the muse can talk them out of a bad situation."

Jezebel shrugged. "There is that. But when you break down someone's door you're not exactly giving the muse much of a chance to talk you out of it."

Catalina looked over and shook her head. "I've got nothing."

Rufus glanced over his shoulder. "Meanwhile, we're a day late on rebuilding Mortimer, and I can guarantee that we'll be fined again if we turn up with another fictional golem. This one needs to be built with legitimate parts."

"Then we'll need two golems," said Kingston.

Rufus nearly threw himself back into the sofa in utter defeat. *"Two?"*

"Yeah. Old Mortimer to start and finish the show to avoid the fines, and new Mortimer to do all of the heavy smackage during the middle portion."

John nodded. "And a third Mortimer with me in that suit thing."

Rufus spluttered in trying to argue against Kingston, but he saw Joanna and even Jezebel nodding their heads.

"Competing with fictional parts is the only way we can do this cheaply," said Joanna. "And it's all about attrition. If no one can make it to the last hour because they're broke and out of resources then we'll win."

Rufus looked from face to face in utter despair. "But there just aren't enough hours in the day to do all of that!"

"Then we start with new Mortimer, because he can be cheaply built and repaired, and we'll just risk a fine if we can't get old Mortimer up and running as well."

"But ... but!"

Kingston looked over. "Any questions?"

"It takes ten years to build an entrant!" cried Rufus.

"Stop being a baby," said John. "You built two golems in just a couple of months."

"And so now you think it's reasonable to build three golems in just a couple of days?"

John bobbed his head. "I'm sure the other teams are panicking right now as well, so we're not at that much of a disadvantage."

"I'm sure of it," said Jezebel.

Rufus ran his hands over his face and groaned. "This would be a lot easier if we could get everyone to forfeit before round three begins. Then we just spend five days in the arena with no one to fight. That's how you win the tournament. You stop people from turning up!"

"I'm happy to consider that as Plan A, but Plan B means building and repairing lots of Mortimers," said Kingston. "So, we're all going to be incredibly busy for the next two weeks and we need to get up to speed on how to repair Mortimer and replace spare parts. Any final ideas of genius?" He looked around the table and hoped that someone had a saving grace hidden away. "Then let's get to it. Joanna and I will get spare parts. Catalina, can you work on appealing the fine we just received?"

Catalina shrugged. "I can try."

"Good. John? We have a few fictional supplies from the vaults that need to be brought up. Rufus? Repair new Mortimer. Jezebel? Help him."

John looked back to Kingston. "Are you sure you two will be okay? It seems like every time you go into Fiction something awful happens."

"Yeah," said Kingston. "I have noticed that pattern."

"You like stirring up trouble," said Catalina.

"Trouble just finds me," said Kingston.

"But I've got his back," said Joanna, and she patted his knee.

"As adorable as you two are, this is a disaster," said Catalina.

Joanna shrugged. "To be fair, it is the only kind of life we know."

Catalina arched an eyebrow at them. "In that case you two should probably never have kids."

XIX

That night, Kingston and Joanna burst back into the lobby of their apartment building with a trunk of components for Mortimer, and jumped when Catalina yelped in surprise.

"Ay, where the hell have you two been?" Catalina cried.

"... Out," said Kingston, hoping that no one was able to read his mind when clearly he and Joanna had been plundering their way through Fiction.

"I've been waiting here for hours!" She looked as though she was about to tear her hair out in panic.

Joanna lowered the trunk to the ground. "What's going on?"

"Chloe Stuyvescent is waiting in your office!"

Kingston and Joanna looked back at each other, half expecting the other to remember some kind of meeting that they had set up, but they were both taken by complete surprise. "Is she trashing the place?" asked Kingston.

Catalina pushed them towards the door. "No. John is with her. While you two were gone Rufus thought it was a good idea to try and get Stuyvescent onto our side, so he set up a meeting with her and you, but you two weren't here. She agreed to meet and we've been left trying to contact you for hours! John waited in the office and had to get a teleport lock set in place in case you two burst inside with all of this illegal junk!"

Kingston and Joanna turned to face each other. "That would explain why -"

"He was trying to stop you from being fined by another team," said Catalina. "So go! Now! Talk to her!" Catalina pushed them towards the door.

"Talk to her about what?" asked Joanna.

"I don't know! Whatever it was that Rufus promised. And hurry! John is on his own trying to handle this meeting as best he can."

Kingston looked down to the chest. "What do we do about that?"

"Send John back," said Catalina. "I'll keep an eye on it and he can carry it over to the bank."

"Okay," said Kingston. He grabbed Joanna's hand and they teleported to the corner of Anubis and Niamh. Two and a half minutes later they knocked on their office door.

John sprung forward and unlocked it. He was wearing his best suit. "Ah! Kingston! And Joanna! How good to see you again. Please come in."

Kingston and Joanna did so, and they saw Chloe sitting impatiently in front of the desk. She held her arms tightly against her stomach and sat with her legs crossed. She took one look at Kingston and turned her attention away.

"I've just been telling Madam Chloe here about Catalina and Joanna's harrowing trip through the underworld. We were just up to the part of meeting Satan in his palace."

"I'm sorry I missed it," said Kingston. He came forward and offered his hand to Chloe. "How are you?" She didn't take it.

"The meeting was for seven o'clock. That was a while ago."

"I do apologise," said Kingston, and he waved his hand towards Joanna. "This is Joanna York."

John leaned forward and smiled at Chloe. "She accompanied Catalina through the depths of Hell."

"How do you do?" asked Joanna.

"I am well," said Chloe. "Can we hurry this up, or am I going to hear more stories about the inspiration behind some paintings?"

"Certainly," said Kingston, and he looked back to John, hoping for some clue as to what they were supposed to talk about. "Catalina is expecting you in the lobby of the apartment."

"Oh," said John. When he glanced over to Joanna he saw her nod, and realised that his moment in the spotlight was over. He waved back to Chloe. "It was a pleasure meeting you."

"Yes," said Chloe, and John left them in peace. She looked back to Kingston and Joanna as they settled themselves down. "Now, what do you want?" she asked.

Kingston went for broke and hoped it would work. "An alliance during the third round."

Chloe sighed and turned away. "I've been fielding offers like that all day."

Kingston turned to regain her attention. "From whom?"

Chloe rolled her eyes at him, clearly insulted that she could attract such enviable attention, and Joanna stepped in to take control.

"I'm sorry, Chloe," said Joanna. "Subtlety is not one of Kingston's strong points. We just wanted to find some way to make the most out of this tournament, and we were hoping you would be open to recouping a little money."

Chloe still looked as though she was ready to throw something in Kingston's face. "I'm still pissed at Rufus for competing again."

"Would you care for something to drink?" asked Joanna.

Chloe squinted back at Kingston, trying to unsettle him. "Sure."

Joanna tapped Kingston and he went to fetch a couple of glasses, while Joanna led the wheeling and dealing.

"Well done for making it into the second division," said Chloe.

"Thank you," smiled Joanna.

"Perhaps if Rufus sold me whatever it was that he sold you, *I* might have made it into the second division."

"He was sincere in trying to never compete again," said Joanna. "He did hope to sit this one out."

"Let me guess, you convinced him that he would win."

"We agreed to fund his build," said Joanna.

Chloe snorted in disbelief, stared back across the table, and then she realised that Joanna might actually be telling the truth. "Really?"

"Yeah," said Joanna.

"He's the most incompetent builder in Limbo!"

"He's also terrible at handling his finances," said Joanna.

"I've heard the same thing about you and Kingston."

Joanna paused, considered Chloe carefully, and resumed. "If we all team up we stand a greater chance at making it into the finale."

Chloe agreed, but it was just one of a dozen offers she had heard that day. Kingston returned with three vodkas and pineapple juice with a drop of red grenadine in each and passed them around. Joanna stared at the drink and felt her stomach almost backflip, as the night of gin and vermouth still haunted her.

Joanna continued. "If we team up and agree to a strategy then we can pick off the other teams and do our best to get both of us into the finale. Rufus can even ramp up some of the capabilities on your machine. He -"

"You mean he short changed my machine's capabilities?" Chloe asked.

"Not at all, but we can provide Helix's Gambit, for example, which might -"

"So you're saying I'm not a good enough builder to make it on my own?" Chloe held her hand up quickly, gritted her teeth, glared at Joanna, and turned to face Kingston. "I don't like her anymore. You try again."

Kingston sat down behind his desk. "Rufus has a vault full of spare parts that are specifically designed for his old machines. You already know how to enchant them. That supply will keep you in the arena long after the other teams are forced to forfeit because they've run out of components."

Chloe thought it over, briefly considered it, and then shrugged it away. "It's tempting, but I've had other offers." She turned her nose upwards and looked away.

Kingston and Joanna shared a look, both thinking that it was unlikely that Chloe had been offered anything better than what she had just received. "Like what?"

"I have non-aggression pacts with teams Foster and Newell."

"That would still stand," said Kingston.

"Except they don't like you," said Chloe.

For some reason, that one stung Kingston more than he expected. "Why not?"

Chloe shrugged. "I don't like you and I have more of a reason."

"Because we're sponsoring Rufus?" Kingston asked.

Chloe sighed, leaned back in her chair, and shook her head. "When's my birthday? Where do I work? What did I want to do when I was a little girl? How have I acquired all of the components to build Persephone? What will I do with any money I win? Why am I even competing when I would surely be thumped by every team from Hell?" She looked back at Kingston and Joanna and rolled her eyes. "You two have a reputation about caring for yourselves rather than helping anyone else."

Kingston opened his mouth to protest, and then he realised that Chloe, in all likelihood, was right. Even Joanna was hit hard by that revelation, all the more so because she prided herself on breaking down every problem by getting to know the people involved, and to tug on their sympathy strings. She knew the useless essentials, like how old Chloe was and where she worked, but Joanna was at a loss for what Chloe was actually like or how she enjoyed herself.

"Exactly," said Chloe. "You two aren't so hot right now, are you?"

Kingston looked over at Joanna and hoped they were able to play the sympathy card just right, except he realised that was exactly what Chloe was talking about. "I guess not."

Chloe shrugged. "But what can you expect, we're in the middle of the Games and everyone loses their mind, right?"

"I suppose," said Kingston.

"Except you've been in Limbo for almost two years and you've caused chaos wherever you've gone. People from Limbo compete because they enjoy the challenge, they love the mechanics of building something new, learning new skills, and having a moment of glory that you can talk about for years, regardless of the sacrifice and humiliation. You two are here for the money."

Kingston leaned back, sighed, and realised his eyes had gone wide. "I take full responsibility for that. I dragged the others along for a ride, so don't blame them."

"You don't need to fall on your sword to save the whole team," said Chloe.

"Well, you sure know how to drop people down a few pegs."

"I used to be a teacher," said Chloe.

Kingston glanced over to Joanna. He never knew their reputation was this bad.

Joanna looked back to Chloe. "What would you like us to do?"

Chloe leaned forward. "Look, everyone in Limbo wants a team from here to win, and you lot have a reasonable chance. Horatio is in division one so he's still the favourite, but he's up against the worst competition. Six teams from Hell against him. They'll take him out first, so really, you and Rufus are in with a fighting chance. But in terms of popularity, your team is probably last. Rufus is a joke, you waste so much money, and you've never even seen a tournament before yet you're expecting to win on your first go."

Chloe looked from Kingston to Joanna and knew that they were both dying inside at hearing their reputation ripped to shreds. She took a sip from her cocktail and placed it back on the desk.

Kingston launched himself into full damage control. There was one way to salvage his dignity with the other teams, but he knew it was going to cost him dearly. He had to quickly consult Joanna. "What if we helped the other teams?" he whispered.

"All the ones from Limbo?"

"Yeah. We have some resources."

"You know that will soon become illegal," whispered Joanna.

"That's in the future. Right now, though, it might level the playing field."

Joanna thought it over, and knew, tactically, it was a mistake. Still, hearing that her reputation was so crappy had all but ruined her day. She turned back to Chloe. "So like Kingston was saying, what if we helped all of the other teams from Limbo?"

Chloe arched an eyebrow. "How?"

"We could supply you with some amber," said Kingston.

Chloe thought it through and started bobbing her head. "The apothecaries won't be pleased. And I don't need amber. I found out I'm allergic to it."

"Then how about each team from Limbo asks for one specific component and we'll have it delivered?"

Joanna shot Kingston a look and knew that would backfire.

"I need fifty kilos of wrought iron," said Chloe. "Plus whatever you have in the vault that Rufus built."

"We'll have to look over the details carefully on that one."

"If I get the iron and the old machines from Rufus I will stay by your team's side and risk my own ass in taking down opponents from your division."

Kingston glanced over to Joanna to confirm, and she gave a non-committal nod. "Okay."

"And the only way you can ensure that the teams from Limbo don't ambush you is if you supply them with some materials. That might go some way to rebuilding your reputation and they will be less inclined to sabotage you."

Kingston knew he would have had to bribe his way to victory, but he never expected it would mean bribing every team in the realm. "I'll see what we can do."

"Good," said Chloe. "If you help all of the other teams I'll put in a good word for you with the usual sponsors."

Joanna read a little too much into that comment, and she then realised why the team had been struggling to find even the sponsors they had. "Have potential donors and sponsors been told to stay away from us?"

"Yes," said Chloe.

"Really?" asked Kingston.

Chloe shrugged. "You didn't know? You might need to chat to your thief about that. It's something she should've have looked into."

"How were they told to stay away?" asked Kingston.

"The other teams from Limbo tried to have you lot blacklisted. The Cascade didn't listen, but when enough people started talking about it, it scared away the punters. They didn't want to risk allying themselves with you in case the gaming houses refused to honour any bet they made."

"Huh," said Kingston, and he realised that answered a lot of his concerns. "Okay, we'll help all of the other teams. If you could pass on the information to whoever is responsible that we're not to be blacklisted we would appreciate that."

"I'll do my part. I can't speak for the other teams," said Chloe. She looked up at the time and stood up. "I've already stayed longer than I cared for."

"We'll have to discuss this with the team," said Kingston.

"I need an answer now," said Chloe. "You two are the team bosses."

Kingston glanced back to Joanna and read her expression. It was one of resigned acceptance. "Done," said Kingston.

"I'm glad to hear," said Chloe.

Kingston reached out and Chloe was, at last, willing to shake his hand.

"I'd like those components from Rufus in the next six hours," she said, and she left.

Joanna closed the door after Chloe and collapsed onto the sofa. "We just got screwed."

"I know," said Kingston, and he rubbed his hands over his face.

"We can't supply them all with anything fictional because it won't react properly with what they've already built. We'll have to buy all of this legitimately."

"No kidding," said Kingston. "Thirteen other teams wanting the most expensive item on the menu, and lots of it so they can keep the repairs going over five days."

"We're going to need another loan," said Joanna.

When they told Rufus of their new arrangement he slumped over on the table and demanded another bottle of scotch, or else he wasn't going to be able to stand up again.

Jezebel looked nervously from Kingston to Joanna.

"Be honest," said Joanna. "Do the other teams hate us?"

"Every team hates every other team to some degree," said Jezebel. "It's part of the Games. It's just the way things are. Then the dust settles and everyone realises that they had a good time."

"So how is our reputation doing?" asked Kingston.

"I wouldn't worry about it," said Jezebel.

"It's too late for that. How is our reputation doing?"

Jezebel pulled back and winced. "It's not great. By now you should have at least twice the number of donors. It doesn't help that you are best friends with Death and Satan, that you are always chasing the limelight ..."

"We don't chase the limelight," said Joanna. "And believe it or not we are somewhat retired."

"I think there's a big difference in what you do and what you think you do. The first thing you all did was host a great big party to draw as much attention to yourselves as possible."

"That's how it's done in Life," said Kingston.

"That's not how it's done here," said Jezebel. "You also built a great big golem instead of something more practical."

"That was to attract interest in our team." Kingston realised what he had just said and he sighed at his own stupidity.

"You might find that people are weary of you because whenever you lot are involved, things kinda blow out of proportion. So, the locals will try to keep to themselves or else they risk getting dragged into your mess."

Kingston slumped his shoulders and shook his head.

"Maybe public relations just aren't your thing," said Jezebel.

Kingston glanced over to Joanna. "If we're going to partially fund everyone else's build then we're going to need a lot more second opinions."

"That sounds like pouring lemon juice on an open wound," said Joanna.

"I'm afraid you're disqualified from getting another loan," said Sebastian Burrows.

Kingston leaned forward in shock. "What? Why?"

Burrows pulled forward a sheet of paper. "This comes from the gaming commission. Your machine exploded in the player's booth, breaching safety guidelines, and five members of the commission required urgent medical attention, which was delayed by your team by an hour."

"And why does this stop me from getting a loan?"

"Because you are using your machine as collateral against this loan, and the gaming commission has put you on notice for breaching safety guidelines. Your machine may be seized at any moment, so you don't actually have any collateral."

"What if I got some more machine parts?"

Burrows shook his head. "As long as they are parts for the tournament then they too are under notice."

"Could Joanna York get a loan instead of me?"

"No. This affects everyone in the team."

Kingston gritted his teeth and knew he hated asking this, but he had to do so anyway. "If someone else, not related to our team, received a loan for my teams' benefit, is that doable?"

"That is fine," said Burrows. "But they wouldn't be able to use any of your assets as collateral. They would have to use their own machine to back yours."

Kingston felt another groan coming along as their problems doubled.

Kingston met with Roger again and offered him a case of beer.

"How's the fantasy tournament going?" asked Kingston.

Roger winced. "Well ... it's been a bit hit and miss, actually."

"How did fake Mortimer go?"

"Oh, in the game he did fantastic!"

"But not in reality?"

"Well, no, and some of the guys think I've been fudging the stats because we've seen him run at different speeds, and I didn't expect him to throw his war hammer either, but really, you guys getting hit by those bricks ... that was just unfair."

Kingston pulled out a pen and paper and began taking notes.

"So, onto this new line up. Who would win in a fight between my team, Sanders, Lucha, Biggins, Wayne, Carver, Creig, and Kazuka?"

"We actually tried that scenario last night. Kazuka was beaten to a pulp and was forced to take out Lucha because that was the only combatant in range. Biggins was able to shoot down Carver, while - "

Kingston held his hand up to stop Roger from babbling away. "Who won?"

"Biggins," said Roger. "With Creig as a close second."

Kingston sighed and felt the life nearly drop out from under him. "How did my team do?"

"Oh, you were a solid fourth."

"Fourth? Out of eight?" Kingston sighed and knew that he now had to listen to Roger go on about the different options, line ups, stats, and how things should have been done better, were it not for Dave or Chris rolling several critical hits. Finally, Kingston asked Roger to replay the game until Mortimer won, and Kingston offered another case of beer to see how that version played out.

Kingston then hurried to the bank to get back to some real work.

"Well look, if it isn't Mr Generosity," said Rufus the moment he saw Kingston. "Care to take anything else from my vault to help our competitors? Perhaps a family heirloom? Maybe even my dignity?"

Kingston rolled his eyes. "I'm sensing a little ... what's the word? Sarcasm."

Rufus glared back at Kingston. "You're being a little liberal with the contents of my vault."

"You arranged a meeting with Stuyvescent and set me up to take it without letting me know," said Kingston.

"Oh, so you handing over all of my most prized possessions to our rival is *my* fault?"

"In a word? Yes."

Rufus shot daggers into Kingston's soul. "Pick a better word."

"Two are springing to mind ..." said Kingston. "How's the rebuild going?"

"We need an extra pair of hands, quickly," said Rufus.

"How about Simon?"

"I've included everyone already on the team. We need more

hands. You have to hire someone. Preferably, two more people." Rufus reached into his back pocket and pulled out a new list. "And we need more brand new projectors from 1920 again. We're going to need lots of those. They get easily broken."

Kingston glanced over the list and raised his eyebrows in surprise. "Fifty projectors?"

Rufus shrugged. "I figure Mortimer will be lucky to survive an hour before needing to be dragged back in for repairs. So we'll replace his visual cortex and send him out again. The change over might take an hour, maybe two depending on the peripheral damage, and then half an hour later he'll be back in to have that whole thing replaced once again. Repeat the process ad nauseam and we'll make it into the final round. Possibly. Our one advantage is that we won't become as bankrupt as the other teams, which right now is our only advantage. We'll need a lot of extra hands building spare parts."

"Do you have any recommendations on who to hire?" asked Kingston.

"We can't trust anyone in Limbo," said Rufus. "Unless Jezebel knows a guy, and chances are she does, but it will be tricky to know if he's working to help us or sabotage us. It's just a whole lot of manual labour, leaving me to do the enchanting in private."

"All right, I'll talk it over with her," said Kingston, and he had the sinking feeling that this was going to get very expensive very quickly.

"And no more looting my vault!" Rufus cried out.

XX

Joc Biggins kept the location of his workshop as secret as possible, though Jezebel assured Kingston that it was on the top floor of building Six of Death Inc., which was home to the Department of Approvals. Joc had sectioned off a corner of the building where he operated in perfect secrecy, until six months ago when his rolling tornado caught fire and set off the sprinkler systems.

Kingston had paid close attention to Joc's machine during the first two rounds and was impressed by the concept. It was designed after a flying wind turbine. It shot out grey smoke to shield its location and floated in the air, surrounded by a tornado, which was capable of throwing the enemy against walls, launching them up into the air, or crushing them under the air pressure. But like all machines in the competition it was prone to not working as well as the builder first imagined.

Kingston met with Joc in the Café Rotunda, off Duat Avenue, which was just a short walk from Kingston's office. Kingston spent the first couple of minutes alone, waiting patiently with a cappuccino and a cinnamon bun, then he felt a slight shift in the air. He was sure Joc's brother Henry Biggins was scouting the area to make sure it was safe for Joc to enter. Soon enough, Joc came in, peered at Kingston suspiciously, and listened to Kingston's baffling offer.

After several minutes of silence, Joc squinted at Kingston. "You're going to give me anything I like?"

Kingston nodded as politely as he could. "Anything you need to help your team make it through this round."

"You do know that we are both in the same division," said Joc.

"And I'd rather see a team from Limbo win than one from

Hell."

Joc stared back at Kingston and weighed up the odds of whether Kingston was telling the truth or not. "You wouldn't object to me investigating you, would you?"

Kingston had a feeling that Joc's brother was about to peer into Kingston's past and unearth every last secret he had held onto during the tournament. "I don't object, but I do mind. What do you need the most of to make it to the end of round three?"

"Oil," said Joc, without missing a beat. "I'd need five barrels of the stuff." He peered at Kingston, and Kingston got the impression that this request wasn't as simple as it appeared to be.

"Oil, teleported through fire," said Kingston.

"Exactly," said Joc. "The teleport aspect of it plays havoc with the chemical components. They get distorted and tend to break down if it is teleported incorrectly."

"What's the best method of bringing it to Limbo?" asked Kingston.

"Ideally? It has to be transported inside someone's stomach."

If there was ever a time when Kingston would talk about when he realised that Stuyvescent had screwed him over, he would look back to this moment and know it was then. He was no longer inspired to finish his cinnamon bun. "Each barrel contains, what, a hundred and forty litres of oil?"

"Yes," said Joc.

"And each person would be able to carry just half a litre at a time inside their stomachs."

"That's right," said Joc.

Kingston knew that his perfect plan of making a fortune through this tournament had just been blown to pieces, all to rebuild his tattered reputation. "And in exchange for this you and I will have a non-aggression pact until the final ten minutes of round three?"

"I think that's fair," said Joc.

Kingston thought it over and knew he had no other choice but to say yes. If he didn't he risked alienating the entire realm. "I'll see what I can do."

"Thank you," said Joc. "I will still investigate you, of course."

"I have no doubt," said Kingston, and he hoped that the other teams would be as welcoming as Joc.

In the back of a Chilean restaurant on Barzakh Way, Joanna met with a very suspicious Kazuka.

"Silver," said Kazuka. "Lots of silver."

"How much?" asked Joanna.

"Lots."

"One kilogram?"

"Ha!" cried Kazuka, and he shook his head. "No less than seventeen kilograms of silver."

Joanna thought it through and gave a non-committal nod. "And if we supply you with the silver you'll work on taking out every other team except us?"

"We will save you for last," said Kazuka. "But you will not be immune to our attacks."

She knew that Kazuka was desperate for parts, having thrown together a machine out of the wreck of several explosions, but even Joanna knew that seventeen kilograms of silver was ludicrous. "We will have to supply it in increments."

Kazuka quickly shook his head. "We need it all before the third round. It must be prepared."

"We can get half of the silver before the round begins but the rest will have to come in stages."

"No! We will not be held hostage like this!"

Joanna cocked her head to one side and she took a confident step forward. "We are offering to *give* you this component for free, and all we ask for is that you don't attack us until your team and ours are the last teams standing in the entire arena."

"We need all of the silver at the beginning otherwise we will have to forfeit!" snapped Kazuka.

Jezebel stared at the increasingly long list of items needed for the other teams. She looked back at Kingston and Joanna in dismay. "Do you have any idea how difficult it is to get all of this?"

"I have an idea, yeah," said Kingston. He had just spent the last twelve hours trying to sweet talk seven other teams into accepting his help, and only three of them had accepted. He knew he would have to try again over the next few days and with any luck the other teams would start to vouch for his good behaviour.

"I'm sure you know a guy," said Joanna.

"This requires *all* of my guys, and some of them have been detained in Hell," said Jezebel.

"We also need a couple of people to help Rufus as well," said Kingston.

Jezebel gritted her teeth. "I'll look into it, but all of the builders are kinda busy. Most still pull down a regular job."

"How much would it cost?" asked Kingston.

"Rufus wants two people at all times, right?" asked Jezebel. "They're going to work their usual eight hour shift, then potentially eight hours with us, so we'll need six well trained people at a moment's notice. That is at least two gold per person per day."

Kingston looked over to Joanna and gave a sigh of relief. "That isn't as bad as I feared."

"But they're going to want to negotiate," said Jezebel. "A minimum of twelve gold a day for the next eleven days? Besides, not all of them are in Limbo. We'll need to ship a lot of this to Hell where they can build the components and have it sent back to us."

"That's going to be a problem," said Joanna. "These components are fictional."

"Then you should probably hire some fictional people," said Jezebel.

"And as soon as we're done with these teams we'll need to spread the word to the others that we are offering our help legitimately," said Joanna.

"I'll try, but at the very least they might look for financial backing as well." Jezebel looked over the list and glanced up to the ceiling as she did some quick maths. "I'm ball parking this, but the silver, the oil, the amber, the entrails of a blue whale ... we're looking at a minimum of eighteen thousand gold."

"Eighteen thousand?" cried Kingston.

"Yep," said Jezebel. "They've gone with the most expensive item on the list and they've gone with lots of it. You know, there's a good chance that they'll just use a tenth of what they get, forfeit the moment they get hit, and sell the rest to earn back some money."

Kingston hung his head, stared at his feet, and he finally glanced over to Joanna. "It's not too late to run away."

"Yes, it is," said Joanna.

"We're going to need a loan of equal that just to gamble with, otherwise there's no way we can earn that back," said Kingston.

"And there's no way to know if they're telling the truth about the quantities they need," said Jezebel. "Except for Joc. I know him and I've looked at his machine. He definitely needs the oil. Kazuka ... yeah, I saw his blueprints a while ago. He needs silver. But that much of it? Hardly. He's probably playing us as idiots and doing what he can to repay his loan."

Kingston took the scenic route back home, which included passing through several parks and idyllic picnic locations, and all the while his head swarmed with bets, debts, and contingency plans. He walked for two hours with his head down until he realised that he had gone one block too far, so he doubled back and found his way to his apartment which, miraculously, wasn't locked or hoodwinked via some design of a mischievous apothecary.

He pushed the door open, kicked his shoes off, laid back on the sofa, and closed his eyes. He *knew* there was still money to be made from the sponsors. He knew that five days of combat was an opportunity that was too good to pass up. He also knew that with the other teams locked in the arena for five days then the entire realm was his for the taking. All he needed was a miracle. He just had no idea how to get one.

As his mind drifted back to how he managed to work his charms in Fiction, he was met with a resounding slap back to reality.

The only reason it worked in Fiction was because you had an author pulling the strings to ensure your victory. Here, everyone is out for themselves, and they know how to play this better than you. And let's not forget that there's a good chance you're not as clever as you thought you were.

He paused when he heard someone coming up the corridor. High heels. A strong walk. It was Joanna.

She opened the front door and saw Kingston lying on the sofa. "That looks like it's becoming your new routine."

Kingston groaned, and surprised himself with the sound that came out of him.

Joanna smirked. "And now you sound like an old man."

"You look as radiant as the first day I met you," said Kingston.

"Well, I am immortal now. It's one of the perks of being in the afterlife." She dropped her keys on the bookshelf beside the door and looked over her exhausted boyfriend. "Rough day?"

"Yeah. I left Horatio's lab and he said something disconcerting."

Joanna felt that knot in her stomach start to build. "Uh huh?"

"Yeah. He used a lot of big words again and said, and I'm paraphrasing: *The other teams never hated you.*"

Joanna bobbed her head, trying to follow Kingston's train of thought, but it was lost on her. "Well of course he would say that, he's messing with us."

"I know, but it was the way he said it."

"How did he say it?" asked Joanna.

"I'm not sure, but the feeling I got from the rest of the builders was this: little Miss Stuyvescent was lying us. They were telling us what she wanted them to say."

Joanna blinked a few times, looked away, and then it dawned on her. "She played us?"

"It makes sense."

"*We* got played?"

"I'm ninety five percent sure that is exactly what happened."

Joanna's jaw dropped open. She flexed her fingers and balled them up into fists, then her anger faded and she collapsed back onto a chair. "Well played."

"Yeah, and now we're kinda committed to following through on her plans, which will financially ruin us."

"Can't we just not give them anything?"

"The problem is our reputation is still in tatters. The teams may not hate us, but no one seems to trust us. That's going to be tough if we're planning to survive as bounty hunters."

Joanna sighed and mumbled to herself. "It's not too late to become a chef."

Kingston stepped forward. "We did actually expect this kind of thing to happen. At this rate we need to win the tournament and every bet we've placed just to break even."

"That would explain why we can't find any decent sponsors," said Joanna. "We have a hundred and ninety of them and they are very tight with their money. There's just no advantage in knowing us when they could bet that kind of money."

"They get free food, free booze, and a party," said Kingston.

"They're effectively paying for the whole party, that's how little their donations are. So, really, the sponsor thing is something of a lost cause." Joanna scowled and headed off into the kitchen. "We need to sabotage every team out there."

Kingston smirked, shook his head, and allowed his mind to wander. It bounced back with a world of clutter. "Do you want to go out tonight?"

Joanna returned. "Out?"

"Yeah, on a date."

Joanna leaned back in surprise. "Are you jealous of John and Catalina?"

Kingston smiled, climbed off the sofa, and went over to Joanna. "I'm saying our minds are fried. We're not thinking straight. You're on a murderous rampage of revenge and I'm trying to figure out a way to soak every last copper out of our sponsors. So let's forget about it for a couple of hours. Let's go out, find a new restaurant that only the statues know about, and do something different."

Joanna sighed, and felt as though she had been on her feet for the last twenty four hours. "We're facing several thousand gold fines ..."

"Yeah, and we have to find a way of coming up with thirty six grand or else we blow all of our sympathy points with the other teams. At this point, spending eight or nine silver hardly matters."

Joanna paused as an idea hit her, and she glanced away quickly.

"I know that look," said Kingston. "You just had a brainwave."

"It's a bad idea," said Joanna.

"No, you had that look as though it was one of the greatest ideas ever. What was it?"

"No. It's probably a quick way to lose our friends."

Kingston glanced around the apartment. "Is this an occasion for vodka, or are you going to let me in on this morally grey idea?"

Joanna sighed and grumbled to herself. "Promise me that you'll keep this to yourself."

"I promise."

"And we're not doing it."

"That's fine."

"Although it is actually a good idea."

"You're not helping."

"And I'm sure we could all convince ourselves that it is a good idea for the team, but individually it's morally questionable."

Kingston bobbed his head. "I am very excited about how excited I will be when I hear about this wonderful brainwave of yours."

Joanna bit down on her lower lip and winced. "I know how we

can get a trustworthy seer, or psychic, working for the team. But it's a bad idea, our friends will *hate* us for considering it, and we might end up getting expelled from Limbo if we try it."

"That does sound severe. Is there someone specific in mind?"

"Yeah. Yurana. John's niece from *Robin Hood*."

Kingston raised his eyebrows in utter shock. "You want to get the one person who John is more protective of than Catalina ..."

"I know."

"Bring her out of Fiction and into Limbo ..."

"I know."

"For the sole purpose of us winning a tournament and making money?"

Joanna gave Kingston a quick nod. "I know. It's a horrible thing to think of, so please don't seriously consider it."

Kingston glanced up towards the ceiling.

"No! Don't consider it!"

"I'm just working it through," said Kingston.

"It's not worth it!"

"But ..."

"No!"

"Hang on ..."

"Not for all the money in Limbo!" cried Joanna.

"I'm sure we could convince the others ..."

"No!" shouted Joanna, and she stamped her foot. "Seriously, we can not do that. Not ever. There is no way we can convince Death that this is or was a good idea. There is no way to rebuild our reputations once the public finds out, and there is no way John will ever want to see us again if anything happens to her, and considering that these are the Games where people are sabotaged day and night we *know* something will happen to her. John will *kill* us the moment something happens to his niece."

Kingston bobbed his head for a few moments and considered everything that Joanna said. "All right, then we're going to need to come up with another brilliant idea that will not cripple us for the rest of eternity."

The next day they had it, and it came from Simon, of all sources.

John pushed Simon into the workshop and stopped him in front of Kingston. "Simon has an idea."

"I do?"

"Yes. Tell Kingston what it was."

"But doesn't he already know about it?"

John rolled his eyes and stared back at Kingston. "Last year we saved the bank, right?"

"Yeah," said Kingston.

"And we recovered more than a hundred thousand gold pieces, right?"

"Yeah, but that went straight back to the bank."

John nudged Simon in the back. "Tell him."

"But he already knows," said Simon.

John rolled his eyes again. "There's a finder's fee reward worth ten percent."

Kingston looked up just as his jaw dropped open. "There is?"

Simon peered at Kingston. "But you already knew that."

"No, I didn't!"

"Why not?"

"I don't know why. Is it true?"

Simon shrugged. "It hasn't been used all that much since I first arrived, but I think that policy is still technically in the books. And it's not a great deal, either. You receive a loan without any interest on it. You still have to pay the loan back."

"It's an interest free loan!" cried John. "And Simon thought of it! Can you believe it?"

Kingston hurried off to see Burrows upstairs, and much to their mutual disbelief Kingston was able to draw a goodwill loan from the bank thanks to his efforts in recovering over a hundred thousand gold pieces. In theory he now had enough to buy just half of the other team's supplies and rebuild his reputation.

XXI

It was one week before the third round began. The team had gathered over Mortimer to finalise the details of their game plan. Then Rufus handed over a list of requirements.

Kingston looked over the list. "Hammocks?"

Rufus rolled his eyes at Kingston. "Have you ever competed in a five day non-stop last man standing battle royale?"

Kingston sighed. "Rufus?"

Rufus sighed in return and repeated himself. "Have you ever competed in a five day non-stop last man standing battle royale?"

"No. And neither have you."

"I know!" said Rufus. "We need somewhere to sleep. We need -"

"That's why we're here," said Kingston. He pulled out a list of his own, and in first place was *'Hammocks'*. Next to it was a big tick.

Rufus gawked, then he saw Joanna, John, and Catalina nod at him. "You lot have been planning this behind my back?"

Joanna pulled out another sheet of paper. "Here's our proposed roster. In the marquee, entertaining the sponsors and giving an update on the score, myself and Catalina."

Rufus arched an eyebrow at Joanna. "For five days?"

"We will be on twelve hour shifts. We'll be smiling and dining our way to success."

"How do you expect to stay awake for that long?" asked Rufus.

"Lots of power naps. And we're not going to be there the whole time either. We'll have greeters and bar staff who will watch over the place while Cat and I are gone."

Rufus peered over at Kingston. "Do we have that in the booth?"

"No," said Kingston. "We'll have power naps, coffee, and sheer force of will to stay awake for that long."

"That's a crap idea," said Rufus.

"Jezebel has offered to help relieve us for a few hours every day."

"That's nice of her," said Rufus.

"Yes, it is," said Jezebel. "Especially because Joanna needs to pop out every few hours to update the bets."

Joanna looked over the team. "Jezebel will be working flat out spying, so we need to stay as fluid with the gambling as possible."

Rufus glared at the team and shook his head. "You do know that after five days of three people in that one room, all drinking coffee and sweating from the stress, that it's going to smell awful, right?"

John grabbed the list of necessities. "I'll just underline the potpourri section."

The newspapers had now doubled in size as everyone wanted an interview with each of the builders, and no article would be complete without the views of an armchair critic speculating on the last man standing. Every team trash talked the other, flooded the realm with false information, left fake blueprints behind, sealed the doors to every team, and tried to blow up every hide out, until everyone became so paranoid that simply making a cup of coffee became an ordeal of testing and re-testing before they could trust the caffeine they were about to drink. Best of all, though, was that Horatio had been fined for hiding a listening device in a coffee mug in the gaming commissioner's office.

After number crunching their missing fortune, Kingston had to veto the extra hired hands. Rufus kicked and screamed, but Kingston assured him that the only way they could afford this was by doing as much of the building on their own as possible.

"You better have some exceptionally gifted fictional people working their magic on your spare parts, because there's no way we're going to have all of this done in time," said Rufus.

Kingston and Joanna were on a constant rotation of diving into Fiction and back again to retrieve all of the items they needed. They got Kazuka's silver, Biggins' oil, Chloe's wrought iron, and everything else on the list from the eight builders who were willing to accept Kingston's help. Jezebel's contacts were paid off with gifts of fictional ice wine and bourbon to take the items down to Hell and bounce them back up again, but this was a process that had to be repeated until the taint from Hell was strong enough to pass off the items as being non-fiction. Even so, the silver, oil, iron, and the like were now considered to be inferior in quality.

"Use it during the middle of the battle royale and save your best stuff for last," said Kingston, and the teams grumbled a 'thank you'.

Meanwhile, there were factories spread across fictional Germany that were working around the clock on building spare parts for Mortimer. The real problem came with the telemetry suit that John was expected to wear, as Rufus barely had enough time to enchant it and the golem for John to get any practice.

And all the while Kingston and Joanna kept their heads in the betting guide, working on every single contingency bet available, every strategy they could use, and every piece of trivia they picked up from Jezebel and her contacts.

At long last, and now well under prepared, Kingston and Joanna returned to Limbo with the first batch of joints for new Mortimer.

Jezebel came bounding down the stairs of the bank, ran around the corner, and almost bumped into Kingston, who was standing in the corridor with a cup of coffee from his favourite café in Vienna.

"Let me guess. *Two minutes, Mr K?*"

Jezebel closed her mouth, smirked, then nodded. "Pretty much."

Kingston took another sip, then headed down towards the workshop. "How are the teams handling our generous donations?"

Jezebel's enthusiasm faltered for a moment. "They are grateful."

"Were we played as fools?"

"Not necessarily, but ..."

"But you think so?"

"It will be a talking point once the Games are done."

"At least there's that," said Kingston. They reached the door into the workshop and found that it was locked. "Rufus? Rise and shine."

After a moment of shuffling about, Rufus pulled the door open and stared out at Kingston. The light in the corridor seemed to blind him. "What?"

"It's time to pack up the workshop and carry everything over to the arena."

Rufus smacked his lips together. "The doors don't open for us until ten o'clock."

Kingston grinned and savoured the moment. "That's in one minute."

"No, it's in an hour and a half. I set my alarm for eight thirty."

Kingston held out his watch to show Rufus the time.

"Your watch is fast."

"No. You overslept."

A very sceptical Rufus shuffled back into his dark room to prove that Kingston was a wrong, and as his eyes adjusted to the darkness he realised that he may have forgotten to set his alarm. *"Oh sweet Jesus, we're late!"*

The team carried as much as they could over to the arena and they were assigned booth twenty eight. It was identical to every other player's booth except this one was painted purple. It took them several trips to move everything across, but by four o'clock John was sure that they had everything they needed. He lowered a chest of tools onto the ground and arched his back to relieve the tension.

"Good," mumbled Rufus. "Now stay here and make sure no one robs us. I'll be back in an hour."

"Ah, no," said John. "I have to help the girls set up the marquee."

"You what? It's already set up! It's been set up for the past month!"

"It's hardly suitable for two women to live in the open for five days like that. We need to establish dressing rooms and showers."

"They don't need any of that! They can teleport back home and shower in private. Just give them a refill of mascara and wait here while I go back to the workshop for more of my supplies!"

"It won't take an hour to teleport to the bank and back again," said John. "What are you hiding? It's not your book of enchantments, is it?"

Rufus spluttered in response. "I need my good luck charm if you must know!"

John reeled back in surprise. "You need a good luck charm?"

"Ever since meeting you four? Yes! I have a new good luck charm for every tournament. So far none of them have exactly worked, and even though I have even less faith in this new one I still need it!"

"What is it? A rabbit's foot?"

"It doesn't matter what it is, I just need to have it."

"It better not be Snowflake," said John.

"Trust me, it's not. Just stay here until Kingston or the girls come back."

Kingston sauntered into the room with a final backpack of food and drinks. "There! That should be it."

"Good! Now you can both watch the room," said Rufus.

"What's going on?" asked Kingston.

"Mr Piddlesworth here has left his good luck charm back in the bank and life can't go on without it," said John.

Kingston arched an eyebrow at Rufus. "This wouldn't be your autographed collector's card for Game One, with you on it, autographed by you, would it?"

Rufus' jaw dropped open. "How did you know about that?"

"Because it was the only thing left in the workshop," said Kingston.

Rufus gasped and hurried out the door.

John stepped forward and broke into a whisper. "Okay, really, how did you find out about that thing?"

"I saw him buy it directly from a seller at the auction," said Kingston. "I guess he's more nostalgic than he lets on."

"Maybe that was his last moment of greatness, before the debt nearly killed him."

Kingston and John continued to set up the room, which was now crammed with a work bench, tools, a hammock, food, bottles of water, a coffee machine, and several trunks of spare parts for Mortimer. The whole room began as the size of a one bedroom apartment. Now it had the free space of a cupboard.

"Is 'cosy' the right word?" asked John.

"It'll get better when Mortimer is out in the arena."

An hour later, Rufus returned, guided by Jezebel.

"You were cutting it pretty close," said Kingston.

"I said I would be gone for an hour and I was gone for an hour," said Rufus. "It's not like we're amateurs at this. We have an hour left before game time."

"We had to take the scenic route," said Jezebel.

"That's not a euphemism, is it?" asked John.

"No, but I'll have to remember that one for the next time. I'll be ducking in and out over the next five days, here to keep you alive, the girls sane, and the opponents miserable. Good luck!" Jezebel backed away and hurried off to the marquee.

Rufus glanced out the window and looked over the crowd. "I really wish I could have sat this one out and watched."

"Montgomery wouldn't have given you a moment's peace," said Kingston.

Rufus shrugged. Already the crowd had filled the arena, lifting the quiet realm into a thunderous roar. Just beyond the glass was a sea of bright colours and teams chanting together. The screens displayed the highlights of the preceding rounds while giving the stats of each builder. Rufus looked away when he saw his list of defeats light up for millions of people to see.

There was a knock at the door and a brunette referee peered inside. "Hello?"

"Yes?" asked Kingston.

"Hi, my name's Henrietta. We are one hour away."

"Thank you," said Kingston.

"We need to listen to this part," murmured Rufus.

Kingston looked back to Henrietta and he saw her nod. She then pulled out the official paperwork.

"This is to prevent any confusion. There will be confusion, but this should help to ease it somewhat. I think." She looked over her speech. "Okay, in case there is any confusion ... I said that already ... there are retrieval times, lock-out times, and re-entry times. Retrieval times will be given a two minute warning and they will last for five minutes. During this time there will be no fighting in the arena otherwise you will receive a fine and a time penalty. This time is to allow damaged entrants to exit the arena for repairs.

"Next are lock-out times. These will last for one hour and they will occur no less than thirty minutes after the end of the previous lock-out time, and no later than two hours after the previous lock-out time. For every lock-out you miss you will receive a time penalty. All penalties are cumulative, and each lasts for two minutes.

"There are also re-entry times. If you miss these then you are locked out for one hour and receive a penalty. On the final day, with ninety minutes remaining in the round, all teams will exit the arena, at which point you may do your final repairs without penalty.

"The final ten minute mark of the round is crucial. If you receive no penalties you may re-enter with ten minutes to go. If you receive a single time penalty you must re-enter with twelve minutes to go, and so on."

"What the hell does all of that mean?" asked John.

Kingston leaned over. "It means the longer Mortimer is fighting in the ring, in theory five days straight without leaving, then he receives no penalties and he can come into the last ten minutes refreshed and repaired, whereas if he's locked out and receives ten time penalties over the five days then the latest he can come into the final ten minutes is with a twenty minute disadvantage, so he'll arrive thirty minutes before the end of the round and risk thirty minutes of carnage, allowing the team with the fewest of penalties a chance to waltz into the finale."

"Exactly," said Henrietta.

"Amateurs," muttered Rufus.

Kingston ignored him. "So there are two real strategies here. The first is to stay in the arena the longest and receive the fewest time penalties. That would allow that team the greatest chance of out lasting their opponents in the final hoorah of the round. The other strategy is to avoid as much punishment over the next five days as possible, receive the longest penalty imaginable, and then spend an hour and a half fighting the strongest, fittest, and cheatiest of opponents."

Henrietta smiled and nodded at Kingston. "I'm glad someone read the information pack."

"What information pack?" asked Kingston.

"The pack we sent you last week with all of this information," said Henrietta.

Kingston looked over to Rufus and John, but they both shook their heads as well. "We didn't get it."

"Then your team would be the first to not get it. Maybe I should report this."

"There's no need," said Kingston.

"No, I think ... that might explain ... wait here, please." Henrietta backed away and closed the door.

Rufus looked over to Kingston. "Does she really think we're

going somewhere else?"

John glanced around their room and looked over the painted walls. "So our team's pack was intercepted."

Rufus nodded. "Makes you paranoid, doesn't it?"

John peered at the wall. "Is there a significance to purple?"

Rufus shook his head. "There is no significance to any of these colours. I'm sure there might even be two purple rooms because, really, how many different colours could there be?"

John arched his eyebrow at Rufus and shook his head. "I'm an artist, you know, so I know the difference between lilac and mauve."

"Yay for you," said Rufus. "And for what it's worth, I've seen your ... 'paintings.'"

John flared his eyes and took a menacing step forward. "What did you say?"

"Gentlemen?" Kingston called out.

Rufus nearly shrieked. "We have five days of uncontrollable mayhem, no sleep, and enough coffee to kill a third world country, and you two are talking about the damned colour on the wall! Do you people not have your priorities in check?"

John gritted his teeth and looked back to Kingston. "Five days of him in this mood."

"Yeah," said Rufus. "Believe it or not, this is me at my most Zen."

There was another knock on the door, and this time Hubert Stance, the gaming commissioner, entered.

"Mr Stance," said Kingston.

"Mr Raine. One of the referees tells me you did not receive your information pack last week. I wanted to make sure you were up to speed on the rules and regulations of the round so I took the liberty of providing you with a copy." Stance held out a small booklet.

Kingston took it and flipped through the pages. "Cheers."

Stance glanced up at Mortimer and peered at the machine inquisitively. "This doesn't seem to be the same golem as what was entered last time."

"These things are a constant work in progress," said Kingston.

Stance tapped on Mortimer's chest plate, then snapped his fingers at one of the junior gaming officials, who hurried over and examined Mortimer closely.

"May I ask what you're looking for?"

"Three months ago someone vandalised the ship over in the docks and stole two hundred and fifty kilograms worth of iron."

Kingston felt a gulp building in his chest. "We bought our iron from the auction."

The junior gaming official looked back to Stance and shook his head.

"Hmm," said Stance, and he nearly smirked at Kingston. "We will need to investigate this golem. It appears as though he is made up of stolen material belonging to the realm of Limbo."

Kingston knew that was likely to carry another thousand gold fine. "He's due for combat any minute now."

"Don't worry, Mr Raine, we aren't picking on you unnecessarily. All of the teams are under scrutiny before the competition." Stance tapped Mortimer's chest again. "We'll have a look at him after the round comes to an end." He turned and took the gaming officials away with him.

John closed the door on them, looked back at Kingston and Rufus, and exhaled loudly. "What a pugnacious little man."

Rufus cocked his head to one side. "Pugnacious?"

John shrugged. "I heard Horatio call me that a while ago. Had to look it up in the dictionary."

Kingston looked over to Rufus. "Any ideas?"

"Not really," said Rufus. "If we hand over old Mortimer here we'll be fined a thousand gold pieces for using stolen property. If we hand over new Mortimer we'll be fined a thousand gold pieces for using components from Fiction."

"At least we're not being disqualified," said John.

Kingston stared out through the glass and watched as the thousands of fans began doing a wave around the stands. The first hour was bound to see the most amount of carnage and mayhem the Games had ever experienced. Front row tickets were selling for ten gold pieces. Even the cheap seats were going for five gold a piece.

There was also more than a million gold pieces riding on various outcomes by thousands of punters in Limbo alone. Most bets were friendly wagers among friends, but the more serious of strategists went to the gambling houses to try their luck. By all accounts, Mortimer was the third most likely team from division two to make it into the finale. Joc Biggins was first with his flying tornado, Sanders and his drill were second.

For once, Kingston had taken a very conservative approach to gambling. It was virtually impossible to pick a winner in the first few minutes of a battle royale, although Kingston did place several contingent bets. *If Aurelius begins next to Kwon, Aurelius will attack Kwon first.* He had a hundred of those, but he was only willing to bet one silver piece on each. Most of his more serious bets scaled up towards the end. *If Horatio is still competing twenty four hours after round three begins he will compete in the final twenty four hours.* He had placed ten gold pieces on that one.

All up, Kingston had twelve thousand gold pieces riding on the outcome of this round. Ten thousand of those were contingency bets, so if none of those possibilities occurred then at least he would get his money back. Then again, if everything worked out perfectly then he stood to win thirty thousand gold. Even the outcome of that was available for the public to bet on. *Kingston Raine to win every bet in round three – 500:1.* Three people had bet on that one. Kingston was not one of them.

There was finally a knock on their door and one of the referees came to invite the team to take their place on the arena floor.

Kingston beamed a smile at Rufus and John. "Well, here goes nothing."

John patted Mortimer on the shoulder. "Do us proud, Pinky."

Rufus rolled his head. "For crying out loud, his name is not Pinky!"

John grinned at the builder and gave Mortimer another pat. "Do us proud, Not Pinky." He then glanced back to Rufus and waited for the inevitable retort.

"Five days of this," muttered Rufus. "Five days in the one tiny room with buffoons."

They took their positions in front of the main doors and waited for their cue. They could already hear the crowd chanting some kind of song, and for a moment it felt as though the finale was upon them instead of the beginning of round three. Kingston stood next to Mortimer as he rolled his shoulders back and forth to get some life into him. Regardless of his reputation, he had to own the next few days and work out some kind of master plan sabotage everyone else.

The doors buzzed and swung inwards. The crowd cheered in delight as every team made their way into the arena. Mortimer took his position. For everyone involved it was the first time they got to see their starting position.

"Nineteen tournaments," said Rufus, as he shook his head. Five days of hell were about to begin. The crowd pointed excitedly at the various teams while they all braced themselves for the marathon event. Kingston looked across the faces and hoped to recognise someone, but they all blurred together among a mass of colourful scarves, hats, and banners. Thankfully he saw a couple of his own team's shawls from Muira's Apothecary, but they were few and far between. He hoped to see a friendly smile or two, maybe even a thumbs up for encouragement, but there was too much happening for anyone to pick out just one team from the thirty others.

Kingston didn't like the look of the team next to him. Cove, from division one, had built a chain link spider that was half the height of Mortimer, but looked as though it had several layers of redundant chains, allowing it to take one hell of a punishment while still being able to attack with up to eight whip-like legs at once. Cove had made some improvements on the build since the last round, and Kingston could see that some of the newer chain links were a brighter colour than the old and damaged ones.

John pulled out a pen and sheet of paper. There was a large circle drawn on it with thirty one evenly spaced lines sticking out. "Ready," he said.

"Good," said Kingston, and he looked to their left. "Start with us at six o'clock."

John positioned their team on his map. "Yep."

"Cove to our left."

"Cove," repeated John.

"Then Redding, Semper, Gibbs ..."

They continued marking down the starting positions of each team, and Kingston quickly checked his own notes. "We're between Cove and Newell. The closest in our division is Kazuka, two spaces over on our right."

"We want to avoid him," said Rufus. "His strategy is to explode."

"So we avoid going right altogether?"

"If we can," said Rufus.

"That means our closest opponent to our left is Carmen Lucha, also from Limbo. It'd be nice if we had someone from Hell there, as that would be an easy choice."

Rufus grumbled. "We're one of the division favourites, so we're not going to have much choice in who we fight. I'd be wary of Milliara pulverising us within the first ten seconds."

"He's in division one," said Kingston.

"You'll find that in a few minutes it doesn't matter which division you are in, because you're still going to face three of these teams in the finale, and if you can obliterate them now then you have a better chance of winning the tournament."

John quickly wrote up the order of combatants again.

"What's that for?" Rufus asked.

"It's so the girls have a copy," said John.

The ten minute wait before the final trumpet couldn't come soon enough. Kingston kept one eye on Lawnston's team and wasn't the least bit surprised when two familiar looking brutes walked over to Ernie Sanders and chased him away from his machine. Kingston knew that if the brutes even touched a rival's team Lawnston would be disqualified. But there was nothing in the rules about chasing away the builder, and thus preventing him from doing his final checks. The referees were called in, and Lawnston was fined, but it didn't stop the brutes from coming over for a second time to chase Sanders away. Horatio kept his cannon pointed at Aurelius, Scamp's car was focussed on Stuyvescent's machine, and every team had their own codes and signals relayed to everyone around them.

With two minutes to go, the teams were ushered inside to take their positions in the player's booth. Kingston took his position behind the glass and had one last look around their cluttered room. He hoped like hell that they had brought everything they would need, but a nagging feeling in the pit of his stomach told him that he had forgotten something vital.

Rufus stared out through the window. His hand was poised over the control panel and he gave his final instructions to Mortimer. "Look over to Kazuka. Good. Avoid him at all costs. Focus on Lucha. Use the whip. Keep moving but don't run unless it is to escape." He turned to John. "Double espresso. Quickly."

John considered his options carefully, and with great reluctance he set the machine going.

"You'll need to be quicker than that if we're to make it through to the finale. No lay abouts!"

Kingston nodded towards the window. "Rufus?"

"I need to focus!"

"The ten second countdown timer has begun," said Kingston.

Rufus turned just as the trumpets blared, and the crowd burst into cheers. "Lucha! Whip!"

Mortimer shot his left hand out and the chain link whip snapped through the air. Redding's machine moved forward, crossed into the firing line, and was caught by the whip. A pulse of electricity burst through the air and Redding's machine fell backwards.

"Sorry Mazoe," muttered John.

"I said Lucha! Not ... not him!" cried Rufus.

Mortimer fired off the whip again in quick succession, hitting Semper, then Gibbs, as they both crossed into the firing line.

"They're in the wrong division!" shouted Rufus.

Cove's chain link spider, standing next to Mortimer, turned and realised that Mortimer was too much of a threat for her to risk advancing into the centre of the arena. The spider turned and shot two of her legs out to grab at Mortimer. She instead caught the whip, received a blast of electricity, and Rufus was forced into a new approach.

"Ah hell, just smash the spider!"

Mortimer yanked the whip back, bringing the spider along with him, and he smashed Titan down onto what would have been the head. The links gave way and the whole creature crumpled to the ground.

"Use the spike!" shouted Rufus.

The spider started to regather herself. She shot two other legs around Mortimer's ankles and pulled herself closer. Mortimer spun Titan around and clobbered her body with the spike. She fell back down and several of the links broke apart, but they were too well connected to give up completely. Redding, and Semper, having all been stung by the chain link whip, turned on Mortimer.

Kingston's eyes lit up in a moment of sincere panic. "RUN!"

"He's trying!" shouted Rufus.

Mortimer flailed about with the hammer, creating a whirlwind around him. The moment Redding stepped into the firing line he was smacked back into Semper. Mortimer then yanked on the whip to break free from Cove's spider, but the spider latched on with more of her tentacle-like legs and tried to rend Mortimer apart.

Meanwhile, in the marquee half a kilometre from the action, Joanna and Catalina were entertaining just forty sponsors. One,

Earl, looked as though he had never used shampoo in his life. Joanna did her best to smile at him. "How are you, Earl?"

"Oh, can't complain, can't complain," he said. He then checked over his shoulder and leaned in close. "I've heard something on the grapevine." He gave a knowing nod and leaned back, now quite pleased with himself.

Joanna resisted the temptation to roll her eyes. "What did you hear?"

"That if we make a few requests, those requests might be met. You know."

Joanna feared this was about to turn creepy and seedy very quickly. "I'm lost."

Earl looked over his shoulder again and stepped in closer to Joanna. "I heard that you can go into Fiction whenever you like."

Joanna's defences flared against receiving another fine and she shook her head. "I'm afraid those stories have been exaggerated."

"But for the right price, could they be true?"

Joanna paused and considered this line of thinking quickly. "What exactly are you after?"

Earl gave a sheepish grin. "Book one Joanna."

Joanna shook her head in confusion. "Can you elaborate?"

Earl looked around, now baffled, as though what he said should have been the most obvious phrase in the world. "Book one Joanna," he said again.

"That's not elaborating, sweetie," Joanna said.

"Oh," said Earl, and he realised she was telling the truth. "I mean, you can introduce us to people from Fiction, right?"

"Yes," said Joanna, and now it was taking all the strength in the world not to shout at her greasy haired sponsor. "What, exactly, do you want?"

"You," said Earl. "But from book one."

Joanna jolted back in surprise. "You want to meet me?"

"The younger you, yes."

Joanna shuddered, pulled a face, and that was too much for her. "Ew! What the hell, Earl?"

"Shhhh!" said Earl, and he looked around in a panic to see who had overheard him. "It was just an idea."

"No! You're not going to meet the younger me so you can drool all over her!"

"But she was sexy and mysterious."

"I'm *still* sexy and mysterious!"

"Yeah, but ... this one is younger."

Joanna walked over to Catalina. "Punch him."

"I can't," said Catalina. "I might never get the grease off my hands."

Another sponsor smiled at the pair. "I have a request."

Joanna gave Elmore a chance. "What did you have in mind?"

"The Wandering Jew," said Elmore, and he gave a sincere nod.

Joanna cocked her head to one side, and she was certainly surprised to hear that one.

Catalina turned to Joanna and dropped into a whisper. "It looks as though one of the other teams has found a way to sabotage us."

Joanna looked back to Elmore. "The Wandering Jew? Why him?"

Elmore shrugged. "I always thought he would know a thing or two about philosophy, considering how old he is by now. I know it's a little unorthodox, but I had always been intrigued by the regret and superstitions he would have gone through."

Joanna turned from being a sceptic to a saleswoman. "Make the team an offer."

Catalina grabbed onto Joanna's wrist. "No, no, absolutely not."

"But -"

"Do you remember how illegal it was to kidnap Don Keaton from Life?"

"No, because I wasn't around when that went down," said Joanna.

"Okay. It's just ... as far as getting into trouble goes, kidnapping someone is going to be frowned upon."

Joanna sighed, realised that Catalina was right, and had to turn Elmore down.

"Even for twenty gold?" Elmore asked.

Meanwhile, Mortimer was fighting off three opponents at once. Whenever Cove's spider reached back to take another swipe she ended up smacking Redding's machine in the face and getting entangled. Mortimer thrashed about with Titan, hitting Semper's machine in the shoulder, and then the spider released her grip on Mortimer and locked onto the war hammer.

"Fling him!" shouted Rufus.

Mortimer pulled Titan back, bringing the spider with him, and slammed her down from left to right as quickly as he could, breaking several of the links, until the spider released her grip and was flung into the air.

"Finally!" said Rufus, breathing a sigh of relief.

Mortimer was then bull rushed by Semper's and Redding's machines, and he was pushed down onto the ground.

"And now we're screwed," grumbled Rufus.

Half a kilometre away ... Catalina sidled up to Joanna. "We're getting more requests."

"Do we really want to know?" asked Joanna.

Catalina shrugged. "It's bringing in the sponsors. They all want to meet someone famous from Fiction."

"That will get us expelled quicker than anything," said Joanna. She then considered a distant idea and turned to face the Spaniard. "If you could meet anyone from Fiction, who would it be?"

Catalina smiled weakly. "My mamá."

Joanna shrugged with a look of 'of course'. "I suppose John would want to see his niece again."

"I think more than anything he'd want to know what happened to his sister, but that's a little risky."

Joanna cocked her head to one side. "Why?"

Catalina stared back with a curious look. "Kingston never told you?"

"I'm not sure what he did or did not tell me. What happened to John's sister?"

"She babysat him when he was little. He walked off. She got shouted at. She and everyone else in the forest went out looking for him. He came back. His sister did not. His mum never forgave him."

Joanna reeled back in surprise. "I never heard that before."

"Oh. I thought you two talked about everything."

It was Joanna's turn to smile weakly. "Yeah. We're pretty good at keeping secrets, you know?"

Catalina glanced over her shoulder. "In that case, who would you want to see most of all?"

Joanna rolled her eyes up towards the ceiling. "Cleopatra?"

"But she's real. You could probably go down to Hell and meet her yourself."

"Then, I guess, Mr Darcy?"

Catalina shook her head. "Who's that?"

"Where the hell is Stuyvescent?" cried Rufus.

"She's pinned down, like us," said Kingston. He looked out onto the battlefield and was thrilled to see the first defeat in the round - Zamba, from Hell. He was also in division four, so he had little influence on Kingston's fight. Unfortunately that freed up Sequa, who turned his machine against Mortimer.

"What!?" cried Rufus. "Is three against one not good enough for these people? Now we need *four* against one?"

Kingston felt his stomach lurch as Sequa's machine crashed into Mortimer. Mortimer tried to raise one arm to push Sequa away, but the pummelling from the other teams was too much for him to handle.

Then, in the space of three seconds, Milliara's anvil broke up the fight. It smashed down onto Semper, then Redding, ignored Zamba and went straight for Mortimer. Mortimer's right shoulder was caught under the sudden weight of the anvil and it crumpled under the stress.

"Damn it!" shouted Rufus.

"Pull him back quickly!" shouted Kingston.

Rufus flicked the controls and Mortimer pushed back just in time. The anvil dropped onto the ground right in front of the golem and smacked itself into the arena floor.

"Smash it!" shouted Rufus.

Mortimer clumsily swung his right arm around, grinding the gears of his broken shoulder, and he clobbered the anvil with Titan. The resounding blast knocked Zamba back, and Milliara teleported to somewhere safer. Mortimer climbed back to his feet and struggled to move his arm with any kind of precision.

There was a random timer set up on the main screens to show the crowd when the lock-out times began. The timer flashed across every screen to show that it would begin in ten minutes.

"The longer old Mortimer stays out there, the better we'll be in the long run," said Rufus.

"That's an expensive gamble," said Kingston.

Rufus glanced over his shoulder. "You read the rules about Last Man Standing?"

"Of course. The less opportunities we come in for repairs, the fewer time penalties we'll have for the whole round."

"I'm glad you agree," said Rufus. "So leaving Mortimer out there until the second lock-out will do us a world of good."

"Old Mortimer is worth eight thousand gold pieces. New

Mortimer is worth far less and can take on much more damage. We can sell old Mortimer later and turn a profit."

Mortimer flung his whip out and clobbered Jones' wrecking ball.

"Where the hell is Stuyvescent, anyway?" shouted Rufus.

John checked his notes. "She was eighteenth from our left."

"So she should've started directly opposite us? Great. She's on the other side of the arena."

"And she's bogged down by Aurelius," said Kingston.

Milliara's anvil reappeared and narrowly missed Mortimer.

"He needs to run if he's going to have a chance."

"Run!" shouted Rufus.

Mortimer was facing the arena wall and ran full steam into it.

"Not that way, you idiot!"

Mortimer bounced off the brick wall and stumbled backwards. The anvil dropped out of the air and landed just behind Mortimer, missing his back by an inch.

At that point, Horatio's cannon turned on Mortimer and fired. The cannon ball struck Titan and bounced away in a resounding *clink*. The crowd cheered in surprise, but the momentum from the cannon ball pushed Mortimer off balance, and he toppled over. Then the anvil returned and smashed into Mortimer's left leg.

"That one might need him to be repaired," said Rufus.

John rolled his eyes at Rufus. "I might have to be the judge on this one, but I say: as long as he can move, he's going to stay out."

"All he can do right now is hobble," said Rufus.

"Then let him hobble. He still has the whip, right?"

"I need more coffee!"

"You still have one cup in front of you."

"I need one in my hand!"

"Then pick it up! Jeez Louise."

The trumpets blared and the crowd cheered in delight as they saw that half of the field had been dropped completely.

"Moment of truth," said Rufus. "He can barely stand, barely fight. Do we bring him in?"

Kingston glanced towards John, and John shook his head.

"We need as much advantage at the end of the round as possible," said John.

"Then let's keep Mortimer out there," said Kingston, though repairing Mortimer was now going to be all the more difficult in the coming hours.

The entrants all backed away as the referees were able to move out onto the arena floor, where they then pulled the fallen units back through the doorways. The time to bring Mortimer in for repairs came and went, and the fight resumed with fifteen fighters all slugging it out.

"Smash him!" cried Rufus.

Maurice walked through the marquee and smiled at Joanna. "You guys are doing better than expected."

"Thanks," said Joanna. "I don't suppose you have any advice?"

"Nothing really at this point," said Maurice. "I came here hoping to hear something from your end."

Joanna rolled her eyes to the screen. "Take a look for yourself."

"Yeah. Rufus should have brought the golem in for repairs. It won't survive long against the other fourteen opponents."

"He'll do his best," said Joanna.

As she said that, Milliara's anvil dropped over Mortimer and found its mark. The battered golem crumpled in a heap and had to wait another hour and a half before being rescued by the referees.

It was hour nine of round three. Mortimer was being repaired, again, and the first wave of fatigue settled across the realm. The party goers had started to drift away from all of the free drinks and were forced to go home, sleep off their intoxication, and get ready for work the following day. Kingston returned to the player's booth with a small chest of spare parts from Munich.

"You almost missed the lock-out," said Rufus.

"Then if it's any consolation I have four elbows, three knees, and two helmets for you."

Rufus peered at Kingston. "What the hell am I going to do with three knees?"

"Hopefully one of them will survive long enough so we don't need to change it out."

Even Joanna and Catalina were fighting the battle against tiredness. Their cheeks ached from smiling, their brains were fried from holding the same small talk topic of conversation over and over again, and their feet were killing them. They had one hundred and eleven hours remaining. Joanna had already updated their betting guide based on some report of Denoa heading home in defeat, as she was sure that Denoa wouldn't be back for the final showdown.

During a lull in the evening, Joanna came over to Catalina with a plate of hors-d'oeuvres and sat down at the bar next to her. Catalina had removed her shoes and was busy rubbing her feet.

"We need to swap places with Kingston and John," said Joanna.

"I agree. I don't know how much more staring at the screen I can do." She glanced around the marquee and saw just a dozen people lingering about. "We need more money."

"I'll go out in a minute and grab a few people from off the street. They'll be coming or going from the arena and some will want to come in and stay."

Catalina looked her up and down. "No body armour today?"

"Being in that thing for a couple of hours was murder, so no. Never again." Joanna then glanced over her shoulder. "In the meantime, I'm going to ..."

Something caught her attention. Catalina glanced up at the entry to the marquee and yelped in surprise.

Satan had arrived.

"No ..." mumbled Catalina.

Satan glanced over to Joanna and Catalina, beamed with a smile, and walked on over.

"Game face," whispered Joanna. "Quickly."

"Joanna my dear!" said Satan.

Joanna stepped away from the bar and greeted their guest. "Satan, how are you?"

"Please, call me Luc."

"I'd rather -"

"And I must say: thank you for inviting me." Satan held out his hand and showed Joanna the official invitation that Kingston had sent, which was now a month old and had been issued for one of the six pre-tournament parties. "It's good to see you again."

"Likewise," said Joanna, though she felt her strength start to falter as the idea of making small talk with the Devil got the better of her. Then she remembered that he had a crush on her, and that Kingston was going to be away for another four and a half days.

Satan glanced over to Catalina and bobbed his head at her. "Catalina dear, how are you?"

"I'm well, thank you."

Satan looked around the marquee and nodded approvingly. "So

... you've been cheating."

Joanna held herself steady at the sound of that. "Nothing out of the ordinary."

Satan smirked and winked at her. "Oh, come on, everyone does it. Milliara's been cheating since day one."

Joanna glanced to the side at the sound of that and she found an impossible moment present itself. "How exactly has he been cheating?"

"Ooooo, I think that will cost you, say, a drink."

"Catalina? A martini for the Devil, with Stalactite Vermouth."

"Good choice," said Satan. He glanced over the faces of everyone else in the marquee and saw the rest of the guests hurry towards the exit. "Well, I can certainly clear a room. I guess we'll be a threesome for the evening."

Joanna glared at Satan. "Stop that."

"A *ménage à* ..."

"I get it," said Joanna. Then she cocked her head to one side. "You were speaking French."

"*Ah mais oui,* I have, what would you say, a gift for language."

"How are you speaking French in Limbo? Isn't there only one language here?"

"That only applies to mortals," said Satan.

"Aren't we all immortal in the afterlife?"

"Yes, but the people up here were mortal at one point."

"I wasn't. I'm one hundred percent fictional."

"You were created by a mortal."

"So if you wrote a book ..."

"I've written many."

"And if the main character died ..."

"The results would be so catastrophic that every woman's heart would need piecing back together by a trained professional."

"Aren't professionals usually trained?"

"And here I thought you were about to have a go at me for not mentioning anything about the breaking of a man's heart."

"They are just as easy to break as a woman's," said Joanna.

Catalina came over and handed Satan his martini.

"Thank you, *ma chéri.*"

"I don't speak French," said Catalina, and she did her best to hold her tongue.

Satan smirked at her with his best bedroom eyes. He turned to

Joanna and held one hand out for her.

"What's this for?"

"A dance."

Joanna snorted. "Why?"

"It's a party, I'm Lucifer, I have a drink, and I have inside dirt on every team in the competition." He beckoned her to take his hand. "Incidentally, you smell like cherries."

"Thank you?"

"My pleasure. Now come on and let me tell you how one of Milliara's contacts in Limbo snuck into every player's booth and sprayed the ceiling with hickory ash."

"What would that result it?"

"It lightly falls on the combatants and helps an anvil find its target without a lot of guess work from a psychic." Satan beckoned again.

Joanna reluctantly took his hand and now wished that she was wearing body armour.

Sixteen hours in. Mortimer was being repaired again for a busted helmet, and Rufus shook his head in dismay.

"This is going to require two whole days to repair."

John then beamed with a grin. "Then it's time for me to suit up!"

Rufus sighed and gave the most feeble of shrugs. "I guess it is."

Kingston helped John into the telemetry suit, while Rufus fired up the newest Mortimer. John only had access to the arms and torso of new Mortimer, while Kingston was able to control the legs via a control panel. If John had been fitted with legs then he was limited to the area of the player's booth, which would be a dead giveaway to anyone watching.

The whole suit was an unyielding mess of spokes and joints, and when it sat on John it made him look more like a demon from a steam-punk horror story. It took half an hour just to climb into it and get everything fitted.

"We're about to miss out on the timer," said John. The lock-out for re-entry would begin in two minutes.

"We'll be okay," said Rufus, and he plugged the last of the cables into John's back. "There we go. Try that."

John stretched his arms out and new Mortimer did the same.

"Great! Send me in there."

"We're going to have problems with the whip since you're not calibrated for using it."

"Yes, yes, just send me in there!"

"Which means we won't be using it with the suit."

"Fine. Just give me the hammer."

"Then pick it up," said Rufus.

John fumbled about as new Mortimer swayed back and forth. They both reached out into thin air to try and grab onto Titan, and as soon as Mortimer had a decent hold of it John flexed his fingers and dropped the war hammer to the ground.

"Sorry," mumbled John.

Rufus sighed and gave John a small steel bar to hold onto, except he had to hold it out at the correct angle so that when John grabbed the bar he was also able to grab Titan. "There. Don't let that go."

"Hurry," said Kingston.

"We're good to go," said Rufus.

Kingston walked Mortimer forward but misjudged the side of the door frame. Mortimer clunked to a stop, needed to take a step back, and they all tried again.

"We're going to miss the re-entry point," said John.

"We'll be fine," said Rufus.

Mortimer banged into the far wall in the corridor and shuddered.

"This is why telemetry suits are a complicated mess."

Kingston turned Mortimer around and walked him towards the stairs. Then they realised a flaw in their plan. Old Mortimer had been trained to go down stairs and he could recognise the distance between each step. New Mortimer was not so fortunate. He took one step forward and Kingston saw in a moment of panic that ...

Yep, Mortimer stepped out into thin air and toppled forward, slamming face first into the ground beneath it.

"Drag yourself forward!" cried Rufus.

John did his best to push against the air, hoping that Mortimer would push himself forward, but they hadn't even practiced standing up from a prone position.

The trumpets blared, and the lock-out for one hour began.

The three men sighed and stared at each other. "Let's get him back on his feet," said Kingston. "We have an hour until we can get back out there."

"Do I have to stay in this thing?" John asked.

"It will take fifteen minutes to power Mortimer down, and then you can move about."

"But it takes half an hour to get into it," said John.

"Yes, it does."

"And half an hour to get out of it."

"Exactly."

"So ..."

"So if you need to go to the bathroom in the next half an hour you'll be wearing that hulking suit. And, you'll have to whiz in private, because if any of the referees see you then they might pass on to the other teams that we're using a telemetry suit."

Kingston stepped back as a letter burst out in front of him. It was from Joanna.

'We're locked out?'

'Yes. Technical difficulties,' answered Kingston. He helped Mortimer up onto his feet and they prepared themselves for the next round of combat. Rufus then hurried back into their makeshift workshop and started repairing old Mortimer.

"This isn't going exactly to plan," said John, while he stood in the hulking contraption strapped to his chest and arms.

"No." He checked his notes and started to feel his eyes blur some of the information. "We're at six time penalties right now which means we're doing averagely. Unfortunately, all of the teams from division one have less penalties than us."

John stretched his arms out and nearly whacked Rufus in the side of the head with New Mortimer.

"Hey!"

"Sorry! Sorry."

Kingston scribbled a note back to Joanna and hoped that she was having a better time with the sponsors.

Joanna was onto her sixth drink, and sixth dance with Satan, who explained how the sixth team from Hell were cheating.

"You know, I notice that before every new dance you skip off to the bathroom."

"That's because I'm writing down everything you tell me before I forget," said Joanna. "And that's not very gentlemanly of you, pointing out something like that."

"How are the sponsors doing?" Satan asked.

"They're very generous," said Joanna.

"Of course they are. You should be up to, what, five thousand gold pieces by now? Maybe even six?"

Joanna hesitated for a moment too long.

"Don't tell me it's half that," said Satan. Then he caught Joanna's reaction. "*Less* than half? Please tell me it's more than a thousand gold a night?"

"*A night?*" shrieked Joanna.

Satan's jaw dropped open. "Wow, okay, something is seriously wrong with the people up here. You have four of Limbo's only celebrities teaming up and you can't even raise enough money to compete?"

"What are we doing wrong?" asked Joanna.

Satan winced and shook his head. "If I had to guess I'd say that there are rumours of you lot being blacklisted."

"Is that a guess or are there actual rumours?"

"Rumours. It's a self-fulfilling prophecy, really. You spread enough lies about a team being blacklisted and no one puts any money into them because there's no way they will see a return on their investment. Pretty sad, really."

"How is that self-fulfilling?" asked Joanna.

"*Ménage à troi.*"

Joanna rolled her eyes.

"Seriously, though, you should look into that, because Aurelius has been holding sponsorship parties with all of his celebrity builders and he's been raking it in. They've earned two hundred and eighty million sterling by now."

"How much is that up here?"

"Nineteen thousand gold, eight silver, three copper. Basically, it's enough to build his dragon." He smirked and peered over at Catalina. "If you convince her to have a dance with me I'll tell you how to beat that dragon."

Joanna glanced over to the bar. "She's playing with her nails, so I'd advise against it."

"I take it then she's not bored?"

"Far from it. She's primed to fight for her life." She looked back to Satan. "Let me ask you something."

"By all means."

"There are only so many variations of what people look like, so there have to be thousands of people in Hell who look like me,

329

right?"

"Oh yes. And thousands who look like Kingston. In fact, you're the spitting image of Joan of Arc."

"No, I'm not," said Joanna.

"Nah, you're not. Would be cool if you were."

"Not especially."

Satan smiled at Joanna. "Kingston is the spitting image of Alfred the Great. I guess the only way to find out for sure is to come down to Hell for a few days and meet the guy."

"Or I could check the Library of Limbo and find a picture of whoever it was you said my boyfriend looks like."

Satan smacked his lips together. "Okay, I may have been exaggerating a little."

"And for that penalty you can tell me how to defeat Aurelius."

"Well, considering that Catalina lied to me about not speaking French I think that makes us even. Let's have another drink."

XXII

It was twenty four hours until the end of round three. Coffee sales were at an all time high, and yet only a handful of Limbo residents were able to function at some kind of coherent level. Kingston had gone to Fiction three times already to refresh their supplies for the battered golem. Whenever he came back he was always met by John beaming with a grin.

"Carver is being investigated for cheating," he would say, or: "The Sequa's have just been fined for using illegal parts." The list of teams being investigated seemed to grow by the hour, and Kingston was always suspecting that Mortimer would be hauled off to the side by the referees and found guilty of breaking every rule in the book, but curiously that hadn't happened yet.

Then, on Kingston's final return to the player's booth, he was met by a soaked John and Rufus.

"What the hell happened here?" Kingston asked.

"It's been raining on and off for two hours," grumbled John.

"Inside?"

"Yeah. Someone figured out how to make us even more miserable."

Then Kingston got a taste of it as well. A thick rumble of thunder ran from one wall to the next and the down-pour began.

"It could be worse," said John. "It looks like a disco from hell in some of the booths over there."

Kingston glanced out and saw strobe lights flashing back and forth, and all of a sudden the rain was a lot easier to handle.

"Smack the scorpion!" shouted Kingston.

John swung his arm down and telemetry Mortimer did the same. He connected with one of the scorpion's legs and broke the knee clean off. The scorpion retreated, but it still had five good legs and one stinger.

"Well done," said Kingston.

"Ta."

Rufus snored behind them. Kingston then scanned the arena looking for their next target. He consulted his list from Joanna, through Satan, and delivered by Jezebel, about their opponents.

"Creig's tank is susceptible to Orion's Flame." Kingston glanced over his shoulder and tried to remember which chest that had been stored in. "I know we have some of that. If we coat the end of the whip in that stuff and get a good hit on that tank it will explode."

"That's if he appears in the next round," said John.

"He's been in repairs for the last three hours so he's bound to make an appearance sooner or later."

John glanced out through the window. "There's another lock-out due in ten minutes."

Kingston raised himself up and found a possible moment of glory. There were only three teams still competing in the arena, the other twenty eight were busy being repaired. "We have to make sure we're the only ones left standing in the next ten minutes."

"Is this a show boating thing?"

"Yep. We'll have an hour to ourselves in the arena. All of the attention will be on us."

John bobbed his head and turned back to face Bonaparte. "Ten minutes to take out the wall of spinning spikes and the scorpion."

"Make it happen."

Back in the marquee, the level of fatigue was similar. Some of the more drunken sponsors had lost their voices from shouting at the screens, and most of them staggered from side to side. Catalina reappeared from the bathroom now wearing jeans and a jacket, and she wore one of Muira's black shawls across her head.

Joanna crept away from Satan and looked over Catalina's curious change in attire. "What's that for?"

"I have to duck out for a couple of hours," said Catalina.

"Okay, why?"

Catalina pulled Joanna over to the side of the marquee. "I need you to keep a secret for the next day. Absolute secrecy, yes? Not one other person, okay?"

"Sure. What's up?"

"I can't tell you because it's a secret. But if you could ..."

Catalina fished out John's list of every combatant, along with what booth the teams occupied. "Who would you most like to see in the finale?"

Joanna smirked at Catalina. She had no idea what Catalina was playing at but from what she knew of her ... actually Catalina was the sneakiest of the entire group, and everyone underestimated her. Joanna looked over the list and noticed that Horatio was crossed out. "Why division -"

"Because like it or not we're going to be up against Milliara in round four. He can teleport. The others can't. But who would you like to see from division three?"

"Stuyvescent," said Joanna.

"Okay. And division four?"

"Urisha."

"I will see what I can do, but you may need to buy those two back into the tournament. Remember: absolute secrecy. No one else can know." Catalina stuffed the paperwork into her pocket and she hurried out through the rear of the marquee.

Satan sauntered over to Joanna and smirked at her. "No one else can know? Very interesting."

Joanna turned and groaned when she realised what Satan had just seen. "How much is this going to cost me?"

"Let's start with another drink and keep going from there."

"I've had thirty drinks with you and thirty dances in the last four days with almost no sleep."

"And you've been having the time of your life!" said Satan. "Trust me, I can see it in your eyes. You're faking this whole tired thing because inside they are screaming, 'I should totally follow this guy back to his palace.' Especially now that our chaperone has given us some peace and quiet."

"Tell me, how much of this five day slugfest was your idea?" Joanna asked.

Satan beamed a grin at her. "I'm not nearly drunk enough to tell you the truth about that."

Mortimer slammed Titan into the side of the scorpion, knocking it into Bonaparte's spinning spikes.

"Hoo yeah!" cried Kingston, and he saw both machines rip each other apart. The lock-out began and the referees retrieved Kwon's and Bonaparte's combatants, leaving Mortimer alone in the arena. John lifted his arms into the air and Mortimer did the same.

"Here come the sponsors!" said Kingston. "Time to pull some poses and make the most of it."

John glanced over his shoulder and saw Rufus was still asleep. "This is probably his finest moment and he's sleeping through it."

Kingston nudged his builder.

Rufus snorted and looked up. "Huh?"

"I thought you might want to have a look at this," said Kingston.

John jolted back in surprise. "Hey! What the hell just happened?"

Kingston and Rufus looked over. A jet of sticky ink had exploded in front of their window, blocking their view of the arena floor.

"I can't see anything!" said John.

Rufus groaned. "Are we in a lock-out?"

"Yeah," said Kingston.

Rufus leaned back into his hammock and closed his eyes. "Then there's nothing we can do until the lock-out ends."

Back in the marquee, Joanna winced as she saw Mortimer stumbling around, obviously matching John's movements in the player's booth. Then she saw Milliara's anvil break the lock-out rules and it smashed into Mortimer, crumpling him to the ground. The anvil then teleported away, leaving Mortimer lifeless with fifty nine minutes of the lock-out remaining.

An hour later four more teams ventured out, but no one could remove Mortimer until the next round of retrievals. By then, Rufus had caught up on a few hours of sleep, and Kingston and John seethed in their booth. Soon enough, though, they were able to drag Mortimer back inside and clean off the gunk on their window.

Catalina ducked back into the marquee.

"You were gone longer than I expected," said Joanna.

"Yeah, sorry."

"Were you successful?"

"Hopefully," said Catalina. She hurried into the bathroom and changed back into her dress.

Joanna glanced back to Satan. "Any ideas?"

"Our little Spanish friend is about to make a lot of people very unhappy."

Joanna looked around the marquee quickly. "I have to make a quick trip to the bookies."

All across the realm, thirty one statues started to make their way towards the arena.

The final lock-out came ninety minutes before the end of round three, and this required every team competing. Every machine was dragged back into the player's booths and haphazardly repaired in anticipation of the royal rumble that was soon to begin.

The monitors all blared with an official order of time penalties, indicating who would be allowed out into the arena at what time. Kingston then felt five days worth of exhaustion catch up to him in a hurry. He glanced over his shoulder and saw Rufus with his eyes closed, breathing deeply. Kingston nudged him.

Rufus opened his eyes quickly. "Huh?"

"We have twenty three time penalties."

Rufus sat forward and looked at the monitor. "That puts us in the middle."

The team with the most time penalties was Denoa, whose machine had been battered beyond recognition in the first half an hour. He hadn't competed again. The team with the fewest penalties was Aurelius, who had just three.

Kingston looked over the list of names and he felt another groan coming along. "What are the chances of everyone with worse times than us actually going out there and competing?"

"Slim," said Rufus.

"So Aurelius will be out with sixteen minutes to go, Kwon will be out with twenty four minutes to go ... and then there are five more teams from Hell before Biggins has a chance, and he's the one from Limbo with the fewest penalties."

"I'm impressed," said Rufus. "Five days of flying that tornado around with as few break downs as he's had ... you should have sponsored him."

"Yeah. And we're out with forty six minutes to go." Kingston blinked slowly as he tried to process that information again. "*Fifty* six minutes to go. Not forty six."

John nodded. "Did you forget about the ten minute block added to the end?"

"Briefly."

"We're doomed," said Rufus. "Big guy, how about some coffee?"

"First tell me how Mortimer is holding up," said Kingston.

"Fantastically." Rufus went over to the coffee machine.

"You didn't lie to me just then, did you?"

"I'm a lot more honest after I've had some caffeine in me. And Mortimer could be anywhere from fantastically screwed to fantastically awesome. Thankfully old Mortimer blew up so we've got new Mortimer, who is completely fictional. We're going to be fined quite a bit by the referees, but he's our best bet at making it into round four."

John grunted. "And it's either getting fined for him being fictional, or we get fined for having robbed that ship of its iron."

"Okay, strategy time," said Kingston. "We focus on everyone in the second division, primarily any team from Hell. As long as there is a Limbo showdown in round four we stand a pretty good chance of being able to influence them."

"I guess we can finally use that Orion's Flame," said John.

"I don't know if we should be trusting the girls with that kind of information," said Rufus.

"It comes from a very reliable source," said Kingston.

John gave Rufus a nod. "Satan."

Rufus spluttered into his coffee. "You what?"

"Yeah," said Kingston, with a groan.

"What the hell did I sleep through?" asked Rufus.

John and Kingston exchanged a concerned look. "We've mentioned Satan like five times already!" said John.

"And Jezebel gives us an update on him every time she comes in here," said Kingston.

"I thought that was some stupid code!" cried Rufus.

"How?" asked John.

"Like how some people say 'He's the Devil.' They don't actually mean he's the real Devil, just that he's an asshole."

"Then surprise! We're telling the truth," said John. "And by the sound of things Joanna has been off her face for the last five days. Now come on, we need to fix new Mortimer and get him out there."

The two brutes from Lawnston's team stood close to the front of the player's entrance to the arena. They were on the look out for anything that might jeopardise their team's chances. They noticed something all right. The march of thirty one statues was hard to miss.

"Are those statues or golems?" one brute asked.

"We should tell Lawnston about this."

They were interrupted when a smoke bomb from Jezebel exploded in front of them, sending them into a fit of coughing that took an hour to recover from. By then the statues had pushed their way inside the arena and had taken their places.

Cove was the first to notice, with a time penalty of one hour and six minutes. The other teams with a greater penalty all decided to forfeit. Cove's team, with the chain-link spider, tried to leave their player's booth to re-enter the arena and found the door handle wouldn't open. The team fought with the door and wrestled against the handle, then they tried to smash the door down with the spider, but the door had been especially enchanted by the referees to prevent any team from breaking it down, thanks to previous occasions of one team interfering with another.

"Help!" Cove cried.

Meanwhile, standing just on the outside of Cove's door was the statue of Alexander Radishchev, who was simply holding onto the door handle with a tight grip and wouldn't let go, despite the frantic demands of the referees surrounding him.

Elsewhere, the statue of Fernando de Herrera couldn't help but grin as he stood in front of Horatio's door, refusing to let his arch nemesis through. "Let that be a lesson to you, you stupid man," muttered Fernando.

The only three doors that were unburdened by statues were Kingston's, from division two, Stuyvescent's, from division three, and Urisha's, from division four.

As the countdown timer elapsed, team after team were forced into forfeit as their combatants were unable to enter the arena.

Kingston pulled the door open to his booth and stepped back in surprise when he found a statue standing outside. "Archimedes?"

Archimedes smiled at Kingston and he stepped to the side.

John walked up to the doorway. "What's going on?"

"Beats me," said Kingston.

"This stays between us," said Archimedes. "No one else is to know that I let you out."

"Okay," said Kingston, though he still wasn't sure why that was an issue.

Mortimer went out and stood in the arena, looking around for the next entrant to face. The trumpets blared and another team was forced to forfeit.

Rufus peered at Kingston. "Did you do this?"

"I honestly have no idea what's going on," said Kingston.

In the marquee, Joanna felt a grin spread across her face. "Ohhhhh, Catalina ..."

"Yes?" said Catalina.

"Oh, I like you."

"I know," smirked Catalina.

"What did you do?"

Catalina gave an innocent shrug. "On the very first day of brainstorming it was mentioned that if the teams can't make it onto the arena floor then they would be disqualified. So while you and Kingston went with your overly complicated plans to sabotage just one team at a time, I sweet talked Fernando the statue into convincing his friends to help us out. Right now they're blocking as many teams as possible. Fernando, I'm pleased to say, is currently having his revenge on Horatio."

Joanna burst into laughter. "Oh, Catalina ..."

"If you're going to cheat, you might as well *really* cheat."

Satan snorted. "The bookies will be pissing themselves right about now."

And they were. All across Limbo and Hell millions of fans were up in arms, screaming at what they saw as a great betrayal of their teams, as no one had any idea what was delaying their teams from walking onto the arena floor. They watched as Mortimer stood to one side, taking his time, and they watched as Stuyvescent's machine lumbered about, and then came Urisha's spinning top. None attacked the other, since they were all from different divisions, and there was still a few minutes remaining before the last team could enter.

Kingston peered out through the glass and started to put everything together. He quickly looked over their supplies. "We have to scramble. Get everything packed up and back to the bank!"

"But we're still fighting," said Rufus.

"You stay here and avoid everyone you can. John and I have to haul ass before anyone comes looking for revenge."

John gave Kingston a solemn nod. "I'm on it."

Sure enough, one team from Hell found a way out of their

player's booth. Milliara. His psychic, Frederika, told him exactly what was going on and Raquel, the muse, simply stood by the door and sweet talked the statue of Georg Büchner into standing back.

"I can't," said the statue. "I have to stand here and keep the door closed."

"But you have the wrong door," said Raquel.

That caught Georg by surprise. "Are you sure? I'm supposed to keep door number three closed."

"No, no, you're supposed to keep door twenty three closed."

"Then why was I told about door number three?"

"It was an unfortunate mistake, but you better hurry to get to twenty three before you get in trouble."

The statue released his grip and the door swung open. Milliara had twenty seconds to drag his anvil out into the arena or be disqualified. He ducked around Georg's body and dragged the anvil along the ground.

"Who the hell is behind this?" screamed Milliara, but he was sure it had to be Kingston Raine. Since his was only one of three teams currently in the arena, it had to be him.

Kingston saw Milliara's arena door swing open. "Get Mortimer moving! And make it unpredictable!"

With five seconds to go, Milliara hurled his anvil through the open doors and entered the royal rumble. The anvil teleported away and reappeared above where Mortimer had been standing. It kept teleporting in and out, always dropping over Mortimer. Mortimer swung up and knocked the anvil away with Titan, but to no avail. The anvil simply teleported back and dropped over Mortimer again.

Kingston and John threw everything they had into the trunks and lugged them outside, then they teleported back to the bank.

The trumpets blared and every other team in the tournament was forced to forfeit. The Games had their finalists with still ten minutes to go in round three. The anvil quickly smashed on top of Stuyvescent's machine, crumpling it to smithereens, and then it destroyed Urisha's spinning top. It then chased Mortimer around for another nine minutes.

Kingston and John burst back inside their player's booth just as the final set of trumpets blared.

"We did it!" shouted Kingston, and he threw his hands into the air.

"Huzzah!" cried John.

"Yep," said Rufus. "Of course, there are now twenty seven teams who absolutely hate us, so we can expect twenty seven acts of revenge."

The first act came seconds later, when a barrel of glue landed on top of Mortimer. The golem was now stuck to the arena floor.

XXIII

The fury of such blatant cheating was eventually watered down when the residents of Limbo realised that they had three combatants in the final against just one from Hell. Furthermore, there was a cheeky level of admiration pointed towards Kingston and his team. Even though nearly everyone lost money on their various bets, they did admire that Kingston found a way into the finale that no one else had been able to pull off. That level of philosophy would come later. Right now every gambler was still struggling to come to terms with being ripped off from the fight to end all fights.

Before the gang could even leave the marquee they were greeted by an envelope appearing out of thin air, from Michelle.

'Well done. Now you have to hide. No place is safe.'

They could hear the rattle of the angry crowd and the hundreds of team members out looking for revenge. Kingston took one look at his team mates and knew that this required some drastic measures.

Pop.

Kingston, Joanna, John, Catalina, and Rufus all appeared in a narrow corridor to a book repair store. At the far end was a secret room hidden from scouts, seers, psychics, and teleporting. It was called Cleaver Hall, and had most recently been the site of a secret organisation operating within Limbo for nefarious purposes.

"We should be okay in here," said Kingston, as he led everyone into the small room, which held just a few chairs and two round tables.

Rufus sniffed the air and turned his nose up. "This place hasn't been aired out in decades."

"It has been vacant for just one year, but close enough," said Kingston. He closed the door and beamed at Catalina. "That was a *fantastic* idea!"

"Thank you," said Catalina. "It took months to organise but I'm glad it paid off."

"Did you bet on us?" asked John.

"Of course. One gold piece on the final four line up."

John grinned. "One gold piece?"

"It was all I was willing to bet," said Catalina. "And I think that means I won seventy two gold, so that has me dancing on air."

Kingston leaned in towards Joanna. "I don't suppose you bet on that outcome?"

"I didn't know it was going to happen," whispered Joanna.

"Everyone's going to know it was us playing silly buggers with the statues," said Rufus.

"But we didn't do anything illegal," said Catalina. "I read the rules. We shouldn't be fined for this."

"But public perception," mumbled Rufus.

"The referees will know that there were thirty one statues blocking thirty one doors. Luckily, four teams were able to get out. I figured Milliara would escape, his team was a given, and really I wanted Bonaparte in the finale, but I couldn't take the risk. I thought it might be best if everyone from division one was disqualified."

John looked around the small room and did a quick survey of their options. "So now what? Are we moving in here completely?"

"We're going to have to lie low until the anger ebbs away," said Kingston.

"Someone should tell Jezebel what's happened," said Joanna. "She'll be able to tell us when it is safe to come out of hiding."

Kingston pointed to the door. "We do have a corridor, you know. And notes that can teleport."

"Fine," said Joanna.

Kingston scribbled a note to Jezebel, sent it off, and came back into the room. "I asked her to report back in one hour."

"You should have asked her to send a deck of cards as well," said Rufus, and he made himself at home at one of the round tables.

"Cheer up, you little man!" cried John. "We've made it into the finale! This is the best you've ever done!"

"My beautiful creations haven't walked out of a single round.

The only reason we're still competing is not through any talent of mine but because of you four being tricky!" Rufus slumped forward and rested his head on the table. "I'm going to get some shut eye. I haven't slept properly in five days. If anyone objects ..." Rufus raised his middle finger at the group.

An hour later, Jezebel responded. Kingston read through her note and groaned.

"We've not been robbed, have we?" asked Joanna.

"No. John and I moved all of our supplies into one of the vaults in case such a thing might happen. Our marquee has been trashed, we're being investigated for vandalising the ship and carrying off a whole lotta metal, and we've been fined for Mortimer still being glued to the surface of the arena."

"That's not so bad," said Joanna.

Another hour later, they had a second update.

"The marquee rental company is asking us to pay for damages," said Kingston.

"Is it cheaper to buy the marquee outright?" asked Joanna.

"It would be, except they're saying it's not for sale. And it looks as though we're being investigated by the bank for illegally using their premises."

"Preposterous," said John. "We have authorisation from Simon."

"Two can play at that game," said Joanna. She pulled out her list of team secrets from Satan and began writing an anonymous complaint to the gaming commission. She had dirt on every team out there and if they were going to be fined then she was determined to bring every other team down to even the score.

It took five hours to clear all of the teams from Hell out of Limbo. By then the news of the statues blocking the doors of the player's booths had spread and the tactic was admired by many. It also made the gambling houses very rich, since very few people actually bet on the final line up being Milliara, Rufus, Stuyvescent, and Urisha.

The team crept back to the bank as discreetly as they could, but their workshop was now locked.

"Maybe we should use Cleaver Hall?" suggested John.

"It's on the other side of the realm and would take far too long to walk Mortimer to the arena," said Kingston. "He'd be prone to all kinds of sabotage."

Joanna glanced along the corridor. "Not to be weird or anything, but all we really have to do is find a spare door and screw the hinges into one of these walls. That would turn the corridor into a room."

Kingston looked over to Rufus, and the little builder shrugged.

"Yeah, fine, whatever."

Kingston waved his hands in the air. "I'm sensing some kind of defeat coming from you."

"Yeah, it looks a lot like cautious optimism. It's my thing. I don't have many things, but this one I do really well. You should try it sometime. Aside from me bouncing up and down like a new man, ready to take on the world with a burst of confidence, I really want to know what happens now. Are you going to bet everything you have on us winning? Because as of yesterday we're going to be the target of every disgruntled team out there."

Kingston looked over his notes and shrugged. "Right now we're in debt by seventy one thousand gold. If we sell all of our excess components we might be able to earn back ten grand, but that's pushing it. Chances are we'll need to hold onto a lot of this for another ten years and sell it at an auction to anyone desperate enough to bid. And our best odds at winning, right now, are three to one. Thankfully I do already have some money on us winning from the previous rounds when our odds were higher, but even so I would need another loan of thirty five thousand gold and bet on us winning to cancel out all of our debts, and then we can ride high with the prize money, sell off Mortimer, and hopefully win some surprise bets that come our way." He turned to Joanna. "How did we do with sponsors and donations?"

"We're up two hundred and ninety gold pieces."

"Isn't that a relief," muttered Rufus.

John smirked at Kingston. "You sound like you're starting to get cold feet about us winning."

Kingston sighed. "Yeah. I can't imagine anyone is going to let us get away with what happened at the end of round three. There's going to be some kind of epic revenge and we're not going to make it to the end of round four. So gambling away thirty five thousand gold does seem like throwing it down the toilet."

"Especially with Milliara out there, and he's never been defeated," said John.

Kingston gave that one some thought. "You know at the end of round three when they dropped a whole bunch of glue on top of Mortimer?"

"Yep?"

"What if we did that to Milliara? Or, just fill one Mortimer with glue and send out another to replace him? Milliara crashes down, crushes Mortimer, then gets stuck to the floor. He's out."

"It could work," said John. "Aside from this whole second Mortimer thing. If we took a fall we might earn some money."

Kingston snorted. "Take a fall?"

"Sure. We're here to earn money, not necessarily to win. If everyone is out for revenge then we simply ..." John's eyes drifted to the side and he was suddenly hit by a brilliant idea. "What if we just didn't turn up! That would really irritate them."

"That would forfeit a lot of our bets," said Kingston. "And we're here to earn money, not to lose it."

Catalina glanced from one dour face to another. "Believe it or not, we're going to need to host another party. And we need to get Stuyvescent and Urisha on our side to help us all take on Milliara."

Kingston and Joanna head back to their apartment.

Kingston reached out and took Joanna by the hand. "Please tell me we won some money from what Catalina did."

"Some, but not a lot. I was able to place, all up, eighty two gold, spread out anonymously."

Kingston looked up to the sky and quickly worked that out. "Five thousand nine hundred gold?"

"Yeah."

Kingston grinned and pulled Joanna in for a hug. "Thank you."

"You'd think with a haul like that we would be bouncing off the walls with joy."

They returned to their apartment and were unsurprised to find that the door wouldn't open. They called the superintendent once more, who called the apothecary, to find it was another round of Skunk Breath that had to be removed from the doorway.

John and Catalina went out for pizza, and the whole time he couldn't stop smiling at her.

Catalina did a few double takes before she finally shook her head. "What's that look for?"

"For outsmarting Kingston and Joanna," said John.

"I should tell you I had to dance with Satan a few times. He pinched my bum."

John growled.

"But on the bright side I'm now rich, so I'm paying for dinner, and repaying a few loans, and ... actually that will wipe me out again." Catalina shook her head in despair. "At least now I'm only twenty ... *three* ... maybe, gold in debt. That will only take ten months to pay off." She then caught John's puzzled expression.

"What about all of the dresses that came from Fiction?"

"I wore them, but I've kept a running tally of everything else that Kingston and Joanna have paid for me."

"Those were gifts, babe."

"I don't want to appear ungrateful."

"Then say 'thank you' by spending money."

Catalina shrugged it off.

"And it's funny knowing that of the four of us, you're probably the richest."

"Have you taken out any loans?"

"Not a single one. And if you don't pay Kingston and Joanna back then you're still richer than me."

Catalina shook her head again and glanced around the pizzeria. "Just so you know, I have a whole pizza with my name on it, so you will probably have to carry me back home."

"With pleasure!"

Catalina started to space out after the exhausting week, and just before she fell asleep at their table John nudged her awake. "Huh?"

"How come you never told me you were reading to Fernando?"

"He asked me to keep it to ourselves," said Catalina. She then saw John's face crease with a puzzled look. "I know how that sounds if he was human, but he's not. And he was something of a nervous wreck. Considering everyone in the realm seems to know what we are doing, and that we're being spied on and sabotaged everywhere we go, it was a relief to have something quiet and away from prying eyes. Besides, the longer I kept this thing a secret, the greater the payoff. He pulled through for us without needing any bribes or back door deals. All I did was talk to him when everyone else ignored him and he liked that." It was Catalina's turn to peer at John. "We were in that hidden room for hours. How come you only asked me this now, in private?"

"I knew that you had been reading to Fernando. Kingston knew as well. I didn't really want to find out if Rufus and Jezebel were in on it too."

"Yeah, I'd rather not find out if my friends were spying on me."

Their pizza came, and the inevitable food coma soon kicked in. John carried Catalina back to their apartment and laid her down in bed, before he promptly passed out with tiredness as well.

The next day the team gathered in the bank to read over the highlights of round three in the newspaper.

"Pfft," said John. "*Limbo team cheats its way into the final round.*'Nonsense."

Rufus nodded to the rest of the team. "On the bright side, that might actually help us win sponsors, now that we're obviously the best at cheating and one of only four teams left standing."

"Yay us!" cried Jezebel.

Catalina winced away. "It's too bad you had to pay the other Limbo teams off with supplies."

"Nah," said Joanna. "That one actually plays to our advantage, because everyone will be trying to figure out why we did that and then cheated the way we did. They'll know there must be a strategy involved, so they'll spend a lot of time trying to figure out what we're up to, trying to make sense of it, and they won't come up with anything because there is no sense to be made."

Kingston smiled and had to agree with Joanna, but on the inside he wished he hadn't just sunk so many thousands of gold pieces on the other teams just to salvage his reputation.

John shook his head over several statements in the newspaper. "They're complaining about how legitimate the whole sport is if it is this rife with cheating."

"Ha!" cried Rufus. "We're only cheating to keep up with everyone else!"

"Right," said Kingston. "There is so much of that happening behind the scenes that it would probably make your average spectator's head spin."

Jezebel gave the team a weak smile. "Not to play devil's advocate, but while that is true this whole thing has to appear to be fair on the outside. Whatever happens back stage is acceptable because there's always the element of plausible deniability." She quickly turned to Catalina. "It was still brilliant, by the way, and people will be talking about it for years."

"Thank you?" said Catalina.

"So what's the problem then?" asked John. "Those of us in the player's booth had nothing to do with the statues preventing the other teams from entering the arena, and no one actually saw anyone from the team do it. They didn't actually catch us cheating, they only think we did it. Which we did, but that's beside the point."

"Because it's the only thing in the newspapers," said Jezebel. "Every team is shouting high and loud that round three was won through nothing but cheating. There was no skill there."

"There was a good deal of skill involved!" said Kingston. "Honestly, if there was a medal for skill in cheating, I expect we would win gold, silver, and bronze. And they'd all go to Catalina."

Catalina blushed and shied away. "Thank you, but no."

Joanna dropped her newspaper onto the coffee table and looked over to Kingston. "I think it's time to go see Urisha and Stuyvescent."

"Why?" asked Rufus.

"We effectively got them into the finale, so they owe us. Plus we need to pay them off so that we all take on Milliara."

"Yeah," said Kingston. "Any ideas how anyone is going to take on a teleporting anvil?"

"I'll see what I can do," said Rufus.

On one of her few moments to herself, Joanna ducked downstairs to the corner shop to pick up the makings for dinner that evening. On the outside of the front door was a billboard advertising the next batch of cooking courses. This time it was Moroccan. Joanna put her and Kingston's name down.

Inside the store she was met by several glares from the customers. She smiled at each of them as she wandered from aisle to aisle, but after the sixth person snubbed her she felt like going back upstairs and hiding under a blanket. The store owner did his best to be hospitable, but Joanna knew that he was a Biggins supporter, and the small talk was icy.

Outside, Joanna noticed that her and Kingston's names had been scribbled out from the cooking course.

The team stood in the marquee, greeting the guests and donors, for what was hopefully the final party of the tournament. Joanna was stiff again and barely able to breathe, thanks to her body armour. Kingston looked quite buff under his suit, thanks to his armour as well. John stood next to Catalina without a care in the world, while Rufus hid behind the bar, knowing that he was now the best target for revenge against their rivals.

Maurice wandered in, found Kingston talking to some of the newspaper folks, and stole Kingston away.

"How's the Cascade doing?" asked Kingston.

Maurice grimaced. "Not well, I'm afraid. That little stunt with the statues has cost us, since we spent a lot of money predicting the line up to the finale."

"Was my team in any of these predictions?"

"Some, but not a lot," said Maurice. "I'm here to advise you that you're being dropped as a client."

"Ah," said Kingston, and he felt that one sting harder than it should have. "Because I didn't let you know about the statues ahead of time?"

"Yes," said Maurice. "Also, the shouting I had to endure from my partners was not pleasant. It was my call to drop you. Your team is too unpredictable."

Kingston studied Maurice carefully and took a gamble. "I take full responsibility for not telling you about our plans."

Maurice glanced around the marquee. "You were just telling the newspaper folks that you had nothing to do with the statues."

"Well, we have to manage the public's perception somehow. The plan has always been to overwhelm them with different versions without anything official being released and let them try to figure out what really happened. But come on, do you really think that I had no idea about the statues?"

Maurice sighed with a shrug. "If you had mentioned something to me we could have all made a lot of money."

"I looked into that, but suddenly dumping all of our money into the final line up would have frozen the gambling houses. They wouldn't pay up. I guarantee it. They'd cite some clause about cheating and refuse to hand over a single gold piece. It's either that or they face being bankrupt, and they like their money more than I like mine. But anyway, we are now staring down the barrel of round four. I know we've just parted ways as business partners but there is still a chance for the two of us to make some money. You scratch my back one last time and I'll scratch yours." Kingston peered at Maurice hopefully.

"I wish I had more to tell you. Chloe Stuyvescent is one of my clients. Urisha is not. I can't speak for what they have planned. They are also bearing the brunt of public hate right now because they are the only teams that are mysteriously not being investigated by the gaming commission for cheating during the third round."

"That's a shame," said Kingston, with a smile.

"And all of the other teams were ratted on by the same anonymous source."

"Well, what are you going to do?"

"Although there was one other team that was not ratted on."

"You don't say."

"And the penmanship was quite lovely on the anonymous notes."

Kingston glanced over to Joanna and knew that her skills at keeping Satan entertained had paid off. It was too bad that she now broke into a sweat whenever she saw a bottle of vermouth.

Maurice looked back in bewilderment. "Not only did you cheat the other teams out of a fair fight, you ratted on the losers as well?"

Kingston beamed with a smile. "We are good at what we do."

Maurice held out his hand for Kingston to shake. "Well then, I wish you all the luck in round four."

Kingston shook Maurice's hand in return. "I know they're going to cheat against us."

"That's a given. On the bright side you have turned this year's tournament into one hell of an interesting one. They'll be talking about it for decades." Maurice turned and headed outside.

Kingston casually walked over to Joanna. "I have a feeling we're not going to do very well in the fourth round."

"Don't worry sweetie, we don't do well in any round."

"And we've been dropped from the Cascade."

Joanna sighed and looked over the crowd. "That's fair, since the gambling houses don't want us anywhere near them as well."

"So somehow we need to raise fifty thousand gold pieces from this one party."

They both looked around in quiet defeat, took a moment to gather themselves from the sheer impossibility of making that happen, and then they went to work the crowd for all it was worth.

XXIV

Round Four.

"Stand!" shouted Rufus.

Mortimer sat up on the makeshift bench, swung his legs over, and stood upright. Rufus gave him a quick pat on the shoulder.

"This is the last time we'll be doing this, at least for ten years. I have a feeling, though, that Kingston is going to try to sell you to make some money. If that happens then this is goodbye." Rufus looked over his shoulder to make sure the coast was clear, then he whispered: "Make us proud, Pinky."

The teams of Rufus, Milliara, Stuyvescent, and Urisha all made their way into the arena, and the crowd roared with the new round of blatant cheating.

"What the hell is that?" cried Kingston, as he looked across the arena floor.

Rufus glanced over, groaned, and patted Mortimer gently on the shoulder. "It was nice knowing you."

To Mortimer's right was Milliara's anvil. To Mortimer's left was Horatio's cannon, pointing directly at Mortimer. And on the other side of the arena was Aurelius' dragon. Curiously, both Stuyvescent and Urisha were present on the arena floor.

Kingston spluttered. "Did someone pay those two off?"

"Yup," said Rufus.

"But *we* paid them off first!"

"We sure did," said Rufus.

John sneered at the other teams. "Would it irritate them if we forfeited?"

"It would irritate them more if we won," said Kingston.

"Yeeeaaah, that's not going to happen," said Rufus. "Obviously Horatio has paid off Stuyvescent to replace her machine with his cannon, and Aurelius did the same with Urisha to get his dragon in under her name. It's not illegal, it's just against the rules, so they're going to be fined, no question there, but they won't be disqualified. And we're facing the wrath of every other team out there, so you can bet your ass that they're going to take us out first just to prove a point, and then they'll have a go at each other."

Kingston pulled out his betting sheet and saw that it had updated his chances of success. He was 9:1 to win. All of a sudden his lucky cufflinks didn't feel so lucky. "Great. So the gambling houses are aware of some extra trickery that we haven't seen yet."

Rufus glanced at the sheet. "Meh. I'd say that works in our favour. See, if we were doomed then we would be twenty to one. Even if we actually are twenty to one the houses believe that we have something up our sleeves, which brings us back to nine to one. Yes?"

"Do we have anything up our sleeves?" asked John.

Rufus shrugged. "I'm not sure. What has your girlfriend got planned?"

"A bottle of brandy and croissants, mostly," said John.

"I'm down with that," said Rufus.

"You're not invited," said John, then he squinted into the distance. "What happens if I go over there and pick a fight?"

"We'd be disqualified," said Rufus.

"*That* gets someone disqualified?" asked Kingston.

Rufus nodded. "If you have any last moments of genius, now is a good time to do something about it."

It was two minutes to go and the trumpets blared.

"I swear the lead in time is getting shorter and shorter," said John.

Rufus nodded again. "Last tournament the trumpets began with a ten minute warning. By the last round it was down to thirty seconds. It keeps you on your toes."

Mortimer shuddered with a spurt of energy, causing John to step back in concern.

"We'll be fine," said Rufus.

"Just what kind of berserker rage are you expecting here?"

"Chances are he will blow up, which should be pretty

interesting to watch." Rufus clapped his hands together and he looked up at both Kingston and Rufus. "Well, this must be quite an exciting moment for the both of you. Into the finale on your first tournament. Well done. I'll say my congratulations now because in about three minutes Montgomery Stup and his brother will be looking for me once again, as will a hundred other people I owe money to. And we do have a contract where you'll pay me twelve gold pieces per day's work if we made it into the finale, plus splitting all of the profits."

"It was eight gold a day to get into the finale and twelve if we win," said Kingston. "Besides, you were drunk for most of that."

"Sure was," said Rufus. "I'll be needing that money in cash, soon. Very soon."

The trumpets blared again and all of the team members started to hurry into their player booths.

"See ya, Pinky," said John, and he headed inside. Rufus turned and followed the giant, which left Kingston to take one final look across the arena, hoping for some kind of miracle. He then stepped away and heard the frenzy of the audience build to a crescendo. They all counted through the final minute, and Kingston took his position in the player's booth.

"Who first?" asked Rufus, as he fixed his headset across his ears.

"Dodge Horatio and take him out first. Smash him to smithereens," said Kingston. "Just ... obliterate him."

"You mean his cannon?"

"Sure, let's start with the cannon," said Kingston, as he scowled across the arena floor.

John kept an eye on the countdown timer and saw it reach ten seconds. "Here we go!"

The trumpets blared, and the cannon shot a net out towards Mortimer. Mortimer dodged out of the way, just as Milliara's anvil dropped in on where Mortimer was standing. Aurelius' dragon, likewise, made a bee-line towards Mortimer.

"Holy crap!" shrieked Rufus. "They're ganging up on us!"

"Then smash something!" shouted Kingston.

Mortimer shot the whip out at the cannon, just as it fired another net. The two met in the middle and their momentum broke. On the bright side, the net was now caught around the whip. Mortimer spun towards the dragon, catching it in mid air and snaring its wings in the process.

"Do I let go of the whip?" asked Rufus.

"No, just keep going for Horatio!" shouted Kingston.

Mortimer tried to lumber forward, but the dragon was trying to break itself free by pulling in the opposite direction. Meanwhile, the anvil dropped in over Mortimer.

"Side step!" shouted Rufus.

Mortimer did so just in time, and the anvil slammed into the ground next to Mortimer's toes.

"I can't keep going after Horatio if I have to drag that stupid dragon along!"

"Then focus on the dragon!"

Mortimer spun around and raised Titan over his head. The cannon redirected itself and fired another blast at Mortimer. This one connected and it knocked Mortimer to the ground.

"Stand!" shouted Rufus.

The anvil dropped in just above Mortimer and missed by an inch as the golem lifted itself up onto its feet. The cannon fired again but was off target, while the dragon pulled against the net and whip with all its might.

Mortimer yanked back on the whip, but the force was too much to handle between the golem and heavy dragon, and the links fractured into a hundred pieces and spluttered to the ground.

"Ah crap, we needed that for later!" cried Rufus.

"Stop crying about it," said Kingston.

"I'm not crying!" cried Rufus. "It's just we could have sold that whip tomorrow for two thousand gold pieces."

While the dragon was still entangled, the cannon was now free for Mortimer to seize. Mortimer bounded across the arena with Titan raised in the air. The cannon released its brakes and fired several times, pushing itself around the arena as it struggled to hit Mortimer. The anvil kept dropping in and out of the air, landing perilously close to Mortimer.

"We're not gaining on Horatio," said John.

"Throw Titan," said Kingston.

Rufus groaned and gave the command. Mortimer hurled Titan across the arena, missed the cannon, and the war hammer slammed into the wall scaring the bejesus out of a hundred spectators.

"Do it again," said Kingston.

Mortimer dodged out of the way of the anvil and the cannon blasts and managed to scoop Titan back up in his hand. He hurled it at the cannon once again. This time it connected and the hit spun the cannon around just as it fired off another round.

"Bull rush!" Kingston, John, and Rufus shouted all at the same time.

Mortimer charged in, braced his shoulder against the impact, and slammed himself against the cannon. It shuddered onto one wheel and Mortimer dug his heels deeper into the round.

"Pull back from the anvil!" shouted Kingston.

Mortimer stepped back just as the anvil crashed into where he had been standing, which coincided with the cannon rocking back into place. The anvil sliced through one wheel and teleported away again. Mortimer threw himself against the cannon again, forcing it to tip over and fall onto its side.

The crowd roared in delight as Horatio's machine was now rendered immobile. But, it could still turn and shoot everything in the arena. Mortimer hurried over to Titan and by now Milliara figured out where to best position the anvil. It dropped out of the air and slammed into the war hammer's handle. Titan flipped up as the handle broke, and the anvil tried again to target Mortimer.

"No Titan, no whip," said Rufus. "Now what?"

"Use the cannon as a baseball bat," said Kingston.

Mortimer tried, but the cannon was too heavy.

"And don't stand in the one spot for too long!"

"Well, what do you want, a baseball bat or him to keep moving?" asked Rufus.

"Keep moving!"

"Ay yai yai, it's like arguing with your wife all over again."

"Girlfriend."

John rolled his eyes at the pair of grown boys in front of him. "Is this really the best time to squabble like this?"

Mortimer dodged out of the way of the anvil but came into range of Aurelius' dragon, who still fought his way through the net. Then, much to the delight of the crowd, the dragon drew in a deep breath and shot out a plume of fire, burning through the net in seconds.

Kingston raised his eyebrows in surprise. "That's new."

"Well, we *are* in the finals and teams usually try to hold onto their best tricks until then," said Rufus.

The dragon was now free and it flew in towards Mortimer. It drew in another lungful of air and spat out a jet of flames.

"Run!" shouted Rufus.

Mortimer hurried away and was pursued by the flying dragon. The anvil kept dropping in and out, missing Mortimer as he zigzagged across the arena, and the cannon kept taking pot shots at the golem from its awkward position.

Rufus glanced over to Kingston with a resigned look in his face. "There is an expensive way out of this."

Kingston sighed and felt the weight of a seventy thousand gold loan crash around him. "Let's hear it."

"If we happen to be standing next to the cannon, with the dragon and the anvil in range, and we detonate Mortimer, then we would technically win because we took out the other teams."

"And if our timing is off?"

"Then we take out Horatio, Aurelius, and Mortimer, and hand the victory, in all likelihood, over to Milliara."

While Kingston thought it over, Mortimer kept running around the arena as the three teams continued to fire, shoot, and drop at him. Kingston finally looked over to John. "What do you think?"

John shook his head. "We'd never get the timing right, and self destructing is not exactly ... our ..." He spied Kingston carefully, and then he shook his head again. "I mean, self destructing shouldn't be our way of doing things."

Kingston peered at John suspiciously. "I'm trying very hard not to read between the lines to what you just said."

John shrugged. "If we miss we lose out on fifteen grand."

Kingston looked back to Rufus. "We keep on fighting."

"As you wish," said Rufus.

"Stay close to the cannon. Hopefully the dragon or anvil will take it out by accident."

The cannon spun around to face Kingston's player's booth and fired. Kingston and the gang jolted back in surprise as a thick, black goo covered most of the window, blocking their vision of the arena.

"I can still see," said Rufus, and he stared at the monitor to get an in-helmet view from Mortimer.

"But we have no idea what's happening around us!" said Kingston.

"We could use a muse right about now."

"I could go and punch one of the other teams," said John.

Kingston stepped over to the side of the window, where one tiny section of glass was free from the dripping goo. "The dragon is coming in behind us."

Mortimer turned, raised both hands into the air, and was slammed to the ground by the flying dragon.

"Grab it!" shouted Kingston.

"I'm doing what I can!"

Mortimer latched onto one of the dragon's wings and began punching the creature with his free hand. The crowd cheered in delight, especially when Mortimer swung the dragon down to shield himself from the cannon, which fired and hit the dragon in the back.

"The anvil's coming!"

Mortimer stepped back and pulled the dragon along with him, just as the anvil dropped into view. At the last second the anvil teleported away, keeping the dragon in one piece as it tried again to focus on Mortimer.

"I'm going for the self destruct," said Rufus.

"Don't you dare."

Mortimer pulled the dragon in towards the cannon, avoiding the near misses of the anvil as it continued to teleport over Mortimer's head, and then Mortimer reached relative safety by standing next to the cannon.

"Don't!" shouted Kingston.

Rufus thumped one of the large buttons on his control panel and sighed with a great deal of resignation. Then his mood soured even further as he thumped the button again and again. "Uh oh."

"Please tell me the self destruct isn't working," said Kingston.

Rufus squished the button as hard as he could. "Damn it, that was my epic surprise!"

Kingston stepped back in relief. He looked over to John, who had found a small corner of the window that was free from the goo.

"The anvil is lying on the ground," said John.

Kingston looked over to Rufus as his suspicions got the better of him. "What exactly was that button of yours supposed to do?"

"Don't just stand there!" shouted John. "Beat the stuffing out of that dragon!"

Mortimer began to bat the dragon into the side of the cannon. The dragon fought back, using its wings and four legs to slash at Mortimer, until one swipe knocked Mortimer's helmet loose.

"I can't see," said Rufus, and he yelped when John lifted him off the ground and held him in front of the clear space of the window.

The dragon attacked again, knocking Mortimer backwards. The cannon fired and knocked Mortimer forwards, back into the dragon, which took another swipe at Mortimer.

Rufus punched down on the self destruct button again, but whatever he had planned didn't work. "That was supposed to be Lady Luck!"

John smirked. "Then you are shit out of -"

"Shut up!"

The cannon blasted Mortimer again. The iron golem fell backwards and landed with a sickening crunch. Rufus' control panel lit up in a mix of blue and red lights. The cannon quickly turned on the dragon and fired shot after shot until the beast lost a wing, then a leg, and finally had its head hanging off at an angle.

Mortimer did his best to stand up but half of his functions were now kaput. The cannon shot again, hit Mortimer in the leg and took it clean off.

Rufus sighed and lowered his head. "We're done. We can't exactly crawl our way to victory."

The cannon fired its remaining shots at the dragon and scored on every single hit. At last the scoreboard lit up, showing Aurelius' defeat.

"We have a chance," said Kingston. "We can out last Horatio."

The cannon turned to follow Mortimer and clicked in desperation, but no shots were fired. Mortimer crawled around in a circle, while the anvil remained in one place. Then, one of Rufus' lights started flashing.

"Uh oh."

Smoke and flames crept out from under Mortimer's armour.

"Roll him over," said Kingston. "We have to stay out there long enough to keep ourselves from being disqualified."

Mortimer struggled to turn himself over. Then the crowd cheered as a ten minute countdown timer began.

"We have to keep smashing that cannon," said John. "Throw the dragon at it."

"I'll try, but that thing is far too heavy when Mortimer is prone."

At eight minutes Mortimer reached the carcase of the dragon. At six minutes he was able to push it halfway towards the cannon. At four minutes he had the dragon nudged all the way up to Horatio's machine, but Mortimer was now on fire.

"Keep rolling over," said Kingston.

"And punch the cannon at least once," said John.

Mortimer gave the flimsiest of slaps at the barrel of the cannon.

Kingston looked over to Rufus. "Is there any chance Mortimer can set fire to the dragon and have the dragon explode under the cannon while Mortimer crawls away?"

Rufus shrugged and tried his best. Then with two and a half minutes remaining the flames became too much and Mortimer exploded, sending the dragon and cannon flying off to the side. The crowd erupted and stared back at the scoreboard, hoping to see that Mortimer had just taken out the cannon, but nothing came up.

Kingston raised his hands in disbelief. "Are the referees blind? We just blew up the cannon!"

"But we didn't defeat it," said Rufus.

The scoreboard showed the answer as well. *~~Rufus~~ – critical failure.'*

"I ... I think we just came third," mumbled Rufus. "Third! In the finale!" He beamed with pride.

"So what do we win?" asked John.

"Two and a half thousand gold," said Kingston, and deep down he knew that he still had a fifty thousand gold piece deficit.

There was nothing left of Mortimer. The countdown timer continued towards zero and at last the trumpets blared. The crowd clapped politely as just about everyone tried to figure out if they had won money or lost it, then the sickening realisation kicked in that they were about to go another nine years and nine months without another tournament.

The scoreboard showed another update. *'Knock Out Decision.'*

Kingston sighed. John growled. Rufus stared quietly at his control panel.

"How long does it take to come to a decision?" asked John.

"Anywhere from five minutes to an hour," said Rufus. "But it's never happened in a finale before."

There was a knock at the door and Kenneth the referee appeared. "Gentlemen, if you could just wait in here until we've cleared the arena floor? Thank you." He closed the door and left the three men in peace.

"So what are the chances that someone is sneaking up on us?" asked John.

"Meh, slim," said Rufus. "The tournament's over. Anything they do now carries serious consequences, so we're just going to sit around and wait until this whole thing blows over."

It took two hours. Kingston and John both paced around the player's booth with nothing to do, while Rufus sat in the corner and stared at the collector's card of himself.

John glanced over to Kingston and Rufus. "Is there likely to be any winner other than Horatio?"

"It wouldn't be Horatio," said Kingston. "He wasn't technically competing. It would be Chloe."

"Can we complain that it wasn't actually her and that it was Horatio instead?"

"That's probably why there has been a delay of two hours already," said Rufus.

The crowd had started to dwindle. Most of the spectators remained where they were to soak up the atmosphere for all it was worth, but even a two hour wait with no end in sight was too much for a lot of people. Then, finally, the scoreboard lit up and the crowd cheered. Rufus climbed to his feet and peered out of the only visible spot on the window.

The Winner Of The XIX Games ... Chloe Stuyvescent. Second: Milliara. Third: Rufus Winston. Fourth: Urisha L.'

There was another knock on the door and Kenneth reappeared. "Thank you, gentlemen. The arena floor has been cleared. You may collect your combatant in two hours." He closed the door again.

Rufus glanced over to Kingston. "*That* has me worried."

Kingston rolled his eyes. "Oh, I'm sure this is all perfectly normal in the finals, it's just that it's our first time experiencing this."

"Right," muttered Rufus. Then something occurred to him and he sat up straighter. "Hang on ... I actually made it through the whole tournament! Me! Something I built made it to the end!" A broad smile crept over his face and his eyes lit up in delight. He rummaged through his pockets and pulled out his collector's card of himself from the very first tournament. "I actually got to the end!"

His smile then faded and was replaced by despair. "Montgomery is still after me. And everyone else. I better run." Rufus hurried to the door and ran out into the corridor.

Kingston glanced up at John. "So what'd you think?"

"I think we could've cheated more," said John.

"Well, there's always next time."

"Ahhhhh, I don't know if there is a next time. My good lady wife isn't too keen on all of this stealing business."

"Just get her drunk and convince her that it was all her idea to begin with," said Kingston.

"Sure, because nothing can go wrong with that idea."

"Exactly, it's utterly fool proof."

John sighed and took one last look over the player's booth. "I guess it's time to go see the ladies."

After dodging the crowd and spending another three hours celebrating in the marquee with all of their investors, who were now less interested in investing than ever, Kingston, Joanna, John, and Catalina all headed back to the bank to clean up and return everything as to how it was when they first arrived. Not surprisingly, Rufus had holed himself up in the corridor workshop, drinking himself stupid with Simon's stash of whiskey.

"What are ya doing to ma drink?" Simon asked.

"I don't have your drink, this one's mine!" cried Rufus.

"It's all ma drink, ya know?"

"And I will thank you in the morning!"

Kingston glanced at Joanna and rolled his eyes. "They're destined for each other."

"Great news Mr K!" called out Jezebel, as she ran around the corner. "We're the talk of the town!"

"Wonderful," said Kingston. "How much does talk pay?"

"Nothing, but if we're back in ten years then we'll make twice as much money!"

"So does that mean we'll lose only half as much?" asked Kingston.

Catalina glanced at John when she heard that, and he had to quickly gesture for her to remain quiet.

"We'll need to think about that one before trying it again," said Kingston.

Jezebel could hear Rufus coming around the corner. She looked herself up and down and tussled her hair. "How do I look?" She was met with four pairs of bewildered eyes, and then she cowered back in horror. "I have something up my nose, don't I?"

"No," said Joanna. "It just sounded like you were about to proposition Rufus."

"I am," said Jezebel. "He's a local celebrity, you know." She bounced up and down on her tiptoes and grinned at the foursome. "So seriously, hair is okay? Make up is fine?"

"You look good, sweetie," said Catalina.

"Thank you," said Jezebel. She winked at Catalina and sauntered off down the corridor.

Kingston watched Jezebel walk away and he turned to Joanna. "Seriously, where were the girls like that when I was growing up?"

"You went to an all boy's school," said Joanna. "And even when I first met you, Kim was giving you the most obvious of signals and you missed them all."

Kingston smacked his lips together and peered at Joanna suspiciously. "Tall Kim or Blonde Kim?"

"Blonde Kim."

"She was never interested in me," said Kingston.

"She was more of a sure thing than Jezebel, and you missed every signal she threw at you."

John bellowed in laughter and clapped his hand against Kingston's back. "Don't worry, it happens to even the best of us. Well, maybe not all of us. Catalina?"

"Yes, my love?"

"Did I miss any of your signals when we first met?"

"None."

John looked back at Kingston and grinned. "Must be just you, then."

A flash of light burst into the air and an envelope fell to Kingston's feet. He scooped it up, grateful for a distraction, and then he dropped his shoulders in dismay. "Would you look at this? It's another fine. Two hundred and fifty gold pieces."

Joanna checked the time. "And we have four hours to collect our money from the gambling house before they declare all bets null and void."

"I'll bring John."

"Hazzah!" cried John. "How much did we make?"

Kingston pulled out his great big list of every bet he made. "We made a total of fifty six thousand gold from the gambling houses."

John's eyes grew to the size of dinner plates. "Pfft, *what?*"

"A lot of those were roll over bets. At no point did I actually have that kind of money sitting around. And, truth be told, we ... *I* ... spent thirty nine thousand on gambling."

"Still, that's pretty damn good."

"And we made one thousand and seven gold from the donors and sponsors. Of course, I did spend a fortune on Mortimer, supplies, loans, fines, and paying off the competition. But with the winnings and earnings I'm down by forty two thousand."

Jezebel led Rufus back through the corridor. He was already drunk and had clumsily stuffed his book of enchantments down his pants, thinking that it was as incognito as he could get.

Another flash of light burst into the air and an envelope fell to Kingston's feet. "Oh, look, another one," he said.

Joanna gave him a sympathetic smile, but she was also feeling the sting of seeing too many fines and investigations come their way.

Kingston picked up the envelope and ran his thumb over the seal. There was a stamp from *'The Office of Death'*, and he felt a drop in his stomach, knowing that he was about to be summoned by Death himself. Kingston broke the seal and pulled out the letter within.

"Huh," he said. "There's a party with all of the teams from Limbo, hosted by Death."

Rufus staggered sideways while trying to steady his balance and he shook his head. "I'm not going."

"There are free drinks," said Kingston.

"The team is done and dusted, and I'd rather get back on with my life." Rufus looked over the faces in his team and he gave a slight shrug. "I'd just like to say that you four are now famous for all of the wrong reasons." He nodded at the group, turned, and walked away with Jezebel in one arm.

"Until next time!" called out Jezebel.

Catalina sighed and looked over the state of the basement. "I don't think I can go to this party either."

"Why not?" asked Joanna.

"The last couple of months have highlighted a serious need in following my own path in the afterlife, and that focus is leading me towards being a lawyer. I have studying to do."

"It's just one party," said Joanna.

"I love you two to bits, but it's never just one thing with you guys, there is always some kind of catastrophe waiting to happen.

Besides, I've spent far too long in tight dresses trying to mingle. I just want to curl up on the sofa with a book and a blanket, and watch John dabble with watercolour."

John grinned at her and squeezed her knee. "I guess that's my evening booked as well."

"Fair enough," said Kingston. He looked back to Joanna and did his best to withhold a sigh. "All right Charlotte Deveraux, let's go be social for one last time."

XXV

The final night of the XIX Games were marked by parties across the realms, and the premiere event was held on the rooftop of Death Inc.

Kingston and Joanna stepped out from the elevator and looked around in wonder. From the street it looked as though the building held a solid curved roof over its head, but it was mostly cutaway to provide an open top for entertaining. There were several clusters of outdoor lounges, rows of flowers, statues, and water features. Death, Michelle, and the various heads of department gathered to congratulate the fourteen teams from Limbo, and Michelle smiled at Kingston and Joanna from across the rooftop.

"Any last words?" asked Joanna.

"It's not too late to run away," said Kingston.

Michelle came forward and gave Kingston and Joanna a kiss on the cheek. "I'm glad you could make it."

"Well, who are we to pass up a free party?" asked Kingston.

Michelle smirked at him. "Just how in debt are you?"

"We should have it paid off in just a couple of hundred years. Nothing to really worry about," said Kingston.

Michelle rolled her eyes.

"How did you do with all of the gambling?" asked Joanna.

"I did very well! It was three to one that Rufus would compete again, so I bet almost everything I had on that. I then reclaimed my money and gambled with the rest. I may have taken a few hits but I still came out ahead."

"I'm not surprised," said Kingston.

"You two helped me out," said Michelle.

"If you're feeling generous, a little donation wouldn't go awry."

"I donated a hundred gold already, I think our debts are settled."

Kingston glanced over to Joanna. "I didn't know about that."

"Neither did I," said Joanna.

"Anonymously," said Michelle. "I couldn't appear to be involved. That would just be bad for business. Anyway, I hope you enjoy the party. The Games are over, so there's no more cheating, no more gambling, and no more revenge."

"I'm somewhat relieved by that," said Joanna.

Michelle shook her head in bewilderment. "Somewhat relieved? You English people ..."

"I never caught where you were from," said Kingston.

"Calais," said Michelle. "Though I usually keep that to myself."

"Why?"

Michelle shrugged, smiled, and looked away. "I have to mingle. You'll want to stay for the speech from Death. It's the usual jazz, really. *Thank you for entertaining us, but I should point out that gambling, sabotage, and illegal activities are now over. Please let any grievance you have be a thing of the past.*"

"It's good advice," said Joanna.

"It is, and it's worth reminding everyone because problems still arise." Michelle saw a waiter come by with a tray of champagne. "Now, if you don't mind I'm getting paid to drink on the job, so I'm going to take advantage of that." She slipped away, snagged a drink, and went to talk to some of the other guests."

The final guest of the evening stepped out from the elevator and hesitated when she saw Kingston and Joanna.

"Chloe," said Kingston, greeting her with a good deal of reservation.

"Hi," said Chloe, as warmly as she could manage. She held out her hand and Kingston shook it. She did the same for Joanna, but the tension between the three was thick and cold.

"Congratulations," said Kingston.

"Thank you, but it wasn't really how I expected it to play out."

Kingston cocked his head to one side. "If you were blackmailed into it ..."

"No, no, nothing like that," said Chloe. "Milliara loaned me his muse for a few days and everything she said seemed like a good idea at the time."

Joanna sighed and shook her head. "Well, the things we learn for next time."

"Will we see you again in ten years?" Chloe asked.

"It's doubtful," said Kingston. "Tell me ... did all the teams actually hate us, or were you playing on our emotions to try and bankrupt us?"

Chloe gave them a weak smile and shrugged. "A bit of both, really. Either way it worked."

"That ended up costing us a fortune," said Kingston, and he glared at his former rival.

"Welcome to the world where everyone cheats. I'm sure you'll figure out how to pay off that kind of debt." Chloe winked at Kingston and she wandered away to join the rest of the party.

It allowed Kingston a moment of quiet reflection. "What in holy Zeus just happened to us?"

"You got played by a pro," said Joanna. "But don't worry, I didn't see it coming either."

"Next time ..."

Joanna spun around just in time. "*Next* time?"

"Yes. Next time we're getting a muse to tell us if this is really a good idea. And a psychic to tell us when it's a bad idea."

Joanna peered at Kingston, then she shook her head. "I don't think we need a psychic anymore to point out our bad ideas."

Kingston sighed, glanced up to the dark sky and watched the swirls of red drift from one side of Limbo to the other. Then he was struck by another idea, and his attention fell back to Joanna.

She recognised that look and grimaced. "Let's hear it."

"You know all those sporting heroes in Life who retire past their prime, lose all of their money, end up bankrupt, and then fade to almost obscurity? What do they do in their time of crisis? When they don't have a penny to their name? They have someone write their autobiography."

"I'm not having someone write about my past!" said Joanna.

"Why not? We'll have the inside story on Joanna York and Kingston Raine, mastermind extraordinaires, and it will cover our adventures in Fiction, and then in Limbo. We'll sell a hundred thousand copies and be rich!"

"No, we'll sell ten copies, be only slightly less in debt, and after suffering for the last year and a half with the entire realm reading up on our whole life stories don't you think we deserve to have a little privacy now that we're almost bankrupt? We need to behave like normal people."

"Normal people are bored and wish they led more exciting lives," said Kingston.

Joanna pulled on Kingston's tie and led them towards the buffet table.

"'*Chapter one,*'" said Kingston. "'*It began with a saucy debutante strolling through my office door.*'"

"Uh huh," mumbled Joanna, as she glanced over the selection of sushi.

"'*She wore a dress as black as a moonless night.*'"

"No kidding," mumbled Joanna. "Although a moonless night is actually dark blue, not black."

"'*With blonde hair down to her waist.*'"

Joanna perked up and glanced at Kingston. "Who are you talking about?"

Kingston stared wistfully across the crowd. "'*She went by the name of ...*'" He struggled for a moment, which was made all the more difficult when Joanna waved a mouthful of food at him.

"Maybe you should ask Catalina if there's a creative writing course at the University of Limbo."

Kingston snapped his fingers together. "I could be a lecturer!"

"Yeah, because that pays well."

"Hmm. Then we make our own gaming league."

"No," said Joanna. "We're going to hold down regular jobs and try to pay off this incredible debt one day at a time."

"That seems like a gross mismanagement of our talents," said Kingston.

"Well, at least for the next ten years no one will be trying to kill us," said Joanna.

Kingston glanced around the teams of Limbo and he caught a few of them glaring at him. He smiled and waved at them, forcing the disgruntled few to turn away. "It's just we're not very successful as bounty hunters."

"Yes, now that we live in the afterlife we seem to be inconvenienced because it's not as easy as it used to be to become millionaires."

"We should establish Limbo Telecom. Introduce phones and the Internet to the realm."

"That might put all of the statues out of business," said Joanna.

Kingston cocked his head to one side and he thought that one over." He looked through the crowd and focussed on Chloe again and remembered how easily she had crippled his reputation, or at least his perception of their reputation. "She said we did it for the money."

"I'm sure we did it for the thrill," said Joanna.

"Maybe we should work on our people skills for a while, do the right thing, and forget about our crushing debt."

Joanna smiled at Kingston and her look drifted away. "You know I always wanted to write an opera."

"Why didn't you?"

"Because it wouldn't be any good."

Kingston leaned in and kissed Joanna on the forehead. "That's a crap excuse. Look at John. He's showing his paintings to Raphael and getting tips on how to improve, so what's holding you back?"

Joanna nudged Kingston on the arm. "A fear of the mundane."

Death took to the centre of the rooftop. "Ladies and gentlemen, if I may have your attention?"

Half an hour later, in the quiet street of Xolotl Avenue, Kingston and Joanna came upon the statue of Fernando de Herrera.

"We never said thank you," said Kingston.

Fernando smiled and bobbed his head gently. "It was comforting to know that I had not been forgotten, and that I could still be of some use around here. What can I do for you?"

Joanna stepped forward. "For the last three months we put money ahead of people and that was a mistake. It completely bit us in the arse so we're trying to make amends to everyone who knows us."

"Well, friends are more important than money," said Fernando.

"Do you have any ideas on how we start?"

Fernando nodded. "Be more generous and less paranoid. Not everyone is going to like you, not everyone is going to trust your motives, but when in doubt start by saying 'thank you.'"

Kingston nodded as he thought it over. "Start by saying 'thank you.'" Then he was hit by a nauseating feeling. "John and Catalina ..."

Joanna realised it as well. "Did we really forget ..."

"Yep."

"Surely ..."

"No."

"That means we're ..."

"Yeah."

Joanna looked back up to Fernando. "Sorry. And thank you. But we have to go!"

Kingston and Joanna hurried back to their apartment to find John and Catalina. Meanwhile, Fernando was left standing on his own, in the middle of a vacant street, muttering to himself. He glanced up and down the street and grumbled. Then, at long last, he picked himself up and moved back to Vingólf Boulevard.

"Fernando!" cried Socrates. "What brings you back here?"

"I thought it was time," said Fernando, and he took up his old place once again. "What did I miss?"

"Nothing much. Life, Death, the trials in between. I saw an interesting burst of colour in the sky, though."

Fernando smirked as best he could. "Some divine guidance, I gather?"

"Oh yes. A goat carried an eagle across the water," said Socrates. "That's a sign if ever there was one."

"It's red dust in the sky," said Fernando.

"But when have you ever seen a goat carry an eagle?"

"Never. But clearly it meant I was going to come back and chat to my friends like old times."

Socrates kept his mouth shut and decided it was best not to reveal that the fate of the realm would soon plunge into utter chaos.

ACKNOWLEDGEMENTS

Once again, many thanks go to the countless people who endured my ramblings about a make believe world set in the afterlife. Were it not for you humouring me I might have been able to finish this book in half the time.

In particular I'd like to thank Amanda, who yet again picked over Kingston's adventures and highlighted when he really was pushing his luck.

Also to Deirdre, for pointing out several of my stock phrases that were repeated so often that she had to call me up and let me know that I had to find a thesaurus.

And for everyone who ignores a typo in the finished book: I thank you from the bottom of my heart. To those who point it out to me: I hate you.

Kingston Raine's world is turned upside down in just one second as he goes from trying to rescue his girlfriend to waking up in Limbo ... utterly dead, and facing a baffled Grim Reaper who tells Kingston that he is completely fictional and didn't even exist until just a few moments ago.

Having never experienced this problem before, the Grim Reaper isn't sure about what to do with his fictional celebrity. Satan has a few suggestions, but none of them are at all appealing.

If that wasn't bad enough, Limbo is facing an uprising designed to kick the Grim Reaper out of the realm, and news of Kingston's death is exactly what the uprising needs to topple Limbo's ancient government.

Before the day is even over Kingston finds a way to escape reality, where he nearly loses his head to Macbeth, rescues Little John before Robin Hood can save the day, and does everything he can to get back to his own universe before Limbo's bounty hunters can catch up to him.

When one of Life's most despicable businessmen is found murdered in Limbo all suspicions point to Hell. When Satan assures Death that such a thing is impossible within either realm they settle on a truce by hiring an outside investigator: Kingston Raine.

As soon as Kingston and his friends take the job they realise that they are being spied upon by a secret organisation working within the Bank of Limbo, and that this group routinely assists the rich and corrupt in Life. What troubles Kingston is that the bank is not at all concerned about being run by blackmailers and murderers, instead they seem to be focussed on how Kingston and his friends can benefit them and their diabolical schemes.

Now he and his friends stand in immortal peril.

Kingston Raine is at his wits' end as he tries to protect the most dangerous prisoner to have ever escaped from Hell: a Scottish muse driven mad by one of Satan's devils.

The muse has been chased across the realms by millions of bounty hunters, leaving Satan and Death to decide her fate in a political tug of war. Kingston and his friends do their best to track down the devil responsible for driving her insane while also keeping the muse far out of harm's way, but they soon realise just how supernaturally persuasive she can be, which becomes tricky when Kingston is expected to keep her in his sights at all times.

Inevitability, Kingston learns that Satan has an illegitimate child on Earth, and the mere existence of this kid is likely to cause the apocalypse. Right now the child remains hidden in secrecy, but it's only a matter of time before Satan learns of his offspring in Life.

Can Satan be distracted long enough so that everyone else can figure out what to do about hiding his kid? Can the afterlife survive the great unravelling of its origin? And can Kingston ever enjoy a quiet moment where the fate of Limbo does not rest on his shoulders?